Twisted

Christa Simpson

The Twisted Trilogy
Book 1

CHRISTA SIMPSON, CANADA

Twisted

Christa Simpson

Original Front Cover Art by Razzle Dazzle Design
http://razzdazzdesign.com

Edited Front Cover Design by Kellie Dennis of Book Cover By Design
http://www.bookcoverbydesign.co.uk

ACKNOWLEDGEMENTS

Thanks to my husband and girls for putting up with me, while I spent hours finding my way as an indie author. It was slow going at first, but I think I finally have my hubby on board.

Thank you to my mom and sisters for being my sounding board whenever I needed one (which was often).

Thanks to everyone else who has supported me on my publishing journey.

Last, but certainly not least, thanks to you for your interest in my book.

Happy Reading!
~ Christa Simpson

CHAPTER ONE

Feeling anxious and impatient, I sped toward my quaint Victorian house settled snugly in the luscious, green City of Rose Arbour. I swung my car into my double driveway, jammed my foot on the brake, and slammed it into park.

With long strides, I hurried to my front door and slipped inside my house, my heart beating fast, my face covered with a smile. *It was the perfect night for a blind date. What am I saying? There's no such thing!* Regardless, I had to get ready for my night out and fast. I was expecting my mystery man any minute.

Edwin Santora's eyes were on me the second our solid wood door clunked shut. After kicking off my shoes and giving a silent wave to my brooding, shirtless roommate, I rushed directly upstairs taking two steps at a time.

Within seconds, Edwin was flying up the stairs behind me, all brawn and pride. He stalked me down the hall, his large agile physique a shadow of stealth.

No matter how smooth Edwin thought he was, I could always sense when he was lurking around.

I disappeared into the bathroom, ignoring his approach, heart still racing, cheeks flushed with a healthy glow. It had been way too long and it was time for me to move on with my life. The days of Edwin and I were over and I had finally faced that fact. For that reason, I trusted my matchmaking to an eager co-worker. What else could I do? I didn't seem to have any luck finding *myself* a man.

Edwin filled the doorframe with his imposing shoulders. "Where are *you* going all dolled up like that?"

I should have slammed the door shut behind me while I had the chance. The last thing I needed now was Edwin giving me a hard time. It had been months since my last date and let's just say that it's not possible for this one to go any worse than that one had.

After carefully touching up my mascara in the mirror, I twirled around to face him, my glossy, brown hair fanning out behind me. "I got a date!" I smiled from honest excitement, but I really didn't have time to chat about it.

"Who is he?" Edwin pried.

"You don't know him."

Edwin's chest flexed under my warm gaze, his abs held tight, sculpted from stone. *Oh, I love watching him sweat.* He narrowed his aqua eyes in response to my devious smile. Then, as if on cue, the doorbell rang.

I made my way to the bathroom door, but Edwin boxed me out with his hip and took off ahead of me. He hurried down the hall with swift, powerful strides, every muscle in his body twitching with adrenaline. There was no point in trying to fight him for the front door. He had me beat.

"Do you think you could put on a shirt, Eddie? Please?"

Edwin shuffled down the stairs and ignored my request. "I'll get it," he hollered. He was all too eager to answer the door and his mischievous grin gave away his greedy intentions.

"Edwin, be good!" I warned, stopping at the top of the open staircase.

"What? I'm always good." He flashed me a sly smile and raised his dark arched eyebrows.

I knew it meant trouble, as the butterflies danced nervously in my tummy. Edwin had better not blow this one too. He had a tendency of scaring away my dates. It was getting old. I clung to the wooden post, hoping the poor guy would pass the test.

Edwin opened the front door ever so slightly and started in on his usual act, deliberately blocking my view. *Bastard.* Then he cracked the door open a little farther, teasing, his generous back still in the way.

He folded his bulging arms over his impressive chest and stared *down* at my date with eyes dark and voice low. "Can I help you?" he asked firmly, acting all macho.

I nearly burst out laughing and had to hide the smile on

my face to show that I was not amused. Even if I was.

"Is this the home of Abigail Jenkins?" the poor guy asked, hesitantly.

"Yes," Edwin answered, but he didn't invite him in.

"Edwin!" I warned, scowling at his back. I'd had enough. As I started down the stairs to intervene, I struggled to interpret their mumbling. It was time that I took things into my own hands.

"I guess you can come in," Edwin finally offered. He swung the door wide open and smirked at me over his bulky shoulder.

I wanted to throttle him, but decided to save it for later.

"I'm Kerry, by the way. Kerry Malone." My date offered his business card to Edwin and then extended his hand for a shake.

Edwin nodded at him and left him hanging, but took the card. "Isn't Kerry a girl's name? Is there something you're not telling us Kerry?"

Oh boy, here we go. Why Edwin had to pull out the immaturity card at a time like this was beyond me. "That's enough, wise guy," I said, jabbing my elbow into Edwin's rock-hard gut. My cheeks warmed with embarrassment. "Don't mind him," I said, smiling at Kerry.

Kerry flashed me an anxious, selfless smile, his dark chocolate eyes warm with hope.

Not bad. Not bad at all.

Edwin strode off, without another word, but I had a distinct feeling that I wasn't in the clear just yet. I detected a slight sense of annoyance from Edwin, and maybe a little disappointment? I quickly shuffled that thought away.

"Is that pest your brother?" Kerry asked, quietly.

"You could say he's something of the sort," I lied, loud enough for Edwin to hear.

"Hah!" Edwin snapped from the living room, carefully listening in, as I suspected.

Kerry ignored Edwin and totally focused on me. "You look beautiful tonight."

"Thank you," I replied, my cheeks warming all over

again. He must have liked my hair. I had styled long, loose curls in it this morning and it still looked great.

I bent over and slipped on my new stilettos. "Shall we?" I asked, motioning toward the door. I didn't want to leave an opening for Edwin to come back and sabotage Kerry's chances. So far so good.

I stepped out into the heat, as Kerry made his way down the porch steps, the pavement still distributing the warmth from the hot day's sun. It wasn't even summer yet, but the weather was exceptionally warm and I was enjoying every waking moment of it.

Kerry opened my car door and my smile revealed my appreciation. *Check.* The soft music and laidback conversation was encouraging. *Check.* He drove his car steadily to the restaurant, without trying to make a show of it. *Check.*

Kerry's body language was promising. I noticed how his shoulders slanted toward me and his left hand casually dangled over the top of the steering wheel, as he smoothly shifted gears. He seemed kind and attentive on the trip to the restaurant. Finally, this night had turned right.

When he monitored the oncoming traffic, I took the opportunity to check him out some more. His face was attractive, especially when he was donning that anxious smile that curved up a little higher on the left. All in all, the combination of his short black hair, dark brown eyes and appealing smile was actually quite charming.

When his car came to a halt, I got my own door. I rounded the front of the car and met up with him before we approached the restaurant on foot. Suddenly, everything took a turn for the worst. Everything always had a way of doing that for me.

It started with an enormous bulge jutting out from Kerry's back pocket. How did I not notice that before? I let him take one full stride ahead of me and decided his wallet looked more like a pocket dictionary; totally ridiculous. It made me second-guess my assessment of his character.

Then there was our obvious height difference. I

supposed it didn't help that I was wearing four inch heels, but he couldn't have been an inch over five foot six on a good day. After having dated Edwin, an easy six foot two, with tree trunks for legs, Kerry seemed to me like half a man. Considering the fact that I had him beat by a couple of inches standing flat-footed, it was official that this date was hopeless.

The restaurant was his selection, an average run-of-the mill chain restaurant. The music was too loud, the lights too dim and the patio lanterns set the stage for an awful night.

I tossed my voluminous hair over my shoulder, inspecting the embarrassing distance from his shoulders to mine, my confidence wavering from his shortcomings. I literally towered over Kerry, as the petite, young hostess asked for his name. He handed her his business card.

Okay then.

I wanted to keep an open mind, but I had already come to terms with the fact that it would be a hard fight with myself to win this one. Weak and unimpressive were words that came to mind, when I preferred strong and commanding.

I smiled at Kerry when he looked up at me, but when he opened his mouth, that just put the icing on his goodbye cake. His breath reeked of liquor and I started to wonder how I hadn't noticed his slight slur before now. That would explain why he was driving so carefully.

For lack of a good escape plan, I figured I might as well get a good meal out of the deal. His wallet was fat enough. I was sure he could afford it.

Soon a waitress led us to a booth near the bar. Thoughtfully, Kerry offered for me to take my seat first. I slid into the middle of the leather covered bench seat. Seconds later I realized that Kerry was feeling daring tonight, and he slid in next to me. There was nowhere for me to go, shoved up against the wall, so I dropped my purse in between us. I could only hope that it was enough to keep him at bay.

"Could I please have a glass of water?" I asked the

waitress.

Despite my strongest efforts to redirect Kerry's attention away, he leaned in toward me and overpowered me with his beer breath. I forced out a smile and quickly reached for a menu, lifting it in front of my face to block the stale stench from my sensitive nose. I glanced over the menu quickly, selected the first item I saw and, when his nose was safely in his menu, I put mine down on the table.

"Wow. You already know what you want? That was quick," he said, giving me another dose of his rank breath.

Holding my own breath, I grinned and nodded.

"I like a woman who knows what she wants." He raised his eyebrows suggestively, as I took a drink from my water.

Gag me. Literally. I choked on my water and turned away to gasp for air as discreetly as possible. The last thing I needed was for him to pull a stunt like the Heimlich on me.

When the waitress finished taking Kerry's drink order, I insisted that she take our meals too. Not surprisingly, he ordered a tall beer along with his steak.

The first course came quickly and I tried to keep my mouth full, so I didn't have to talk much. I ate half of my meal and while it tasted surprisingly delicious, there was no way I could enjoy it. I pushed it into the middle of the table mid-way through the meal and dropped my napkin on top to show that I was done.

"Didn't you like it?" Kerry asked.

"It was fine. I'm not that hungry. I'm actually feeling a little sick," I lied, hoping to speed up the night. *BINGO!*

Kerry took the bait and finished his meal promptly. With a wave of his hand, he called the waitress over and asked for our bill. She nodded studiously and went to her station to print it up. Kerry briefly glanced toward the waitress and it looked like he was anticipating payment. As the waitress approached our table with the bill, he quickly stood up.

"Can you please excuse me for a minute? I need to use the restroom," he said, then rushed off, without waiting for a response.

Oh no he didn't! As he walked away I noted that his wallet, being as fat as a tennis ball, was most certainly big enough to pay for my dinner. He must have had a huge wad of cash in there for it to be that thick. Then it finally dawned on me: *business cards.* His wallet was likely stacked full of them. He had been handing them to every person we passed, much to my embarrassment. The waitress handed me the bill and I peeked at it, before slipping it back into the leather folder.

"How would you like to pay for that?" the woman asked me.

"I'm going to wait for my date," I explained, a smug smile in place.

"Okay, I'll be back in a minute then," she replied, and I was satisfied she gathered exactly what was going on.

As Kerry returned to the table, the waitress followed up behind him. I was happy that she had decidedly rephrased her question for him. "Will you be paying the entire bill tonight, sir?" she asked.

He looked at me restlessly and smiled. I smiled back, that appreciative smile, showing no indication that I planned to chip in. He leaned over and pulled out the big, unattractive wad from his pants. He was damn lucky too, because there would have been a fight if I had to pay a dime for this disaster.

As the waitress went off with his credit card, I forced a harsh frown and held my stomach as though I wasn't well. I think he started to figure out my deal. I never was a very good actress when it came to those sorts of things, but he didn't ask and I didn't tell him.

When we went out to his car, he didn't offer to get my door, and when he pulled out of the parking lot, he squealed his tires like an ass. If he was trying to offend me, he had succeeded. It was incredibly immature and very unappealing, and if I wasn't actually sick before, I was now from his reckless driving.

After the awkward silence back to my house, I hoped I could make a quick exit, but it looked to me that he still expected a goodnight kiss. *Not gonna happen beer breath!* I stared out the tinted window at the darkness, seeking inspirational words to express my disgust.

"I had a great time tonight. I was hoping we could stay out later, but maybe next time," he said, pulling the emergency break.

"Mmm hmm," I mumbled, as I desperately scratched for the door handle in the dark. There was no avoiding his brutal man breath when he leaned toward me. I turned my head, just missing his sloppy, repulsive kiss. His lips mashed against my cheek.

"Good night," I said firmly, as I finally found the handle. I dove out of the door and rushed up to my house, feeling nauseous and offended. I quickly jammed my key in the lock to let myself in and slammed the door shut behind me. I rolled over the deadbolt and leaned against the door for support, before banging my head against it. *Why me?*

I tried to find something positive from the situation. At least I managed to bolt from his car before he could ask for my number. *Yes. I'd done good.* As for Maddison Walker, the one who set me up with this drunkard, there would be hell to pay.

I heard Edwin walking down the hall, so I collected myself before he stopped at the top of the stairs. It was dark and I hadn't turned on the lights. I was thankful that Edwin hadn't either.

"You're home early. I take it he's the man of your dreams," he teased.

Suddenly I was mounting with anger. I straightened myself and headed up the stairs with a vicious stomp. I wanted to appear angry, but my words came off as pouting. "Not good."

Amused, Edwin followed me to my room. "Was it something I did?"

Was he intentionally trying to rub it in? He leaned against my bedroom doorway, flaunting all his manly beauty. *Remind me again why I broke up with this man.*

"I wish it was," I said, dropping my head in defeat. "Let's

just chalk this one up to a natural disaster."

"You really had nothing to work with. That guy's hardly even a man. Besides, I told you that dating's no good for you. Why do you need another man in your life when you've got me?"

I wasn't comfortable letting that conversation go where it was heading, so I quickly changed the topic, forcing a smile onto my pouty face. "Shouldn't you be getting ready for bed? Tomorrow's a big day for you."

"It's my first day at your office, not my first day of kindergarten; and it's nine thirty. I think I'll be alright."

"Aren't you nervous though?"

"Not really," he admitted confidently.

Such a sexy quality.

"Well, I'm getting in the shower," I said, as I pulled off my delicate knit top and exposed my silky, strapless bra.

Edwin smiled at me and seductively raised his arched eyebrows.

"Alone!" I added with a growl, answering Edwin's unspoken question.

"Didn't you just take a bath this morning?" Edwin recalled, as he freed himself from the doorway.

"I'm suddenly feeling very dirty."

CHAPTER TWO

The birds were chirping when I awoke in the morning, and I was happy that last night was already in the past. It was Edwin's first day on the job and I was dead set on being the first to welcome him to my law firm.

I went into the office extra early to get a head start on the day, but as the clock approached eight thirty., my attention span was shot. I promised Edwin I would be the first to greet him when he got to the office and I'd make good on that promise.

I slipped out of my cubicle and crossed the hall to the spare office where a wall of blue glass windows faced the main road. Leaning against the solid wood desk, I anxiously waited for Edwin to show. When I finally saw his loaded black truck pull up, I scurried to the front lobby to meet him.

When Edwin made his way through the double doors, I couldn't wipe the smile from my face; partly out of nervousness for him, but mostly because he looked so damn handsome in his new attire. His gorgeous aqua eyes gleamed in the early morning sun, in amazing contrast to his gun metal grey suit. I was stunned, elated, but I did my best to keep it together.

"Abigail Jenkins," he said. "Nice to finally meet you." He strolled up next to me and reached his hand out for a shake, keeping up his charade. I playfully swatted it away.

"Cut it out. Come on, I'll show you to your new home." We turned right, stepped past the empty reception desk and skipped by the first office.

"This is it," I said, pointing to the next room.

His office was conveniently and yet awkwardly placed directly between the two Partners in the firm. It was a large space, with a long strip of blue-tinted windows spanning the entire exterior wall. A subdivision of new town houses was rapidly being built, just outside his window. A tall bookcase, half filled with chunky books and binders, took up a good portion of one of the interior walls.

It was an incredible space, but unfortunately the rear of the room was covered in banker's boxes, stacked five high, not having found a place in our filing system yet. Edwin didn't seem to notice.

He walked to his desk, put down his things and turned on the computer. He spun around in his chair and peered at me from behind the huge stack of files already waiting for him. He flashed me a big distinguished grin. "Now what, boss?"

I pointed back toward the front corner office that we had passed. "That's Jacob Miller's office. He's your boss. The cubicle across from his is Maddison Walker's. I'm sure she'll act like she's your boss, but don't be fooled." My teasing smile didn't go unnoticed.

"Oh boy. Maddison Walker."

"Be nice," I warned him. "She's good at what she does."

Edwin was good friends with Maddison's younger brother, TJ. Edwin knew that, if you let her, Maddison would walk all over you. In other words, she's a bitch.

"Well, here goes nothing," Edwin said. He raised his sharp, dark eyebrows and smiled, as he brushed past me and approached Miller's office.

"Good luck," I whispered, then admired his firm knock on the boss' door. I ducked away as he shook Miller's hand and followed him inside.

Before heading back to my desk, which was on the very opposite side of the entire building, I passed by my friend Aliah's desk. Aliah Brooklin was by far my best girlfriend. Her cubicle was only a few strides away from Edwin's door, which was rather convenient, but while most of the staff had already arrived for the morning, Aliah was not among them.

I strolled around the interior hall, passed the oversized copier room and headed for my desk. When I reached my destination, I pulled out my chair and slumped into it.

My cubicle was spacious, planted in the middle of a modern floor plan with extremely high ceilings. A hallway circled around all of the inner cubicles, where the walls reached only 8 feet in height. The ceiling, being much higher, left the interior space a network of inter-office noise. As for privacy, there was none.

With a sigh, I lifted open the file I had been working on and got right back down to business. There were three enormous piles of files, neatly stacked down the length of my desk, and they weren't going anywhere unless I did something with them.

The morning was going by quickly and, just as I started to wonder how I managed to avoid Edwin so far, he appeared like magic, quietly passing by my office and disappearing into the washroom. After a minute or so, I heard some commotion across the way and wondered what could possibly be going on. Before I could worry too much, Edwin appeared at my desk-side with a growing look of concern on his face.

"What's wrong?" I asked.

He moved his hands away from his pants and I immediately saw his trouble. Shocked, my mouth dropped open and a hysterical gasp escaped my smiling lips. It wasn't until I saw how agitated he was that I bit my tongue. When I finally collected myself enough to speak, I cleared my throat and pressed my lips together to force away the smirk, as I stared at the dampness on the crotch of his expensive pants.

"Sorry. What happened?"

"The damn sink in there. It's like a glass bowl sitting on the counter. I turned on the water, apparently a little too hard, and it splashed right up the rim of bowl and all over me."

"Yeah, I can see that. It looks like you wet yourself." I giggled, at his expense, and I could see that he was not pleased with me.

"They really need to post a warning or something."

I couldn't help but snicker again. "Yeah, that's real classy."

"Enough already. Now what am I supposed to do? I didn't bring a change of clothes and I can't go home. This is my first day!" Edwin wasn't typically one to be bothered with anything, but this was obviously terrorizing him.

"Well, you could go tell Miller that you had an accident..." Tears formed in my eyes as I burst into laughter. "I'm sorry, you asked for that. This is too much like kindergarten."

Unable to see the humour in it, Edwin's face soured, his eyes narrowed. He meant business. "Seriously Abigail, this isn't funny."

"Relax. You're overreacting. It's fine, really," I reassured him, knowing he was a sucker for reason. "Why don't you just hang low for the next half hour or so? I'm sure it'll dry a bit. Then you can go home on your lunch hour to change."

"Yeah, I can do that."

"You'd better make a beeline straight for your office though, before anyone notices. I could just imagine all the nicknames and rumours, if anyone gets a hold of this one," I teased.

"No one will though, will they, Abigail?" he threatened, his eyes darkening.

I shrugged my shoulders to tease. "You might be safe for now, but you owe me big if you don't want this to come out later."

"Thanks, I think." Scowling, he bolted for his office covering the wet zone.

I giggled a little more before I started thinking about the two of us. It was no surprise to me that seeing Edwin at work would be more than a little distracting. Staring off into space, I smiled, and I was gone.

Edwin and I had lived in the same neighbourhood as children. We went to different schools, his parents being very particular about raising him in a good catholic household, while my parents were a little more liberal when it came to religion. Regardless of his mother's intentions, Edwin and I became good friends at a young age, and it was never a secret that he had always hoped for something more.

Persistent, he was, and by the time we hit high school, I finally gave in to him. After I let my guard down, it wasn't long before I fell madly in love with him. I can still remember those days like it was yesterday. We were inseparable. Edwin was infatuated with me and I was no less smitten with him. People called us high school sweethearts, but my sister always said it was more like an addiction.

All that changed when Edwin decided to go away to an elaborate university in the big city and I stayed behind, content with the local community college. Our lives were leading us in different directions and we were both young and stubborn.

After being apart for two long years, our only connection being through random emails and the occasional messenger chat, I decided to tell him that he had grown too distant, and maybe I should stop contacting him.

Though he had a lot going on, less than a month after my last message to him, he called to tell me he was coming back home and transferring to a local university.

Not long after he returned to Rose Arbour, we decided to buy a house together, as a business arrangement. *Strictly business.* We were spending every free minute together anyway and it seemed like a smart financial decision. Going ahead with the plan, we purchased a fixer-upper in no time at all and spent the entire summer renovating, pouring our heart and souls into the promising Victorian, making it our own.

We fell back in love, our flame reignited, but while I was working a full-time job, he was out partying with friends. When I would go out, he'd be at home studying for exams. It just wasn't working for us then and that brings us to now.

Though our on again off again relationship has been difficult to keep up with, now that Edwin has graduated from law school with honours, our close friendship was back in business.

Having successfully articled with a notable law firm, Edwin could pretty much work wherever he wanted; and yet of all the lawyers' offices, government buildings and corporate headquarters in the City of Rose Arbour, Edwin decided to accept a job at my small firm.

After my morning filled with dreams and smiles, the rest of the day surprisingly zoomed by. It was nearly over when I finally ran into Edwin again, this time at the photocopy machine.

"Look at you. Bone dry," I teased.

"I'll bone you one," Edwin said, smirking.

Distressed, my eyes darted toward each of the exits to check for nosy neighbours. "You'd better watch your mouth. There are ears everywhere in here, you know. I'd bet you've already been had."

He chuckled, unconcerned. "It's all in good fun. No one heard me. You worry too much."

After our brief, unprofessional chat, he hurried back to whatever it was that he was so diligently working at. I was a little disappointed that I only crossed his path for all of two minutes and it played out like that, but what was I expecting? I took a deep breath, stacked my papers on the copier and pressed start.

"Abby." A voice called to me from the reception desk and rang in my ears.

I glanced through the doorway to find Maddison Walker standing there next to Taylor, the office receptionist. Maddie's long, silky black hair shimmered in the neon light as she scowled at me with her large brown eyes. Such a pretty girl, with a long narrow face, and dark olive skin, and yet it always amazed me that she was even related to Edwin's friend, TJ. He was such a nice person. Unfortunately, I couldn't say the same for her.

She stalked me like a demon, approaching with an evil look in her chocolate brown eyes. "What about Kerry? I thought you and Edwin weren't an item anymore," she hissed.

I wasn't about to bring up that horrid date now. I backed up a step. "We're not," I replied, forcefully genuine.

She reached her hand to the counter, leaning against it, and blocked my path to the copier. "Oh, so you're just doing him on the side then?"

"Maddie, mind your own business." I pushed her gently aside and picked up my papers from the tray.

An evil laugh shimmered through the long cavernous room. "I'll take that as a yes then," she sneered.

I peeked up at the front desk again, where Taylor was listening intently. Her dark brown hair, pulled up in the front, left her no protection to hide from my annoyed gaze. Her plump, pale skin, and friendly smile made you think you could trust her but Taylor was not the lovely older lady from next door, as she appeared to be. In fact, she was the office gossip queen, and she tended to feed off of Maddie's craziness. To make a point I twisted my smile and narrowed my emerald eyes at her.

Hers turned wide with understanding, as she scurried to her seat.

"It's not like that. But if it was, you'd be the last to find out," I said.

"Not with his big mouth. You'd think he'd be a little more careful on his first day. But don't worry, your secrets are safe with me," she said, wicked and blunt.

I rolled my eyes and reluctantly played her depraved game. "And what secret is that?"

"Oh, you don't know? It's so obvious. Edwin's still in love with you. It's so cute how you two are playing the cat-and-mouse game."

I rolled my eyes in disbelief. "Whatever, Maddie." I was unwillingly to listen to this insincere snob.

"Oh, you don't like that? Allow me to rephrase. *Hot pursuit.* Need I say more?"

"No, you've said enough," I insisted, though I had already stopped listening two seconds ago.

"If you can't see it, then you're blind. Roll the shades, Abigail; you're either doing him or you need to cut the cord." She paused momentarily, retrieved the dagger from my gut, then took another stab. "I see your date with Kerry was obviously a bust."

"Right, thanks for that by the way," I moaned sarcastically.

"Kerry's a nice guy. That was all you."

"Like I said before, mind your own." I was so angry now I could have growled.

"If you say so. You and Edwin really need to work that out. Just remember who told you first. Then we'll see who your real friends are," she said, smooth and scandalous, before slinking back to Taylor's desk.

I rolled my eyes again, when she wasn't watching, and went back to my desk with my blood boiling. Why had I ever decided to befriend Maddison Walker? Oh, yes: *Keep your friends close and your enemies closer.*

"Get ready, girl, or we're going to be late!" Aliah peeked into my desk area with obvious urgency. I jumped a little and it took a second for my mind to snap back into reality. Aliah was dressed in a cute yoga outfit and raring to go. But she was always a little high strung.

I looked at the clock to see what the hype was all about. "Oh shit! I didn't realize what time it was."

"Then hurry up!"

I pulled my exercise getup from my bottom drawer and leapt out of my cubicle at full speed. I wiggled into my spandex as fast as humanly possible, and gracelessly scurried back toward my desk, bumping right into my boss, Owen Wallace. Too late to stop the forward motion, I knocked every last loose paper from his hands. Some slammed onto the floor in a pile and others fluttered through the air, scattering in a disorganized mess.

"Oh my gosh! I'm so sorry, Owen." I knelt to the floor

and shuffled up the scattered papers with him.

"No worries. It was my fault."

I smiled at him, knowing he was only being nice. Who was I to argue with the most successful, young litigator in the City? When I handed Owen the remainder of his tousled papers he took them from me and smiled. My mind had been running on autopilot for the better part of the day and it kind of threw me for a loop, sending me into a blank stare.

Aliah was standing behind me now. "Hello? Earth to Abigail. We're going to be late! What's with you today?" She was clearly annoyed with me, but the feeling was mutual.

I looked back briefly to scowl at her, then flashed my award winning smile at Owen.

"I don't mean to keep you," he said.

"Yeah, yeah. Let's go," Aliah said, as she pulled me away. She had all of our bags in her arms and still managed to yank me past Owen.

He was still standing there, a little stunned, with his pile of messed up papers. I knew the second we disappeared he would be feverishly reorganizing them.

"I really am sorry," I insisted, with a backward glance, before disappearing around the corner.

"See you, Owen," Aliah hollered, as we raced toward the exit. "You're coming with me."

CHAPTER THREE

Aliah Brooklin always got what she wanted, ever since she was a little girl. It may have been related to the fact that her father was the head of the City fire department or maybe it was that she was exceptionally good looking. Either way, she did what she wanted, and everyone else had to deal with her wrath if they got in the way of that.

I turned away from Aliah, who was driving like a madwoman to get us to the Westmount Fit Club for our exercise class. I glanced out my window as she pulled into the freshly paved parking lot, just minutes before class was about to start.

Aliah clutched the steering wheel, feverishly driving through the many rows of parked cars. The lot was packed and she was clearly not satisfied with the spaces littered at the back of the lot. I watched her eyes darting back and forth as her adrenaline pumped and her anger quickly mounted. Quite frankly, it was amusing.

"Can I ask what you're doing?" I asked, teasing.

"What's it look like? I'm finding a good spot!"

"Well, I thought that maybe since we're going to the gym, it wouldn't kill us to do a little walking."

"Good point," she admitted, to my surprise.

Without a second thought, Aliah swung her car around and sped to the back of the lot. She pulled past a few of the open spots and rammed right into the farthest space available. "How's that?" she asked, like a smart ass.

"I didn't say I wanted to walk a marathon."

"Make up your mind, woman. You either want the exercise or you don't." She threw the car into park and turned it off. "Let's move or we're going to be late!" she hollered, like a drill sergeant, as she barrelled for the doors.

I reached into the backseat for my yoga mat and hurried

out of the car after her. I jogged all the way into the Westmount, until Aliah came to a screeching halt and nearly tripped me onto the hard, ceramic floor.

Gawking at a guy, through the window separating us from the room of weights, she whispered to herself. "Whoa. When did that happen?" Her voice was so soft that if I weren't standing right next to her, I wouldn't have heard it.

"What's up?" I asked, confused, but she ignored me. My eyes followed her longing gaze until it landed on the sweaty stud exiting the weight room.

"Hunter Wight. How's it going?" Aliah left my side and walked right up to the attractive man, with dark hair and even darker eyes. She jumped into his arms like they were long lost lovers and his bulging biceps wrapped around her.

When Aliah finally released his hard, muscled body, and lowered her legs to the floor, I checked her reaction to read this unusual situation. They stared into each other's eyes, with ridiculous smiles plastered on their faces. I came up blank. Aliah never talked about Hunter, so who knew where this guy fit into her life.

"When did you get so buff?" Aliah said, finally giving me a hint.

He smiled arrogantly, acknowledging his accomplishment, but I didn't get the impression that he was an egotistical ass, like most of the muscle heads who worked out at the Westmount.

"Come on now, I've always been buff."

She snickered. Yes. Aliah snickered. Then a huge, honest grin formed on her face. Oh, she had it bad.

"I work here you know. Have for like six months now. I'm a personal trainer in my spare time," he said.

"No way! I've been coming here for years. Can you believe I've been coming here for the past six months and never ran into him?" Aliah asked me, superficially shocked, but not expecting an answer. She couldn't remove her eyes from him.

He poked her in the belly, jokingly. "Maybe you should come here more often then," he said.

Aliah absolutely had no need to be at the gym, being blessed with a petite frame and slim build. Now, feeling the awkward silence as they gazed all starry-eyed at each other, I turned toward the classroom, just as the door began to close. I knew how mad Jasmine got whenever someone came in late and disrupted her class, and it looked like class was about to start without us.

"Well... I'm gonna go to class now," I said, interrupting their trance.

Aliah huffed. "Yeah, I'd better go too. But it was nice seeing you, Hunter. We should get together and catch up real soon," she said, batting her eyelashes.

"Absolutely. Here, let me get you my card." Hunter swiftly headed for the reception desk and pulled a card from a hidden compartment. He scribbled a number on the back and reached it out to Aliah. "I put my cell number on the back. You can get me on there anytime."

Aliah flipped over the card and smiled, then turned it face up. It read: Rose Arbour Fire Department, Rescue Division. Aliah stared at the writing then flashed him an even more seductive smile. She was absolutely glowing. "I'm impressed," she said.

I knew she was only saying what he wanted to hear, since she had a handful of hot firefighters waiting on her doorstep, but he didn't know that. Her attraction to him was blindingly obvious and there was no doubt in my mind that their previous relationship was nothing more than friendship. Regardless, I was sure I'd be seeing this guy around again, if Aliah had anything to do with it.

"I'm Abigail, by the way."

"Good to meet you, Abigail."

"It's nice meeting you too, and I do apologize, but I really have to go. Sounds like maybe I'll see you again soon."

"Looking forward to it."

That comment was blatantly meant for Aliah. He smiled at her once again and she wiggled her fingers in a cute little wave as we paced quickly to our class. Late.

The warm-ups were in full swing and Jasmine flashed us

an evil eye when we interrupted their count. "Nice of you ladies to join us," she exclaimed, scowling into the mirror for the whole class to see. We joined in at the back of the classroom, and stretched out our tight muscles.

I knew I should wait, but I had a bundle of questions for Aliah. "What was that all about?" I finally asked her, with a whisper.

"I know, right? Damn, he looks good, eh? I haven't seen him in years. He's really filled out."

"Ladies," Jasmine called, raising her voice. She raised one eyebrow at us in disgust.

We took the hint and zipped our lips.

After class, Aliah told me that Hunter was a long-time friend of hers. Apparently they hadn't seen each other in six or seven years. I didn't have to ask Aliah to know that she was attracted to him, now that he was all grown up and in his physical prime. By the time we had our yoga mats rolled up, I was convinced that Aliah was officially on a mission, and she wasted no time putting her plan into action.

She exited the classroom ahead of me and came to a dead freeze in the hallway. "What is that bitch doing with Hunter?" Aliah's eyes were red with rage.

Of all people to interrupt her game, Maddison Walker was chatting Hunter up in the weight room. It was obvious to me that Hunter was only giving Maddison a private session, but Aliah didn't seem to care why she was with him, only that she was. If it were physically possible, daggers would have been blasting from her eyes.

"Maybe we should go," I suggested.

"Yeah, let's get out of here. I can't stand to watch that girl another minute," Aliah snorted. She pulled out the business card that Hunter had given her and looked it over carefully as we moseyed to the door. She flipped it over to make sure the cell number hadn't disappeared. I struggled to keep up with her as she heatedly rushed to her car. Sure enough, before she even got the key in the ignition, her cell was being drawn from her purse. I watched her feverishly press his number onto the keypad and wait impatiently as it rang off the hook.

"Hey, Hunter.   It's me, Aliah.   I was actually calling because I have this party coming up.   It's just a little promotion party for Abby's boss and I was thinking that maybe you'd want to come. It could be the perfect chance for us to hook up; I mean catch up. Anyways, give me a call back. Talk to you soon."

She ended the call and slapped herself on the forehead. "I have serious issues. He is so going to see right through that message."

"Transparent? Yes. But honestly Aliah, I don't think it's going to be a problem. He seemed pretty happy to see you too."

"You think? I hope so. He's so hot. I can't believe how much he's filled out. And that growly voice. It's so sexy." As I laughed at her obsessive remarks, she motioned her hands back toward the club. "I just have to invite him to the party before *that witch* does!"

When I looked up, I saw Maddie already making her way toward us, her bag slung from her slim shoulder. I put the window down to be friendly.

"Hey, Maddie. What's going on?" I asked, though I knew exactly what was up.

"Oh, I just finished a really tough workout session with my new trainer. Did you see him? Damn, he's fine."

I ignored the ghastly remarks Aliah made under her breath and nodded my head at Maddie, smiling. "Yeah I saw you in there with him. He is cute."

"Cute doesn't even begin to explain it. I just wanted to touch his muscles. It's so distracting. Isn't he gorgeous? I tell you, it's hard when you're trying to work out without sweating." Her smile was wicked.

Aliah's narrowed eyes left no room for question. She was getting more annoyed by the second.

"Well we have to get going," I said. My car's still at the office and we haven't even eaten dinner yet. See you tomorrow?"

"Kay, laters," Maddie answered.

Aliah put the car into gear and sped off rudely, before I even got my window up. "Ugh! Can you believe her? Oogling my man like that."

"He's your man now, is he?" I teased.

"You know what I mean. Besides, if I have anything to do with it, he'll be my man before the summer is over," she stated, unmistakably.

"Don't be the crazy lady, calling Hunter a million times. He *will* call you back."

After a few minutes of bantering back and forth, I was getting tired of hearing her many ideas for plotting against Maddie. For once I was happy that Aliah was a wild driver. Before long, she pulled up to the office where my lonely car sat in the empty parking lot.

"You really need to consider taking some anger management classes or something," I said, as I got out of her car.

"Don't you start on me..." Suddenly her phone began to ring. She lifted her cell and a massive smile instantly formed on her lips when she saw the number. "Hah! He'll be mine sooner than you know!" she cheered, proud and buoyant. She answered her phone in a sweet tone, all too sweet for Aliah.

Good luck, I mouthed leaning into the car. I nudged the door shut and retrieved my keys from my bag. She was busy and I'd give her some privacy.

It was a cool night and so I zipped my pink yoga jacket to my chin the second I stood up. The sun had decided to disappear behind the clouds, making it feel even cooler yet, so I hurried inside my car and sped off toward home.

At home, Edwin was hanging out in living room listening to music, already out of his suit. *What a shame.* I lazily plopped on the couch next to him, to hear about his first day. "And so?" I asked.

"What?"

"How was your day?" I asked. *Obviously.*

"It was alright."

"That's it? It was just alright?"

"What do you want me to say? I had so much fun researching the *Ontario Corporations Act* today," he said, sarcastically.

I laughed and smiled. "Okay, okay."

"No, it was good. Jake seems like a good guy to work for."

"Jake? Nobody calls him that," I teased.

"Well get used to it, because I do. He told me to call him that."

"Whatever you say, Eddie." I smirked at him as I undid my fitted jacket.

Edwin, easily distracted, quickly changed the subject. "Look at you, all sweaty."

"Hey, I worked hard. What do you expect?"

"Oh, don't get me wrong. It's hot," he said, smiling. "I have to come check out your class some time and see you all shaking your asses. I hear your teacher is pretty hot too."

I narrowed my eyes into a scowl that spread across my face, as Edwin humped the air, mocking our sassy dance class. "You're such a perv!" I got up from the couch and made my way to the fridge.

Edwin followed me casually to the kitchen. "So, I'm not getting in your way at work?"

Oh, he's suddenly concerned with what I think? "Please. I saw you for like two minutes. Besides, I like having you there."

"Yeah, it's hard not to like this," he said, groping his own hard body.

I rolled my eyes and guzzled a bottle of water.

"No, I think I'm going to like it there too. My office is huge. At least it will be, once they get those damn boxes out of there."

"Yeah, that room was originally built for an associate, but it's turned into more like a storage room. I don't know where Owen's going to put all those files."

"What about that empty office near yours?"

"Well, it may be empty now, but it won't be vacant much longer. Ever since Connor Stevens left, we've been drowning in work. Owen has to hire on another lawyer like yesterday."

"No shit. That sucks."

"Yeah, especially for my social life. That's why I've been working so late these days."

"I see you had time to hit the gym tonight though."

"Hey, be fair. I needed some *me time*. I haven't even eaten dinner yet!"

"What are we having?"

"What do you mean we? You're on your own, Eddie boy."

"Come on. I haven't eaten either. We might as well go in on something."

"Why don't you get us Chinese then?" I demanded, pressing my finger on his chest to poke him as I passed.

"Doesn't that defeat the purpose of your exercise class?" he teased, following me again.

I twirled around instantly to face him and pushed him back. "Do you want to eat or not? I went to that class for fun. Now go order the damn food."

"I'll order it, but why don't you come with me to pick it up?"

"Aw, is Eddie feeling lonely?" I teased, flattening my hands on his chest and gently brushing my fingers across the solid muscles. *It's fun to play.*

His blue eyes darkened and his mouth widened with excitement, much like another body part awakened by the trickery. "Very," he growled.

"Too bad. You'll have to go it alone. I want to get in the shower," I said, as I pulled away from him and peeled off my jacket. I started toward the bathroom and Edwin followed me like a lost puppy.

"Okay. If I order the food now, we'll have time for that," he said, vulgar and certain. He stripped of his shirt in one swift motion and chased me up the stairs.

"Has anyone ever told you you're obsessed?" I seriously wondered if he ever thought about anything other than sex.

"Um, yes. You do all the time," he reminded me, looking

up with dark, dazzling eyes. His chest muscles flexed, capturing my attention and testing my resolve, but he made no move to continue up the stairs.

Phew! "Not gonna happen," I said, regaining my composure. I walked away, tearing my eyes from his delicious hand-out. Yes I *want* to touch. I am alive. "I'm having a shower. You're going to get me some Chinese."

I slipped into the bathroom and listened carefully. I was satisfied that he finally gave in when I heard him stomping down the stairs.

"You're no fun!" he hollered, scooping up his shirt and pulling it back over his head.

Good boy.

CHAPTER FOUR

"To celebrate Edwin joining the firm, I thought we could take a trip to the beach," Aliah had said.

I suggested we make a weekend of it. As far I as I knew, Edwin didn't have anything planned for the long weekend and I could use a little R & R. Aliah was all game, but another week passed before we found a free minute to do some planning.

Finally, one night after work, we sat down in the office kitchen, sipping on iced cappuccinos and brainstormed ideas.

"Grand Bend...Wasaga Beach? How far do we want to drive?" I asked, looking for Aliah's input.

Just then, Joshua Bailey hurried into the room and went right for the fridge. "Ladies," he greeted, with a nod.

I smiled back and he yanked open the fridge door. Joshua Bailey was Aliah's boss, one of the Partners at the firm. He was an interesting individual, comedic, not particularly handsome, but very dark and convincing. He was likely *the man* in his day, but that day had certainly passed.

"What keeps you ladies here on such a lovely night?" he asked, once he escaped from the frosty depths of the fridge.

"We were actually just talking about this trip we're planning for the long weekend. You and Emily are welcome to come along?" Aliah suggested, in an obvious attempt to play the goody-goody.

It's true, his wife was youthful and amusing, but I couldn't fathom the thought of having them around for our entire weekend.

A deep throaty laugh came from Bailey in response, instantly relieving my worry. "Thank you for the offer, but I think we're a little too old for that. You young ones go and enjoy yourselves. You don't need us old folkies slowing you down." He laughed again as he tossed his apple high into the air and caught it above his shoulder. "Have a good night, ladies." He promptly stepped away and disappeared into the hall.

I waited enough seconds to be sure that Bailey was a safe distance away before letting Aliah have it. "Are you kidding me, Aliah? Bailey?"

"What? I knew he would say no."

"Ass kiss."

Aliah didn't care. She shrugged her shoulders, unconcerned with what I thought of her.

"Who all's coming anyway?" I asked, anxious to hear the short list.

"Let's see. Me, you, Hunter, Edwin and TJ," she said, tapping all of the fingers on one hand.

"I thought we were making it six, three to each cabin. We've got room for one more."

"Right," she said, hesitantly. The look on Aliah's face told me she was hiding something.

"What is it?"

"Hunter and TJ think we should invite Maddison. I think it's a bad idea," she said, unimpressed.

"Please tell me you're joking."

"Afraid not. You said it. We need another person to put three to a room. It'll be cheaper that way."

"Or we could split the difference and save ourselves the suffering," I mumbled.

"She can stay in the other cabin. It'll be fine," Aliah said. "We don't even have to talk to her."

"Yeah, I'm sure that'll go over well." I knew better than that.

"Now that we have our six, we just have to work out the where. What are you doing for dinner?"

"Why don't you come to my place. We can Google it before making our decision."

"Alright. Let's get up out of here then. I've had enough of this place."

Aliah decided to drive her own car over to my place, which is too bad for her because I was suddenly in a wicked good mood. She rode right on my tail most of the way home, until she couldn't handle five over the speed limit any longer. She pulled out into the traffic and passed me like the psycho that she is.

I accelerated a little, just enough to keep Aliah's car in my sights, until I hit a red light. She was leaning against her car when I pulled up to my house, her arms folded over her chest.

"What took you so long?" she called out impatiently, as I clambered to the front door.

"You're a maniac," I said.

She only smiled.

After a couple of hours of serious research, we were certain that we had found the place for us. With one more click, the Southwind Inn was as good as ours. It wasn't too far away and they had only two cabins left. It was meant to be.

"This is going to be awesome," Aliah squealed with excitement.

I was nodding my head at her when Edwin walked in the room.

"What's up, ladies?"

"We just booked the trip," I said.

"Right on." He slipped up behind me and glanced over my shoulder at the image on the computer screen. "Is that the place?"

"Yup. The Southwind Inn."

"You've done good. I've heard good things about that place."

Aliah and I slapped hands in the air, smiling at each other.

"So, I was thinking," Aliah said, looking to Edwin, "since we had to get two places, what if the girls share the two bedroom and the guys share the other cabin?"

"What?" *What happened to getting Maddie far, far away from us?*

"That's good by me," Edwin said.

"Why would you do that?"

"I was just thinking: Do you want the guys pissing all over our toilet seat and farting up the whole place?" Aliah asked.

She would know having lived with a family of four brothers. I guess Maddie wasn't *that* bad. She was at least clean. "Well, you're in my bed then, because I will not share a room with Maddison."

"Yeah, and like I want to be put with her. I'd rather take the couch," Aliah said, snarling.

We both snickered at our own snootiness.

Edwin was watching us intently, with eyebrows raised. "Maybe I want to be in your room!" he said, with a smirk.

I shook my head at him and narrowed my eyes without responding.

"What? Hunter will probably be disappointed too, you know. It'll dampen his odds of getting laid," he explained.

"Get out of here Edwin!" I yelled, shoving him away.

His smirk only grew as he moseyed for the other room.

Aliah pitched the throw pillow she had been hugging at Edwin's head, but it missed by a long shot. He left the room laughing and now Aliah was the one shaking her head.

The next few weeks went super slow, as we impatiently waited for the break. Edwin had settled into the firm nicely and we were finally used to our new daily routine. Since we had the same schedule now, it didn't take long for Edwin to figure out who gets to use the bathroom first in the mornings. *I do.*

Bright and early one morning, Aliah called me demanding that I go to the gym with her after work, to work on our bikini bods. *How could I say no to that?*

Edwin agreed that I could drive in with him, so I hurried to pack a lunch and finish my morning routine. While staring long and hard at my sizable shoe collection, I heard the rev and rumble of Edwin's truck out front and knew that it was my one minute notice that the train was leaving the station.

Luckily, I had already packed my exercise clothes and so I slipped on some sensible heels, grabbed my bag, and hurried out to him before he took off without me. *Because he so would.*

I lifted myself up into his huge truck, hooking my heel on the chrome tube before tossing my things in ahead of me. When I slid into the seat next to him, he blasted me with a charming smile that flooded me with an unexpected awareness.

For some reason, seeing Edwin all sexy in his business suit this morning was getting to me. He looked so incredibly handsome, his suit hugging his broad shoulders, his smile shining with roguish pride. And when he glanced over at me a second time, with his dark boomerang eyebrows hovering over his bright aqua eyes, I couldn't even hide my fascination. He looked delicious, and that was the only explanation for the hunger burning inside me.

A smile curled on my trembling lips, as I tried to explain the exhilaration suddenly pulsing through my veins. Butterflies danced in my belly and the hairs on the nape of my neck stood on end. Unfortunately, the tingling sensations didn't stop there. *Am I sick? I certainly didn't feel ill this morning.*

"Everything okay?" Edwin asked, noticing my internal conflict.

It was written all over my face. "I'm okay, I guess. My stomach's just a little upset," I said, trying hard to find something unappetizing about him.

"You ragging?"

"Edwin! No, I'm not ragging," I screeched, angered by his insinuation.

"You know what I always say. Never trust anything that

bleeds for five days straight and doesn't die," he teased.

"You stop it!"

"Just sayin'."

As we motored off, I had to hand it to him, I was acting rather strange. I had felt that feeling for Edwin before and I knew exactly what it was.

But could it really be that?

My eyes trailed back to Edwin when I was sure he was enveloped in driving, to see what had gotten me in such a tizzy. The air thickened between us as I admired his dark, handsome features again. Ignoring his bold sarcastic remarks made it easy to leave him untouched in my fantasy land, at least in theory, because in my dreams my hands were all over him.

Edwin looked at me suddenly.

Shit! He totally caught me gazing at him. Though I quickly turned away and glanced out the window, trying to act casual, my reaction to his eyes on me didn't go unnoticed.

He smirked at my jumpy reaction. "What's with you today?" He paused. Even his thoughtful look was god-damned gorgeous. "I hope you're not coming down with something. That would blow. And I doubt we could find someone to go to the Southwind in your place."

I nodded and continued to stare out the side window, as dangerous daydreams danced in my head.

You'd better not replace me.

Even though Edwin and I weren't *together*, it was hard even for a stranger not to notice our elemental bond. I'd always struggled with the fact that Edwin had took up shop on a pedestal in my heart early on and, despite his well-timed immaturity, I'd never demanded that he step down.

My mind drifted to the only other serious relationship in my life. *Spencer Caldwell.* He had been the only man who had what it took to outlast Edwin's strict conditions and ridiculous scare tactics.

At one time, Spencer would have done anything to be with me. Though he wasn't my typical type, with a much slimmer build than Edwin and a much colder sex appeal than I was used to, I think his ability to irk and avert Edwin's angered advances was part of my strong attraction to him. Spencer was not afraid of a little competition, and he was the only one who didn't fail Edwin's tests.

Edwin's large, rough hand grasped heavily on my shoulder, breaking me out of my dreamland. We were already parked in front of the office. "Are you coming, or what?" he said, drawing his hand away as he got out of the truck.

I gasped for air when his door clicked shut. "Yeah, I'm coming."

CHAPTER FIVE

After lunch, I walked up to the copier desk to pick up my printing.

"We did it!" Maddie yelped.

"What are you talking about?" Her enthusiasm was annoying.

"We made it! We leave tomorrow! I can't wait!" she squealed, excitedly.

"Yeah, it's definitely going to be fun. Have you seen this place? It's gorgeous."

"Yeah, been there, done that. You know another thing that's gorgeous? Hunter."

"About that," I said. "Aliah and him go way back. You think you could tone it down a bit when she's around? She seems to get a little antsy when you talk about him like that."

"Oh, please. She can handle it. And I know she can't deny the fact that he's fine."

Aliah suddenly walked in the room like a ghostly figure from the underworld and I was sure she had heard everything. "So, you were talking about the trip?" Aliah asked, calm and cool. I could sense the fire burning beneath the surface.

"Yeah. It's going to be the trip of the year!" Maddison exclaimed.

"Okay, your energy is really irritating. We still have to get through today, you know," Aliah said, clearly annoyed.

"But when you know what's coming, it's so worth the wait," Maddie said, as she spun around and dashed through the front reception door, taking a shortcut to her desk.

"I can see she's going to get annoying real fast," Aliah said, knowing that Maddie could still hear her.

I made a face at her and she smiled. "It'll be whatever

we make it. But if I want to go at all, I'd better get back to work. I'm kind of in the middle of something right now, so I'll talk to you later?"

"Whatevs. Later." Aliah scooped up her papers and took off.

Back at my desk, I quickly squinted at Owen's calendar for the afternoon. It looked like I was in the clear, but Owen had booked a couple of interviews with prospective lawyers to join his practice. Owen was still holding his own, but if we didn't get help soon, it would only be a matter of time before his clients started to suffer the consequences of a staff shortage.

I worked super hard that afternoon and was feeling a little exhausted, though I kept in the back of my head the promise to Aliah that I would hit the gym with her after work. I was ready on time for a change and Aliah was pleasantly surprised, though it didn't stop her from driving us to the club in her usual flurry of speed.

We had made it one block away from the club when I noticed an unmarked police car pulling out behind us. Glancing in the side mirror, I saw the black car increase its speed. It gained on us, until it got so close I couldn't see the headlights. That's when the cherries started flashing erratically.

"Shit!" Aliah screeched, dawning with realization.

"Pull over, dumb ass!"

She ignored my comment and continued the rest of the way, since the driveway to the Westmount was very near. She pulled into the parking lot and parked the car in the first empty space. "Can you believe this?" she asked.

"What do you expect when you drive like a crazy lady?"

"Don't worry I can handle it," she said, tousling her hair and checking herself in the rear-view mirror.

Aliah was in luck. The male police officer was alone. I glanced out the angled rear view, getting a perfect shot of his long solid legs as he stepped out of his car. He adjusted his hat, lowering it over his eyes and approached her side of the car, smooth and stealthy. Dressed in full uniform, complete with aviator sunglasses, he looked like a walking wet dream. *Ooh, I love a man in uniform.* He knocked at her window before she put it down.

"Yes, officer?" she said coyly, leaving the window only half open.

"Do you realize how fast you were driving?" he said, voice flat and strong, with an incredibly appealing accent. His eyes were shadowed beneath his brimmed hat and I couldn't help but stare at his amazing lips.

"Well, my friend and I were just heading to the Westmount, after a long day's work, as you can see. We really didn't want to be late for our class. I apologize, officer. I promise it won't happen again."

I rolled my eyes and glanced out my window, noting the growing crowd inside the Westmount's large front window.

The officer chuckled, amused for some unknown reason. Being awfully bold, he reached inside the window and pressed the button to ease it all the way down. That dark, troubled chuckle caught my attention. My eyes tore from my window and flashed out Aliah's in an instant.

The officer tipped up his hat to get a good look at me. "Is this true, sweetheart?" he asked.

I thought I recognized those lips. How could I be so ignorant? "Spencer!" I said, sounding completely shocked. How could I have mistaken that terribly sexy accent? The officer removed his aviators, hooked them onto his collared shirt, then readjusted the brim of his hat, all while gazing at me with his mysteriously icy blue eyes.

"Good to see you. How are things going?" he asked. His stance became less formal, as he clutched the top of the car and leaned closer, his duty blowing away with the wind.

"Things are good. The house is finally done. I'm still working with Owen. Same old, I guess. How've you been?" I asked, curiously attentive.

"Alright, I guess. You look great! Are you still single?" he asked, his accent straight out of England.

Flustered, both from his offensive suggestion and his sexy voice, I stuttered. "Uhh..."

"I apologize. I realize how that sounded and I didn't mean to insult you. Let me rephrase my question, if you will. If you aren't seeing someone right now, would you like to get a coffee sometime? With me. You know, to catch up."

I smiled at his save but was not incredibly intrigued by his invitation. *What was I thinking? I was intrigued. And clearly I wasn't thinking.* "I'd like that." I'd been having a draught in the man department lately and that accent of his was irresistible. I would do coffee with him anytime, if only to sit and listen to him talk.

Aliah knew I was carefully working her out of a speeding ticket, but she still couldn't keep her mouth shut. "You didn't recognize *me*, Spence?"

"No, but I should have recognized your reckless driving."

"Could you blame me? This car just begs you to drive fast," she said, not helping her situation.

"I'll tell you what. I may be willing to bargain with you. But if I don't give you a ticket here, today, you'll have to give me something in exchange," he said to Aliah.

"Anything." She even raised her eyebrows to be sure he understood that point.

I shook my head out of embarrassment, with my hand over my eyes, though Aliah was clearly unaffected by her lack of humility.

"You have Abigail call me," he said. Spencer plucked his pad of paper from his pocket and scribbled something on it. As he ripped the paper off, I overheard a call come in over his radio.

"Is that even legal, what you're doing there, Mr. Officer?" Aliah taunted, yanking the paper from his fingers.

"Don't push your luck. What you just offered me could be considered bribing a police officer," he said bluntly, then smiled at me.

He looked wicked and sexy as hell. His mysterious eyes sparkled and dazzled me even more than I had remembered they could. "I have to take care of this call. You ladies should probably get to that class you were racing to. And you make sure Abby calls me, or I'll get you next time." He curled his lips into another mysterious smile and hustled back to his car. In seconds he was speeding off with lights and sirens and just like that, Spencer was gone.

"Mmm, mmm. There's just something about a man in uniform," Aliah said. "Tell me again why you never got back with him?"

"Funny you say that. I'm having a hard time remembering that myself right now." I laughed, but there were plenty of reasons not to get involved with Spencer.

Aliah pulled her keys from the ignition and together we jogged up to the building. The bystanders had scattered from the window by time we reached the doors. We had even made it to class with a few minutes to spare.

After class, I showered at the club and it reenergized me; gave me a sense of vibrant wellbeing. Aliah drove me home, faster than necessary, despite what had transpired earlier.

"Thanks for the ride, *Danica*."

"Hey. If it weren't for my speedy driving, you wouldn't have seen Spencer Caldwell at all."

"Whatever you have to tell yourself," I teased. "Laters." I walked past Edwin's truck and clutched the antiqued bronze door handle. The door was locked. After digging through my bag, at last I found my key and slid it into the lock. It turned over with ease.

I let myself inside and dropped my bag on the floor. "Hello?" I hollered, not hearing Edwin anywhere on the main floor. I walked around, but he wasn't anywhere to be found. *That's strange.*

I strapped by bag back onto my shoulder and jogged up stairs. His bedroom door was shut. *I hope he's not ill.* I dropped my things inside my bedroom door and finger combed my hair as I headed for his room. I tapped on his door and peeked inside, expecting the worst.

Edwin was lying on his bed relaxing, with headphones on, but he appeared to be alive and well. He saw me as soon as I opened his door and waved for me to come in. He pulled off his headphones and swung his feet over the side of the bed. "I've been waiting for you. I wanted to talk to you about something," Edwin said, patting the bed next to himself.

"Did you eat dinner yet?" I asked, hoping to put it off.

"No, but this is important. I want to discuss it with you first." His face looked troubled, yet his body was as laid-back as usual.

I instantly got a pain in my side, wondering if this had something to do with my googly eyes for him earlier. *Shit.* He's probably feeling like he has to let me down before I get my hopes up. *This is awkward.* I hesitantly crept closer to the bed.

Edwin had been watching me. He raised an eyebrow and smiled. "Don't look so worried. Come here." His smile kicked up a notch. He knew I was fretting and was somehow pleased by that.

My anxiety mounted considerably when it hit me. *Is he ready to move on without me?* I knew our joint home ownership couldn't last forever and it was only a matter of time before one of us made the decision to either move out or try to give the other the boot. But now? *I can't believe he's doing this to me.* He must want a fresh start. New job. New space. New life. I took a seat a safe distance away from him.

"Come on now, am I that scary?"

I shimmied a little closer, but he wasn't satisfied, shifting himself until our legs were touching. I rested my hands on my thighs, with nowhere else for them to go, and stared at them in silent agony. Sitting so close to Edwin, I couldn't help but inhale his fresh scent, lemony bleach and fabric softener. I couldn't escape the urge to snuggle up against his chest and run my fingers over his tight, rigid abs.

"You know that I've had a bit of a dry spell with the ladies lately."

"Okay," I said, hesitantly. I wondered if he thought our living arrangement was the cause of that. It had definitely not made things easy for me.

"So, I was thinking. Maybe we could give the whole friends-with-benefits thing a shot." Though his words flowed serious and honest, he could not wipe the huge smile off his face. His amusement invoked an urge within me to attack him.

I didn't know whether it had formed out of anger, relief or attraction, but I went with it anyway, acting on impulse. I tackled Edwin and pinned him down on the bed. "Is that all you ever think about?" I raised my eyebrows at him waiting for a thoughtful response.

He sensed my anger and tried to manage his smile, but his lips still curled handsomely at the edges. "You have no idea how much that just turned me on."

"Ugh!" I screeched, jumping up off of him. I bounced to my butt and hopped off the bed swiftly. I stomped a few steps away to show my annoyance, though my heart was racing and my head was thrilled.

Not knowing how to deal with the feelings coursing through me, I scurried out his door and got a head start on the stairs. My exhilaration was seeping out onto my face and I was having a hell of a time controlling it. Edwin was hot on my tail.

"I see you're feeling better," he called behind me.

Obviously I am, because I was never sick, dumb ass. I masked my facial expressions as best I could, by pressing a frown onto my lips. "Yes, I am, thank you very much."

I made it to the kitchen and opened the fridge quickly, tucking my head inside the french doors. I didn't find anything enticing, since I hadn't stocked it this week, knowing we'd be away for the weekend. I stared a little longer than needed, hoping to regain my composure. When I thought I had it together, I shut the fridge, turned around and looked at Edwin.

He was smiling, teeth and all. But damn, he looked good.

I rolled my eyes then scowled at him, since it was the only logical response without totally giving myself away. "You know that shit never works out."

"Oh, but it'd be so much fun trying. No strings attached. And I know it's been a while for you too. Come on. I'll follow your rules," he begged. And it was so hot.

I was offended that he was keeping tabs on my sex life, but I was happy to hear that he didn't sleep with that last floozy he was dating. *Unless he was only telling me what I wanted to hear.*

Wait a minute. Am I actually considering this? This is insane.

When I broke out of the daze, I realized that Edwin's smile hadn't faded. He knew I was considering it and he approved. His enthusiasm was actually quite charming. He *was* looking incredibly sexy today.

Such a dangerous decision, and even though I knew it was a bad idea, I also knew what I was missing out on. If I couldn't bring myself to indulge, I could at least press his buttons a little, right? It'd be harmless to be a tease, and wind him up just for the fun of it.

Yes. That's what I'll do.

"Are you that hard up?" I teased, finally letting a soft smile sneak out. "What about Aleshia from a few weeks ago? I thought she was a sure thing."

"Nope. She couldn't shut her mouth long enough and I couldn't bring myself to do it. I have standards you know."

"Oh, I see, and somehow this is way classier than sleeping with a girlfriend."

"It's the safest bet. You know what you're getting into and you don't have to worry about the awkward morning after."

"True. And it's not like I'd be hanging out in your bed by morning anyway."

"Is that so? Then you forget. This isn't new to us, Abs. I know what you like. When I'm done with you, you won't be going anywhere."

I gulped as a liquid heat pooled between my thighs. I squeezed them tightly together and shrugged my shoulders, playing the part of a dainty innocent. How had he gotten me all flustered again?

"I'm really hungry though," I insisted, being provocative and playful.

My turn.

I drew close to him, acting seductive and inviting. Excitement flickered in Edwin's glorious blue eyes. I watched the colour darken and stir before me, swirling like a thunderstorm. I stopped only inches away from his face and gazed up into his stormy eyes. It messed with my self-control.

"Hungry for love?" Edwin wrapped his arms securely around my waist and pulled me close.

I'd be damned if I didn't admit it felt good to be in his big, protective arms again. When I caught his warm, alluring scent, I had lost all control. My knees grew weak, and I knew if it weren't for him holding me firmly in place, I would have crumbled to the floor.

I couldn't resist him anymore. I had to kiss him. Breathless, my eyes fluttered shut and my lips parted. Edwin tightened his hold on me, then gently brushed his lips across mine in a silent seduction. We shared a sweet breath as our passion collided, old feelings renewed in a moment of undeniable chemistry. His lips touched mine again, so gentle and passionate. I softened beneath him, an unforgiving whimper escaping my lips.

His smile touched my mouth as he deepened the kiss, his tongue softly swiping mine. He kissed me breathless, stealing my air, jolting my heart from its sweet ache. Desperate for air, I forced myself to break away from his mouth. Still clinging to his broad muscled shoulder and swimming with desire, I gasped for air. I couldn't see his face, but I knew he was smiling. I shouldn't have let him get to me like that, and feeling slightly mortified from my whimsical reaction, I decided it was time to throw a wrench in it.

I whispered softly in his ear, remembering his last words before I lost myself. "I'm hungry for food."

He sighed, his disappointment obvious. "Really?" he asked, staring me down, his eyes so warm and full of promise.

"Yes, Eddie. I'm starving." I withdrew my nails from his shoulder and smoothed them down his triangular back. I smirked at him as I slipped my hands into the back pockets of his jeans. I raised my eyebrows, and held them there, showing him that I'd do what I wanted. Then I squeezed his irresistible butt.

He raised his eyebrows, intrigued once again. He seemed happy that I hadn't let him go, but his eyes glazed over as he sunk deep in thought. Then, "I know just the thing."

"Huh?"

He cupped my face and brushed his thumb over my cheek, then dropped a delicious kiss on my mouth. "Just to change it up a bit."

Concerned, I released my hands from his pants. "I hope you're talking food," I said. But I knew he wasn't. I could almost guarantee his plan was going to be trouble.

"I'm going to go get us our pizza. It should be ready soon. I know we've never done anything quite like this before, but just go with it. Please, Abs." He kissed me on my cheek and ran out the door. Before I could bombard him with questions, the door slammed shut.

"Go with what?" I said softly, knowing he couldn't hear me anymore.

There was no point in trying to figure out how his wacky brain worked. Not needing the undue stress, I flopped down on the couch and kicked up my feet. Wow. What had just happened? It had been too long since I had felt such a spark. I forgot how it was supposed to feel.

Emotions that I had tucked away after our last breakup had resurfaced with a vengeance. That meant trouble. Especially since Edwin made it clear that he was only looking for a little bit of fun. *No strings attached,* is what he had said, to be exact.

Interesting, Edwin used to always say that *every* man who claims he's *just friends* with a girl, secretly hopes that it turns into something more. I've trusted that truth and it has proven to be accurate to this day. That only means that dangerous waters lie ahead and I need to tread carefully.

CHAPTER SIX

I could still feel the touch of his lips on mine when I closed my eyes. My stomach growled loudly, startling me out of my daydream, just seconds before the doorbell rang. Was Edwin expecting company? Curious to see who it was, I hurried to the door and peered out the sidelight. *That's peculiar. What in the world is he doing?*

I opened the door to Edwin standing there with the pizza in hand, leaning against the house with a ball cap pulled low over his eyes. "Pizza delivery," he said, his voice deep and serious.

"Eddie, what are you doing?"

"Delivering this pizza ma'am."

"What if the neighbours see you like this?" I scoffed.

"It says right here, 608 Stewart," he replied, refusing to break character. "That is you, right?" he added, pointing at the matching number on the house.

"I didn't order a pizza." I held my lips in a pout and stared at him, unmoving. When I realized he wasn't going to give it up that easily, I decided to up the ante. He was obviously taking his cues from this old porn we used to watch together and it was absolutely hilarious, though I'd be lying if I didn't admit it kind of turned me on.

"Well, I'd hate for this delicious pizza to go to waste ma'am," he said, licking his full curvaceous lips.

Ahh, hell. What did I have to lose? "Actually, suddenly I'm feeling terribly hungry. Would you like to come in?" I asked, getting into character.

"I really shouldn't. You know, I have to work and all."

I grabbed him by the shirt and pulled him in the house, slamming the door shut behind us.

"Okay!" he replied willingly, after I manhandled him. He glanced around the room anxiously, as though he had never been there before.

"Don't worry. My husband isn't expected back for hours," I said, as I pulled off his cap and tossed it on the floor.

Pizza still in hand, he shuffled backwards, like a shy young man trying to avoid my advances, until I had his back pressed up against the wall.

I slid my hand down his solid abs and grabbed him through his pants. He was already as hard as a rock. A blast of heat swept through me again, reminding me of our passionate kiss. Edwin squeezed his eyes shut on a sharp intake of breath, reveling in the moment, as I teased him gently with my hand. Stealing his breath entirely, my lips lightly brushed across his, barely touching, like a forgotten whisper.

Then my stomach growled. "Do you think maybe we could eat first?" I asked, voice low and husky.

Edwin opened his eyes and raised his eyebrows at me, suggesting that there was no way we were stopping now. "Screw this," he said, throwing the pizza onto the foyer table. Grabbing my wrist, he pulled me upstairs to his bedroom.

I didn't put up a fight, being even more turned on by his loss of control.

Once we got in his room, he let go of my arm. When he closed his door, the room suddenly felt a lot smaller. Hotter. He looped around me, but I quickly walked away from him, swaying my hips as I slowly moved toward his bed. I knew he was watching and when I glanced back, my eyes warm with thoughtful curiosity, I saw that he was.

"You're sure you want to do this?" Edwin swiftly closed the distance between us, his eyes burning with desire, flames licking the air around me.

"You've gotten this far. Are you saying you've changed your mind?"

"Absolutely not. I'm all about it. As long as you're good with it," he said, as he pulled me in tight against him.

"I'm all about it," I whispered.

He certainly was too, because I could still feel him bursting from his pants, solid, rigid and erect.

His hands became aggressive, as he kissed me with passionate, insatiable lips. He slipped off my shirt, not missing a breath, his lips crashing back into mine. Desperate to feel skin on skin, I peeled his shirt from his back. He was warm, smooth and hard all over.

We scuffled to the bed and crashed onto it, with limbs tangled together as we knocked over his bed-side lamp. Startled, we both laughed, but there was nothing funny about the intensity in the atmosphere. A storm of sensations continued to brew and collide around us.

Craving his touch, I directed his hands, his full weight resting heavy on me, as his lips reminded me what I had been missing out on. I ran my fingers through his short, dark hair and pulled, trying to decipher whether this was reality or illusion.

Edwin smiled. "Hey." He brought both of his hands to my face and cradled my head, before delivering an intimate, breathtaking kiss. He lowered me onto his pillows, without ever taking his eyes from mine. "I don't want to rush it," he whispered, hovering over me like a dark angel.

While I appreciated the gesture, I was fine with the thrashing. Confusion balled up in the pit of my stomach. *Suddenly he wants to go slow?*

Make up your mind!

"You have no idea how long I've waited for this, Abs." His bold statement left me breathless, exposing that there was more to this little escapade than he was letting on.

"What sexing me up?" I asked. I tried to stay playful, but secretly hoped it was enough to get him to spit it out.

"Not just that, but that's a part of it. I miss you, Abs. *In every way.* And I think you know that." He laid back down on top of me, pinning with his weight, our legs interlaced together. At that moment, I knew he needed me as much as I needed him.

"I miss you too," I said softly.

He didn't seem convinced. "I don't want you to do this if

you're not feeling it, and it's okay if you're not. I can handle it." He paused, not leaving any breathing room for me. "So, are you?"

I gulped to clear the lump from my throat, suddenly feeling put on the spot. "You said *no strings attached*. You've got me all revved up. Are you reneging now?" I asked, kissing his soft lips. I paused thoughtfully, deciding whether I should satisfy his curiosity or just distract him with incredible, mindless sex. I left my lips lingering close to his and let out a sigh. "You know how I was kind of acting funny this morning?"

"Great, you *are* ragging! That explains the mood swings. He untangled our legs and lifted himself off of me.

"No! Will you shut up for a minute so I can tell you this?"

"Okay, I'm sorry." He propped himself up beside me and looked me in the eyes, giving me his full attention.

That in turn gave me a sudden loss of nerve. I looked away and reconsidered whether I was giving up too much information in the moment. Maybe I was only responding to his raging hormones and mine. The room fell awkwardly silent.

"That answers my question," he said. Crushed, he sat up and turned away, shutting me out. "You don't have to say another word."

"Just like that?" I said, watching his reaction.

The suspense was obviously still killing him. I crawled up next to him and took his strong jaw in my hands, turning it toward me against his will, until he was paying close attention.

"Don't freak out, but I think I still love you." I released his face, suddenly feeling incredibly self-conscious. *Shit, did I just say that?* I held my breath, waiting for his response, but mostly afraid to hear it.

Edwin's eyes never left my face. He had to have known that my words were drawn from pure, raw emotion, yet he broke out in full on laughter. Obviously I was the only one who had caught feelings.

"That's it? That's what you were having such a hard time

saying?" he said, still smirking.

I tried not to feel the hurt that was engulfing my heart, but it was there throbbing at the seams.

"I love you too, Abs," Edwin said, low and sure.

My eyes widened, but I wasn't smiling. "It's not funny, Eddie, and I don't think you get it. I don't love you like a friend. I love you more than that. I still get butterflies. It's ridiculous, I know," I rambled, angry at him and angry at myself.

His face turned serious, but his smile seemed a little too amused for me to feel like I was in the safe zone. "I'm sorry for laughing," he said, though he looked like he was ready to explode, his huge smile bursting from his face.

"Ugh! I've said too much," I gushed embarrassedly, covering my eyes.

"No, you haven't. I love you like that too. Is it really that surprising to you? Do you really need to hear me say it to believe it?"

"Yes," I demanded selfishly.

"I - L-O-V-E - YOU! You really don't know how hard you've made it for me lately, do you?"

The pain eased away from my heart, allowing it to pound strong and steady, and yet I didn't know what to say to that. So I said nothing at all.

"It's cool that you still get butterflies, being that we live together and all," he added.

A sudden flicker of embarrassment warmed my cheeks, flushing a rosy red colour over them. I *had* said too much. *What a disaster.* So much for a little harmless fun. I shifted on his bed and dropped my head on the pillow with a sigh.

I should have felt relieved from getting it all off my chest, but I didn't. I blew out a harsh breath, my head pounding at the temples. "I guess we kind of blew the moment."

Edwin sprawled out next to me and reached his hand for my face. "Hardly. I want you now more than ever."

Love burst from my eyes as he slid closer to me and brought his lips to mine, his touch more passionate than ever. I looped my arms around his neck and he pulled me onto his lap. We took our time, slowly peeling each other's clothes off, piece by piece. Touching. Feeling. The blankets swallowed us whole, Edwin giving careful attention to every inch of my body, his caress so strong yet so gentle. His lips found mine and I devoured him, slow and deep, tasting everything he had to offer. He touched me until I was ready to explode, then his lips tickled my ear, his whisper making me tremble with desire.

"I need you. Now. Do you want me to get a condom?" He nibbled on my ear and brushed soft, wet kisses across my neck and up my chin.

"Will you?" I rasped softly, releasing his body without removing my lips from his. I didn't want to let him go, but I had to feel him inside of me.

Edwin rolled away and pulled a condom from the bedside table, allowing cool air under the steamy covers. I trembled as he tore open the package and quickly rolled it on. He smiled sweetly and when his lips came back to mine, so did my raging desire, surging back to the point of eruption.

"Now," he insisted, desperation laced in his deep, smooth voice.

He slowly glided over me and I groaned softly as he pressed himself inside, transporting me to another world. I gasped for air, clinging to his strong shoulders, as a rush of pleasure built deep inside me. Deliberate, but unhurried, he kissed my mouth as he filled me with long, steady strokes.

"Oh, God!" I cried, unable to quiet my enjoyment.

Edwin quickened his pace, heightening my arousal with every thrust.

"Yes," I screamed, unable to stop the incredible force bearing down on me. Clung tight to Edwin's back, my climax hit me like violent tidal wave.

Edwin pressed on, eager to deliver, as my raging satisfaction baited his own release. Every muscle in my body twitched in agreement, with Edwin packed deep inside me, his mouth covering my gasps of glorious pleasure, his moans delivering me delicious vibrations.

After the tremors subsided, joined in a moment of quiet contemplation, Edwin rolled beside me.

"Wow!" he managed, breathless and satisfied.

"Yes," I replied, in agreement.

CHAPTER SEVEN

I was happy to have the mind-numbing conversation out of the way and was hoping it was lost in the back of Edwin's sex-crazed mind. After slipping on my panties, I got back into his bed. We laid there for a long time, silently staring into each other's eyes, each of us wondering what the other was thinking.

Finally, Edwin leaned in and kissed me again. "Are you still hungry?"

"Hungry for love," I teased, as I pushed him away from me and jumped up to look for the rest of my clothes. I was actually very hungry and suddenly pretty concerned about my pizza. "I'm sure the pizza's cold by now."

"Maybe if you could've kept your hands off the pizza man, you would've had it hot. Instead, you're stuck with me, a warm bed and cold pizza."

Maybe if my pizza man wasn't so damn fine I could keep my hands off of him. I stared briefly at Edwin's male perfection, lazy like a lion; a big, strong, dangerous lion. Before the moment could pass, I quickly pulled my shirt over my head, slipped my arms through the holes and took full advantage of that warm bed. I jumped back on top of Edwin and kissed him affectionately.

"I'll take that over hot pizza any day," I said, brushing my hands over his hard chest.

He pulled me in for another kiss, pressing his lips purposefully against mine, and holding me tight. "I love you, Abby," he reminded me.

Unable to meet his eyes, I laid my head on his shoulder. "I love you too, Eddie," I said, with a soft sigh.

I'd never thought I'd hear myself saying that out loud any time soon.

After a moment of peaceful silence, my stomach growled

reminding me just how hungry I was. I propped my elbows up on Edwin's chest. "Are you going to come have some pizza with me?" I asked.

"Yup. I'll be down in a minute."

After one last smooch, I hopped up to go looking for the pizza. The box hadn't made it far from the front door and it made me giggle when I recalled Edwin's little pizza delivery act. I carried the cold box of pizza to the table, threw a few slices on a couple of plates and popped them into the microwave, one at a time. I pulled two icy cold bottles of Coors Light from the fridge. I was sure Edwin would agree that they were warranted.

I put one warm plate on the table and twisted the cap off my bottle. I took a sip of the cold beer and it slid delightfully down my throat. I went back to the microwave for the other plate of warmed pizza and dropped it onto Edwin's spot at the table. What was taking him so long?

"Your pizza's getting cold," I hollered. Before I could swallow my first bite, Edwin was seated across from me. And damn he looked good. So put together. The exact opposite of how I felt at this very moment.

"It wouldn't be the first time." He chuckled as he lifted a slice of pizza to his open mouth. "You'd better watch it, a guy could get used to this." Smiling, he brought his bottle to his lips and took a healthy swig.

"We wouldn't want that," I said, sarcastically, then had another bite of pizza. Unable to stay away from him, *my man*, I gathered all my courage. I walked around the table and took a seat on his lap, with a half-eaten slice of pizza in my hand.

"Yup, already used to it," he teased, smiling. He put down his pizza to kiss me, his hand cupped in my hair.

After a few seconds, I pulled away and took another bite of my slice. "Okay, I'll leave you to yours. It's not like I'm going anywhere," I said, drawing his eyes to my body as I walked back to my chair.

I took a seat and looked up at him, to find him still eyeing me. He was already finishing off his last slice, his beer nearly gone. I couldn't help but notice that mine was still half full.

He caught me gawking at my half full bottle. "Drink up. You'll need the practice for this weekend."

"Shit! We're leaving tomorrow and I haven't even started packing!" I was suddenly aware of how little time was left.

"Oh no! And you only have twenty-four hours to do it!" He laughed at my girly crisis.

I scowled at him, but I wasn't actually mad. Good vibes still coursed through my veins.

"I know a few things you should bring," Edwin said, his voice a low, sexy growl. "That skimpy, pink bikini for one. Oh and that short white dress that looks like you took the scissors to the bottom."

"It's cream coloured, but I'll pack it. Any other requests?"

"Nope, as long as you're coming, I'll have everything I need."

His words stroked me like a big, steady hand, my insides flickering with a warm and fuzzy sensation. My lips refused to stop smiling, though I wasn't done messing with him yet. "Eddie. It's no strings attached. Remember?" After tossing my crust into the garbage pail, I rinsed my plate in the sink.

Edwin came up behind me, wrapped his arms around my waist and started showering my neck with soft, intimate kisses. "You know there's more to it than that. I need you, Abigail; in my arms and in my bed."

I twirled around and laced my fingers behind his neck. His aqua blue eyes glinted with confidence. A girl could get lost in those gorgeous, deep eyes. With a soft smile, I chewed on my lip.

"Don't act all shy around me," Edwin said. "I know you better than you know yourself. Like I said, there's more to it than that; and you know it."

The quieter I kept, the more he bombarded me with his confessions of love.

"I love everything about you, Abby; even that you're

often stubborn, usually sarcastic and always demanding."

Gee thanks. "You'd better quit being so sweet, because a girl could get used to that you know." I was being sarcastic.

Edwin drew his hands up from my curvaceous hips and closed them around my waist. "Maybe you should," he said. "I didn't even get started on how mesmerizing your hips are, or that glimmer in your eyes that tells me your mine. And I guarantee there's more where that came from."

"Yup, already used to it."

His smile was effortless, as he leaned in for another kiss.

The work day was going by fast and no one seemed to notice that Edwin and I were a little *closer* than normal. In need of short break in the afternoon, I went to the kitchen for a drink. Unexpectedly, Edwin was standing there, sharing a few words with Miller over coffee. They were deep in conversation about a particular file but, unable to help myself, I had to intrude.

"Excuse me," I interrupted, so I could squeeze by and get into the fridge.

Edwin trained his eyes on me and a slight smile curled on the edge of his lips. I ducked my head in the fridge, relieved to have the cool refuge from my suddenly rosy cheeks and Edwin's burning stare. *How is it that he can still have that effect on me?*

After rummaging something up, I heard Miller start back in on the file. I figured it was safe to make my exit. I immediately glanced up at Edwin, whose eyes wandered toward my hips. Staggered by the attention, I swayed seductively toward a table and selected a seat.

Taylor appeared out of nowhere in the doorway. "Mr. Miller, Derrick Marshall is here again. Did you want to talk to him?"

"I guess I'll have to. Tell him I'll be a few minutes," he said, rather unhappily.

I winked at her with understanding and lowered into my

seat. Taylor walked away quickly and Miller shook his head, showing his disappointment.

"This is his third visit today. Give me a break!" he said to Edwin, then briskly walked to the door. "We'll have to talk about this again another time."

Edwin chuckled and I looked away, so he didn't think I was listening in, though I totally was. I stared at the wall, trying to mind my own business, waiting for Edwin's reaction to running into me at the office after last night.

Boldly enough, he walked right up behind me. "Real convincing," he said. Then with a sexy whisper, close to my ear, "Hey."

A tingling sensation sprinkled down my body and my smile couldn't resist. "Hey," I replied seductively, glancing at him over my shoulder.

His arched eyebrow rose inquisitively. "There's, uh, this paper in the shredding room that is giving me some trouble. I thought maybe you could give me *a hand.*" He briskly walked away, not waiting for an answer.

CHAPTER EIGHT

A paper jam. I'm sure. I know it's a bad idea, but how can I say no to this man? I brushed away all logic, ignored the consequences of what I was about to do, and focused on the desire. I wanted Edwin as bad as he wanted me.

Edwin bolted for the door and nodded his head at Taylor as she re-entered the lunchroom.

"Hi," Taylor said, flashing a warm, friendly smile. She continued on to the fridge.

"Hey Taylor," I replied cheerfully, remaining seated. *No. She couldn't possibly know and I was ready to take my chances.*

Making an immediate getaway, I tore out of the room before Taylor could even catch which way I was heading. I rushed straight for the paper shredding room, anxiously glancing around to be sure no one caught me entering the door.

The odds of someone else going into that room was slim to none, being that the students had already gone home for the day; yet I carefully double checked both directions before grabbing onto the door handle. With my excitement kicked into a higher gear, I snuck inside the room. It was small enough to be a closet.

"You came." Edwin's voice was a low, smooth growl.

"You didn't think I would?"

A smile crept onto his lips as he flipped the light switch. In total darkness, I was suddenly feeling totally at ease with the situation, every sense deliciously heightened. When his fingers whispered over my arm I shivered, but it didn't relieve the temperature in the room that had spiked up several degrees in a matter of seconds.

The sexual tension in the room was like a tight knot that I intended to unravel. I hooked my arms around Edwin's neck and his hands were on my thighs, hauling me up against him, before I could realize which way was up. His lips crashed into mine, hot and hungry, setting off a fire through my blood stream. His excitement felt as sharp as my own, jabbed hard against my belly. I let out a gentle moan and my eyes suddenly popped open, fear colliding with all the other emotions swirling in the warm air. I could feel Edwin's smile on my lips.

"It's okay, baby. No one can hear us in here," he breathed.

He nudged my lips apart and it was like a live wire tapped into my heart. His mouth felt amazing, his kiss incredibly arousing, the sounds a tornado of echoes in my head. The sound of the rustling of my clothes under his hands, his tongue sucking on mine, his lips smacking against me, all set off an alarm in my overactive brain. *Really? Is this amusing to you? Two can play that game.*

I lowered my feet to the floor, reached my hand down and grabbed the rod protruding from his pants. Edwin gasped with enthusiasm and pressed himself deeper into my grasp. Controlling him like a manual transmission car, I sucked on his upper lip and tugged on his lower one with my teeth.

"Mmm," he growled.

I tilted my head so he'd have better access to my exposed neck and he wasted no time working his magical lips. My hand was clutched in his hair, holding him firmly against me. It felt so good I wanted to scream out. Stifling those feelings only caused my arousal to rage even hotter. I dug my nails into his light, suit jacket and he squeezed me even closer, as his mouth covered mine, his hand slipping inside my panties.

Right when I thought a dry hump would be enough to send me over the edge, a co-worker stopped just outside our door, putting an abrupt end to my rise. I turned toward the door and froze in place, breath on hold, while Edwin continued to devour me.

"Do you know where I might find Abigail?" Owen asked.

Edwin stopped mid-nibble, as a loud gasp of horror escaped me. He cupped his free hand over my mouth, buffering the sound, as we both stood in place like statues.

"Sorry, Owen. I don't. She was just in the lunchroom a few minutes ago. Maybe she went for a coffee. I'll let her know you're looking for her if I see her."

If we got caught, we would be screwed in every sense of the word. My head started to feel light. Then I realized I was still holding my breath under Edwin's heavy hand. I struggled to break free from him, but he barely lightened his hold on me. We both held our stillness until an entire minute passed, and even then I was still too scared to make a sound.

Edwin let out a sigh of relief. "Breathe," he whispered, smiling as he retrieved his hand from my pants and flicked on the light switch.

After holding my breath so long I thought I might pass out, I gasped for air. "Do you really think this is funny?" I whispered. My arousal was quickly substituted with anger.

Edwin didn't answer, but he also couldn't wipe his unregulated smile from his face. He caught my chin and gave me a soft kiss, easing my anger oh so slightly, though any amount of affection wasn't going to be enough to take away all of my anxiety right now.

"I think that might be our warning," I said softly, eyes still closed.

"Yeah, I suppose it is," Edwin agreed.

I relaxed, trying to steady my ragged breaths, and reopened my eyes so they could adjust to the bright, white light.

"Pull yourself together, woman; seducing me like that. And at the office no less. It's just not right," he teased.

I slapped him on the shoulder and flashed him a dirty look, though I couldn't help but be amused by his harmless antics. "Go straight to your office," I ordered. And after adjusting his tie, I passionately kissed him off, knowing full well it'd be the last until tonight. "Oh, and Edwin? Don't blow it."

He smiled anxiously and my heart fluttered. "Here goes nothing." With a quick rise and fall of his brows, he strolled casually out of the room.

I closed the door behind him, refusing to head out at the same time. After waiting another long minute, I cracked the door open. When I slipped out the door, I nearly peed my pants. Edwin was still standing there. I was sure we were toast.

"The coast is clear," he whispered.

Not taking any chances of being caught with Edwin, still looking all mussed up, I hightailed it back to my desk. *Men. They can't follow simple instructions.*

After resisting the urge to go to Owen's office to see what was up, I struggled through drafting an Affidavit. When Owen took his next client into the boardroom, I decided enough time had passed and so it was safe for me to roam the office again. I desperately wanted to tell Aliah about me and Edwin. *Now. I had to get it off my shoulders and off my mind.*

A brisk walk to Aliah's desk, rounding the reception desk to skip Edwin's doorway, was useless. Aliah wasn't in her chair and, being so dangerously close, I couldn't help but steal a glance at Edwin. He stood just inside his door, staring blankly at his shelf of books. *I know the feeling.* Going against every grain of womanly intuition, I slipped into his room to see how his afternoon was turning out.

"There's trouble," Edwin said, smiling. He was amused by my own lack of focus, but it was apparent from the frustration hiding beneath his smile that he was experiencing the same problem.

"You're busy. I should let you get back to work." I clambered toward his door regretting the bothersome visit.

"Abigail."

I twisted around, to find his eyes blazing. *Is that torment in his eyes? Is it because I'm leaving?* He extended his arms, begging for me to come to him and I recklessly obeyed.

"I always have time for you," he whispered, before tugging me closer and nuzzling his nose in my hair.

I couldn't resist him as he inhaled me like a fragrance. He was already standing so utterly close to me. I had to touch him. The doorway was empty. There was no one in sight.

Reading my mind, Edwin stepped farther into the corner of his office, frantically pulling me into a blind spot from the door. He didn't stop me when I put my hand on his face. Running my fingers over his light stubble, I kissed him long and soft.

When I finally drew my lips away, Edwin's reaction told me I had lingered a little too long. *Busted.* I was certain there was someone standing in his doorway behind me and a pang of distress clenched my insides as I turned around to see who it was.

"It's not what it looks like," Edwin blurted out.

With my thoughts still scrambled, I couldn't find my tongue.

"Holy shit, guys. What's going on here?" Aliah asked, entering the doorway. She approached us quietly. "You didn't tell me you guys were an item again. I should've known. I saw this coming from a mile away."

"Is that so?" Edwin asked, amused.

I pulled free from Edwin's tight grip. "Were not exactly... I mean... it just happened. It's complicated."

Edwin stood there silently, clearly amused by my stammering.

"It happened just now?" Aliah bellowed.

Terrified that someone had heard her, my eyes grew wide. I laughed nervously and looked to Edwin for some assistance. His boss suddenly materialized in the door behind Aliah.

"Hey, Jake. I was just getting that book for you," Edwin said, stepping away from me.

Miller stepped past Edwin and pulled the book off the shelf, knowing right where to find it. "Sorry to break up the party, but..."

"I apologize, Mr. Miller," I interrupted. "It's my fault."

"I know you kids are excited for the long weekend, but

Edwin has some work to do if he plans to get out of here for four."

"That's very nice of you, Jake. But I don't mind staying until five," Edwin insisted. Kissing his bosses ass was very becoming of him and Miller seemed to agree.

"I insist. I won't take no for an answer." Miller nodded at me and walked out the door, without making any further conversation.

I could feel the heat rising to my cheeks. I pressed my cool hand against my burning forehead. "Oh my gosh, that was close."

"Too close," Edwin added.

"Well, if you are going to give it a go, you'll have to learn how to keep your hands off each other at work," Aliah said, smirking.

"We'd better let Edwin get back to work," I said, gazing up at him through long, dark lashes. I gave him a quick peck on the cheek and, as I turned to leave, he playfully swatted my ass.

"Later, baby," he said, smirking.

"Yes. Save it for later," I stammered. I couldn't believe he didn't learn anything from our run-in with his boss. Though my eyes were narrowed, I still caught a glimpse of that amazing smile before I hooked Aliah's arm and walked with her out the door. I smiled back at Edwin, unable to help myself.

"You'd better quit looking at him like that, or everyone's going to know," Aliah said, quietly

Edwin's disturbingly sexy chuckle told me that he had heard her. She was lucky he was the only one, or I would have had to kill her. I didn't want everyone else up in our business, and privacy in our office was practically non-existent, but I couldn't wipe the ecstatic look from my face.

"I can't help it. It's like I picked the lock to a treasure chest and now that I found my treasure, I can't stop staring at it... and touching it," I added, giggling. *What a relief to finally get it off my chest.*

"Good for you. I'm sure you'll work out all the minor

details this weekend. I'm looking forward to *working it out* with Hunter this weekend too." She raised her eyebrows suggestively and her tone was vulgar. *What a slut.* We both broke out in laughter.

"Aliah?" Bailey called, from the depths of his corner office. "Can I see you for a minute?" he boomed.

"Gotta go!" Aliah breezed past me and rushed into Bailey's office.

As if he hadn't heard us babbling in the hall, I waited a few seconds before I passed his door and got back to work.

Excited to pick up my last papers of the day, I stood from my desk with a bounce.

Owen popped his head in my doorway, startling me. "Are you ready to call it a night?" he asked, noticing my smiles.

I looked at my computer, feeling confused. "Night? It's only three thirty, Owen."

"Yeah, but you and a group of others are leaving for that trip tonight right? I thought you could use the time so you don't have to rush. It's a long weekend after all. I bet traffic will be hell."

"Owen, since when did we leave the office early on a long weekend? You don't have to do that."

"Since now. You've been working really hard lately. You deserve it. Get out of here."

"You're sure?"

"Yes. Go."

"Okay. I really appreciate it. I'm just finishing up the report on the Chancellor file. I'll clean up once I get it on your desk."

"If you insist, but it'll still be here on Tuesday."

Owen headed back to his office and excitement drove me to the copier at lightning speed. Maddie was standing at the long counter binding some documents.

"Hey, Maddie! If you can believe it, Owen just told me I

can go now!"

"Miller agreed to let us go at four!" she said, equally as enthusiastic.

"Are we driving up together then?" I asked.

"Yeah. I might as well catch a ride with you and Edwin since we'll all be ready early. TJ isn't off work until six. Aliah can catch a ride with him and Hunter. She won't mind; will she?"

I imagined Aliah's assault on Hunter in the backseat of TJ's jeep and smirked. "Um, no. I'm sure she won't mind. At least then *we* can get there before dark. What do you say we pick you up around five?"

"Great! I just have a few things left to pack. It shouldn't take long at all."

"Okay, we'll see you then."

I hustled back to my desk and read over my report. Everything was in order, so I packaged it up and put it on Owen's desk for signing. He was nowhere to be found. I slipped past Edwin's office, to have a quick chat with Aliah, since it was still a few minutes before Edwin's quitting time.

"Hey, girl. Are you getting off early?" I asked.

"No. Bailey never goes for that. Seriously...it's not even worth my breath."

"You'll be happy to know then, that you get to drive up with Hunter. Edwin and I are going to take Maddie with us. You can thank me later." I had a feeling that her smile would still be plastered on her face when she joined me later tonight.

"Sweet! No offence, but I'm glad not to be stuck with you two love birds and Monster Maddie."

"Oh, thanks. What am I, chop liver?"

"Sorry, but Hunter is much more appealing to me. Sorry 'bout your luck!"

I laughed at her snarky comments. Typical Aliah. "Don't have too much fun without me."

"I will," she said smiling, as I walked away.

I looked in Edwin's door before I knocked on it. He didn't respond. He was working away and didn't even notice me when I stopped right in front of his desk. I knocked lightly on his desktop to get his attention, but still his eyes were glued to his computer screen.

Putting both hands flat on his desk, I leaned toward him. "Excuse me, Mr. Santora. Can I get some attention here for a minute?"

Breaking his concentration at last, Edwin's eyes flashed up at me. "Oh, Abby. I didn't see you there." He pulled some seemingly invisible ear plugs from his ears.

"Are you almost done here? The Southwind Inn awaits us."

He looked at the clock. It was three fifty-nine. "I've got one more minute to go," he said, smirking.

"Well, on my watch, you're two minutes overdue."

He slammed the thick book shut on the papers he was marking up and started clicking his mouse erratically. "Do you think I could ride with you?" he asked.

"Do you really have to ask? Of course you can. I told Maddie she can ride with us. The others have to work late."

He nodded his head as he shut down his computer. "Works for me. As long as I've got you."

Edwin's words never ceased to amaze me and his body was no exception in the amazing department. When he stood from his manager's chair and stretched out, his solid muscles flexed beneath his crisp white shirt. I turned away to stop the urge to go to him. With one step closer to the door, Edwin slung his laptop bag over his shoulder and caught up to me in three, long strides. He turned off his lights and, with the blinds drawn, the spacious room was now draped in heavy shadows.

"I told Maddie we'd pick her up at five."

"Maddie can wait." Edwin tugged me back inside and leaned against me, plastering me to his bookshelf. His kiss was hot, his eyes intense, satisfying my naughty thoughts.

So much for that ice barrier I had put in place for myself at work. Edwin had melted it in two seconds flat. I broke my mouth free from his demanding lips. "You're bad," I breathed.

"I know you like it though." He nuzzled his nose against mine and kissed me again, throwing all caution to the wind.

I pulled away from him again, terrified of getting caught by any number of people. "Why don't we take this party home?"

"Mmm, I like where you're going with this." He gripped me possessively and kissed me one last time before granting my release.

"I'll meet you at the truck. I just have to grab my purse." I left his dark room first, feeling entirely exposed, my lips as pink as my cheeks. With fingers on my bottom lip, I glanced back in time to see Edwin duck down the hall. I wanted him so bad.

Edwin was already backing his truck up to the curb, when I walked out the front door of the office. He jumped out of the truck and beat me to the passenger door. "My lady," he said, opening the door for me.

"Edwin! Could you be any more obvious?"

"What?"

"Since when did you give me curbside service?"

"Since now."

He was not going to back down. But neither was I.

"I rest my case."

His smile tugged at my heart.   "Afraid of a little attention? Let 'em stare. You're mine."

CHAPTER NINE

When we got home from work, Edwin loaded all of our bags into the trunk before coming back inside. I was still up in my room, changing into something more comfortable; travelling clothes. Edwin swiftly climbed the stairs. I glanced out my bedroom door to catch a glimpse of him passing by. My cheeks burned scarlet when he appeared in my doorway and caught me staring. He knew I was waiting to catch a glimpse of him.

He stood there very still, as his eyes zeroed in on mine. He gave no indication that he was leaving. I stood by my closet, only half dressed in a fitted tank and sexy panties, hugging my shorts to my chest.

"Mmm, look at you. Delicious," he growled.

I smiled and chewed on my swollen lip. "I've wanted you all day, Eddie."

His response seemed to confirm that he felt the same. His hands reached for his trousers and undid them before I could blink. He came at me fast, crashing aggressively into my body and lifting me off the floor.

Instinctively, I wrapped my legs around him and kissed him with urgent desperation. He tugged on my clinging shirt and pulled it over my head with one yank, his suit jacket already carelessly tossed onto the floor.

His pants dropped, a condom clenched in his teeth, as I worked feverishly on his shirt buttons. He made quick work of the last two buttons, while I yanked off his tie. Pressing me to the wall, his hand glided down between my legs and he took a deep, exhilarating breath. "Oh, Abby." He swiftly slid the condom on and yanked down the scrap that was my panties.

I panted with excitement, the urgency growing as he touched me with his hands, his mouth, his tongue. I arched my back, my body begging for more. Edwin delivered. He slammed inside me, his sculpted muscles pressing against me as he mashed me like potatoes.

I hooked my hand around his neck demanding that he come closer. He complied and kissed me hard, slamming me into a realm of unexpected bliss. I grabbed onto my dresser, clinging to reality, but when the low growl rumbled deep in Edwin's throat, all was lost. Combining his forces with gravity, he drew me into the vortex of mind-blowing ecstasy. I threw my head back and convulsed with pleasure.

"Yes," I wailed, wanton and breathless, recklessly pushing Edwin over the edge.

I sighed with amusement, after a moment of silence, when I realized how swiftly Edwin had taken me. "That was fast," I said, grinning from ear to ear.

Edwin still had me nailed to the wall. "What do you expect when you do that to me?"

"Who, me?" I chimed, batting my eyelashes.

He flashed his charming smile and loosened his grip on my hips. After peeling me off the wall, he lowered me to the floor. "I hate to put my mitts in the oven and run, but I want to get in the shower before we go."

I flashed him a sassy smile and swaggered daintily toward the door. "Get out of here then."

I was done with him. He was dismissed. He smirked as he collected his scattered clothes and took off to his room, covering his slick abs and semi-erect body with the dangling fabric.

When I got to the bathroom I decided that, though our encounter was sweaty and delicious, a shower wasn't a bad idea. I leapt into the stall as quick as I could, to beat out Edwin. I hurriedly washed myself then closed my eyes to rinse my hair.

I couldn't stop thinking about our sexy rendezvous, but pushed all thoughts aside when Edwin joined me in the bathroom. Leaving the water running, I hopped out of the tub to switch him places. I rushed to my room, dressed as quickly as I could and hurried down the hall.

Edwin was still faster than me. Fully dressed and standing at the foot of the stairs. "Do you mind if I drive?" he asked, staring up at me.

What kind of question was that after what we just did? It was like a hit and run. I yanked my purse off its hook and rummaged around for my keys. I tossed them out to him, as I opened the front door and walked out. "Drive, if you want to drive." The words came out even colder than I planned for them to.

"Well, I am the man of the relationship." He knew that would get under my skin and I would have to bite back.

I spun around, with hands on my hips, and squinted at him, unamused. "Relationship? You think what we just did constitutes a relationship?"

"Sure do. You're stuck with me now, baby!" he teased.

"Whatever. We should probably figure out what's going on here, before other people start filling in the blanks for us."

"I thought we did all the talking last night."

"Eddie, I can't take anything you say when we're having sex seriously. You'd tell me anything I want to hear if it means you'll get laid."

"That's not true. Well maybe a little... but that's not what happened last night and you know it. What are you so afraid of?"

Oh let's see... everything! "I don't know."

"Abs, you're overthinking it. It's real simple. You're single. I'm single. We're both undeniably attracted to each other. I may even love you," he added, smiling.

I folded my arms over my chest and gave him another narrowed glance.

"Okay...I do love you. Do you really want to pass that up? I know it hasn't worked out in the past, but this is different."

"Oh? And how is that?"

"We're older now. I've got a solid job. It's just different."

He was right. As annoying as it was, he was always right. I pushed aside my haunting intuition and dropped my defences. If anything, the man made a good argument.

"You realize Maddie is going to have a heyday with this, right?"

"They will all know soon enough. How they deal with it is their problem." He tugged gently on my arm, pulling me into his chest. He kissed me slow and sweet. "Right now, I can't see any reason why I wouldn't do everything in my power to keep you in these arms for the rest of my life."

Oh, my. I love this man.

He kissed me again and we gazed contently into each other's eyes. A smile crept onto his lips, then he gave me a wink and headed for the driver seat of my car. By the time my seat belt clicked, the car purred to life and we sped off to Maddie's house. Passing the tree-lined city streets, I daydreamed about us spending the rest of our lives together.

"Eddie?"

"Mmm, hmm?"

"I've been thinking. Would you be opposed to saving the news for later? I really don't want to deal with Maddie's jibber jabber all the way there."

"Suit yourself," he said.

"Are you mad?"

Edwin's face remained neutral, as he pulled the car into Maddie's driveway. "I'm pretty sure she'll figure it out for herself, but I'm all for waiting if that's what you want."

"Thank you." I slipped out the door and walked up Maddie's drive.

Edwin eased his window down and whistled at me like a horny construction worker, with a huge smile plastered on his face. I looked back at him to roll my eyes, but I couldn't hide my smile.

With two knocks on Maddie's door, her friend Samantha opened it, looking as posh as ever with her shiny, short, dark hair.

"Come on in," she said. "She's going to be another minute."

I knew that meant Maddie would be at least ten, so I

waved at Edwin to come in. I heard him cut the engine as I went inside. "I thought you'd be ready," I hollered to Maddie, who was nowhere to be seen.

"Um, no," Maddie hollered back.

I looked to Samantha for an explanation of her visit. "Moral support?"

"She's having a hard time picking out what bathing suits to bring. She's so concerned about what colour Hunter will like most. She told me it was an emergency." Samantha rolled her eyes, seemingly uninterested and impatient.

Maddie entered at the far end of the room with a hoard of skimpy bathing suits dangling from each of her arms. It looked like I would have to take it upon myself to make a hasty decision before Edwin came in and had a bird.

"Let's see 'em then," I said, waving at the suits.

She instantly started flashing her hoard of suits to me. "What do you think?"

"Oh, definitely the black one piece. I love that one," I said.

"And the orange one too. You look hot in it," Samantha chimed.

"You think?"

Edwin finally walked in the front door, without so much as a knock. "Oh, no. What did I just get myself into?" he asked wearily, blocking his eyes with his hand.

"Don't listen to him. Those are my favs by far," I said.

"Do you think two will be enough?" Maddie asked.

"Yeah, for sure. We're only going for a few days. It won't kill you to wear one twice if you have to," I said.

"It might," Samantha added sarcastically, knowing Maddie all too well.

"Yeah. I think I'd better bring one more, just in case," Maddie agreed. "I hate wearing a wet bathing suit. That's just nasty." Maddie cringed at the thought. "Okay, so what other one do you think? Maybe this white one?"

Edwin dropped his hands in defeat, his eyes slanting toward the skimpy, frilly white thing Maddie dangled from her fingers. "Oh, yes; definitely that one! And maybe Abby can borrow it for a night," Edwin said, with renewed interest.

Maddie stood there thoughtfully for a minute, confused by Edwin's comment, then shrugged her shoulders. Seemingly satisfied, she packed the suit up. Samantha on the other hand, who was no stranger to Edwin and I, glanced at me with a stunned look on her face. I just shrugged my shoulders in response, hoping that'd be enough to curb her curiosity. *She is onto us.*

"So, are we ready then?" I asked Maddie, animatedly.

"Yes, I'm ready."

Samantha suddenly seemed equally as eager to get out of there, pulling on her shoes and stringing her purse over her shoulder. "Have fun, guys. Catch ya later."

"See ya, Sam. Thanks for your help," Maddie said, as Samantha took off.

Edwin picked up the two bags at the door, as Maddie pulled her tote toward me.

My mouth dropped open. "Did you dump your whole wardrobe in there?" I laughed, as I looked at the amount of things Maddie had packed for such a short trip.

"You'll thank me later," she said, smirking.

I glanced at Edwin, wide-eyed, and he smiled back at me, acknowledging that she was as crazy as I thought she was. I headed outside to pop the trunk and Maddie nearly tumbled over me, trying to get to the car first.

"Shotgun!" she hollered, dropping her bag at Edwin's feet. She held onto the passenger door like it was a life line.

"Um, no. Edwin's driving. I get shotgun. My car, my rules," I said.

"Edwin's driving? That's weird." Maddie sighed and grudgingly got into the back seat.

I couldn't help but smile. I waved at Samantha as she pulled away from the curb, then took my seat next to Edwin. I couldn't wipe the smile from my face. I was happy.

Edwin drove us away, leaving the craziness of the city behind and disappearing into the serenity of the country. After a good hour passed, I was ready to dump Maddie. She would not stop talking. I swear if that woman didn't shut up, I would have to dispose of her in some other unfriendly way.

Edwin's brow furrowed. He felt the same way. Then, shaking things up, his hand slowly wandered to my thigh. He squeezed and brushed his fingers higher. I gasped for air, shocked by his brazen act, but also incredibly intrigued. Heat electrified my body from my thighs to my mouth.

Edwin smiled and smoothed his hand back down my thigh. He slowly scooped my hand into his and I gave him a guarded glance. Ignoring my wide eyes, showing me more attention than I cared for, he brushed his thumb over my knuckles. Such a soft touch and yet it stirred so many feelings.

I chewed my lip and squeezed my eyes shut, trying to steady my rapid breaths. When I thought I was in the safe zone, I locked my eyes on Edwin, until he finally smiled and gave me a wink. Maddie didn't even seem to notice, too caught up in her own story.

When we pulled into the resort, the sun was still shining high in the sky, and Maddie hadn't said anything about our handholding. The road quickly turned from pavement to gravel and Edwin slowed the car so we didn't kick up too much dust when we winded down the narrow drive.

The land was naturally beautiful. Native flowers covered the forest floor. Lush, green trees hovered protectively over the secluded road. We reached a clearing, leading us to what looked like an over-sized log house. It overlooked the natural lakeside, a stunning display of nature at its finest.

The first bout of silence went on, as Maddie watched out the window, equally as taken by the amazing view.

"I can run in and get our keys if you want," I suggested.

"Okay," Maddie said.

Edwin put the car in park. "I'll come with you."

"Can you at least leave the music on?" Maddie asked, not suspecting anything.

Edwin indulged her and then walked around the front of the car, where I waited for him. We both directed our attention to the two storey log house.

"I take it that's where we have to go," Edwin guessed, pointing at the doorway marked *Registration*. Edwin put his hand on the small of my back, gentle yet possessive, and guided me toward the wooden stairs. Two steps up and Edwin still hadn't removed his hand from my back, his fingers slipping beneath my shirt and skimming across my skin.

I turned back to flash a warning smile. "I have a feeling Maddie's watching us right now."

Edwin was one step behind, but when I turned back we stood eye to eye. He didn't leave me any room to breathe. His warm breath touched my lips and I nearly expired. "We're here now. Let her watch." He brushed a kiss across my lips and my dark lashes fluttered shut.

That was one devastatingly sexy kiss.

I waited for another kiss but, after a second of silence, I opened my eyes to find Edwin smiling.

He raised an eyebrow. "Registration?"

"Tease," I said, then shuffled up the rest of the stairs ahead of him.

He reached past me, to get the door, and I gladly let him open it for me. I stepped inside the registration room. It was as rustic as bark on a tree, raw wood touching every surface in the place. A beautiful young girl sat behind a heavy wooden desk. She looked innocent enough, wearing her ruffled white blouse and honest smile, until she turned that innocent smile on my man.

Jealousy raged deep in my chest, my teeth clenched, and my emerald eyes darkened, as I narrowed them at her. She didn't seem to notice, her fascination with Edwin obvious, as she turned all of her attention to him. Her lips parted, and her lashes fluttered. Could she be any more obvious?

Edwin certainly noticed the fact that she was ignoring me entirely. He cleared his throat and linked our fingers together, then drew my hand to his mouth. His eyes reached mine when his lips touched the back of my hand, relieving enough of my tension for me to wipe the scowl from my face. A soft smile took its place.

After sharing a warm smile with Edwin, I was confident my claim had been staked. The young lady drew her eyes away from my prize and redirected her attention to me, like I had suddenly appeared before her.

"Welcome to the Southwind Inn," she said. *So annoying. And fake.*

"Thank you," I chimed, equally as cheerful. *Also fake.*

"Do you have reservations?"

I do, but Edwin doesn't seem to have any. "We do. Jenkins. Abigail Jenkins. I have two rooms for the weekend."

Edwin looked at me and smiled, but remained silent. The girl typed quickly on her keyboard in an attempt to find some information about our stay.

"Oh, yes! Here you are. You have the studio cabin and the two-bedroom reserved. Can I see some photo ID please?"

I pulled out my wallet and handed her my Driver's License. She looked at the card and up at me to compare, then scribbled down my number.

"Thank you," she announced, as she handed it back to me.

I stood there, boredom consuming me, as she fumbled around behind her desk. She finally reached out four keys, dangling them before me. I extended out my hand and she dropped them dramatically, as if I might burn her if she got too close.

"I seem to have your MasterCard on file already, so you're all set." She passed me a couple of pamphlets and started into a speech about the resort. "This is where you'll find everything you need to know about our grounds. A map to help you find the cabins. You'll find the hours of operation for the restaurant on the back there. There are fresh towels at the poolside. Oh, and if you need anything else, there is always someone in the office."

"Thank you so much," I said, scooping up the brochures. I smiled, but I was not happy with her.

She had a wide smile for me and a wink for Edwin. I wanted to wrap my hands around her skinny little throat and strangle her.

"Yes, thank you," Edwin added, kindly nodding his head at her and smiling back at me. He pulled me toward the door, before I could give her a piece of my mind.

The girl stood from her chair, the legs scraping across the floor. "I must say, you two make an awfully cute couple," she gushed. Then, after a harsh sigh, "I wish I were so lucky to have what you two share."

"Uh, thanks?" I said, gazing into Edwin's eyes in search of his reaction.

He winked at me and put his arm around my back as we turned to go.

"Enjoy your stay!" she called after us.

"What was that all about?" I asked, after the door banged shut.

"We must be giving off vibes. You certainly were," Edwin said, with a chuckle.

"Puh-lease. She was totally ogling you. It was disgusting."

"Can you blame her?"

I rolled my eyes and dropped Edwin's hand, then pulled open the passenger door and slid onto the soft leather seat.

"Where to?" Edwin asked, with his eyes on me.

I opened up one of the pamphlets to find our cabins. After leaving me to squint at it in confusion for a minute, Edwin yanked it from my hands with one swift tug. "Give me that. I can figure it out way faster than you ever will."

"Whatever," I sniped.

He ran his finger over the map. "Got it. What did I say, huh? I'm the man," he insisted. "Say it."

"You're so full of yourself," I retorted, unwilling to give him any props.

"Say it!" he repeated.

"I'm not saying it!" I also couldn't stop smiling.

"Please stop! You two sound like an old married couple," Maddie shouted.

I snickered to myself and flashed Edwin a knowing smile. He subtly acknowledged my glance. Maddie obviously hadn't been paying us any attention. We were hardly sneaking around, but it had become a bit of a game.

Edwin took his time driving down the dirt path and had no trouble locating the cabins. He parked the car in the oversized, gravel parking space next to the rustic wooden cabins.

"Huh," he said, as he glanced over the resort's map. "That place we just passed seems to be the studio. It looks like we have shared parking."

"Perf! We're so close to the guys. Hunter won't be able to hide from me," Maddie said, smiling.

"Great," Edwin moaned.

Maddie hit Edwin on the shoulder, before I could. "Give me the key," she insisted.

I reached my arm into the backseat and dangled it out to her. Maddie yanked the key out of my grip. After retrieving my arm, I dropped the other key into my purse and handed Edwin the others before getting out of the car.

While Edwin stopped to take a good stretch, Maddie hurled herself past me to get to the cabin first.

"Take 'er easy," Edwin hollered.

"This is so great! Our cabins are right next to each other. Hunter won't know what to do with himself," she chimed.

She was right. Hunter was stuck with her whether he liked it or not. The only thing separating our cabins was a couple of overgrown hedges and a few large, bushy trees in the surrounding yard.

Being a little less excited about the accommodations and a little more excited about the handsome man unlocking the trunk, I stepped around the car to see him. Maddie began to squeal with excitement inside the cabin.

"I guess it's as good as it looked," I said, smirking.

Edwin hooked an arm around my waist and pulled me toward him possessively, our bodies colliding. Standing there, behind the open trunk, Maddie couldn't see a thing.

"I'm here with you. That's enough for me," Edwin said,

in a low sexy growl, then covered my mouth with his.

When I came up for breath, I fluttered my dainty eyelashes hoping it would help my situation. "I just wish that *we* could share a cabin."

"We'll be together. Don't you worry about that."

When I pulled out of his arms he gave my rear a swat, then grabbed my bags from the trunk. He flashed me a dangerous smile as he carried my bags behind me.

"I think I'm starting to have fun with this secret lover thing," Edwin said. "It's so..."

"Stimulating?" I finished.

"I was going to say arousing, but I could definitely do stimulating." His lips curled into a devious smile.

I liked it. Unable to stop myself, I spun around and linked my arms around his waist for another lingering kiss.

"I'm definitely going along with the secret scheming, if it turns you on that much," Edwin said against my lips. His fingers skimmed over my nipples. They were already straining against my shirt.

"You have no idea how hard I am right now," he breathed in my ear.

I squeezed my eyes shut, imagining him in all his naked glory. Then on a sharp breath, I turned on my heel and continued up the sandy, flagstone path. When I walked in the cabin, any chance for intimate conversation vanished in an instant.

"You snooze you lose! I get this room," Maddie boasted. She jumped into the doorway of the corner room, blocking my entry like a child.

I approached her casually and shoved her aside to peek inside the room. It was smallish, but tidy, with a queen-sized bed and an amazing, picturesque lake-view. Brushing quickly past Maddie, I headed for the other room.

"I'll deal." *I don't plan to spend a whole lot of time indoors anyway.* My room was a bit smaller than the first, but otherwise it was the same. One queen bed was pushed up against the front wall of the cabin, and covered in clean blankets of soft blues and warm whites. The room smelled surprisingly fresh and felt like an airy, ocean-like oasis.

Edwin took one step into the room and plunked my bags to the floor, snapping my attention up from the bed. A sexual charge heated the room and, with him blocking the door, it suddenly felt like especially tight quarters.

He turned away from me and leaned out the door. "Your bags are in the trunk. Close it when you're finished," Edwin hollered to Maddie. He swung back around to face me, brandishing a wickedly sexy smile. He slammed the door shut and locked it securely behind his back, not removing his eyes from mine.

After glancing out the side window at the lush, green forest, I dropped myself backward onto the fresh, fluffy bed, with eyes closed, to hide from Edwin's heated stare. Reveling in the relaxed atmosphere, in the confines of my temporarily private room, I stretched my arms over my head and took a deep breath.

At last, I found one downfall of the place. The walls were paper thin. I heard every angry slur Maddie made about Edwin's rudeness. I giggled softly, in my uninterrupted oasis. "So, what do you think?" I asked.

Edwin made his stealthy approach. "I think it's perfect," he said, his voice deep and serious. "I think you're perfect." He drew his knee onto the bed and locked his darkened, blue eyes on mine. "And I think this is the perfect time to see if this bed can hold up to our high standards." He raised his arched eyebrows, his eyes full of promise, and crawled onto the bed like a savage animal, aggressive and hungry.

Frozen on the bed beneath him, my emotions swayed between exhilaration and anxiety. He hovered over me, waiting for me to give in. I locked my eyes shut, but his body continued to call my name. When Edwin's lips hooked onto mine, wild and ravenous, I whimpered for more.

The delicious pressure of his hard, heavy body, rocking against me only intensified every flick of his tongue. Floating among the fluffy clouds, Edwin's firm, possessive hold on me threatened to steal my only connection to reality.

I heard a woman's faint cry of desire. The sound was coming from my room. I abruptly opened my eyes and Edwin lifted up as I froze in a state of panic, until I realized that cry was my own. Still fiercely clung to Edwin, he smiled at me, amused. I released his shoulders and dropped to the bed.

"You realize I can hear you in there," Maddie hollered.

After a moment of silence, staring into each other's eyes, we both broke into an uncontrollable laughter. It felt like we had gotten caught by my mother and were being warned to stop before she came in and made us. I wasn't even sure that Maddie knew what she thought she heard, because aside from my soft, desperate cry for more, we weren't saying anything at all.

I covered my face with my hands. "I'm sorry. But I don't think Aliah would appreciate it very much if we did the dirty in her bed."

"If we don't now, it's only a matter of time before we do," Edwin said. "Would you rather Aliah and Hunter break the bed in first?"

"Ugh," I groaned, fighting the urge to rip off his clothes. I bunched his shirt in one hand and pulled hard until he was on top of me bracing himself for a one, long, delicious kiss. Before his roaming tongue could convince me to stay, I shoved him off of me and leapt from the bed, prowling toward the door.

"You can blame me," he pleaded desperately.

"Oh, I will. Let's go check out your place. You should get there first so you can claim the King." The truth was we needed privacy, and fast. I flashed a look at Edwin, then blasted out of the room into the common area. I walked straight out the exterior door leaving it wide open.

Predictably, Edwin jogged out of the cabin and chased after me.

CHAPTER TEN

Edwin flung the door open and I stepped inside his cabin, curious and amazed. My mouth dropped open. *Wow!* The ladies definitely got shortchanged in this deal. Edwin only smiled and nodded, taking it all in with me.

The suite was fit for a honeymoon, much more elegant than I expected for a friendly weekend retreat. The room was complete with a wood burning fireplace, Jacuzzi tub, modern décor and panoramic views of the forest and lakeside. The windows were trimmed with wispy, transparent drapes that fluttered delicately in the warm breeze.

I lost myself in the whimsical atmosphere, without noticing that Edwin was admiring me while I admired the space.

He closed the door and locked the deadbolt. "You realize I have both of the keys, right?" he asked, in a deep, growly voice.

His approach was slow and deliberate, but I didn't dare turn around. His big hands landed on my hips and skimmed up my waist, dragging my shirt up with them. He tugged me back against him and I could feel his fierce erection pressed against the small of my back.

"What are you getting at?" I whispered, trying not to squirm like a school girl.

His fingers brushed the hair from my shoulder and his lips caressed my neck. "While I can appreciate your morals - and I do, don't get me wrong - I need you."

My mind wandered, as Edwin swept me up into his arms and effortlessly lowered me onto the oversized bed. Edwin stood over me, with a sensual grin on his face, before he lowered himself on top of me. Our lips locked and our bodies moulded together. Edwin's hands were touching me everywhere, as he scrambled to kick off his shoes.

Edwin rolled me on top of him until I pinned his solid body to the bed. With my knees spread wide, I ran my hands under his shirt, exposing a set of full, chiseled abs. His eyes were closed but that didn't cool the wave of urgency flooding me.

I lifted his shirt over his head, eager to uncover his entire body. I flattened my palms on his firm, bare chest.

"What do you say?" I pressed myself against the crowded bulge in his pants.

He moaned, and didn't hesitate for another breath. "Yes!"

Amused with his impatience, I lightly circled my tongue around his nipple, before closing my mouth over it. My hand found him through his pants and he grunted again, raring to go.

After working open the button on his pants, I slowly eased down his zipper. I slipped my cool hand in his pants and wrapped my fingers around him, only a thin veil of fabric separating our skin.

"How would you like it?" I whispered, squeezing tighter.

A bead of moisture soaked his shorts and a muffled groan sounded from his throat as I pulled him free. I twisted my grip and stroked his length, not that he needed any more foreplay. He was ready to go.

Before I knew what hit me, Edwin had me flat on my back, stripped of my summer clothes. "Off," he said, reaching for the snap on my bra.

When I wiggled free from it, I was completely naked. So was he, like a naked statue, only bigger and stronger and real.

He pressed his firm erection against my soft inner-thigh and frantically dropped wet kisses all over me, until my head was spinning with anticipation. When he glided over top of me, every nerve ending sparked alive. The urge to have him inside me was pulsing at high capacity. My legs trembled with anticipation.

"Now," I begged, arching my back and bucking against

him.

When Edwin's mouth reached mine, he slid over me again, taunting, tempting me.

My intuition begged me to open my eyes. I refused.

Focusing on the thrilling energy swirling around us, and the wet tension between my thighs, I refused to be drawn back to reality. Edwin's tongue slipped inside my mouth and his lips muffled my moan as he dipped toward me.

That's when I heard it. Again. This time it startled me enough to break me from my sexual daze.

I tried to push Edwin off of me, but failed miserably. Wanting to scream, ready to cry, I sat up as best I could and froze against his hot, hard body.

"Did I hurt you?" he asked.

"No! Shh!" I huffed, listening carefully.

Two seconds of stillness was all it took to confirm that we were no longer alone. *There was someone outside the cabin!*

"Aww, man! What's it gonna take to get laid around here?" Edwin grumbled, slamming his fist on the soft bed.

I pulled myself free from him and hurriedly collected my clothes. "Ditto," I said, equally as frustrated. "I'll get you later," I promised, as I attempted to refasten my bra.

I swiftly pulled on my clothes and checked myself in the mirror. After straightening my tousled hair, I paced to the window and pulled aside the dainty fabric that hardly covered it. Just as I had suspected, TJ's burnt orange Wrangler was parked next to my car.

Aliah and Hunter were standing next to the jeep, while TJ locked it up. Aliah immediately caught a glimpse of me through the window and hollered out, waving hysterically. "Hey, girl. We made it!"

I dropped the panel and headed for the door. Edwin followed behind me with his shirt in hand.

"Nice timing, guys," he moaned sarcastically, slamming the door shut behind him.

"Ohhh!" TJ hollered back, bumbling around and acknowledging Edwin's sexual frustration.

I rolled my eyes at them both and shook my head in annoyance. There would be more of that over the course of the weekend, I was sure.

The bright sunlight was already starting to fade to a light glow, as the sun began to set in the sky. TJ and Hunter pulled out their bags and headed for the cabin, shoving and tripping each other, trying to get to the cabin first.

"You're outta luck, brothers. You get your choice of the cot, couch or floor. I've already called the King," Edwin hollered, laughing at them as he grabbed his bag from my trunk. "If you were a few minutes later, I would have christened it too."

He slid my car keys into my hand and dropped a peck on my cheek, before following TJ inside.

"You coming or what?" Aliah called out, already half way up the path to the ladies cabin.

"Be there in a sec," I said, appreciating the well-groomed, flowering gardens, and the full green bushes.

The birds chirped as I gazed over the panoramic views and took in the fluffy clouds bouncing in the bright blue sky. It was breathtaking. The trip of the year, for sure. After taking in a good breath of fresh air, I happily strolled up the path.

I caught Edwin peeking out the window at me and I wiggled my fingers at him, with a super feminine wave. He flashed me a handsome smile and then disappeared behind the whimsical drapes.

I hurried up the flagstone path, unable to avoid the excitement welling up inside me. I turned the door knob and let myself inside. Aliah was sitting on the sofa, rummaging through her bag.

I cheerily planted myself snuggly next to her and reached my arm over her shoulder, as she proceeded to tell me about their drive up to the Southwind. After her long-winded explanation, mostly about Hunter's bulging biceps, dark eyes and dimpled smile, I quickly changed the subject.

"What's the plan for tonight, ladies?" I asked, as I released her neck from my playful grip.

"You're in a good mood," Aliah said, smirking.

Maddie plowed into the room, physically demanding our immediate attention. "How do I look?" she asked, as she pranced around in a cute little summer dress like she was a model. "I got it for Hunter."

"You wasted your money then," Aliah growled.

"Oh, boy. This is going to be a fun weekend," I said, smiling. There was no need to fight now, there'd be plenty of time for that later, but it didn't stop Aliah from scowling at Maddie.

"I'm thinking maybe we should just settle in tonight; hang out here," I suggested.

Maddie nodded in agreement. "That's cool."

"I like it. That way I can set Maddie straight," Aliah snapped.

"What?" Maddie said, as if she didn't know why Aliah was scowling at her.

We all three froze momentarily and listened to the menacing silence, until a muffled hoot and holler came from next door.

Aliah hooked onto my arm and pulled me off the couch. "Hear that?"

"It sounds like the guys are starting without us," I said, nodding. "Let's go see what they're up to."

"I'm coming too," Maddie shrieked.

"Whatever," Aliah called back, rudely. She walked straight for the door, our arms still linked together.

"Oh, Ally. Can't you two get along for like two seconds?"

"Not likely."

"You're making this harder than it has to be. Why don't you let Hunter decide who he wants? Did you ever think of that?"

"Hah! That's suggesting Maddison has a shot up against me. Not a chance in hell," Aliah said, cold and confident.

As we approached the guys' place, I could hardly hear the loud music over their roars of laughter and ridiculous argument. I skipped past Aliah and lightly tapped on the door. Surprise. No answer. So I let us right in.

They didn't even hear me, but it took two short seconds before they realized that the ladies were in the house. Every one of them froze as I stepped into the roomy oasis. Edwin flashed me a heavenly smile.

"Carry on," Aliah announced, taking a seat on the floor next to Hunter. "You're hitting the booze already?"

"Why am I not surprised?" I said, smiling at Edwin. I slipped my butt onto the sofa's armrest, next to him.

Each of the guys were holding a recently emptied shot glass and it was obvious that the liquor had already started to affect TJ. Hunter wasn't far behind him, sprawled out comfortably on the floor. He piped up first.

"It wasn't me... peer pressure!" Hunter blurted, grinning from ear to ear.

All the guys started laughing hysterically. Aliah and I shared a disturbed glance. It was just not that funny.

"How many have you had?" I asked Edwin, out of pure curiosity.

"Three, four maybe."

Looking at the nearly emptied bottles of liquor cluttered on the floor, I found that hard to believe.

"Five," TJ blurted, throwing Edwin under the bus, then laughed some more with Hunter.

Just then Maddie tromped into the room unannounced.

"It looks like you guys are sleeping alone tonight then," I said, a slight threat in my tone.

"Uh, oh. Edwin's in trouble!" TJ hooted, drunkenly.

"Why is Edwin in trouble?" Maddie asked, foolishly. She still hadn't figured us out yet.

"I know *we* won't be sleeping alone," Aliah said to me, to tease the boys.

"I'm with them tonight!" Hunter hollered, captivated by Aliah's suggestion.

Aliah laughed. "In your dreams, Hunter."

"Mmm, I hope so," he replied, sending everyone into another fit of laughter.

Maddie didn't appreciate Hunter giving anyone else his attention and her disappointment was written all over her face. Even worse, I could tell she was secretly plotting against Aliah that very minute. Edwin tilted his shot glass to me, in an attempt to steal my eyes.

"Want one?" he asked.

"Oh, come on, do it," TJ taunted.

"Oh... I don't know. It's probably not a good idea. You know how I get when I do shots," I said.

Edwin smirked. "Yes. I. Do."

"That's funny because you're always double fisting it in my dreams," Hunter slurred, laughing again.

Another roaring sensation filled the room. Aliah gazed lovingly at Hunter, clearly liking his wild side, while Maddie scowled at them.

"Why is it that whenever men get drunk they have to act like outrageously horny perverts?" Maddie announced.

Aliah shrugged her shoulders and gave up the fight. "Fill 'er up!" she shouted, then pulled Hunter's glass from his hand. "Fill hers up too," she told TJ, who was holding the bottle of liquor.

Edwin held up the shot glass in front of me and TJ filled it to the brim, spilling some on the floor.

"Do you think you could've at least filled it up for me?" I licked the liquid off the side of the glass, still in Edwin's hand, then ran my tongue over my smiling lips.

"Oh, God! Do that again," Edwin begged, staring at my mouth.

Smiling, I took the wet glass from his hand.

"Cheers!" Aliah shouted, then clinked her glass against mine, spilling even more liquor on the hardwood floor.

Annoyed, Maddie rushed to soak up the spilled liquor. I shrugged at Edwin, who was giving me his intrigued attention, then tilted my head back to help down the strong liquor. Aliah and I both made funny faces from the taste and all the guys found that to be hilarious.

"Give me one of those," Maddie demanded. She tossed the damp towel on the floor, slapped her brother and stole his glass from his hand.

After downing the shot, she held it out for a refill. TJ

wasn't fast enough, so she yanked the bottle away from him and took a huge swig, choking it back.

Next, Maddie passed the bottle to me. "Drink up," she said.

When I was done laughing at her, I had a drink.

"That's my girl," Edwin said, shoving over to make room for me on the sofa.

Before long, *everyone* was laughing like hyenas and acting all crazy. Hunter took another drink from the bottle and handed it back to Aliah. "One more," he insisted.

She took a big gulp and winked at him. "That one was for you." She sounded so sleazy, but Hunter was definitely not complaining.

It cracked me right up.

"You shut up," Aliah hollered at me.

Edwin wrapped his arm around me and I curled into his chest. Though the drinks slowed, the party went on. After hours of slurs, hollering and fighting, one by one our peeps started to fall to the liquor. Hunter was half asleep, Maddie and Aliah arguing on either side of him, and TJ was already hugging the toilet bowl.

Listening to the gagging, tied my stomach in knots. "That's it for me," I said, holding my hand up to the pile of empty bottles.

"I'm done too," Edwin agreed.

He took my hand in his and, after dropping a soft kiss on it, slowly laced our fingers together. His gaze was wondrously intoxicating and I was definitely intoxicated. We hadn't exactly notified the others of our blooming romance, but the fact that we'd been attached at the hip the entire night should've tipped them off.

I gazed up into his eyes and ran my hand across his sexy, five o'clock shadow. My fingers traced over his parted, soft, pink lips. He was looking particularly sexy tonight. Edwin closed his eyes, as my fingers weaved through his short, dark hair.

Without a care, he pulled me into his lap and kissed me without regard to the others. His soft, wet lips touched against mine and his warm, sweet tongue swept inside my mouth. He tasted so good, like sweet, juicy, black cherries. I didn't care if anyone noticed. I couldn't stop now if I wanted to.

Maddie and Aliah were so intent on fighting over Hunter that they didn't even catch our public display of affection.

"Mmm. You're delicious," Edwin whispered, licking his lips. "I could drink you right up."

He lifted me up, so I could spread my legs over him and kiss him more deeply. His hands cupped my rear and pulled me onto his growing erection. I whimpered in response, an equally fast growing need aching in my belly.

When Edwin released my tempted lips from his spell, he brushed my hair from my face. "What do you say we go for a walk?"

I'd say he read my mind. I nodded at him and he offered me his sweater. I slipped it on, then took his hand again, to head for the door. A dizzy spell overcame me when I took to my feet, but Edwin was there to keep me standing.

Aliah and Maddie were having a full blown bitch-fest and though Hunter was the main topic of conversation, he looked like he had passed out from boredom.

"We're going for a walk," I said. "Don't wait up for me."

Edwin grabbed his jacket and pulled open the door without waiting for a response. While he was high on my list of things to do, the fresh air reminded me just how stumbling drunk I was. I pulled his sweater over my nose. It smelled of fresh fabric softener, rich cologne and Edwin.

"Mmm," I moaned.

"You need to quit with those sounds or I'm going to lay you out right here." Edwin scooped up my arm and pulled me away from the cabin.

A silly giggle sounded from my mouth, before I could catch my breath. "What else have you got planned for this weekend?" I asked.

"I have no idea. You?"

"Honestly? I'm always planning and fitting everything into a tight schedule. It's just too stressful," I admitted. "I think I'm gonna just go with the flow for a change and see what happens."

Edwin's curved eyebrow shot up, intrigued. "I like it," he said, beaming.

I couldn't tell if it was the liquor enhancing our attraction or if our old feelings were falling back into place, but I couldn't remove the smile that was plastered on my face.

We continued down the manicured path, until a couple nearly bumped into us as they passed in the darkness, clearly caught up in each other.

"He's getting laid for sure," Edwin whispered.

I peered over my shoulder and watched the couple. They were holding hands, but not too close. It was obvious to me that it was a new relationship. "I don't think so," I wagered.

Edwin casually stopped us, so he could see whether the guy sealed the deal. "If I win, we do what I want tonight. You win, it's up to you."

"Deal," I answered, then peeked over my shoulder to watch the couple hovering near the front door of the cabin. I glanced back just in time to see that their kiss goodnight was becoming rather heated. The guy even went so far as to pull his shirt off on the front porch and the girl had her hands all over him.

Edwin had to look at me to confirm I was seeing it to. "Ahh?" he said, nudging me.

Stunned, my mouth gaped open and I nodded. "Dammit!" I said, a little too loud.

The couple stopped and turned to see what we were doing, both having heard me.

"Shit. It looks like he's gonna come over here," I whispered, looking up at Edwin anxiously.

"I'll put a stop to that." Edwin laced his hands in my hair and pulled my lips inches away from his.

My heart started to race and my breath caught in my throat, even though I knew he was only acting. "What are you doing?" I breathed, against his lips.

Edwin smiled his killer smile. "Just go with it."

Looking forward to it, I bit my lower lip, and he wasted no time finding my mouth. His lips sealed over mine and his tongue gently explored my mouth. I tilted my head even farther, making an unbreakable seal between us. I nearly forgot about the couple as Edwin made me drunk with passion.

"Look," he whispered, his lips hovering over mine.

Squinting out of the corner of my eye, I watched the girl yank the guy inside her cabin by his belt. I gulped, collecting my bearings. "I was not expecting that."

A slanted smile curved on Edwin's lips. "A deal's a deal. Now you have to do whatever I want," he said. "Hmm, let me think about what that's going to be." He stepped away, taunting me, as he pondered a suitable reward.

"Let me guess. Now I have to satisfy your every sexual desire," I said, rolling my eyes, though not totally against the idea.

He smiled his sexy smile, flashing all of his beaming, white teeth, clearly amused with my idea. "Is that punishment to you?"

"No. Not really." By the time my smile touched my lips, I found myself tucked back in Edwin's warm arms.

"You could tie me up and have your way with me," he teased.

I looped my arms around his waist and we walked down the trail together. "It's always about sex with you."

"It doesn't have to be about sex. I mean, unless you're cool with that," he said, his face totally serious.

"Edwin!"

He smiled again. "No really, I'm kidding. Abs, you know I love you. I can't help it if I enjoy making love to you."

My heart melted as we approached a decision. The path spilt into two ahead of us and we both came to a stop to consider our options.

Edwin glanced off in the distance thoughtfully, then he kissed me swiftly on the corner of my mouth. "I have an idea."

CHAPTER ELEVEN

I gulped in anticipation. "Okay, what is it, Eddie?"

"Do you remember seeing the groomed trail out behind your cabin?" he asked.

"Yeah, why?"

"Walk back that way and I'll meet up with you in a couple of minutes."

"Are you sure this is a good idea?" I slurred, incoherently. I was scared of being alone in the dark on a good night, but now my senses were shot from my unrestrained drinking.

"Come on, Abs. You're with me. You know I won't let anything happen to you. That is if you're up for it."

I sighed, without answering, since I didn't know what I was getting myself into. How could I possibly know if I was up for it?

Edwin took my hand in his and led me off the trail, into the spooky, dark woods. He pointed off in the distance, where I could see a few lights shining at what I supposed led to the rear of our cabins.

"You'll be fine," he said, noticing my concern. He kissed me long and slow. "I'll meet you there in a few, I swear," he promised. He kissed my cheek and nudged me off.

Though it was difficult to see anything through the thick of the trees and ground cover, I tried to set off in the direction Edwin had pointed me to. The branches snapped beneath my feet and insects crawled through the undergrowth, as I hiked deeper into the dark, freaky forest. When Edwin's rustling was out of my ear shot, an eerie feeling overcame me. My heart was already beating heavy in my ears and my quick, shallow breaths were becoming deafening.

Cutting through the thick brush, the light in the distance

faded into oblivion. Unfamiliar sounds broadcast from every bush and tree. My eyes darted back and forth, but they couldn't adjust to the blackness, the only light being that from the sliver of a moon in the black night sky. My nerves were starting to get the best of me.

Seconds crept by as I continued bush whacking, my own sounds in the wilderness startling me still. A shrill whine sounded from my throat, as I pressed on into the darkness. An overwhelming loneliness began to suffocate me. I never should have agreed to tromp through this unchartered territory solo.

As lonely as I felt, I was not alone. Someone was following me. I stopped and listened carefully, then glared over my shoulder in the direction of the sounds. The rustling stopped and there was nothing or no one there.

"Edwin? Is that you?" I asked, softly. If he was playing tricks, it was so not funny.

I crept ahead, shakily, and the rustling resumed. Determined to figure it out, I stopped again. This time my stomach threatened emptying its contents. I waited. Nothing.

I gulped the thick lump from the back of my throat and took one more step. I could hear whatever it was approaching me quicker now and the sound didn't stop this time. Terrified and panicked, I started to run, tripping over tree stumps, branches scratching at my face. Fearful cries escaped my mouth with every shaky breath.

Where's the damn trail?

Faster. I have to move faster.

The darkness taking me, I tumbled over a fallen log and crashed to my knees in the dirt. On all fours I heaved, my stomach testing my wits, but I managed to gag it back.

My eyes flashed up with fear, but the threat didn't show itself. I could feel the impending attack looming behind me. I fumbled back to my feet and with three, long strides, I could finally see the lights peeking out from the cabins. A few more strides and I was on the empty, dirt path, but it gave me no security.

I panted, sick, tired, and fearful for my life, as I jogged for the lights with all I had left. A high pitched scream rang out from behind me. I stopped to cover my ears with both of my hands, but it was no less loud.

I would recognize that scream any day. *It was my sister.*

The shriek filled my ears and haunted my heart, just as it had since my sixth birthday. With it came every insecurity and doubt, flooding back to life with a vengeance, rattling my brain.

Yes, Jennifer Jenkins was my identical twin. *But Jenny: she is dead.*

I wished screaming out loud would make it go away, but it wouldn't. And though I'd never believed in ghosts, I didn't know what to believe at this point in my life, her voice ringing loud and true. I pressed my hands hard against my ears, but it was like the blood curdling scream was coming from within. I cried, as I struggled with the deathly squeal ringing in my head.

Then it stopped.

I eased my eyes open. Total darkness. I fell to my knees and cried in my hands. It had been years since my last episode and I thought I was in the clear. I had managed to avoid the mental institute this long, but not by much.

This unwelcome setback would not be well received by my psychiatrist, or Edwin for that matter. The hope that I would become detached from Jenny over time was but a distant dream.

I knew it was true: There is no disconnecting yourself from your identical twin. Dead or alive.

Jenny would haunt me with her death for the rest of my life.

A motorized vehicle ripped me from my thoughts, buzzing up the trail in a flurry of speed and dust. A new terror settled in as the large intruder slowed its' steady approach. I leapt to my feet and edged to the side of the trail, examining the new threat. Though I lifted my arm to block my eyes, the light of the menacing machine blinded me, as the vehicle crept forward and finally came to a full stop only a few feet away.

My heart pounded from my chest as I stood frozen on the side of the path. When I finally caught a glimpse of the man, his helmet disguised any notable features. The man cut the engine. If he wanted to kill me, he could. As for any reserves left to save myself, I had none.

My panicking caused me to choke on my last breath, as I prepared to kick the man in the balls and scramble for help. But the man just stared at me, unmoving.

"You getting on or are you just going to stand there all night?" he finally called out to me, removing his helmet.

"Edwin? What are you doing?" I screeched with relief.

"I told you I would come. Just go with it."

Overcome with relief I sprang at him and threw my arms around his strong shoulders. I squeezed my eyes shut and wiped the tears from my burning cheeks with the neck his soft t-shirt.

"I don't know what's gotten into you, but I think I like it," Edwin said. His lips found mine and softly kissed my worries away. He had no idea. But I was safe now.

"You okay?" he asked, realizing there was more to it than a fear of the dark.

"I am now," I said, sobbing.

"You want to talk about it?"

I shook my head no and, once I caught my breath, I straddled the machine behind him. He handed me a spare helmet and I put it on over my tangled hair. My arms tightened around his waist and I pressed close to his back. It was such a comfort to be in his fearless presence and soaking up his body heat.

He turned back to face me. "You're sure you're good?"

I was still shaken up, but I wasn't about to tell him that. "I am."

He cupped his hand over mine and gave it a squeeze, then gripped the handle bar and kick started the ATV. "Here we go then," he said.

There was no time to second guess my decision, or evaluate my overactive imagination, as Edwin sped off in a hurry. Adrenaline coursed through my veins again, but I was more relaxed now.

We shot through the darkness for miles, passing rushing rivers, and small lakes, that I'm sure would have been lovely during the day. The well-manicured path made for a smooth ride through the pristine, dark forest. In the darkness though, all I could do was watch the moon glistening on the water, listen to the constant revving engine and absorb the thrill of Edwin speeding through it all.

I closed my eyes and pressed the helmet firmly against Edwin's back, as the trail grew steadily rougher. Eventually, after crisscrossing through the extensive network of trails, I couldn't see any trail ahead of us at all.

A feeling of unease snuck up on me as we winded through the unknown wilderness, bumping and crawling slowly through the grooves and obstacles of the rough, rocky terrain. Edwin loved every minute of it. He was a total adventure seeker, even if his adventurous side had tended to get him into trouble.

Edwin slowed our pace to a crawl, waterways winding around our heels. I feared for my life, as the vehicle rocked beneath us. If we lost the machine now, we would be left in total darkness only miles from the middle of nowhere.

I squeezed Edwin tighter and the bright beam of light that shone from the front of the four-wheeler flickered as we bumped along. Things seemed to creep in the shadows and slink out of the black depths of the wilderness.

When we met a large rock, we were going so slow that the tires refused to take us any further. Edwin cut the engine, leaving us in pitch blackness. My heart rammed into my throat.

"What are you doing? Are you crazy?" I squealed. My eyes darted around us, but I couldn't see a thing.

"Listen," Edwin whispered, as he pulled off his helmet.

I listened, but all I could hear was heavy breathing and a racing heartbeat. "What?"

"You hear that?" he asked again.

"No. I don't know what you're talking about and this is really starting to freak me out."

"Calm down. It's white water. We must be near some falls. The path ends here so we need to decide what we're going to do next. I'd really hate to turn back now. We've come so far," Edwin said, pleading with me to stay and explore.

A whirlwind of emotions flowed through me, as Edwin got off the machine and took a few steps away. He climbed up onto a nearby rock, enjoying nature in its purest of forms. I certainly didn't want to stay, but I would do anything if it meant I didn't have to be alone.

I pulled off my helmet and shook out my hair before lifting my leg over the seat. I stayed seated, my feet dangling over the side of the ATV, as my eyes scattered over the forest.

When I glanced back toward the rocks, Edwin had disappeared into the darkness, striking me with full blown terror. All survival tactics went away with the cool, summer breeze as logic left me and I began to suffer from fear of abandonment. My eyes darted through the darkness, trying to make sense of what was real and what was bogus, but my mind was quickly succumbing to its worst fears.

My quick, shallow breaths didn't help to calm my nerves and the chill that ran down my spine was nothing compared to the shock spiking through my body when I heard sudden motion behind me. The noises were distinctly that of the forest floor. The sounds crept closer, but I could barely see my own hand extended before me let alone whatever or whoever it was.

An unwelcome icy-hot intuition warned me with one word. Danger. There was nowhere to run, so I sat there paralysed with fear. Every muscle in my body was clenched when the sounds subsided.

Perhaps the monster didn't see me there and headed off in another direction. I tempted fate by slowly turning my head to glance in the direction of the noises. I squinted my eyes, but struggled to focus on the creature that was positioned only ten feet away from me.

Suddenly she locked onto my gaze, her eyes glowing blood red, holding my stare against my wishes. I gasped for air, my voice failing me, as the red-eyed monster started to slink toward me.

My hands were motionless, heavy like ice, cold as stone in the winter. I could feel that the colour had drained out of my face and, despite my terror, my lips wouldn't move, no matter how hard I tried to scream.

I had an eerie lack of control over my limbs, my eyes frantically scanning the dark woods in search of Edwin. Nothing. I squeezed my eyes shut, ready to succumb to my shattered nerves.

This creature doesn't exist. It couldn't possibly, could it? Edwin. I needed him to protect me and tell me that monsters don't exist; to tell me that I was safe in his arms. But Edwin was gone.

Fighting for control, my head slammed heavily to the right in search of Edwin. He was just not there. The monster started to move closer, now only steps away. I shuddered, as I forced myself to look back.

There, in the darkness, stood a small, non-threatening silhouette of a child. I was fine, until the glaring eyes burned red again and locked onto mine, the monster inching closer.

With a snap of a branch, I blinked my eyes shut and silently begged for a miracle while waiting for my demise. My breath failed me. It wouldn't be long now.

Eyes squeezed shut, I could still see the red globes burning through my eyelids. I could feel her hot breath on my neck. I was living a nightmare, listening to her steady breaths in my ears. Gagged of sound, there was nothing I could do.

Suddenly a shrill scream rang through my ears as fresh as the day I first heard it, eighteen years earlier. The force blistered my ear drums and knocked me from my seat. Laying on the hard forest floor, I covered my head and sobbed hysterically.

"Edwin!" I finally shrieked, but it sounded more like a whisper in the night, compared to the blood curdling scream ringing in my ears.

It was like it was happening all over again. Jenny was screaming, burning in the fire. The man tried to help her, but it was too late. "No," I screamed. There was nothing we could do but sit there and watch the car now engulfed in flames. I could smell death in the air, the singed hair and burning flesh of my identical twin sister. *"It should have been me. It should have been me," I cried.*

Edwin scuffled to my side and fell to his knees. "Whoa. Abs. What's going on here?" he breathed, stuffing me into his arms.

The screaming dwindled off and when I opened my tear-filled eyes, Edwin scooped me up and pressed me against his chest. He took a seat on the four-wheeler and rocked me in comfort.

I wished I could shake the icy feeling that had fallen over me, but the danger was still there. I shivered with grief and he squeezed me even tighter.

"It's okay, baby, I'm here. It's okay," Edwin said.

"Did you see her?" I cried.

"Did I see who? There's no one out here, babe. It's just me and you."

Jenny had vanished and now I was alone with Edwin in the eerie, unquiet darkness. I shook my head hysterically. "Edwin she was here. Please... I'm scared," I cried.

He loosened his grip on me, pulled us both to our feet, and stood at my side assessing our surroundings.

"Please don't leave me again." My fear far outweighed the guilt and grief that had settled on my shoulders.

Edwin sighed, his concern apparent, as he lifted me back onto the seat. "I'm not going anywhere."

Exhaustion overwhelmed my body, an anxious trembling controlled my limbs, and each breath revealed a shriek of fear. "I just thought..." I said, snuffling.

Edwin nudged my legs apart with his and rested between my thighs, pinning me to the machine. He took both of my hands in his and took a deep breath. "Babe, you have to know I would never leave you. There's nothing out there. It must have been your imagination."

He wrapped my arms around his hips and I locked my hands together in response. He ran his fingers through my hair and pulled my head up against his hard middle.

A warm tear fell from my eye and ran down my cheek as I listened to his heartbeat, strong and steady, like him. I took a deep breath. It felt like the first breath I had taken in hours. Edwin was my rock.

"I'm here, Abs. You're okay. Everything's going to be okay," he said, reassuring me while he stroked my hair.

My senses were slowly returning to me, but the alcohol didn't help to speed up the process. When I realized that I must have been hallucinating, tears sprang from my eyes. "I'm so sorry. I overreacted. I don't know what's come over me," I cried, softly.

Edwin chuckled, a little amused now. "It could have something to do with those shots you did."

"That's the only reasonable explanation. I was hallucinating. But I really thought there was a monster coming to kill me." *And that monster was my dead sister.*

Edwin chuckled again. "It happens."

"Not to me!"

Edwin squeezed me hard against him. "Well, if you're going to have delusions, why not concentrate real hard on making it a raunchy fantasy about me? You can tell me all about it in the morning."

"Edwin, I'm serious. I've never been so scared in my life. Well... maybe once before," I said, being struck again with my dreadful memories of the accident that claimed my sister's life.

Edwin didn't want to dredge up my devastation. "There's nothing to be scared of. Listen. There's nothing out there. It's so peaceful... just nature. It couldn't be more perfect out here to me." He gazed down into my eyes, lifted my chin and planted a soft kiss on my mouth. "Best of all, I know it's just you and me. I've been working on that all night."

I smiled for the first time since we left the resort and it felt good. I was feeling more like myself by the minute.

"Are you smiling?" Edwin teased.

"Yes," I said, then tucked my head into his arm to stifle a giggle.

He pulled away from me and straddled over the seat behind me. "Come here," he ordered, patting the seat in front of him.

I turned to face him and swung my leg over to reflect his position. He grasped my hips to slide me closer to him and pulled my thighs over the top of his, until my feet rested on the seat behind him. His mouth kicked up in a sweet smile, his face only inches from mine. His aqua eyes sparkled in the moonlight as he leaned down to kiss me.

When his lips brushed across mine, every worry and fear seemed to evaporate, all bad thoughts being driven from my mind.

"I won't ever leave you again," he whispered, his forehead pressed against mine.

Tears instantly streamed from my eyes and he kissed them as they fell down my cheeks. Embarrassed, I turned away and tried to make them disappear, but they just kept coming.

Edwin dried my eyes with the sleeve of his jacket. "What am I going to do with you?"

"Can we blame the tears on the liquor too?" I asked, still crying.

"You have nothing to be ashamed of, Abs. I know I kind of threw you for a loop the other night. Telling you I love you. The sex. I half expected your emotions to follow suit." He swept the back of his fingers under my eye. "As long as those are happy tears, cry away."

Drying my eyes on Edwin's chest, I pressed out a smile. Everything had been going great up until my delusional outburst.

Edwin looked very concerned, but in a sweet sense, and not at all concerned about our predicament. The last thing I wanted to do is ruin his whole night.

I snuffed unattractively and took a deep breath. "What were you saying before I dragged you out of your sanctuary?"

He chuckled, as he stood up and stepped past me, then put his foot on the front tire and gave it a good shake. "We can't go any farther on this thing. But you know me, I like to check things out. I saw a sandy path at the bottom of the rocks there and I think it leads to a lake. I was going to go have a look, but I'm glad I never went that far. Who knows what would have happened if I had?"

I nodded my head. "I would've passed out for sure. Probably would've conked my head off a rock too."

Edwin scowled at me, unimpressed with my attitude. "I certainly can't leave you here with *your optimism* and that wild imagination of yours. Are we going down there or what?"

I took a deep breath to muster up some courage. "Okay, I guess. As long as you promise not to leave my side for the rest of the night."

"I wouldn't dream of it," he said, smiling. He reached a hand out for me and I slipped my fingers between his.

Hand in hand we scaled the boulders. When we met a large rock face, Edwin hopped up first and pulled me up behind him like I was a dependent child.

He watched me as the faint moonlight glinted off my hair and the wind picked up speed, whipping it away from my face. I tried to act like my nerves hadn't returned, but the spaces between the rocks grew wider and I couldn't see the ground beneath them.

Tilting my chin up, I held Edwin's hand tight, guided by blind trust, until I climbed down to where the rocks met the ground.

Just as Edwin had suggested, there was a narrow row of sand right at the base of the rocks. It was a rough, winding path, but it seemed to lead us toward the sound of crashing waves.

The closer we got to the lake the sound of the waves

drowned out those of the nearby rapids. Relief rushed me like a football player when we were met with a clearing. It felt like the monster couldn't get me anymore.

On the narrow beach we were met with twinkling stars that glimmered off the water in the clear night. The silhouette of trees in the distance, the same canopy that had engulfed me earlier, was now a serene picture of absolute tranquility. I took a deep, exaggerated breath.

Edwin sighed. "See what I mean?"

I had to admit it. "It's beautiful."

Still holding my hand, Edwin gazed into my eyes. "Yeah, it is."

We stood there together on the remote, deserted beach, just staring into each other's eyes. Eddie could be so romantic sometimes. It was hard to believe this was the same man who was just delivering my pizza the other night. I smiled and blushed.

"Isn't it kind of funny how quickly things can take a turn for the better?" he said, stealing my very thoughts.

"I know what you mean. It's like we've been living in the same house all this time and yet we couldn't have been farther apart."

Edwin's lips brushed mine softly. "I had to take you to this place to finally get you alone."

I nodded in agreement and a chilly breeze swept past us. I shivered and rubbed my arms briskly, to settle the goose bumps creeping up on me. Edwin's big, warm hands smoothed over my arms, soothing the chill and warming my heart.

"Come on," he said, softly.

Relinking our hands, Edwin led me farther down the narrow beach. I hugged his incredibly big arm and rested my head against his broad shoulder. An extended yawn escaped my mouth and I covered it with my hand.

"Tired?"

"I am. And my feet are ouchy too. So much for those cute sandals I brought for tomorrow."

"You can blame me if you have ouchy feet when you

wake up in the morning," he said, teasing.

I smiled. "Oh, I will."

"Oh yeah, you think it's all on me?" Edwin said, raising his voice. He picked me up and flipped me over his shoulder, clasping my legs with one arm. He ran us out to the water, playfully threatening to drop me in.

I squealed, pleaded, slapped his back, but he wouldn't listen. "Put me down!"

"If you insist!" He flung me off of his shoulder and swept me close to the water.

"Edwin! No!" I was convinced he was going to dunk me, but to my surprise he swooped me back up and maneuvered me into his arms, like he was carrying me over the threshold. I hooked my arms around his neck and gazed into his aqua eyes. They were glimmering in the moonlight.

"Seriously though," he said, his voice a low, sexy growl, his lips only a breath away from mine, "blame me for your sore feet. It was definitely worth it to me." Edwin dropped a soft peck on my lips and hugged me close as he carried me away from the water.

He shuffled a bit, before he went down to one knee and leaned me over it. "Okay, now you can kiss me." His smile was radiant; breathtaking.

I tugged him down until his hot mouth covered mine. He tasted so sweet, but it couldn't stop me from yawning again. This time against his mouth.

"Am I boring you?" he asked, a quizzical look raising his brow.

I smiled softly. "I'm just a little tired."

Edwin scooped me back up into his arms and, though I enjoyed the fact that this massive man could throw me around like a small child, I started to feel self-conscious about my weight. "You don't have to carry me around."

"I like to."

Edwin carried me over to a huge, old, fallen tree. He took a seat against it and effortlessly sat me on his lap. I savoured the silence, as he rested his chin on top of my head. I knew, before long, I would have to ask Edwin how he felt about *us*. *What are we doing here?*

"We're quite the pair, eh?" I asked.

"Yeah, we definitely are." Edwin's chest rose on a deep intake of breath and fell with an exaggerated exhale. At that moment, I knew he was as content as I was. "There's something about this place. I don't want to leave," he whispered.

I felt it too. "We don't have to go," I said softly.

I pulled myself off his lap and sat next to him on the massive branch, our legs still touching, my head resting on his arm. The moonlight sparkled on the gentle waves and the night was filled with serene sounds only nature could provide. The quiet night set the stage for a flood of thoughts to come to me.

Just days ago, I was denying my feelings for Edwin and calling him *just a friend*, though I knew in my heart that our flame had never died out. The love we'd shared could never be erased. So, why did the word *safe* always come to mind?

Edwin made me feel safe. Being in a relationship with Edwin was easy. Those should be good things. The fear of ultimately losing each other altogether seemed to be the glue that always pulled us back together.

There was never any shortage of love, but now there was a new piece to the puzzle. *I want a baby. And soon.*

Edwin has always known how important a family is to me and he's never denied that he wants to have children in the future, but I was worried that the pieces just wouldn't fit together.

He was always reiterating how important it is to be secure in a career before making such a huge investment in life. I doubted a few weeks on the job had given him a warm, fuzzy feeling when it came to financial security.

He's so not ready.

I shook my head to clear the new disturbing thoughts suddenly crowding my mind.

Edwin looked at me funny. I wondered how long he had been watching me. I returned a smile and turned away, suddenly wondering if he was even ready to commit to a permanent relationship.

Was this just another fling for him? A relationship of convenience? One way or another, I would find out by week-end.

CHAPTER TWELVE

Edwin planted his hand on my thigh and gave it a gentle squeeze. "What are you thinking about?" he asked, breaking the long silence.

I shrugged my shoulders. "Things. And how amazing things are right now. Just being with you."

"Yeah, I am the man," he said, with confidence.

The lack of sarcasm in his voice made me laugh out loud, but it was stifled with an all-consuming yawn. I stretched my arms out over my head. I was fading fast.

"We'd better get you back," he said, brushing his fingers through my tangled hair.

"I'm not ready to go." We couldn't leave now. I had made it this far and I wasn't about to trade this dreamy atmosphere for the world. Our connection felt so special tonight, despite my self-deprecating thoughts. It was the perfect chance to tell him how I felt.

Edwin got up from the log and took off his jacket, spreading it before me on the damp sand.

"What are you doing? You're gonna get all wet."

Without any words he laid down in the sand facing the log and patted the jacket for me to join him. I clambered down from the log and curled up on the warm, soft jacket in front of him. Edwin draped his bare arm over my curvaceous hip, giving me more of his grizzly warmth. It was only then that I realized just how tired I was.

"I knew that you wouldn't lay with me if I'd asked you to lie in the dirt. Am I right?"

I hid my inner giggle, because of course he was right. The wind was blowing strong and the waves crashed on the nearby rocks, occasionally spraying us with a cool mist.

The way Edwin cocooned around me, made me feel so utterly happy. When I shivered, he reached forward and collected my hands in his. Though the old, dry log was blocking the brunt of the mist, it didn't protect us entirely.

Edwin squeezed around me tighter, his skin rough and exposed, but he seemed unscathed by the cool, moist air around us. With Edwin's massive body wrapped around me I felt so cozy and safe.

"I love you Abigail," he whispered in my ear.

"Mmm," I mumbled, shimmying to remove the only pocket of air between our bodies. We fit together perfectly.

"You good?" Edwin asked.

"Yeah, but I'm afraid to close my eyes. I don't want to wake up and find that this was all just a dream."

Edwin's chuckle rumbled against my back. He combed my hair back with his fingers and tucked it behind my ear. My eyes fell closed. I was so calm and secure in his arms.

"I'm gonna rest my eyes for a few seconds," I whispered, though we were the only two people for miles.

"Be my guest, babe. I'm not going anywhere," he said, then nuzzled his nose in my hair.

As we lay together on the warm bed of sand, my lack of sleep, recent hysteria and alcoholism hit me with a daze of emotions. *So much for that discussion.* And Edwin wasn't even trying to seduce me. It wasn't like him to put off sex. Not for a whole night.

I forced my eyes open, eager for answers, but they fluttered involuntarily, compelling me to close them again. Regardless of how badly I wanted to talk to Edwin, my mouth refused to speak and my mind shut down. Darkness encircled me and I lost the battle.

When I reopened my eyes, the sun was starting to rise in the sky. Rays of sunshine peeked out over the trees. I lifted my head and was dazzled by the blur of golden colours glimmering on the soft, wavy water. I laid there very still, unable to take my eyes from the natural beauty.

I thought Edwin was still asleep, until I felt him twitch

behind me. He rubbed my arm gently and enfolded me in an affectionate squeeze. I fumbled to a sitting position. My back ached, but other than that I felt pretty darn good, all things considered.

"Morning," I said, my voice rough and raspy.

Edwin stretched out his thick muscles, having been clamped around me all night. "Good morning," he growled, then drew me back into his arms, wrapping me in his manly armour.

Neither of us spoke as we watched the soothing waves roll off the rocks, my head against his warm chest. Edwin smoothed his hand over my hair, warm and tender, then tilted my chin and sealed my lips with a soft, *good morning* kiss. In an instant, I felt like the luckiest woman in the world. I knew, at this very moment, everything was just perfect. Everything else could wait.

It was nearly eight, by the time we reached the ATV. In the morning light, the path was an easy find. To our surprise, not far from where we had scaled the rocks last night, a sandy trail continued on to a manmade, rock stairway.

At the top of the climb, we glanced past the large boulders we had travelled over only hours earlier. The bright yellow ATV was an easy twenty feet away from us, still parked with its tires resting firmly against the rock wall that it had refused to climb.

Where there are man-made stairs, there is man. After starting the machine, Edwin pointed off in the distance. He caught the sun reflecting off of a car passing on a nearby roadway. I guess the beach wasn't as secluded as we had thought.

The return trip seemed so much less demonic in the light of day. The lush plant growth dripped with dew and the warm sunshine beat away any eerie thoughts of what had transpired last night.

Edwin ignored the path less travelled and crawled through the brush, heading straight for the gravel road. It was now deserted, barely wide enough to accommodate one car, and so he pulled onto it and gunned it without looking back.

Edwin sped back to the Southwind at record speed, turning back into the forest onto a trail that let us right into the resort. Edwin pulled up behind his neighbour's cabin and cut the engine.

"Our place is over there. What are you doing?" I asked.

"We should probably be getting this beast back to its owner. He was so nice to loan it to me last night, in exchange for a small fee of course. I promised I would get it back to him by nine o'clock."

"Are you kidding me?" He knew we were going to spend the night in the wild?

Edwin ignored my scowl and glanced at his wrist. "Damn, I'm good." He showed me his wrist watch. There was two minutes to spare.

I rolled my eyes and pushed him aside, having blown off the dreamy stupor on the trip back. Feeling back to normal, though hung over, I plucked the helmet off my head and dropped it onto the empty seat. "I'm gonna head in," I said, then walked off.

As I reached the flagstone path, I was surprised to find Maddie sitting on the patio furniture playing on her phone. I was even more surprised, when Edwin jogged up behind me.

"Hold up," he hollered.

I spun around and he collected me into his arms for a kiss.

"Mmm. Love you," he growled.

I raised an eyebrow and hinted that we had a visitor. "You sure about that?" I whispered.

His lips brushed mine again, ignoring my terrible morning breath and Maddie's squeal when she finally figured it out.

"Love you too, Eddie," I said softly, struggling to break

free from his amorous grip. I flattened my hands on his shirt and smoothed them over his chest. "You realize I'm all sweaty and hung over, not to mention my bedhead. Real attractive." I pushed him off of me, trying to get some distance.

"You look fine to me," he said, smiling.

"You need your eyes checked!" He was obviously looking through some rose coloured glasses this morning.

The need to discuss our relationship was more urgent than ever and I wanted it to happen sooner rather than later. Sooner, but not this soon. I couldn't bear to get into it now, while my aching head steadily reminded me that drinking is bad.

Maddie took two steps up the path, unable to wait another second for us to reach her. "Where have you two been?" she prodded.

"Uhh..." I said.

"We were just out for a little cruise. Then we stopped to check something out. Hmm, we must have fallen asleep," Edwin suggested, as if it were all just a faint memory.

"Do you realize what time it is?" Maddie asked.

"Yes, mother. It won't happen again," Edwin mocked.

While they bickered, I scooted past Maddie. "I'm going to take a shower. I don't want to be caught in public looking like this," I said.

Luckily, short of Maddie, none of our friends had risen from the dead yet.

"Can I at least get one last kiss goodbye?" Edwin asked, stalking up behind me.

"Awww," Maddie said, but it was like she wasn't even there.

"No... but you can have a good morning one." I wrapped my arms around his neck and he swung me around in a circle. A smile lit up my face and our eyes met, as he slowly lowered my body, brushing it sensitively against his, until my toes touched the ground.

Edwin leaned down slowly and when our lips touched, glorious flutters filled my stomach. When his soft lips caressed mine, I felt like I was the only woman in his world. "Mmm... good morning," he said.

I pecked his smiling lips. "Don't be a stranger." I spun away and pranced inside the cabin, feeling exceptionally giddy. I couldn't fight the urge to peek out the window at him. He hadn't moved a muscle, and it sent another round of flutters in my chest when I saw him still gazing at the door I had just entered. I sighed, expressing my contentment, before I realized I had company.

"Oh, girl. You've got it bad! Where the hell have you been?" Aliah was resting on the couch, with a blanket covering her, and she had been watching me the entire time.

"I promise to tell you all about it...later."

"But..."

"...but I desperately need a hot shower right now."

"Make it a quick one. I've got to hear this."

I turned for the bathroom in time to see Hunter materialize from my bedroom, wearing nothing but some fitted boxers that left nothing to the imagination. He tiredly stretched for the ceiling. Every bulging muscle flexed.

"Oh, no you don't!" I hollered. My head start was just enough. Before Hunter even knew what was happening, I disappeared into the bathroom and slammed the door shut behind me, being sure to click the lock. "Morning, Hunter!" I announced cheerily through the door. It was bad enough he slept in my bed, he could go piss on his own toilet seat.

He mumbled, confused, on the other side of the door, but I ignored him, leaving it up to Aliah to explain. He had his own place. He could use his own damn bathroom.

After using up all of the hot water, I tip-toed out the bathroom door and peeked in my bedroom. It was clear, so I closed the door behind me and quickly dressed, feeling as fresh as a morning glory. When there was a knock at my bedroom door, I skipped over to see who it was and smiled at Aliah as I pulled the door wide open for her.

"What's with you this morning?" she asked, disturbed and jealous. "Oh, yes. You're in love."

"Enough about love. I'm starving! Let's go get something to eat," I said.

"Sorry. I've already eaten breakfast. You took too long. You do realize you've been in there for like an hour."

I joined Maddie in the living area. "Maddie?"

"No thanks. You can have my banana, if you want," she offered.

"No, that's alright. I'll go check it out myself."

"You're sure?" Aliah asked, but not seeming too interested to join me.

"Yeah. I could use the time to think. Were the guys there when you went? Eddie?" I asked.

"TJ left with me and Hunter," Aliah said. "I didn't see Edwin."

"Okay. I'll be back soon," I muttered, then scurried off.

The heat of the day was progressively getting warmer and I was glad that I had opted for my short, white, flowing, halter dress this morning. I walked down the dusty road in my heeled sandals, remembering how sore my feet were from the night before, but ignoring it entirely. I refused to let some sore feet stop me from looking totally hot today. My dress fluttered in the warm breeze as I walked up the wooden stairs, onto the raised deck, that overlooked gentle, still water.

I slipped through the sliding glass doors and, after a quick glance around the large room, headed toward the small breakfast bar lining the side wall. A few small, round tables were set up nearby and they were mostly vacant. The few lingering late risers were no one I knew.

I approached the food to eye up what they had to offer. I picked up a cup of fruit and spoon and placed them at a free table, then went back to the small fridge for a vanilla yogurt and bottle of orange juice.

The breakfast attendant caught my attention as I took my seat. She smiled, as though she recognized me, and then approached me watchfully. "A young man was looking for you earlier. I think he's just around the corner. Oh, and he's cute," she added, her cheeks flushing. She flashed me a wink and walked away in that direction.

I sat staring blankly at the wall for a minute and then decided to see who it was. I bundled my breakfast in my arms and slowly walked around the corner to find my mystery man. I watched the lady as she tapped the handsome man on the shoulder, to point out that I had arrived.

He was sitting alone and when the lady left, I suddenly felt the temperature in the room spike a few degrees. I looked behind me, to check on the other guests, but they had already slipped away. When I turned back to the attendant, she was gone too and the handsome man was staring at me with dark, blue eyes. He pushed out his seat and walked toward me.

"May I?" he asked, reaching for the chair across from him.

After pulling it out, he took the bottle of juice from my arm.

"Of course," I said, as I took a seat and placed the rest of my breakfast on the table in front of me. I brushed my skirt under my legs, as he took his seat across from me.

He leaned back in his chair, looking deviously handsome, his arms folded across his massive chest, his eyes dark and intriguing. "I started to think you weren't coming," he said.

"I didn't recognize you. When did you do that to your hair?" I asked. Edwin was donning fresh, blonde highlights in his soft, brown hair and it had turned him into a tanned, beach babe. *Oh. My. God! He looks so damn hot!*

"TJ had some die left over and I knew you'd be a while, so we just did it. You like it?" He scrunched his forehead, looking adorably self-conscious for a change.

"You look so different," I said, smiling.

"Good different, or bad different?"

"Definitely good." I couldn't even remove the smile from my face as I filled my mouth with fruit, and it was difficult to pry my hungry eyes from the buff bod straining against his shirt.

"What took you so long?" Edwin asked.

"Do you think I just wake up looking this good?"

He chuckled at me and lowered his voice. "Actually, I know exactly what you look like when you wake up." He raised his dark eyebrows in seduction.

My, God! "Is that a threat?" I asked, a smile hanging on the edge of my parted lips.

"Abs, you always look good, but I must say you've definitely made it worth my wait."

I smiled, absorbing his compliment. "I'll take that, considering I got all of two hours sleep last night, thanks to you."

"It was nice. Peaceful. At least, I loved it," Edwin said, unwilling to put words into my mouth.

I swallowed some yogurt and fixed my stare on his soft, pink lips. "I liked it to," I agreed. *At least the part where I was in his arms.*

After gazing into each other's eyes, I stole mine away to retrieve my bottle of juice and take a healthy swallow. I was relieved that everything went down and was settling just fine. "Ready?" I asked, standing from the table to toss out my garbage. When I turned to leave, I caught Edwin staring at my ass. *Men.*

"You *do* look really nice today," Edwin said, his words clean but his heated stare dirty. He followed me to the patio doors, his eyes following the gentle sway of my hips. His hand softly cupped my ass. "You look amazing, babe."

I swatted his hand away, but he caught my wrist and clasped our hands together.

"You buttering me up for something?" I asked, raising a suspicious brow. I knew I looked good, but all of those compliments were starting to make me question his intentions.

When he didn't respond, it only ramped up my curiosity, his smile devoid of information. We walked in silence, until we reached the front lawn of our cabins.

"Speaking of buttering you up, I got you something." He stopped me and I gazed up into his striking, aqua eyes, now accentuated by his new, blonde hair. Edwin reached both of his fists out face down. "Don't you want to know what I got you?"

"What is it?" I asked, admiring his new look. Just a hint of highlights, but it made him look super-hot. I couldn't help but stare.

"Pick one," he said, smiling.

I held his stare, expecting him to open his hand, but he didn't budge.

"Pick!" he insisted.

"Fine." I pointed to his right hand.

He opened his left. "You were supposed to pick this one." A dainty bracelet sparkled in the sunlight. He undid the clip and refastened it on my wrist. "Do you like it or what? Don't keep a brotha waiting."

"I love it," I said. I held up the bracelet to get a closer look, and as it dangled from my wrist, the sun made it sparkle. I flashed Edwin an appreciative glance. "Thank you."

His hand cupped my face, then he leaned down to kiss me, soft and slow. "I'm glad you like it. I saw it in the gift shop and thought of you."

He swept a lock of hair from my shoulder and my heart began to race with desire, as his knuckles gently brushed along my collarbone. He propped my chin up with his forefinger.

I closed my eyes and waited for his kiss. When it didn't come, I was left feeling confused and embarrassed. I reopened my eyes and Edwin pierced me with an electrifying gaze, stirring an awareness that any person within fifty feet of us would have detected.

He knew he had my attention. "You're a special breed, Abs. You're one unique woman that can't be classified with anyone else I know."

Suddenly aware of our audience, I was feeling incredibly sensitive about sharing our private conversation. "I may be an individual, but I'm no different than you," I said softly, squinting up at him.

Edwin remained calm and confident, while I was

flustered beneath his penetrating gaze. "Don't fight it, Abs. We love each other. It's no crime that I think you're special and I want others to know that you're with me."

Feeling awkward discussing the depth of our relationship with our friends gathered only paces away, I curled into myself. I needed a minute to collect my scattered thoughts. While there was no doubt that we were very attracted to each other, there had to be more to it. The baby thing was a make or break kind of deal for me.

Instead of giving me another second to pull myself together, his hurt-filled eyes made me respond. It took all I had not to fling my arms around him and gush an apology, but when he looked at me with such intensity, his eyes darkening to a midnight blue, I couldn't resist him any longer.

The edge of his lips curled, with the knowledge that he had worked me over without a word. Ignoring our friends' watchful eyes, he leaned down to kiss me. My lips held firm as he gently caressed my mouth, his hands smoothing over me as he trailed kisses along my jaw, down my neck.

My eyes fluttered shut and my knees grew weak. Edwin's soft, warm tongue on my throat made my head spin. He was right. I was fighting it. But I couldn't fight him off anymore. I was too drawn in to his charming magnetism and the pure allure of kissing him.

When his lips returned to mine, I softened beneath him, whimpering from the delicious give and take of his mouth. It wasn't until his grasp on me relaxed that I realized how tight he had been clutching me. I wasn't going to run off now, but I was still unsteady. He retightened his strong arms around me and titled his head to deepen the kiss. His tongue slipped between my lips, soft and sweet.

Edwin paused, but his lips never left mine, as I gasped on a sharp inhale. "I know, right?" he said, with a soft growl. We shared a smile, our mouths touching, before continuing to lock lips.

Our company was getting impatient, all four sets of eyes gawking at us without shame. Maddie gasped, as we ignored their wandering eyes. She stomped down the path, her anger mounting, as she left the others to interrupt us.

A hard finger poked Edwin's shoulder. "I knew you guys had a secret thing going on. I can't believe you wouldn't admit it to me. Why don't you save it for the bedroom?" she squawked.

"Where's the fun in that?" Edwin said, releasing me from his magical mouth.

Aliah burst out laughing. I was fighting off a grin myself.

"Are you really that surprised?" Aliah asked.

Ignoring them all, Edwin turned his gaze back to me, and I smiled up at him like he was the only other person in the world. My hand dusted over his hulking chest. This hot man was all mine.

"She's just jealous," he said, then initiated another kiss. He tugged on my lower lip with his teeth, testing Maddie's determination.

"Whatever. I'm not hanging around all this." Maddie flailed her hand at us, like we were a single entity, and spun off. "Let's get out of here," she snapped back at Aliah.

Aliah followed Maddie's path of destruction. "Later, Abby. Eddie." She nodded at Edwin, then winked at me as she walked past us.

"Laters," TJ said, moseying after them with a couple of fishing rods and bucket in hand.

Hunter followed with the tackle box, giving us a salute, his smirk unreadable.

"I guess they thought we needed some space," I said, smiling at the suddenly empty lawn.

"Was it that obvious?" Edwin smirked and leaned in for another knee weakening kiss. "What *do* you want to do today? I mean, aside from this; though I'm not saying I'm against doing this all day if that's what you want." A charming smile covered his daring mouth.

"Sorry, I'm a bit off right now. This is all happening so fast. I didn't think..."

"Even after last night?" He seemed surprised, disappointed even.

"I guess I've just been walking around blissfully unaware of where we stand in this relationship," I admitted.

"Blissful though," he said, smirking, "and that's because of me."

CHAPTER THIRTEEN

It was impossible to be serious with Edwin when he was being so damn adorable. *Damn, that sexy smile.* I refused to admit it out loud but, yes: he was the reason I was so blissful. I was having difficulty taking my eyes off of his perfectly tanned skin and full lower lip.

He had decided to skip shaving this morning and it made him that much more rough and appealing. I ran my fingers across his delightful stubble and then playfully chewed on his lip.

How was I ever going to make any progress with serious conversation when Edwin had me going all gaga for him like this?

Going with my gut, I decided to take Edwin's advice. No deep talk was going to crush my vacation weekend. This weekend, I'd just go with it. Better to save it for when we got back to reality; at home.

Edwin gazed into my emerald eyes. "I can think of something else we can do that would make this morning even more blissful," he whispered, stroking my hair.

I chewed on my own lip, to tease. "Oh, and what is that?" I breathed. Both of my hands skimmed over his massive chest, as he drew in a sharp breath. I liked to make him work for it; but then he smiled and all was lost.

"There will be plenty of time for that later," I said, running my finger across his moist lips. "I just got all dolled up and you want to strip me down already?"

"That's exactly what I want," he replied, his eyes darkening.

I started to laugh, trying to break the rigid attraction arching between us. I wanted him so bad, but sweaty bedhead wasn't exactly the look I was going for today. Sex would have to wait.

"We can do that anytime. Why don't we check this place out?"

If he had said no, then there would have been no more arguing.

Edwin sighed in defeat. "If you insist. You name it; let's do it."

"Come on then," I said, pulling him behind me.

I figured our friends hadn't made it far and Aliah wouldn't be too pleased with me if I left her alone with Maddie too long. As Edwin and I neared the main cabin, my suspicions were confirmed. Maddie and Aliah were bickering, hands on hips, chins out.

Would they ever stop arguing?

Surprisingly, they did when we walked up to them.

"Abby. Thank God!" Aliah glared at Edwin, as if it were his fault she was fighting with Maddie. "She's coming with me!" Aliah tugged my arm away from him and started to drag me back the way I came.

"Hold up. What about Edwin?" I asked, stopping her in her tracks.

Aliah glanced over her shoulder at Edwin, whose eyebrows were raised, waiting for her answer.

"Sorry! I'm stealing her away. Girl stuff."

She knew exactly what to say to send Edwin running for the hills.

"Why don't you go find the guys?" Maddie suggested. "They're out fishing. My parents used to bring us here every summer when we were kids. TJ's a creature of habit. I can guarantee that he's gone to his favourite place." Maddie pointed toward a trail in the distance and Edwin nodded.

"See you later?" I said, disappointed by how quickly he gave in.

Maddie headed off, but Aliah didn't budge, still clinging to my arm as if Edwin might steal me away if she let go.

Edwin pried her fingers from my arm and pulled me back to him to hold me close. He dropped a soft, patient kiss on my lips, while Aliah tapped her toe. His gaze locked on mine and he flashed me a reassuring smile before kissing me again. "Have fun, ladies."

"Bye," I breathed, watching him as he walked away. Such a fine ass. Staring after him, I hadn't even noticed that my fingers were lingering on my mouth savouring our last kiss.

"Truly sickening," Aliah snapped, breaking my obsessive gaze.

"What?" I said, my eyes fluttering back to Edwin.

"Okay! Enough of that!" Aliah shouted. "Let's go." She yanked my arm, tearing my gaze away from Edwin, as we headed back to our cabin.

After an in depth debate over who wanted Hunter more, Aliah and Maddie agreed to call a truce so we could at least enjoy our lunch. I nibbled from the spread of cheese and crackers and nuts, and downed an ice cold bottle of water. It was so sweltering hot outside that I couldn't even imagine eating another morsel.

While Aliah cleaned up the mess, I flopped myself on the couch, happy that our place had air conditioning. "So, ladies..."

"What are we going to do now?" Maddie asked, finishing my sentence.

"I could soak up some rays. My skin could use a little colour," Aliah admitted, flashing us her milky white waistline.

"I don't have that trouble," Maddie said, gloating about her naturally tanned skin. "I did bring all of those gorgeous suits though. I'd hate for them to go to waste."

"I'd love to catch a tan," I said.

"It's settled then," Aliah replied. "I'm going to get changed."

"Beach time," Maddie cheered. "Did you know there's a private beach right on the resort? It's for guests only. Why don't we check it out first?"

"That works for me," I said, smiling.

While Aliah gawked at herself in the small mirror, I filled my bag with all the beach essentials: lip balm, sunscreen, bottled water, a towel and a volleyball. It was so hot outside that I pulled on a pair of super short, cut-off jeans over my bikini bottoms and skipped a shirt entirely.

After I slipped on my hot pink flip-flops and put on my shades, I checked out my reflection in the mirror.

"Oh yeah, ladies. I'm ready."

We followed the wooden plank path that travelled right down by the private beach. It was a short enough nature walk, the canopy of trees providing enough shade to make it comfortable, despite the hot sun and rising humidity. A warm breeze graced us with its presence, but my chest was already damp with sweat.

The path directed us out onto the beach and it wrapped back around into the surrounding forest. We stepped onto the sand and I became bizarrely excited. *Girl time! I so needed it.*

"I want to take off my sandals so bad, to feel the sand in my toes," I said. I wanted to, but the afternoon sun was so hot, I was sure the sand would be scalding.

"Oh, me too," Maddie said, excitedly. She flipped off her sandals and bent over to pick them up. After two steps, she started hopping up and down. "It burns!"

Aliah and I laughed, as she hopped on one foot trying to put her other sandal back on. It didn't take long for our girly exchange to get the attention of the mass of guests dispersed on the beach. It was a perfect day for the beach, and the collection of empty towels told me just how inviting those gentle waves were to the lot.

"What do you say we move closer to the water?" I asked, scouting out the perfect spot.

Aliah ignored me and leisurely strolled farther down the beach, keeping her distance from the water. "This is the spot," she said. She lifted her shades, motioned her eyes toward the two, shirtless studs playing Frisbee not far away, and then lowered them, satisfied that she got her point across.

"What about Hunter? Aren't you supposed to be *in love*?" I teased.

"Hey. If Hunter wants to play the indecision card, so will I," she snapped. "At least from here I can get a good look at their bods without them knowing." She smiled at me and tossed her towel down, scattering the hot sand.

I laid mine out next to hers, fumbled with my button, and shimmied my faded shorts to the sand. As I tossed them in my bag, Maddie adjusted the one and only umbrella chair for herself.

Most of the guests were back to their own business, except for the two guys Aliah had set her eyes on; and neither of them were being secretive about their gawking.

I ignored them, as I tousled my hair and slathered on some tanning oil, but I also didn't mind the extra attention. *What can I say? My white bikini is demanding it.*

Amused, I watched out of the corner of my eye, my dark black shades concealing my eyes, as the men tried to continue with their Frisbee game without removing their gaze from us. I lied down next to Aliah and propped myself up on my elbows, a wicked smile lurking on my lips.

"What are you smiling at?" Aliah asked.

"Oh, just concocting master plans over here. Who knows? We'll see." I shrugged my shoulders in an effort to seem careless, but I was stirring the pot and she knew it.

"Uh, oh! That means trouble," Maddie said, duplicating Aliah's thoughts.

"Don't worry, it doesn't involve you. It may involve Aliah though," I said, smiling. "Oh, and maybe those two guys over there." I leaned over to Aliah and lifted my sunglasses to flash a dramatic wink.

A little bit of harmless flirting would never hurt anyone. If anything, I enjoyed causing men a little distress. Edwin included. It was his own fault really, since he always felt the need to compete with other men for my attention.

So what if I help to spark his anger. *He's so hot when he's angry.* A mental image of just how hot Edwin got when he was angry only encouraged me to move ahead with my devious scheme.

"I love it!" Aliah cheered, in support. "Egg-celent." She tapped her fingers together like Mr. Burns on The Simpsons and smiled wickedly. Aliah loved getting me into trouble almost as much as she loved causing it herself.

Smiling, on a deep intake of warm air, I took a second to appreciate the beach, a quarter mile of scenic lake shoreline. So refreshing. So relaxing. The flat blue sky set the scene for a flawless, peaceful day.

I rested my head on my towel to soak up the golden, hot rays, as Maddie and Aliah babbled about random girl things. I lifted my hair from the back of my neck and closed my eyes. My arms were stretched behind my head, knees slightly bent, in a time perfected position to catch the best light and a seamless tan. I was so comfy, until...

"Heads up!" a man called out, breaking me from my relaxation.

As the dirt flew onto my towel, I reacted exactly as I always did when I got startled: I screamed like a school girl.

I swiftly sat up and turned away from the handsome, tanned man, crashing into the sand next to me. His body was glistening with sweat and now entirely covered in sand. After catching the Frisbee, that was right on course to hit me in the face, he rested back in the sand, but his impressive muscles were no less defined.

"Nice catch," I said sarcastically, though I truly was impressed. The troublemaker in me kicked into high gear before I could stop her and, once my plan went into full swing, there was no turning back.

Turning too girly to be true, I stood from my towel paying careful attention to my curves, with my hand on my chest in shock. The men always ate that up.

Time to exploit my target.

While I brushed the sand from my skimpy white bikini, I raised my eyebrows at him, silently demanding an apology.

And right on cue: "Sorry about that..."

"...Abigail," I finished.

"Abigail. Wow, that's a beautiful name." He paused, locking his narrow chestnut eyes on me. "I really didn't mean for all that to happen. It's my buddy... he's such a klutz sometimes... I... uh," he stuttered, and then stopped and smiled.

He didn't look like the nervous type, giving off a very capable vibe, but I returned a smile just the same.

From a distance this guy looked like a total hottie, and up close was no exception. His abs were chiseled to perfection, his thick muscles carved sharply around his hips. He had bulky shoulders and a light dusting of hair over his manly chest. The entire core of his body glistened with sweat in an incredibly sexy way.

He tried to wipe off some of the sand with his hand, as he fumbled with his words, but it wasn't working. *Damn, this man is sexy.*

I dropped the girly act. "Here let me help you." I shook out my towel and stepped toward him to dust off some of the sand.

He lifted his hulking arms up, and every muscle in his body tightened, as I slowly ran my towel over his washboard abs. *Holy hell, this is hot. I should so not be doing this right now.*

My new bracelet jingled on my wrist as a well-timed reminder that I wasn't single anymore. But it was too late to retreat now.

The man had already lowered his arms, turned around, and was waiting for me to brush the sand from his bulky back. Each muscle tensed beneath my touch, and his ass was out of this world. Not that I checked it.

"I appreciate that," he said, glancing at me over his shoulder. His eyes were so warm and kind, and hot.

I nodded and smiled sweetly in response to his striking smile and kind heart.

"Honestly. It sure beats being seen with my buddy groping me over there," he added, pointing to his *klutzy* friend.

Is that what I was doing? Groping?

"Again, I apologize," he said.

"That's really not necessary," I replied. "You saved me from a Frisbee in the face. I should be thanking you." I smiled at Aliah subtly, but kept his eyes on me for her entertainment.

I held my stomach tight and arched my back to accentuate my curves, as I lightly brushed the sand from my white string bikini. He was trying to be polite but, nevertheless, I caught his eyes drifting over my body.

"Yeah. No thanks to my buddy," he finally admitted. "He's really the one that owes you the apology."

Aliah cocked an intrigued brow and I knew what she was thinking. "Maybe he should come on over then," Aliah whispered to me, naughtily.

"His fault?" Maddie interrupted. "It looked pretty damn intentional to me."

I flashed Maddie the look of death, suggesting that she shut her big mouth, but subtlety was never her thing.

"What?" she squawked.

I turned back to my hero and smiled at him, then patiently waited for him to invite his friend over. No intro seemed forthcoming, so I took things into my own hands. "And what do they call you?" *You sexy freak of nature.* I continued to ignore Maddie as the other cutie jogged toward us.

"Tanner. Tanner Bradshaw." He reached for my hand and gave it a friendly shake. "And this is my friend, Jay."

He pointed at his friend, who was less bulky than Tanner, but built with long, sleek muscles. He was still very attractive, athletic and friendly. Jay lifted his hand for a pleasant wave and a nodded at us.

"This is Abigail," Tanner explained, as he unhooked his shirt from his shorts and covered his amazing body.

"Wow. Abigail. That's a beautiful name," Jay said.

Tanner looked to the sand and chuckled. Aliah rolled her eyes and cleared her throat, quietly requesting a proper introduction.

"Thanks," I replied, modestly. "Oh, and this is my friend,

Ally. And Maddie," I added, pointing to Maddison, who rolled her eyes on cue.

"My pleasure," Jay said, with a wave to Maddie, then took Aliah's dainty hand for a shake.

"The pleasure is all mine," Aliah replied.

Jay seemed a bit uncomfortable with Aliah's directness. "Okay then. I was actually coming to see if any of you ladies wanted to play a game of volleyball. Are any of you up for it?" It was rather obvious that Jay was taking full advantage of the instigated opportunity.

Aliah shook her head no. *So much for her making Hunter jealous.* I should probably have stopped while I was ahead too. I shrugged my shoulders with indecision. *Oh, but I love to play.*

"I see you have a volleyball there. You must know how to play," Tanner challenged.

I glanced at Aliah and she shook her head again, suggesting I lie to him. "Yeah, I play," I confessed. "Maddie, what do you think?"

"Oh, it's on," she cheered. "You're going down."

To refrain from smiling was futile. "I'll take it that's a yes," I said, then let out a giggle. No more playing the girly-girl, time to kick some seriously sexy ass.

"I'm a good spectator," Aliah offered. She hopped up and threw her towel over her shoulder.

Leaving my stuff where it was, I picked up my ball and headed for the net after Tanner.

He turned back and flashed me his dangerously sexy smile. "Two on two then?" he asked.

"Girls against boys, so we can show them who's boss!" Maddie shouted, jogging to catch up.

"Actually, I was hoping we could split up. That way Abigail can play with me," Tanner said. *Where was his modesty now?*

"Actually, that's not a bad idea. I wanted big mouth on my team anyway," Jay teased. "She seems pretty frisky. I'd bet she's good for a win."

"The name's Maddie. Get it right," she growled.

"Yes ma'am." Jay saluted her, acting incredibly sarcastic, loving her feistiness.

"Oh, yeah, I see we'll get along just fine," Maddie said, smiling.

"You're mine," he replied, pointing at her.

She couldn't help but widen her smile. Maybe this would work out after all. With Maddie off Hunter's back, Aliah could swoop in for the kill.

"I guess you're with me then," Tanner said softly, too soft for a man of his size. He smiled, all shyness resurfacing, and even that was hot.

Needing to break my ridiculous fascination for this man, I tore my eyes from his arms. "Let's do this," I shouted. "I have to warn you though: I'm pretty competitive, so you better not suck."

Tanner pulled his shirt over his head and tossed it aside. "I'm game," he said, confidently.

I nearly gasped when I saw his core, disturbed by my carnal attraction to him. He was total man candy.

Aliah couldn't seem to pick up her jaw from the ground either. The man was ripped.

Tanner reached his hand out and, after giving him a tag, I forced myself to look away from his tanned flesh, suddenly feeling incredibly guilty.

I tip-toed to the back of the sandy court and exposed my bug eyes to Aliah. *'Oh. My. Gawd.'* I mouthed to her, secretively.

'I know,' she mouthed back, amused.

I looped around when I found the mark. "You ready?" I called to Jay and Maddie.

"Bring it on beoch," Maddie chimed.

When Jay waved in acknowledgement, I threw the ball high in the air. I jumped and hit the ball hard and fast. Time seemed to stand still.

"Ace!" I hollered, as it hit the ground right in between Jay and Maddie. Neither of them had even moved their feet, frozen like statues.

Tanner laughed and pointed at Jay, who was staring at

Maddie with flirty, blame-filled eyes.

"Don't look at me," she shouted. "That was all you."

Jay glanced back to me and shook his head side to side. "Okay. Now that I see how it is, I'm ready," he hollered to me.

"Go, Abby!" Aliah roared, making sure no one forgot she was there.

Tanner picked up the ball, handed it to me, and reached his hand out for another tag. I slapped his hand, so there was no awkward touching and headed back for the service line.

I tossed the ball back in the air and slammed it a little lighter, skipping the showy jump. It was heading right for Maddie, but Jay was not going to let this one go. He stamped in front of her and took the pass. Though Maddie looked pissed, they managed to get it back to us in three hits.

Tanner passed the ball to me and I set him up for a kill. His agile, chiseled frame leapt from the ground and floated in the bright, blue sky before his hand swiftly met the ball, and slammed it to the ground. Jay dove in the sand, but fell just short.

"Impressive," I told him, as I slapped his hand.

I meant the kill, but his bod was pretty damn impressive too. *Dammit. Why does this guy have me fumbling around like a fool? Oh, it can't be those muscles. Shit! I am so going to pay for this.*

The other two got more aggressive as the game went on, but they couldn't compete with Tanner and I. That mostly had something to do with the fact that Jay was more concerned with Maddie's ass than playing the game. After a few more fun, but sweaty rallies, I had had enough.

"I think I'm ready to call it quits," I said, now soaked with sweat.

"Yeah, it's been fun, but it's ridiculously hot," Maddie said.

Tanner wiped his forehead with his hand and smeared it across his long, swim shorts. "Well. It was nice meeting you, Abigail," he said, smiling.

Dammit. His body is glistening again. "You too. Good game," I said, with an unrestrained smile. I walked away from the Greek god of the sand and took my towel from Aliah to dab the sweat from my chest and face.

"What are you doing?" she whispered, and I knew exactly what she was getting at.

"It's harmless," I replied quietly, knowing it was too late now.

"I was thinking," Jay said, then kicked his toe in the sand bashfully. "Since we don't have any other plans for the afternoon, I thought maybe we could go get ice cream. It's on me." He raised his eyebrows hoping Maddie would take the bait. If he only knew Maddie better. She couldn't turn up a free turnip, if you offered it to her nicely.

"Sweet!" Maddie squealed. She put her arm over Jay's sweaty shoulder. "I'm liking you more and more by the minute."

"Abigail? Are you coming?" Jay asked, as they started to head out.

"It's harmless," Aliah mocked, quietly.

"Sure why not," I replied, flashing a quick glance at Aliah.

"I'm sure Edwin won't mind at all if you do," Aliah said. Her quiet sarcasm was really starting to piss me off. "God I hate being the fifth wheel," she said, too loud.

"Ally, cut it out. You're not the fifth wheel, because I'm not with Tanner," I argued, as we collected up our things.

"I'm sure Edwin will see it that way too," Aliah snapped.

What is her problem all of a sudden? Jealous much?

Jay folded up Maddie's towel. "Ready to go?" he asked, tucking it in her bag.

"Absolutely," Aliah replied. And when she realized she couldn't steal Jay's attention from Maddie, she stomped off ahead of us like a child.

It was obvious to me that Aliah was mad because she wasn't the centre of everyone's universe. Ignoring her tantrum, I hustled up behind her in a hurry to reach the wooden boardwalk.

"There's a shop up at the main lodge. We can walk there together," Jay said.

"I'm going to drop my things off at the cabin first then. Here, I'll take your bag," I said to Maddie. "There's no reason for us to carry all this stuff with us. Besides, our place isn't very far out of the way."

Maddie handed me her things. "Thanks, Abby."

"You'll meet us there then?" Tanner asked, all too concerned.

"Why don't you go with her?" Jay pressured, tossing him my volleyball. "Looks like she could use a hand."

"Naw. I don't think she wants me tagging along with her." Tanner handed my ball to me and smiled sweetly, though my hands were nearly full with our things.

"No. It's okay. I mean, if you want," I flushed, pushing the ball back in his hands.

Aliah's eyes nearly bulged out of their sockets. I didn't know what the hell I was doing either.

"Alright. Cool. We'll meet you all there then," Tanner said to Jay.

"Be careful," Jay said, already chuckling as he flashed a look at Tanner. "You know what I always say. Girls are like roads; the more curves they have, the more dangerous they are."

Maddie slapped him for me and I flushed redder yet.

"You're sure you don't want *me* to come with you instead?" Aliah asked, hinting that I should take her up on her offer.

"What are you gonna do, carry my bag for me?" I teased, trying to be reasonable.

"Suit yourself beoch, but don't say I didn't try." Aliah slung her pink bag on Tanner's big, strong shoulder and winked at him. "Oh yeah, that's hot," she said, her scowl finally replaced with a smile.

He smiled back and didn't seem at all embarrassed about having a pink bag hooked on his arm. He must have been more secure with himself than he let on. And why wouldn't he be, when he looked like that?

The others walked off, so I led Tanner directly to my cabin. Tanner walked a step behind me, his shoulders easily carrying the load. I slowed up a step, so he would walk next to me. I didn't need him gawking at my butt.

"What was that all about?" Tanner asked, obviously having picked up on Aliah's intimations.

Telling him about Edwin sooner, rather than later, would prevent any natural disasters from occurring. I sighed. "I think she's hinting that I've taken things with you a little too far."

"What do you mean exactly?" he asked, soft and hesitant.

"I have a boyfriend," I blurted. "It's kind of new, but I think we're pretty serious."

"And?"

"And... she thinks I've given you the wrong impression."

He smirked at me. "It's harmless."

Oh shit! How embarrassing. "You heard that, did you?"

"It's okay. I didn't have any expectations for this weekend either. Just looking for a little fun."

"I really have to watch my mouth," I said, scorning myself.

"Oh, stop. You really haven't done anything wrong. That is unless being beautiful is a crime," he said, breaking out that incredibly dangerous smile.

"Tanner Bradshaw, are you hitting on me?"

"I'm just saying that you can't help it. With that body, you're gonna get men's attention," he said, his eyes rolling over my bare skin like hot coals.

I blushed crimson, though he probably didn't notice, since my cheeks were still flushed from the game. "You're one to talk."

"Miss. Abigail are you hitting on me? And with a boyfriend. Tisk, tisk, tisk."

I had to smile. "You can call me Abby."

"Abby," he said.

To redirect the attention from me, I put him back in the hot seat.

"So, these men giving me all this attention. Are we

talking about all men in general or just you?" I teased.

"I'm sorry.   That was out of line," he said, his embarrassment pliable. "I guess knowing you already have a man does put a slight twist on things."

"Yeah, especially when he owns a gun," I said.

"What?"   Tanner froze outside the cabin door as I unlocked it and let myself it.

"I'm only joking. I'm sorry. Too much too soon?"

He smiled and a hint of relief settled on his brow. He was still hesitant when he followed me into the living room, cautious eyes scanning over the room. He dropped the ladies things on the couch and stood there anxiously. It was obvious that I had made him nervous as hell.

Not making him suffer another minute, I headed back to the door, quickly returning to the hot, afternoon sun. Tanner stood awkwardly outside the door, waiting for me to lock it up, his eyes shooting around the grounds, as though he was looking out for danger.

"You can relax. Edwin's not staying here," I said.

"Edwin? So, that's the lucky bastard's name."

"Quit it. You're making me blush," I said, swatting at him.

Then, giving me another good reason to blush, Tanner removed his shirt. The hot, hot day just got hotter, and it was so hard not to stare.

"You must work out a lot," I said, against my better judgment.

"I do find I have a lot of time on my hands these days." He tossed his shirt over his shoulder and flashed me a smile without revealing any more information.

As we walked toward the lodge, being at a loss for hot topics, I decided to dig into his personal life. "You have a lot of time now? As opposed to before..." I pried.

"... before my wife left me for another man."

Oh shit. I didn't see that coming. "I am so sorry. I really have to learn to mind my own business."

"It's okay. I've come to terms with it, I guess."

"It must be pretty fresh then?" I said, hesitating. *Did I really want to dig any further?*

"It's been over a year now, but it doesn't make it any easier. My divorce was just finalized last month and Jay thought it would be a good idea if we came here to celebrate."

"It doesn't sound like an event worth celebrating, if you ask me," I said. "But that's just my opinion."

"I feel the same way, but I'd bet she's celebrating right about now. She certainly didn't waste any time moving on. I think the court case had been holding up her wedding plans. Now she can go ahead with them. I guess she wants to be married before the baby's born," he said, dropping yet another bomb.

"The baby?"

"Yeah, she's pregnant with his child. We were trying to get pregnant right before she left me, but things don't always work out the way you want. You give a woman everything she wants..." Silence.

"I'm sorry."

"I'm the sorry one. I shouldn't have depressed you with my pitiful life."

"Take it easy on yourself. I don't mind. I won't say I understand because I haven't been there, but I can see why you would be hesitant to move on."

"And now you know why Jay's pushing me on you. I haven't exactly been dating since she left me."

"You will, when you're ready." I rested my hand on his hulking arm and regretted it instantly. It was so hard, and hot.

He didn't seem to notice my squirming. "Jay keeps saying that this is *the* weekend. *My weekend.* He thinks if I mac-it-up with some random chick it will help me to get over her," Tanner said.

"He may have a point there."

"Wait a minute, you're siding with Jay?" He flashed me a slanted smirk.

"I guess I am. Why should you be miserable for the rest of your life, just because this one woman wasted your time?

Is she worth it to you?"

"I used to think so. Now, not so much. Do you know what it's like to hate someone that you're still in love with?" he asked, the pain returning to his soft, brown eyes.

"Sounds pretty messed up to me. A word of advice? You should probably save that one for the second date," I teased.

He laughed, though it was half-hearted. I couldn't blame him.

"That's suggesting that I could get a girl to date this damaged property in the first place. I'm sorry. I don't know why I'm even telling you all of this," he said.

"I'm sure you'll have no problem finding someone. I mean, I'd totally date you, if I didn't have a boyfriend." *Shit! I totally should not have said that. But look at him. Damn!*

"Thanks, that gives me hope," he said, a smile softening his frown.

"Happy to help." I smiled warmly at him and looked up the gravel road. I could see the others seated around the small picnic table, eating their ice cream. Maddie was conveniently attached to Jay's hip, her leg dangling over his.

"I see your friend has taken a liking to Jay," Tanner said, chuckling.

"Yeah, Maddie has no shame. We're friends of convenience. We work together," I said.

Maddie stole her eyes away from the lean, piece of meat, hooked beneath her. "What took you two so long?" she squealed, eyes narrowed at me.

"What are you talking about? Your ice cream hasn't even melted yet, so we couldn't have been that long," I argued.

"Abby, what would you like? I can get it for you," Tanner offered, as Jay tossed him a ten dollar bill.

"I'd love a scoop of moose tracks on a cone, if they have it."

"They do," Maddie said, holding up her half-eaten ice cream.

I smiled at her and nodded. After a short, but heated exchange of looks with Aliah, I sat on the wooden seat next to her. Before long, Tanner returned with my ice cream cone, and not a minute too soon. I could use the refreshment, the sun still beating strong.

Tanner handed me the cone, noticed the pile of bird poop on the only vacant seat across from Aliah, and then moped over to the empty table next to us. "I guess I'll just sit over here all by myself." He was being sarcastic but, feeling for his situation, I shoved closer to Aliah to make room for him next to me.

I slapped the bench beside me. "You're not sitting alone when there's plenty of room right here," I said.

Tanner happily slid into the small place, right next to me, nearly flipping the small table. "Such a nice girl," he teased, giving me a wink.

Aliah gasped and nearly swallowed her cone in one gulp.

In the close proximity, and since Tanner was mocking me, I just couldn't help myself. I bumped his hand intentionally and his ice cream blobbed on his nose.

He grabbed both of my wrists playfully and nudged his nose toward my face. "Now you have to lick it off," he teased.

Aliah let out another gasp, but I was too busy squealing and scuffling to get away from his grip to notice. Jay and Maddie were laughing too, as Tanner tried to force his nose in my mouth. I pressed my lips together, fighting off a smile, when I noticed Aliah's continued horror.

Intuition flaring, I shoved Tanner off of me and he backed away, realizing something was up. Once he leaned back, I glanced around him and saw that Hunter and TJ were already stopped next to the table

Edwin was walking up, and had clearly caught the whole scene. Everyone else had fallen silent, Edwin's anger fueled by my nonchalance.

I gulped back my nerve and managed to draw my eyes up to meet Edwin's. Bad idea. His dark, furious stare was sparking with anger.

"Hey, what's going on?" I said casually, then took a lick of my ice cream. *I was in for it.*

"I was about to ask you the same thing," Edwin snapped,

his features sharp and edgy. He shook his head at me in disgust. "You know what? I don't want to know. I'm outta here. You do what you want." He stomped off toward the cabins and my heart shattered into pieces.

"Wait, Edwin! I can explain." I shoved Tanner aside and clambered away from the table. My ice cream dropped from my hand, but I just left it there to chase after him. He was too fast. "Edwin, please," I cried.

He stopped long enough to shoot me the coldest look from his frosty, aqua eyes. "Don't bother wasting your time. You don't owe me anything," he said snidely, then waved me off. He left me standing there, frozen in place, as our relationship flashed before me.

Tears stung the back of my eyes and I closed them to keep them at bay. One of the guys dared to confront me. He placed his hand on my shoulder and gave it a squeeze.

"Don't touch me." Throwing his arm off of me, anger my driving force, I scowled at him.

"I'll go talk to him," Hunter said, ignoring my overreaction. He had done nothing wrong.

"I'm coming with you," I said. Looking back to the crowd, all eyes were still on me. "I'm sorry," I said, glancing at everyone but Tanner. "Thanks for the ice cream Jay."

"Any time," he replied

I hurried to catch up with Hunter, panic twisting my insides and worry striking my heart.

"What *is* going on?" Hunter said, so accusatory. "Or do I want to know?"

"*Nothing* is going on, Hunter. It was just a misunderstanding. We're friends, that's it," I explained.

"Then I'm sure Edwin will get over it. But it'll probably take some time; as in not now. Maybe you should head back."

I huffed with disappointment, at him and at myself. I couldn't turn back. "He's pretty pissed, eh?"

"Yeah, but wouldn't you be? I know if I saw Aliah sitting next to that guy, I would've been pretty pissed too, and we're not even exclusive."

It hurt my heart to hear him say that, mostly because I couldn't imagine the pain I would feel if Edwin had done the same to me. "It probably looked way worse than it is," I said, but it didn't help.

"Yeah, try telling him that right now. You'll get nowhere fast. Why don't you look at the situation from his perspective?"

Edwin was nearly at the cabin when I finally called out to him again, ignoring Hunter's advice. "Edwin, please. We need to talk."

He stopped at the door and I closed the distance between us. "No. There's nothing to talk about," he boomed. "Why don't you go back to your little boyfriend? You two looked pretty cozy together until I walked up."

I stepped even closer to him, but left a few feet between us. The way he looked at me, with such hatred in his eyes, it was like he was stabbing an icy javelin into my heart.

"Edwin, stop talking or I know you'll say something you'll regret," Hunter insisted.

"No, I have to talk to him," I cried.

Edwin fixed me with a cold, hard stare. "I told you I'm not talking to you. Forget it. It's over."

CHAPTER FOURTEEN

After retrieving the icy javelin from my swollen heart, I stared at the door slammed in my face. I surrounded myself in the sounds that were real to me: birds chirping, flowers swaying, and the leaves rustling in the late afternoon breeze; heart pounding, people laughing and the oxygen draining from my lungs.

"Maybe you should go," Hunter suggested, as he headed for the door. Before he went inside, he turned back and looked at me with concern in his eyes. "I'll do what I can."

"Thanks," I breathed, with a whisper.

Edwin was inconsolable. I was in shock.

What am I going to do?

Lost in my own misery, tears built up in my eyes. I made slow work of the flagstone path, my knees weak with regret. Panic set in as my watery, green gaze returned to the direction of the crime scene.

The clan was heading my way. But I couldn't face them. Not now. In fact, I preferred never to see Tanner Bradshaw's handsome, honest face ever again.

A dreadful tear leaked from my eye, as I hurried behind the cabin. My breath ragged, my insides twisted in a desolate knot of frustration, I dashed through the trees until I reached the trail that Edwin and I had taken the night before.

I ran and I ran, as fast as my legs would carry me. Edwin's cold, aqua eyes haunted me, driving me faster and farther away. Perspiration mingled with my tears, a steady stream flowing from my cheeks and dripping down my bare neck.

As long as I was running then my body was in control and so I ran until I couldn't run anymore.

When my body gave out, I stepped off the trail and bent

over sobbing, holding my side with one hand, a tree in the other. My chest heaved from exertion. I was spent, but I was alive.

Sweat poured from my forehead and my body screamed with ache, as loud as my heart. I tried to fight the imminent despair and depression, but it washed over me like a cold, November rain. I choked on my emotions as my unsteady breathing steered my tattered thoughts.

I fell to one knee, just catching myself before I crashed onto the forest floor. Worried that the few hikers on an intersecting trail might catch up with me, I decided it best to distance myself from this trail and the life attached to it. They would definitely ask me if I was okay.

I am so not okay.

I clawed at the nearby tree, draining what was left of my energy to pull myself to my feet. Drawing on that last reserve, I darted into the wilderness to find a thinking rock. I didn't want to get lost, but I didn't want to be found either.

My blurry eyes scattered franticly across the forest floor, as red eyes loomed fresh in my memories and startled what was left of my rational thoughts. A collection of large boulders were dispersed close by and I decided that one of them would have to suffice. I chose a huge one with a flat face, far enough off the trail that no one could see me, but close enough that I wouldn't get lost if I decided to go back.

I lied back on the rock with a hand over my wet, scalding forehead.

Right now, I can't imagine ever going back.

I knew it wouldn't be long before the bugs came out and I was wearing nothing but a skimpy bikini top and thread-bare jean shorts. *Eat me. See if I care.*

My eyes burned. I squeezed them shut, my worries dancing around like zombies in my head. A loud cry echoed through the wilderness. *I did this.*

How could I make Edwin see that it's him I love? If I could only read his mind; know what he was thinking. I scowled at myself.

Yeah, because I can read minds.

From the haunting look in Edwin's eyes, I knew he wouldn't forgive me. He had never delivered such a cruel eye in all of our years together. Hunter didn't stand a chance. Aliah would only make matters worse. Maddie was only thinking of herself right now. *I'm doomed.*

What were they thinking bringing Tanner and Jay back to our site? Do they want to witness a blood bath? I knew one thing for sure: when Edwin was done with Tanner, he'd finish me off next; as if his words alone weren't already enough to crush me.

My tears boiled over and I sobbed. My sight was near blind again, when I delivered myself some soul destroying news.

What if Edwin refuses to forgive me? Will he move out when we get home? Will he expect me to leave?

This is all my fault.

After hours of lonely torment, I could feel the strain from behind my sockets. It hurt just to open my eyes. I lowered my head and pressed my fingertips into my skull hoping to alleviate some of the pain. It didn't work.

I lied back against the warm rock, my face now shadowed from the dropping sun, as the hot day in hell dragged on. I wondered if it would ever end, or if I had been banished there for life. Miserable. Alone.

My stomach growled, but that was the least of my concerns. Instead, I wished I could just close my eyes and it would all be over. But I wouldn't be so lucky. Instead of being faced with Edwin's painful stare, I was forced to confront red eyes that glowed in the shadows of my darkest memories.

My eyes were squeezed shut and I fought the need to open them. Anything was better than Edwin's pain. I knew it could only be a figment of my imagination, but the memory was so real. Plastered to the rock in fear, I dared myself to face my inner demons.

Holding onto that terrifying image, I relived the moment when the monster approached me, frozen beneath her hot, penetrating stare. But this time Edwin was not there with me. I looked everywhere, thrashing about, but he did not come to my rescue. I was alone.

Almost.

I glared confidently at the entity and it stared back into my soul. I could smell the end of my mortality on its breath, as I swallowed my own, hoping the monster would just relieve me of my life already. As it dominated my strength, it pierced my broken heart. *I give up.*

My sister Aubrey's voice rang loud in my ears: *Winners aren't people who never fail, they're people who never give up.*

As my life flashed before my eyes, and a poisonous burning flowed through my veins, I changed my mind. *I'm not ready to die.* A crying baby startled my thoughts, reminding me of my purpose in life. *A baby.*

My eyes burst open and I forced myself to sit up, as I listened to the echo of my own screaming voice in the empty darkness. Having fallen asleep from exhaustion, the day had passed me by.

Daylight was fading fast, but the fact that the sun hadn't yet disappeared flooded me with relief, the only emotion left in me. It wouldn't be long before I was surrounded in blackness, alone in the wilderness with my wild imagination.

I got to my feet, surprised that my physical pain had subsided, and rushed through the brush toward the path.

My pace was steady, but I had nothing left in me to move my limbs any faster than that. Darkness ushered in around me, though my weary nerves didn't seem to take notice. The hot night fell before I reached the resort. It wasn't far now.

I could see a cabin in the distance, though it was obscured from the combination of my exhausted eyes and the black night. I stopped in my tracks, but the wind kept blowing behind me. I'm not ready to hear Edwin say those words again.

It's over.

My ears rang, my eyes dripped, as I turned down a

narrow sandy path toward the beach. *The beach. Where it all began.*

The boardwalk creaked beneath my feet, the mosquitos stole my blood, goose bumps devoured both of my arms, and still I was dead to the world. The leaves danced with the trees, the waves lapped against the sand, the crickets chirped their mating call and there I walked alone.

I tugged off one sandal, then the other. I sunk my toes in the sand begging to feel something. Anything. *Nothing.*

The sun was gone and it took the warmth with it, leaving me digging my toes through cold, clammy dirt. My eyes scanned the darkened beach, only to find a few couples canoodling in the sand. Just this morning, that was me and Edwin.

It made me sick to my stomach to witness such pure happiness at a time like this. Brooding, I marched down the beach, heading straight for the water, desperately clinging to its raw power.

I hesitantly dipped my toes in the cool waves as they washed ashore. I scooped up some water into my hands and splashed my tear-stained face. Feeling fresh, but far from clean, I started slowly down the beach. *I had nowhere important to be.*

I watched the water ease the hurt from my distressed feet, and nearly stumbled into a man who was walking in the opposite direction. He seemed equally as staggered by me, though it was too dark to be one hundred percent sure.

"Watch where you're going," I said, through gritted teeth, scowling into the darkness. I didn't care that it was as much my fault as it was his. I was mad. Hoping to rid myself of any more human contact, I picked up my speed.

"Abigail? Is that you?"

I cast an evil glare toward the man calling my name. The faceless figure approached me slowly and I cowered away from him in the shadows of night.

"It's me, Tanner," he whispered, as if that would make me want to come any closer.

I let out an exasperated breath, as his face became

clearer. I recognized his flawless profile and the handsome face that caused me all this trouble from the start. "If you knew what was good for you, you would stay away from me," I said, a hard frown pressed on my lips.

"Now why would I do that?" he answered.

"Don't," I warned, my voice disclosing my exhaustion.

"Okay, but you should know everyone is looking for you. They're all worried sick."

"You mean everyone but Edwin. I'm sure they'll get over it." I turned away and took another step, hoping he'd just let me walk.

"I get it you're upset."

I spun back around, my shoulders pressed down. "You think?"

He paused a moment, then stepped closer to me, forcing me to step back. "There's no reason that we should be alone tonight," he whispered, daring me to stop him from coming closer. He moved closer yet, but I refused to let him govern me.

I glared into his chestnut eyes. *How dare he proposition me like this.* "I deserve to be alone."

"No one deserves that. You didn't do anything wrong."

"Please say it one more time, maybe then it will start to sound true," I argued.

"This will all blow over if you just deal with it now," he said, even though his undertones begged me not to.

"Funny, this coming from a guy who's had a year to get over his ex." I regretted spewing the words before they left my mouth.

"Ouch, that hurt. Kick me while I'm down," he said, his hand over his heart.

"I'm sorry. That wasn't fair," I said softly, mad at myself for being so cruel. "Like I said, you're better off staying away from me." I walked away again, and this time I didn't turn back.

I paced slowly down the long, wooden, boat dock and made my way to the end of it. Right at the end, I could see a lone park bench sitting in peace. Board by board, I got closer to the bench, until I finally relieved my aching feet by kicking off my flimsy sandals and taking a seat.

I sighed out loud and glanced out over the wavy water, free flowing and quiet. The dock stretched out so far that it was like I was in the middle of nowhere, right where I wanted to be, away from all the drama that I called my life.

A dark shadow hung heavy over my shoulder. A board creaked, catching my attention. My eyes grew wide when the long shadow fell across the water. Slowly, anxiously, I glanced over my right shoulder.

Ugh! It was Tanner.

Before I could shoo him off, he took a seat without asking my permission. Infuriated, I folded my arms across my chest and shoved over, so my bare legs wouldn't touch him.

I continued to stare out over the water, my chin resting on the palm of my hand, my fingers blocking my eyes from his view, but the warmth that radiated from his bulky body didn't go unnoticed.

"You can't get rid of me that easily. Nice try though," he said.

The bench was small enough and with his considerable size, when he spread his powerful legs and leaned forward, he consumed what was left of the space between us. His warmth penetrated my leg through his thin faded jeans.

I shivered from the reminder of my minimal clothes. "Seriously Tanner, you've got issues. Leave me alone, unless you want a foot to the face," I warned, though I doubted I had the energy to follow through with the threat.

"I do have issues. Why do you think I'm alone?" he asked. "But threatening me won't work. I thrive on threats these days."

Stunned and silenced, I struggled to find a new topic. Why did he have to make me feel bad? I already felt like shit.

"Where's Jay you ask?" he said, igniting a one-sided conversation. "Where do you think?" He glanced out over the water, as he floundered with his own thoughts. "Let's just say he and Maddie like each other, *a lot,* and I wasn't about to hang around and watch them make babies."

"Oh."

"Yeah, I've been pacing the beach for over an hour, but I can't bring myself to go back." He buried his face in his massive hand, leaning against the right side of the bench.

There was a long, comfortable silence. *No talking is good.*

Then he went and opened his mouth. "I'm so selfish," he said. "I can see you have your own problems and here I am making trouble for you. I certainly haven't made your life any easier."

I shuddered from the cool breeze that swept off of the water, no doubt from the dark clouds rolling up, and I instantly wished I had a shirt to hide in. My skin looked like gooseflesh, bumps sprinkled up both of my arms. Tanner noticed immediately.

"You must be freezing. Here, take my jacket." He pulled off his light coat and hung it over my shoulders.

I didn't argue with him. I *was* freezing. But I didn't thank him either. If it weren't for him, I wouldn't be in this mess in the first place. I pulled the jacket tighter around my shoulders, but it didn't stop the trembling. There was only one thing that could make that go away.

"For what it's worth, I'm happy to see that you're okay," Tanner said.

Does this man ever shut up? "What do you care?"

"You obviously have no idea the effect you have on people... on me," he admitted.

"I'm nothing special."

"You're the only woman who has been real with me since my wife left; the only one who came right out and told me to get over it. That makes you special... to me."

"That's not special. You don't know special. Did you ever think that maybe I'm just a bitch like that?"

He grabbed my chin and turned it to face him, startling me from my rant. He looked me in the eyes, his warm and inviting, mine green and wide with alarm. He cupped my cheek, but still held me firmly in place. "Can't you just take the compliment? You are special and I like you; deal with it."

I snagged my chin away from him and glanced off into the darkness. "I have other things to deal with."

He chuckled. "You're more messed up than I thought."

I didn't speak. In the silence, I realized that in the midst of our bickering, Tanner managed to steer my thoughts clear of Edwin. I should have been thankful for such a disruption from my self-deprecating thoughts, but instead I was consumed with guilt.

"Thank you so much for laying that out on the table for me," I said, harsh and sarcastic. "Yes, I've got issues and I don't need some random guy sorting out all of my troubles for me. Especially you. You don't even know me."

"I know that you have good intentions."

I rolled my eyes and turned to face him, angrier than ever. "How can you be so nice to me when I'm trying to rip you a new one?"

He smiled, warmly. "I have my ways."

I waved my arms erratically, knocking his jacket from my shoulders. "You probably think I'm nuts."

"No. A little wild, yes, but not nuts."

Breathless, I smiled. I couldn't believe I was smiling. I am nuts.

"Look at that, she does smile," he breathed. Tanner reached his arm over my shoulder and inched closer as he adjusted the jacket for me.

All at once I was feeling terribly vulnerable. I could taste the flame on my tongue. I was going to get burned. His attraction radiated from his tanned skin, luring me closer. I looked up into the clouded sky for some moral support and a mist of rain answered instantly.

I shuddered involuntarily, pulled my feet onto the bench and tucked my legs into the oversize jacket, wrapping myself into a protective little ball.

Tanner pulled my head onto his shoulder, cradling me in his arm, then wrapped his free arm around my legs, huddling me close to his heart. My arms, tucked neatly inside his jacket, weren't quick enough to avert his advances.

I pressed my eyes shut for a moment and hated to admit that I craved the warmth his arms provided. The warmth was nice, but his safety net was foreign to me. *He was not Edwin.*

Instead of instantly removing myself from his embrace, with eyes shut, I imagined that Edwin and I were okay. To pretend that I was in his arms again felt good. But still, Tanner wasn't Edwin. A sour smile covered my mouth, eyes painfully squeezed closed.

"Abigail?"

Rocked out of my daydream, my eyelids fluttered open. I lifted my head from Tanner's shoulder and stared into the honest eyes of the handsome man before me, his lips aching for a kiss. He slowly leaned in. I did the deer in headlights thing. He stopped, his warm breath tickling my lips.

My alarm faded and Tanner seemed more confused than ever. "Tanner, no," I whispered. "I can't do this." I folded my lips in, stood up next to him and tossed his jacket into his lap.

He glanced at me with a sideways smile. "Of course you can't. You're better than that."

"No. I'm in love with someone else."

I went to pass him, but he put his large leg out to block my way. "I want to hate you, but I feel like this is a step in the right direction," he said.

I smiled at him and he turned his glance timidly to his feet. "Goodbye, Tanner."

CHAPTER FIFTEEN

I rushed away before Tanner could think of something else charming to say. I had to get to Edwin. I had to get through to him. My steady pace turned into a slow jog and then an all-out race. Suddenly, I couldn't get to Edwin fast enough.

Digging deep, my heart driving me forward, I sprinted straight to his cabin. Without stopping for air, or reason, I burst through the door without knocking. I stopped when I got inside, breathless and shaky.

The lights were out, but Edwin was standing in the middle of the dark room, all alone, his eyes glaring out the window.

He turned his shadowed gaze on me. "Abigail?"

Without giving him a chance to throw me out, I marched up to him, flung my arms around his broad shoulders and held on for dear life, eyes pinched shut. He didn't hold me, but he didn't push me away.

Tears started flowing down my cheeks, mistakes upsetting my empty stomach. I dropped my arms and folded them over my bare belly. I was glad the lights were out because I couldn't bear having to look into his accusing eyes again.

"We need to talk, Eddie. And I won't take no for an answer this time."

"No."

My heart rammed into my throat. *Did I hear him correctly?* "What?"

"I said no." He paused as I stood in total confusion, unable to gage his mood without being able to search his heavily shadowed eyes. "Not until you bathe. You smell absolutely repulsive," he said.

My tears fell fast and my heart thumped with relief. If

Edwin could find it in him to fool with me, then I had already won half the battle. He reached up a finger and swept a tear from my moist cheek.

"Don't cry, Abs. I was only messing with you." He wrapped his arms around me and held me, ignoring my sweaty hair and apparent stench. "On second thought, maybe it wouldn't hurt if you hit the shower real quick," he teased.

A nervous chuckle trembled under my breath. Though I couldn't see his face, I knew he wasn't frowning at me, and that was good enough. *For now.*

I wiped away the wetness, as Edwin took my hand and led me to the bathroom. He switched the light on and I cowered from the brightness. My eyes were sore, but focused, like my mind.

"You had us all worried sick. You shouldn't have run off like that," he said, very serious now. He smoothed his thumb over my cheek and ran his fingers down my jaw.

"I'm so sorry. Please give me a chance to explain."

"I will, as soon as you're done in here. I'll go get you some clothes and tell the others that you're okay. I thought something bad had happened to you."

"Something bad did happen. I hurt you. It was cruel and unfair."

"Save it. I'll be back in two."

"Promise?" I said, scared he might change his mind.

"I promise," he whispered.

The warm water wasn't nearly as refreshing as I had hoped it would be. I hurriedly washed my hair and soaped up my body. The scent of Edwin's body wash made the tears start coming again.

I gave myself a quick rinse and forced away the sad thoughts along with the tears, sending them down the drain. I turned off the water and reached for a towel, my clothes already neatly stacked on the vanity. After drying off, I slipped on the fresh t-shirt and pants left out for me.

I stared at my face in the mirror. I was feeling far from refreshed and my reflection was a perfect disaster. I was run ragged. So exhausted. It had been a trying day and a tiresome night.

Having no socks, I tip-toed out of the bathroom barefoot. I found Edwin sitting in the tall bed, leaning against the white, king-sized headboard.

"Feeling better?" he asked.

"Not really." Feeling incredibly anxious, I fidgeted with the towel in my hair. "Where is everyone?"

"They're over at your place. I told them we needed some time."

Relieved that he was at least talking to me, I had a seat next to him on the bed. "Eddie, I am so sorry. I went too far. I hurt you. And that was the last thing I wanted to do. I love you so much. Please forgive me."

Edwin's eyes remained dark, fathomless, unreadable.

I tossed the towel aside. "If you need time, I will give you all the time you need, but please let's work it out together," I blathered on, restless, terrified.

My hand covered his. "I was being selfish. I realize now that it was bad judgment on my part. I shouldn't have done that. I just love when you get all protective over me and you look so darn cute when you're mad. It was stupid." I squeezed his hand and pulled it to my forehead, trying to hide my face.

It sounded so dumb out loud.

Edwin stayed silent. I felt like I had to beg for his forgiveness. Make him see.

"It was rotten of me. God, I'm so sorry. Please, Edwin. Forgive me."

Our hands dropped back to the bed. *Why won't he say anything, damn it?*

"I know I've broken your trust. I'll earn it back. I can. I will. If you'll just let me prove myself to you."

Edwin finally stopped me, his fingers gently covering my lips. "You done?"

"Mmm hmm," I replied, more nervous than ever.

"I did a lot of thinking myself after you took off."

"And?" I asked, anxious, impatient.

"And I realized just how much I need you in my life."

I pressed my lips together to hide an exuberant grin. Tears of joy streamed down my face, but I stopped myself from attacking him. I folded my dry lips in my mouth.

"There's a reason we got back together in the first place," Edwin said. "I'm in love with you. It's amazing how you can spend the afternoon with some hopeless dude and make me madder than ever, and yet you still get my heart racing when you walk in the room."

He paused, and so did my lungs. "After talking to Hunter about it, I've decided to give you the benefit of the doubt. I suppose I overreacted a little." He looked at me with big, blue, puppy dog eyes.

My heart floated, weightless in my chest. "Okay," I said, on a shaky breath.

He stayed serious. "I should have never said those things to you. I feel terrible. It just hurt to see you like that with another guy. I guess what I'm trying to say is, I'm sorry."

Huh? "You're apologizing to me? Here I thought you never wanted to see me again." My eyes threatened rain, but only one happy drop trickled down my cheek.

"Abs, I love you. There's no need to cry anymore."

"I know. I can't help it," I breathed. "I love you so much." I smiled into his dark, dreamy eyes, and Edwin pulled me onto his lap, up and out of the dumps. It felt so good to be in *his* arms again. I rested a hand on his warm, hard chest, his heart beating strong against my ear.

Edwin leaned down, and his lips brushed mine, soft, slow and meaningful. "This is supposed to be *our* weekend, and I know I'm not going to let Arnold Schwarzenegger's son wreck what's left of it."

"Arnold Schwarzenegger?" I said, a huge grin manipulating my dry lips.

"You know what I'm saying," he said, smirking. Edwin brushed the hair from my eyes and then he leaned down slowly, his eyes soft, his kiss passionate.

We kissed and kissed, until my lips hurt from sensory

overload. And then we made good use of his massive bed. Slow and steady, Edwin romanticized make-up sex, touching, feeling and reminding me that I was all his.

Sometime later, blissful silence filled the room, our breaths unified, as we absorbed each other's afterglow. Edwin rolled out of bed and pulled on a fresh pair of sexy, surfer shorts, leaving the top button undone. Damn he looked good. He stood there staring at me, a fascinating package of masculinity, his arms propped out from his body, his biceps too large for his frame.

Then he smirked. "This is what I have to do to get laid around here?" He crawled back on the bed smiling and stretched out all that heavy muscle next to me.

"Don't get any crazy ideas," I said, tangling myself in his long, powerful legs.

"We should probably go next door," Edwin reminded me, his voice a soft growl. He kissed me on the nose and brushed the hair from my face. "But I should warn you, Jay and Tanner are over there."

I winced at the sound of Edwin saying his name. I couldn't even imagine the thought of Tanner and Edwin together in the same room, let alone with me in between them. Edwin could sense the concern that washed over me.

"Would you rather I call him Arnold?"

I laughed, but I was still very anxious. I didn't respond as I pulled away from him and rested back against the soft pillows.

"Don't worry, Abs. I've already talked to Arnold. I can handle it. We had a little chat while you were off practicing for the marathon. I hate to say it, but he seems like a decent guy."

I was sure he wouldn't think that if he knew what had went down at the dock. Better to save that for another time, when Tanner was far, far away.

"I'm sure you and Tanner are best friends now," I said, sarcastically, slinking off the bed for a quick drink.

"Yeah. That's not gonna happen. He apologized for being such a dink and I forgave him. It's not like I'm ever going to see him again after this weekend anyway. We're good now. I mean, we're good, right?" Edwin glanced at me expectantly.

I smiled, as I returned to the bed. "We're very good, Eddie. So good, in fact, that I'd like to spend the rest of the night showing you just how good we are."

With a smile plastered on his face, Edwin leapt up and swept me off of my feet. "Mmm. I hoped you'd say that," he growled. "I'll message TJ to tell them that we need more time."

"You can tell them that I need all night. I don't want to be alone, Eddie."

Edwin pressed a soft kiss to my lips and lowered me to the middle of the bed. I rested, sunken in the feathery sheets, as he bent over the side of the bed to pull his phone from his pants pocket.

"I'm sure TJ will get the hint. He can call it a night at your place. Hunter's already shacked up there with Aliah anyway," Edwin said, then retrieved his phone to notify the others of our plans.

10:46 p.m.
Hey TJ. If the cabin's a rockin, don't come a knockin. I'm serious. STAY AWAY! Edwin (The Stud) Santora

10:47 p.m.
Make me. You've had enough time. ~ TJ

10:49 p.m.
I will make you. Try coming over here and see what happens. I'll take you down with my hands tied behind my back. Don't think I can? Try me. Edwin (The Naked Stud) Santora

10:51 p.m.
Like fuck. Thanks for that nasty image you kinky bastard. Real fucking fair that I have to be here with Maddie and her latest lover, while you're over there getting your fantasy fuck on. ~ TJ

10:52 p.m.
If you don't fuck off, Maddie will be the least of your problems. I need this, bro. I'm not gonna say it again.

10:54 p.m.
Fuck me. Am I the only one not getting laid tonight? ~ TJ

When I returned from the washroom, my curiosity was aroused from Edwin's incessant texting. "What did he say?" I asked.

"No problem," Edwin said. "The place is all ours."

"Sweet. I'm sure if Ally had anything to do with it, Hunter will be in her bed anyway."

"Yeah, they looked like they were getting pretty cozy together earlier tonight. It was actually rather depressing." Edwin tossed his phone onto floor, it skimmed over his pile of clothes and slid across the hard floor, landing a few feet away.

Ignoring that, I got to my knees on the bed and yanked Edwin back onto it with me. After crawling on top of him, I pinned his wrists over his head and kissed him hard. My tongue slipped inside his mouth and he groaned with the knowledge.

With heavy breaths, my lips traveled up his rough jaw toward his ear. I released one of his hands and it instantly skimmed down my back. I eased his zipper down and took him in my hand. He was already ready for round two, and not a second too soon.

"Thank you, Eddie," I breathed, and flicked his lobe with my tongue.

"Like I said before," he growled on a moan, when I squeezed around him, "this is our weekend. You and me, baby. Forget about the rest."

And I did.

The morning came fast and so did my enchantment. To wake attached to my sleepy, but satisfied man, in an amazingly fluffy, king sized bed that overlooked the scenic lakeside, was wonderful to say the least. It was cozy, I was safe, and it was exceptionally quiet in our little corner of heaven.

Not wanting to skip any of the pleasantries, I slipped out from under Edwin's heavy arm, pulled on his oversized t-shirt and tiptoed on the cold, ceramic floor to the kitchen. The fridge was empty except for a half empty bottle of tequila and three bottles of beer. *So much for breakfast in bed*.

Coffee would have to do. The counter held a single cup brewer, courtesy of the Southwind Inn. I was in luck. They had Edwin's favourite flavour.

Moments later his was cup done and I clicked in another flavour disk for me. I heard Edwin tousling around with the blankets, and before I could pull my mug from the machine, Edwin already had his nose nuzzled in my hair.

"Good morning," he growled, deliberately pressing his morning wood against my naked thigh. Edwin was wearing nothing but some revealing tighty whities and they were hard pressed for space. His strong body flexed as he stretched his arms over his head, drawing my eyes to his sharply tapered back and incredible midsection.

"Mmm, good morning. I made you coffee."

Edwin reached around me, gathered his mug into both hands and inhaled the rich flavour. "Mmm. Thanks."

Leaning against the counter, I turned to face him, and enjoyed my own drink. "What's the plan for today?"

"It's late. Want to go for a walk?"

"You don't want to grab some breakfast first?"

"Breakfast can wait. I want to show you something."

"Okay. Give me a minute to make myself presentable. Then we can go." I gulped down my hot drink and rinsed the cup in the sink. When I turned to go to the bathroom, Edwin stopped me with a single arm.

"Not so fast." He put his mug down, pulled me against

his solid chest and, using his fist, he tilted my chin up. His lingering kiss was warm, soft and wet. "Okay, now you can go," he growled.

With hands clasped together, we walked outside in the warm morning sunlight. There wasn't many campers out and about and there was absolutely no sign of life coming from my cabin as we passed it. Edwin led me down the familiar boardwalk and it was obvious that he had a destination in mind.

He dragged me down a narrow dirt trail into the forest. I savoured my curiosity, Edwin's smile bursting from his face.

"We're almost there," he insisted, noting the start of my impatience.

Suddenly, I noticed the trees opening up, their leaves draping over dark teal water. Edwin pulled me from the trail and led me through the lush emerald green grass toward the soft flowing water.

Hanging from a huge old weeping willow tree, that creaked in the light summer breeze, was a hammock for two. It swayed in the wind, hanging over the dark water then swinging back over the land.

"Oh, Eddie," I gasped. "It's beautiful."

"I knew you'd like it," he said. "I thought of you the second I discovered it yesterday. This is where I did all of my thinking. It's so peaceful. You have to try it out."

"Absolutely," I said, following him into the warm, grassy sanctuary.

The wind carried the hammock over the land and Edwin held it for me to hop on. When I did, it swung me out over the water and threatened dropping me in. I giggled and froze as it slowly swayed back and forth, until it came to a stop over the water.

"Give me your hand," Edwin said.

After I reached out to him, he grabbed onto the netting, holding me up in space against gravity's wishes. "You ready?"

I nodded, smiling, and Edwin joined me without too much trouble. He curled his arm under my neck and I shuffled until I had my head on his shoulder.

The swing gently swayed us between the dark water and luscious grass, in the comfort of each other's arms. It was amazing, a euphoric experience.

The weeping branches wisped around us, surrounding us in a magical solace. The air was filled with sounds of nature, soft waves, quivering leaves and small birds singing a harmonious song.

It was incredibly peaceful, lying in Edwin's arms, looking out over the serene, morning lake. We must have lied there silent for an hour, just appreciating nature and each other.

"You see?" Edwin whispered. "This is how much I love you."

I wanted to swoon, but instead I glued my mouth to his. He parted his soft lips and I intertwined them with mine. His mouth was warm and sweet, but his body was rock solid.

He grasped my thigh and pulled me on top of him, his hands gently moving my hips, slowly rocking me against his growing erection. He opened his mouth wide on a groan and his tongue discovered mine, hot and greedy.

The intensity of my emotions was wearing on my self-control. I wanted him right there.

Just then, Aliah and Hunter strolled up the trail and cut through the grass, hand in hand. "Hey, you!" Aliah called, when she realized it was us.

Leave it up to Aliah to disrupt me from my oasis. I reluctantly detached myself from Edwin's mouth and looked back toward the oncoming voices. Edwin held me against him, so as not to expose his condition.

"Good to see you're alive," she added, sarcastically. "Nice of you to pop in and show your face last night."

"Hey, that's my fault. I had other plans for her," Edwin said in my defence, flashing a wickedly sexy smile.

When Edwin gripped onto my butt, Hunter snickered

and Aliah slapped him.

"What do you want, anyway?" I asked.

"Excuuuse me," Aliah whined. "I didn't know I needed a reason to come and say hi to my friend. A-c-t-u-a-l-l-y, I wanted to see if you were up for some shopping in town. There are some local shops I wanted to check out. That is, if Edwin will let you," she teased.

"That sounds like it could be fun," I said, my eyes locked on Edwin. "What do you say?" It was so unlike me to ask for permission, being a headstrong feminist when it came to women's rights, but I did need to know that we were okay.

Edwin raised a sarcastic brow. "I hate to say no, but..."

"I'll save you, bro," Hunter cut in. "Why don't the girls go and we can take our turn soaking some sun on the beach? You know, check out the ladies."

This time Aliah gave Hunter a tight elbow in the gut. He grunted, seemingly unharmed.

"I'm just playing, baby. You know I only have eyes for you," he teased, and Aliah soaked it right up.

I looked to Edwin, unsure whether he would seriously be okay with me leaving his side. I was feeling a bit insecure myself after yesterday's incident.

"I'm cool with that," Edwin said, then brought his lips to my ear. "I trust you, babe," he whispered.

Aliah came to the edge of the water and reached out to me. I grabbed her hand willingly, though reluctant to pull myself from my cozy little bed of joy.

Edwin stumbled his way off the hammock too and instantly I was back in his arms. "Don't make me regret my decision."

I gazed down the narrow tourist packed street. Everyone was dressed for the beach and most were wandering in and out of a collection of little shops lining the road.

Colourful, flowery clothes and bathing suits were

plastered in the windows and hanging from racks on the sidewalks. Tacky souvenirs, cheap jewellery, outrageous sunglasses and a hoard of baseball caps adorned the many shelves and displays. Despite my cold reception, I really couldn't wait to look around.

Aliah and I inspected each and every shop. We pranced around in wild bikini's, played around with random toys, tried on stylin' hats with feathers and struck a pose in our cool shades. After a morning full of girly fun, we managed to pick up a few things that we really didn't need, but got anyway as mementos from our vacation. I even found a little something for Edwin.

Being parched from all that exercise and, after skipping breakfast, I was starved. We approached a cozy restaurant with an outdoor patio and decided it was the place for us. The pink lemonade was refreshing and my meal was delish. I didn't realize how badly I needed this.

"So, you and Edwin, you're good?" Aliah finally asked. She had been avoiding that question all day.

"We're good. Better than good, I think. I should've never done that to him. I don't know what comes over me sometimes."

"I tried to warn you," Aliah said, flashing me an *I told you so* look.

"I know. Sorry for not listening. What can I say? I can't pass up an opportunity for trouble," I teased.

"Now you sound like me."

"I know, right?"

"So, aren't you gonna to ask me about my man?" Aliah pressed, eager to tell.

"Your man?" I could've swore he was only teasing earlier.

"Don't play dumb. Hunter's mine. We had a long talk last night and you were right. He does like me like that."

"I'm happy for you."

"Thanks to Jay for keeping Maddie's attention all night, I had Hunter all to myself. No, really. She went and stayed at Jay's place. What a whore."

"Now tell me how you really feel," I said, laughing.

After finishing our meal and paying the bill, we went on our merry way.

"Hey, check this out. I didn't see this on our way in," Aliah said, just steps away from the restaurant.

We strolled toward the local sea doo rental store. An attractive sales guy approached us before I could redirect Aliah's excitement. His dark tan and darker eyes guaranteed that he would have her attention.

"You ladies look like you're up for some fun. What d'ya say? Two for the price of one for the pretty ladies." He smiled at Aliah with a mouthful of perfect white teeth.

"Now that depends on what you're selling."

The cute salesman smiled, but didn't answer her. It was pretty damn obvious, since he was standing outside a hut full of PFD's and photos of extreme sea doo adventures. There was even an actual sea doo on the sidewalk with a big for rent sign attached to it.

Aliah winked at him. "Excuse us," she said, evidently flustered as she pulled me aside. "Damn, he's fine," she whispered.

"You're hilarious. What were you just telling me about Hunter? You think you're in love. Come on now."

"Stay focused here. It looks like fun. What you think?"

"Seriously? Absolutely. I'm in. But are you up for it?" I asked her.

"One night with him?"

"Aliah! I'm talking about the sea doo you horny beoch."

"Oh, right," she giggled. "Hey a girl has to keep her options open, right?"

I shook my head. "I'm going to tell Hunter you said that."

"No you're not." She kept giggling and it was infectious.

"I say we do it. I think this might be just what I need."

Aliah squealed happily, throwing her hands in the air for a high five. "I wonder if *he* comes with the package."

"Actually, I was thinking we could get another sea doo and invite the guys."

"You're no fun, but... I guess I could settle for that," she replied, sarcastically. "Wait, I have an idea." Aliah walked straight to the guy in the shop, interrupting his sales pitch to some seemingly uninterested male bystanders. "If you have a third machine, you've got yourself a deal."

He looked at the schedule for the day, ignoring the other customers, and smiled at us. "I only have the two machines available right now. I can hold them for you and get another one if you can come back in an hour. I'll need a deposit though," he said.

"That's not a problem. We are so in. That is, if your offer's still good."

Aliah batted her eye lashes at him, and I tuned her out while she worked her magic. Guaranteed her tune would change the second Hunter was back in the mix.

When we returned to the resort, we found Edwin and TJ tossing around a football in the front yard. When I got out of my car, I watched how the ball would disappear high into the trees and then shoot out the other end with a burst of leaves.

Boys and their games.

Hunter was sitting in a white plastic chair, observing the game and critiquing their throws.

"Honey, I'm home," I called out to Edwin.

Edwin caught the football and slammed it on the ground, like a touchdown. "Hey, baby. I missed you."

I slipped into his open arms and kissed him hello.

Aliah headed for Hunter. "We rented some sea doos for the aft. Are you guys in, or what?" she asked.

"Hell yeah," Hunter cheered.

"Edwin?" I asked, looking into his dreamy eyes.

"I'm in if you're in, babe," he said, then brushed my lips with a kiss.

Aliah pried us apart and tugged on my arm. "Oh, she's in. So get your shit together cuz it's time to go."

Before long, we were down at the dock searching for our

afternoon entertainment. We climbed up the steep mound of sand that led to the water's edge.

"There it is down there," I said, pointing to a small aluminum dock. Another random beach hottie was gassing up the machines.

"We only rented three, so someone has to pair up," Aliah explained to Hunter and Edwin.

"Uh, yeah. Right," Edwin said sarcastically, looking to Hunter.

"You riding with me then?" Aliah asked me, smiling.

"No way. I've seen how you drive. I'm not riding with you," I teased.

"We'll see about that," she taunted.

"I take it you're the ones taking out these bad boys. Ladies first," the hottie said. "I'm Kane by the way. If you have any questions or troubles, I'm the man you need to see."

Aliah hopped on first, her smile bursting from her mouth. "Well hello Kane," she said enthusiastically, expressing her obvious obsession with men.

"Before we go any further, you need one of these." Kane pulled out some PFD's and tossed one to each of us. I slipped mine on over my skimpy bikini and Aliah did the same.

Despite my fears of Ally's driving, I knew the guys would like to go it alone, so I got on behind her. Hunter and Edwin seemed equally pleased with the arrangement. Edwin wouldn't stop raising his eyebrows at me, enjoying the half-naked girl on girl action.

"Stop it! I fear for my life," I shouted.

"That's what the life jacket is for," Aliah said. "You'll be fine."

"Drive slow through the canal to keep the wake down. When you get out to the open water you can punch it. You have three hours," Kane said. "Here's a watch for you to wear." He snapped the watch on Aliah's wrist and away we went.

"See you out there suckas!" Aliah called to the guys as

she cranked the gas and zoomed away.

"Slow down!" Kane called after us, though Aliah didn't listen to him. We passed a medium sized boat at the mouth of the water, before we reached the open lake. Aliah punched it as I knew that she would and we sped off at full throttle. The lake water misted steadily in my face, as we jumped the wild waves.

"You're crazy!" I shouted.

"I can't get any lift on this thing, with your fat ass on the back!"

She slowed up a bit and we turned around to see if the guys had made it out of the canal. We could see two small figures heading our way at full speed. It was them alright.

Once the guys got closer, they found it necessary to pull stunts, circling around us. They took turns spraying us in the face with water, and there wasn't a damn thing we could do about it. Nice way to compete for our attention.

"Screw off!" Aliah hollered at Hunter.

"Come on, were just having fun!" he replied smiling.

"Let me throw a bucket of water in your face and see if you think it's fun!"

Despite her scowling, they both laughed and Edwin sprayed us again.

"Oh it's on!" I hollered, switching seats with Aliah.

To my surprise, she dove into the water and swam toward Hunter. *Traitor.*

"Ready?" I called out to Edwin. I crouched up over the seat and gave it gas, hard and fast. I sped off, but Edwin wasn't far behind me. After a minute of proving my coolness, I slowed a bit to let him catch up.

"No fair," he hollered. "Your machine's faster than mine."

I couldn't wipe the smirk from my face. "No, I think it's the awesome driver."

He cocked a competitive brow. "Switch me up then, and we'll see."

"Fine!" I disconnected from my machine and the engine cut out.

Truth was, I'd use any excuse to get closer to him. I dove into the water and adjusted my top. If I hadn't been wearing the PFD, then Edwin would have gotten quite the show. As I stroked closer to him, he cut his engine. I grabbed onto the back of the machine and struggled to get on the back of it.

"A little assistance here please!"

He pulled me onto the back and I wiggled my way closer to him, straddling the seat provocatively. "Mmm, you're all wet and sexy right now," he said, drawing his hands up my thighs.

I kissed him teasingly hard and whispered in his ear. "Let's see how turned on you are..." then louder, "after I beat your ass!"

I pushed him into the water. He didn't drag me in after him, instead with two powerful strokes he reached the other bobbing vehicle and propelled himself out of the water in a matter of seconds.

"You're in trouble now!" he growled.

I squealed anxiously and gathered my wits. "Good luck with that!" I said, spraying him as I stole a head start. I went as fast as the machine would take me, but I could see Edwin gaining on me. I thought I'd be smart and stop, so he'd fly by me. Instead I took a sharp turn to the left. Too sharp! And a wave!

Thrown from the machine, I sailed awkwardly into the air and crashed hard into the choppy water, too dizzy to realize which way was up. I choked on a mouth full of water and was very light headed when I resurfaced, bobbing in the wavy water. If it weren't for the PFD, I doubt I would have resurfaced at all.

Edwin recognized my disorientation and dove off his machine after me. "Abs, are you okay?" he hollered, swimming toward me.

"No," I moaned, wiping my face and gasping for breath, between the coughing and choking.

His arm protectively wrapped around me and he pulled me toward the bobbing death trap. "Abs, you okay?" he repeated.

Treading in place, I finally looked into his aqua eyes. *My gorgeous sea creature.* I stuck out my bottom lip in a pout. "I seem to have bruised my ego, but other than that I think I'll be okay," I said with a raspy voice, and then tried to clear my burning throat.

He laughed, gave me a quick peck and then lifted me onto the Sea Doo. "You're definitely fine. Such a drama queen. You know you can't be the best at everything," he reminded me.

He lifted himself from the water and slipped by me to take the driver's seat. He glanced at me over his shoulder to catch my answer.

"No, but I can try," I said, seductively. I rubbed my slick, wet body suggestively against his back and raised my eye brows to intimate what I wanted. I could show him why I was the best at many things.

Unable to resist, Edwin turned around to face me. I attacked him with my tongue, pinning him against the steering column, groping his powerful body. I was wet with excitement and heavy with heat, kissing and touching and feeling. My hand was tickling above the waistband of his swim trunks when I heard a motor rushing toward us.

Hunter and Aliah pulled up quickly, and their concern faded equally as fast. "You two realize the Sea Doo's floating away, right?" Aliah asked. "I paid for that rental. You should be keeping better tabs on it."

"And here I thought there was an accident," Hunter complained. "Oh well. If you're not going to use it, I am."

Once Hunter got it going, he flashed Aliah a wicked smile.

"Laters," Aliah hollered, as they roared off.

I fluttered my long dark lashes at Edwin. "Looks like you're stuck with me now," I said.

"I'd like to stick it to you now!"

Edwin pulled me up on his lap and I wrapped my legs around him. I was so fiercely hot for him right now. Our lips crashed together, our tongues tasted each other, and Edwin's hands were like fire, sizzling against my skin.

When I was convinced he might take me right there, a large speedboat stole away our attention. The massive ride was coming fast and right in our direction.

Without a word Edwin started us up and got us in motion, before we got ran over. Once we were out of their path, he let off the gas and checked his watch.

"It's almost time. We better head back."

I held him under his jacket and pressed myself against him wickedly close. He smiled back at me and leaned forward, speeding parallel to the beachfront. We pulled up to the dock with only minutes to spare. Hunter and Aliah were waiting for us on the hill.

"Did you guys have fun?" Kane asked, taking my PFD from me.

"A blast," I replied, smiling.

"Yeah, buddy. Thanks a lot," Edwin added.

Kane smiled and nodded. Then after a second of thought, "Hey, there's this nightclub me and my boys like to hit up. It's right on the main drag. It's a pretty fly place, a local hot spot on the long weekends," he said. "You guys should come check it out. There's never a shortage of hot ladies there."

"I got all the hot lady I need right here," he told Kane, as he nuzzled in my hair and gave me a quick kiss.

"I see that. Of course you're invited," Kane said to me, smiling.

Edwin clutched me to his side, strong and possessive.

Kane drew his eyes up to Edwin, acknowledging the limits. "The more hot ladies, the better. Why don't you bring your friends?"

"Okay. Thanks again, brotha," Edwin said, then reached out to exchange some guy handshake with him.

I climbed up the hill, as Aliah stood up with help from Hunter, and dusted herself off. We all walked down the sandy ridge together.

"Do you guys have any plans for tonight?" Edwin asked.

Hunter nodded his head. "We couldn't help but overhear Kane talking about that dance club. Aliah wouldn't mind checking that out."

Aliah smiled at me, over her shoulder. "It's time to get our drink on bichez!"

CHAPTER SIXTEEN

We all congregated outside the ladies place, warming up with a few beers. I could see Maddie coming up the road, dragging Jay along, with Tanner lagging behind them.

"This should be interesting," Aliah mumbled.

"It's fine," I hissed back. I flashed a glance at Edwin, but he was oblivious.

I could have used some downtime. *Too bad there's no rest for the wicked and wicked I am.* Light music flowed from TJ's portable I-pod speakers, and it helped to relax me somewhat, while I waited for dinner to be ready.

TJ was master of the barbeque, and grilled everything from hotdogs to hamburgers to steak. There was probably enough food there to feed half of the resort.

"Do you guys want something?" TJ hollered to the newcomers. "There's lots of food here. Don't be shy."

I had already gobbled down a hotdog and stole a bite from Edwin's second cheeseburger with ketchup and onions. If he was eating onions, then I was too; and man was it tasty.

As night began to flood around us, a cool breeze set a chill in the air. Edwin rubbed my arms to warm me up, but the second his hands left my skin, I trembled again.

"Maybe we should start up a fire," Edwin suggested.

"I can get it," Tanner announced, leaping from his seat, eager to make himself busy.

"I got it," Edwin growled.

I stayed in my seat as the two of them battled it out with words. My heart raced wildly as the two massive men lifted their chests and voiced their expertise. I doubt they were even talking about fire making any more. *Damn. Double damn. This was my doing.*

"You know what?" Tanner said to Edwin. "You go

ahead."

I was relieved when Tanner backed off suddenly to let Edwin tend to the fire, but was stunned when he took a seat in Edwin's lawn chair next to me. Apparently the vacant picnic table next to that wasn't quite as enticing to him.

Aliah's eyes bugged out of her head, and her mouth dropped in shock. Maddie was devoting all of her attention to Jay's rendition of their day together, as Hunter ate it all up.

When Edwin realized Tanner's game, he shot an evil glare in his direction, but Tanner seemed content to ignore it. I tried to ignore them both, but I could feel all of their eyes on me. Tanner was giving me his undivided attention, but I wasn't speaking. Edwin's eyes were angered, waiting for me to say something, but he didn't make a move.

I could see what Tanner was doing, but it wasn't going to work. And I refused to promote his bad behaviour. I told him before I was off limits. I told him I was Edwin's. I told him, but he kept pressing.

"Everything okay?" Tanner finally asked, noticing I was lost in my own thoughts.

I wasn't about to strike up a conversation with him. I'd learned my lesson the hard way. "Everything's great," I said, exaggerating, then left my chair to join Edwin next to the crackling fire. I wrapped my arms around his waist, stroking his ego and making his night.

He held me, his expression proud and possessive. He dipped his lips to my ear, his eyes never leaving Tanner. "I love you," he whispered, though I was sure Tanner could read lips.

"I love you too, Eddie." I slowly tilted my head up until his glimmering eyes met mine. My night was finally complete. When he slowly sunk down for a kiss, I gladly accepted.

Maddie stared at us, tisk tisking. "She pulls a stunt like that and Edwin just comes crawling back to her. Like a dog," Maddie whined. "It's disgusting."

"Shut your hole," Aliah said, to save me from an

argument.

Edwin held me in a trance while Tanner got the hint and decidedly stood from his chair.

"Well, it's been fun, but the nightlife awaits me. If this is *my weekend*, then I better go find myself some hunnies," he said, TJ the only one showing any interest. "You coming, Jay?"

I tried to stay impartial, but I couldn't help but feel sorry for him. Tanner was a decent guy being thrown out to the wolves, after being torn apart by one.

"You know it!" Jay hollered excitedly.

"Wait, what about me?" Maddie pouted.

"Duty calls my lady. I'll check you later," Jay said, pulling her into his arms for an embrace.

"Like hell you will," Maddie said, slapping him off of her. "Don't bother," she snapped, and that was that.

Tanner saw himself off and Jay followed with one hand raised in the air. Funny, it seemed more like a see you later than a wave goodbye. Maddie rolled her eyes and, to my surprise, didn't seem real upset about it when he was gone.

"Over him already?" Aliah teased.

"It was fun while it lasted. I was going to kick him to the curb when I was done with him tonight anyway. He's too high maintenance for me," Maddie said, giving us all a good laugh. She walked across the lawn and took a seat on top of the faded old picnic table. Alone.

While I still felt a little guilty for throwing my relationship in Tanner's face like that, I had to look out for myself. Who knows, maybe now Tanner might actually do something about it for a change.

TJ looked more miserable about Jay leaving than Maddie did. And with Jay out of the picture, Maddie seemed to dwell on me in Edwin's arms. Then she noticed the relationship that had started to blossom between Hunter and Aliah while she was off gallivanting.

"You seem deep in thought," Edwin said. "Nothing I should be worrying about I hope." He stole my stare from the raging fire.

I gazed up through dark lashes, my heart aching for him. "Eddie, I'm all yours." I licked my lips then slowly touched them to Edwin's. Our kiss was soft and sensual.

Edwin smiled and turned his eyes back to the flames. "I didn't doubt it. I just like hearing you say it."

I cupped my hand behind his neck and stole his attention back for another kiss. Moments passed and I was feeling so good. Everything was moving back into place for me.

"You still feel like going out tonight?" Edwin asked. "Or we could always stay in again." He raised his eyebrows suggestively.

I love tapped him on the shoulder so he would release me. "No, I think we should go out. Hey, what do you guys think?" I hollered for everyone to hear. "Want to check out this dance club we heard about?"

"I think that's an excellent idea," Maddie chimed. "I brought all kinds of cute outfits and haven't even worn a single one. We should all clean up and make a night of it."

"Yeah, let's do it!" TJ hollered, getting pumped. He was ready to let loose.

After painting our faces, clothing ourselves in the sexy, but skimpy fashions out of Maddie's massive collection, and covering ourselves in a good helping of body glitter, we were finally ready to go. When I walked out of my room, all of the guys' eyes were on me.

"God damn, Abigail!" TJ choked.

Hunter's eyes were wide, but he didn't say a word, until he couldn't help himself. "Edwin's been known to share, right buddy?" He elbowed TJ, teasing.

Edwin got up from the couch instantly, to see what the huff was all about. He swept across the room and pulled me close. "You look amazing, baby. But you don't know what that does to a man. Look at TJ. And Hunter can't seem to pick his mouth up off the floor."

Hunter snapped his mouth shut.

"I'll take that as a compliment," I said, smiling.

Maddie joined us, not getting the exact response she had hoped for, but she still looked hot. "Aliah, are you almost done in there?" Maddie squealed with impatience. "I'm ready to go!"

"Just one more minute!" she insisted.

"Why don't you call us a couple of cabs?" I tried to distract her, but it was of no use.

"Done and done," Edwin said. "They should be here any minute."

Edwin smelled so good and looked even better, wearing his tight shirt and showing off his incredible physique. Tonight should be fun.

Hunter walked over to the window and peered out. "Our rides are here."

"Come on, TJ. Let's go," Maddie insisted. "Hunter, you too."

"Alright, I guess," Hunter said. "Edwin, you coming with us, brother?"

"I'll catch the next one with Abby. You go ahead."

Hunter jogged out the door behind TJ, Maddie already waiting impatiently in the cab.

"Aliah, let's go!" Edwin hollered, his voice deep and demanding.

"You go ahead and get in the car," I suggested. "I don't want the cabby to take off without us."

I hurried toward the bathroom, as Edwin headed outside. I peered in the door without announcing my arrival. Aliah looked terribly upset.

"What's wrong?" I asked. "Are you sick? I so hope that's not it. That would totally suck."

"I'm freaking out here, Abby," she cried.

Aliah crying? "I'm sorry, you've lost me. What's wrong?"

"Hunter does it for me," she said.

"Huh? He does what?"

"It! You know: *it*," she said, appearing to be extremely frustrated with me. She wasn't usually one to dwell much on emotions. "I'm kind of scared. I've never felt like this before. You must think I'm so stupid."

"No. You're only human. Tell me. What happened?"

"I don't know what happened. But it did. I've fallen so

hard for him, Abby. I think I might even *love* him."

"Oh, no!" I teased.

"Stop it. I'm serious," she whined, so out of her normal character.

"Well I kind of figured as much. That was your plan, right?" I paused to let it sink in. "What does Hunter think about it?"

"I didn't tell him!" she stammered. "Do you think I should tell him?" Worry trumped her expressions of anxiety. "You don't think he knows, do you?"

I laughed, softly. "No. Men aren't that swift. So, telling him might be a good start."

Aliah scowled at me. "What do you think I was getting at earlier today when we saw you and Edwin under that old willow tree? You totally messed with the moment," she said.

"My bad. You can tell him tonight though, right?" *Oh, she's got it bad.*

"Right. No more waiting. I've procrastinated long enough. I'm going to do it," she said with determination.

"Right now?" I asked.

"No better time than the present."

"Oh, shit!" I said aloud, without thinking. "Hunter just took off in the other cab, and yes, Maddie is with him. Sorry to say, but that girl is on a mission tonight."

Aliah's wide eyes narrowed. "That'll change and fast. That bitch better keep her hands off my man or she's gonna have my foot in her face."

A smirk was all I let free. She was even worse than me. "They just left a few minutes ago. If we hurry, we won't be far behind them."

Suddenly Ally grabbed her purse and stomped out of the bathroom. She breezed right passed Edwin, who seemed to be checking up on us.

"What was that about?" Edwin was used to Aliah's outbursts, but seemed stunned by the smear of tears across her face.

"Don't ask," I said, as I locked up for the night.

"I can tell you!" Aliah growled from across the yard. "Maddie had better watch herself or she'll be getting a high-five. In the face. With a chair."

"Okay. Forget I asked," Edwin replied, smirking.

I quickly slipped into the back seat of the dirty yellow car. The interior wasn't much cleaner than the outside, so I sat up tall and made a great effort not to touch anything.

Edwin squeezed in next to me. "Sweet ride," he said sarcastically, then slammed the door shut behind him.

"Let's move buddy! There's an extra twenty in it for ya if you step on it," Aliah said.

The dark haired cabby did just that, shooting dirt from the well-worn tires and leaving a trail of dust behind us, as he sped off.

"That's what I'm talking about!" Aliah cheered, happily. She tossed him an extra twenty when we got out of the car.

We reached the main street just fast enough to catch Hunter disappearing into the club, with Maddie tugging him along. Worse, it didn't look to me like he was putting up much of a fight.

Aliah only saw red. She stalked up the main drag ahead of us, passing the long line of loud, excitable people and up to the door of the club.

Aliah looked back to me, as Edwin and I hurried to catch up with her. I could read her signs too. She wanted me to work my magic on the door man. I nodded to her and Edwin turned away hoping I'd make quick work of it.

First I smiled to get his attention, then lifted my chest and held it out provocatively to distract him. After whispering discreetly in the doorman's ear, with my hand lingering on his buff chest, he was like putty in my hands.

He checked me out, his eyes lingering on my low cut top and glittery cleavage, then he looked Aliah over head to toe. The doorman unlatched the clamp that had blocked our access and Aliah walked in ahead of me, winking at him.

Not bad. I didn't even have to drop Kane's name.

I reached back and twisted Edwin's shirt in my hands, then pulled him through the door. "He's with me," I said, batting my eye lashes as I passed.

The doorman wasn't impressed that I pulled a fast one on him, but he let Edwin pass. As he did, a couple of ladies who were hanging out by the door tried to sneak in with us. There was not a chance in hell that the doorman was going to let another person scam their way in.

"To the back of the line," he told them, simple and stern. "We're at capacity."

We walked through the cool, dark blue hall until we were met with a quirky young woman with short pink and bleached blonde hair, worn straight. She sat on a tall bar stool next to an even taller table.

Standing next to her was a tall, heavyset man, with his head shaved bald and a grim look set on his face. He wore a black collared shirt that showed he was hired muscle. He stood there unsmiling with his hands folded over his sagging chest.

Pinkerella had just stamped Aliah's hand and marked mine next as Edwin paid our cover.

Farther up the way, a group of ladies with dramatic makeup, forced cleavage and tight clothes, congregated on the left side of the hall. As I waited for Edwin, I watched them.

A group of five chicas huddled there, the tallest being the leader of the pack. She stood out from the rest, being very blond, with long lean legs, by far the most striking of the bunch.

The other girls seemed to magnetize to her and were hanging on her every word. Aliah walked right past them, without a look, as they sized her up.

It was clear from the scowling that they pegged her as the competition. It didn't help that TJ greeted her, hugged his arms around her waist and spun her around, with a huge but genuine smile on his face, before she hurried off to find Hunter.

I smiled and watched the ladies drink him up as he came in to meet us. After TJ's recent dry spell, tonight was looking like his lucky night.

He smiled and nodded at the girls as he passed. "Ladies," he said.

They all swooned and smiled, all eyes on him, as they assessed the muscles that pulled his shirt tight in all the right places.

I overheard the blonde chiming to her friends. "I called him first."

"You guys made it," TJ said. He rested his hand on my back and gave it a friendly rub.

We started forward and TJ led the way, all the girls' eyes on him. Just then, the blonde redirected her attention behind me and I knew exactly what she was doing. Her eyes were locked wide on Edwin, devouring his everything.

I slowed up, tucked my arm in Edwin's, and tightened my grip to show her he was mine. I thought that might fend off the vulture's eyes, but it didn't. Edwin didn't seem to notice her and looked at me to see what the sudden attachment was all about. That gave me some satisfaction, but as I glanced over my shoulder, the blonde bimbo continued to devour him.

"Wait, I take that back," the blonde said, with wicked certainty. "This one's mine." Her eyes never left Edwin's ass.

Oh. No. She. Didn't! Unable to let that slide, I tugged on Edwin until he came to a stop. He glanced at me confused.

I went on my tippy toes and cupped my hands over his ear. "There's something I have to do. Be right back," I promised, before planting a soft kiss on his lips.

"Don't be long." Edwin's smile was cute and curious. He carried on down the hall toward TJ and disappeared into the hot, sticky dance room with him.

I couldn't drop what had just happened. I wouldn't. There was an overwhelming, nagging recklessness just begging me to do something about it. Turning on my heel, I spun around to face the whore eyeing up my man and strutted right over to the blonde bimbo and her trampy troop. "Hey you," I called rudely, as I approached.

The bimbo looked me eye to eye, suddenly recognizing

who I was.

"Yeah, I'm talking to you," I said, scowling. "I saw you ogling my man, and I heard what you said. I'm here to tell you to keep your claws off. He's taken."

"I didn't see any ring on his finger," she replied brazenly, flashing a pleased smile to her friends. One of them was grimacing, but all the others only egged her on more.

My eyes never left hers. "Okay, I can play your game then," I projected. "Try and touch him, bitch, and see where that gets you." I whirled around, fuming, and stalked off. I entered the main room. It had low ceilings and insignificant lighting.

"Wait," the blonde girl called out, chasing after me.

Oh, did she want a piece of me? Because I am so ready to knock her block off.

She gazed at me with wide, black trimmed, eyes. She looked horrified, like she was about to deliver some earth shattering announcement.

"No one has ever stood up to me like that. I'm impressed," she admitted, her voice shaking.

I shrugged my bare confident shoulders at her, waiting for the apology. I must be seriously scary.

"I get it. He's off limits. I'll keep my distance." Her pause told me she had a new proposal, but why would that involve me? "But what about that other guy that came in with you?" she asked.

Ah hah! "TJ?"

"Is that his name? Mmm," she said, knee deep into the cocktails.

"He's absolutely available, and a really nice guy," I said, surprised by the turn of conversation.

"It was rude what I did back there. I do apologize. Can you forgive me?" she asked.

One thing was for sure, the girl was hot, and I'd say anything to keep her off my man. "I can do one better. Come with me," I said, reaching for her hand.

She shrugged a dainty shoulder, smiled wickedly and twiddled her fingers in the air to wave goodbye to her infuriated friends. They looked equally as surprised about our new found friendship. I yanked her hand to find TJ and deliver her to him on a silver platter.

We ducked into the crowd to avoid the deafening sound coming from the massive speakers. The place was packed wall to wall. And though it wasn't super classy, the DJ was mixing something fierce, the drinks were flowing steadily and nearly every person was tinged with sweat from dancing up a storm. After scanning the bar, I found TJ and Edwin ordering drinks.

I pulled the girl along until I was at Edwin's side. "You'd better make that two more," I hollered.

TJ turned back to me, taking in my long-legged companion and nodded, a roguish smile creeping onto his lips. TJ handed Edwin a drink, then reached his own out to Blondie.

Hand gripped tight on my wrist, I lifted Blondie's hand up for TJ to take. "TJ, I want you to meet...uh...um..." *Oh shit!* "How rude of me. I don't even know your name," I said to the girl.

Blondie stepped in front of me, took TJ's drink from his hand and passed it off to me, without ever taking her hawk eyes off of him. She slipped her hands over TJ's shoulder and sunk her fingers into his dark well-trimmed hair. "Hey, TJ. I'm Milayna, your next partner in crime and dream come true," she said, with no shame.

"Yes you are, darlin'. You know Abby?" TJ asked, dreadfully intrigued.

"I do now. And now you know me too," she replied. She flashed an appreciative look my way. "I think I can take it from here."

I laughed, but knew how to take a hint. I linked my fingers around Edwin's and pulled him away from the ravenous falcon. Before creating much distance, Aliah found us.

"You still haven't found Hunter?" I asked, my eyes indicating my concern. Though crowded, the dance floor wasn't that large. My only guess was that Maddie was hiding Hunter for her own devious purposes.

"No, I can't find him anywhere. What has she done with him?" Aliah grumbled.

My eyes scanned over the crowd, desperate to locate them before Aliah did. There they were. I shuffled toward them, blocking Aliah's advance. Maddie, the devil in all her glory, was groping Hunter on the dance floor and I'd be damned if I didn't say he was enjoying it.

As soon as Aliah realized what I was doing, she followed my anxious eyes and her instant horror quickly turned to rage. "That bitch is dead!"

Before I could stop her, Aliah got to Maddie and pulled her off of Hunter by the hair. "What the hell do you think you're doing?" she screamed.

Maddie, being a firecracker herself, shoved Aliah off of her. "What's your problem?" she screamed.

"Back off bitch. Hunter's mine."

Maddie got in Aliah's face and I was waiting for Aliah to deck her. To my surprise, she waited to hear what Maddie had to say. Hunter stayed far enough back, knowing that he'd only fuel the fire.

"I think you're barking up the wrong tree," Maddie said, inches from Aliah's mouth. "Hunter's a grown man, he can make his own decisions. The way I see it, he's fair game." She raised an eyebrow, daring Aliah to try something.

The music got so loud that no one but Maddie and Aliah could hear the exchange, but their body language said it all. In one fell swoop, Aliah knocked Maddie's drink from her hand and shoved her viciously into the crowd.

Maddie stumbled over a couple of dancers who, being caught off guard, lost their footing and tumbled onto the beer soaked floor. Hunter reached for Maddie, but was unable to snag her. Maddie toppled on top of them.

Aliah wasn't done. She was hunting Maddie down to mess up her face. Hunter put a stop to it, his hand flat against Aliah's middle.

"Crazy bitch! What is your problem?" Maddie screamed, as she took Hunter's proffered hand and regained her balance.

"I'm crazy? Really?" Aliah screeched, pushing Maddie with both her hands again.

This time, Maddie maintained her stability, with Hunter holding onto her. He raised his hand again.

"That's enough, Ally." Just then, the thumping music stopped. "You're making a fool of yourself!" Hunter hollered, for everyone to hear. His embarrassment from the entire episode was evident.

A couple of large, bald, bouncers, in black collared shirts, had materialized out of the shadows. One grasped firmly onto Aliah's arm. "It's time for you to go," he said.

Aliah yanked her arm away from the man who looked about three times her size. "Get your hands off of me. I'm not going anywhere."

"You're going to leave now or I'll remove you," he said, his deep voice firm. "It's your choice."

"Fine! I'm outta here. I can see when I'm not wanted," she said, flashing a rude glare at Hunter.

Hunter just shook his head, as Aliah stormed away. She pushed through the crowd to the front door, with a bald man following her. The music resumed, as did the dancing, and it was like nothing had even happened.

Hunter hung his head low and stared at the floor, while Maddie rubbed his shoulder to comfort him. Then he turned to face Maddie. "Let me get you a drink. I think we can both use one," he said.

Since it was apparent Hunter wasn't going to check on Aliah, I figured I had better. "I'm gonna go," I told Edwin.

He nodded with understanding as I spun away to chase down the large, bald man. I caught up with Aliah in the dark hall.

"Ally, wait!"

She stopped near the exit, but the man continued to usher her outside. She was clearly very upset when she stepped outside, anger in her eyes and tears on her cheeks.

Ignoring the girl with pink hair, a stamp extended out toward me, I chased after Ally. I crossed the threshold and pulled on her arm to make her face me.

"What's up with you? You just lost it in there."

"I couldn't take it, seeing Maddison throwing herself at Hunter like that. I wanted to smash her face in. She's lucky I didn't get my hands around her neck."

"She *is* lucky, because now she's in there with Hunter and you're out here," I said, making a point.

"In or out ladies," the doorman voiced.

"I just need a minute," I said.

"Don't worry about me. I'll be fine," Aliah lied, as she walked out to the curb.

I pushed past the doorman. "No, I'm coming with you. You're not going off alone."

Aliah stood there, festering, when Tanner and Jay emerged from the club. Jay had a small but spunky girl under his arm, with short spiked hair and full red lips.

"Abigail, Aliah, funny running into you again," Tanner said to me, drunken and sarcastic.

"Yeah, funny," I repeated, unimpressed.

Aliah covered her hands over her face. "Let me guess, you guys saw me in there," she groaned, clearly embarrassed by her behaviour.

"Actually we're just leaving, and I have no idea what you're talking about," Tanner said, uninterested.

"It looks like you could use some company tonight Tanner," Aliah said, motioning toward his empty arm.

He waved a hand at her, suggesting he was fine. Drunk. But fine.

"I know I certainly could use some," Aliah hinted. She was desperate, pleading for his companionship.

"Yes, please," Tanner said, taking her into his arms.

It was depressing to watch them share their heart break and gloom.

"You don't have to do that, Tanner," I said to him. "You don't know what you're doing, Ally. I'll go with you."

"Stop," she said. "I've already ruined my night. There's no need for me to wreck yours too. As for Hunter and Maddie, they can go fuck themselves. I'm with Tanner. I'll be fine," Aliah insisted, rather impressively.

"Seriously, Abigail, I'll take good care of her," Tanner promised.

"That's what I'm afraid of," I replied, smiling.

"It's harmless," he said, as he walked away with Aliah on his arm.

I rolled my eyes at the rat bastard, taking a dose of my own medicine, then flashed some puppy dog eyes at the bouncer to let me back in. I hurried down the hall, pushed my way through the bouncing crowd and headed back toward the bar.

It seemed like every guy I tried to slip by was trying to make a pass at me. They took turns, resting their hands on my hips, grinding against my backside, grabbing at my ass and trying to touch me while I was defenceless.

All I could do was press on toward the bar, where I saw Edwin leaning against a pillar. Being so happy to see him, I curled my arms around his core and inhaled him, my cheek pressed to his warm, buff chest.

He brought his lips down to my ear. "I was getting worried that some horny guy kidnapped you," he teased.

I looked up to meet his loving gaze. "I'm not going anywhere without you." I cupped his neck and pulled him down for an affectionate kiss.

Edwin downed the last of his drink and kissed me again, a little more provocatively. With tongue. His mouth was wet and sweet.

A while later, with a new drink in hand, we went searching for Hunter and Maddie. It wasn't hard to find the two of them dancing together playfully.

"Dance with me?" I begged. I released Edwin and swayed my hips, as I walked out onto the dance floor without giving him any other option.

Edwin smirked, and enjoyed my entertainment from a short distance away, our eyes locked on each other. Before long, a skinny drunken guy, with his pants hanging loosely from his ass, mistook me for fair game.

I caught Edwin's eye, before I even knew what was

happening, when suddenly the tall, Slim Shady pressed his boner against my rear and rubbed against me, with his hands looped around my waist.

"Um, no," I hollered, disgusted. I elbowed him in the gut, and tried to turn around to shun him, but he wouldn't take no for an answer. "Back off! I said I'm not interested."

He tightened his grip around my waist, even more aroused by my struggling. "Oh, come on. You like it," he hollered belligerently, grinding against me.

Edwin stepped in, flexing his chest. He grabbed Slim Shady by the neck of his shirt, and lifted him off the floor. "You'll listen to the lady, if you know what's good for you," he growled, terrifying the grown man. Edwin dropped him, heavy to the floor, and the loser scurried away.

Shocked bystanders pointed and snickered, absorbed in our drama, but Edwin just ignored them and pulled me into his arms. He wrapped himself around me, tucked my hair behind my ear and dropped a soft kiss on my lips. "Are you okay?"

"Mmm hmm," I said, my heart still racing.

"I have to keep my eyes on you. You sure know how to get into trouble," he said, with a low sexy growl.

I was sure no other guy would be bold enough to make a move on me after that. I fluttered my eyelashes at Edwin, begging him to hold me close. "Trouble does have a way of finding me."

"I guess I'd better hold on tighter then." His arms tightened around me, as he dipped his head for another kiss.

We kissed. And we danced. And we kissed some more. The music was dirty, vibrating from the floor to the roof, and I was feeling frisky.

I spun around and grinded him with my body, like sex with clothes on. He was captivated, hard with arousal, aching for more contact. His hands scoured my bare thighs and stroked my behind, his eyes glued to my hips, overwhelmed by my curves.

To be a tease, I bent forward, dipped low, and slowly

returned my back end by brushing against him. Unable to resist me, he clamped his hands on my arms and spun me around to face him, locking his glorious aqua eyes on mine.

Sharing my lust through dark lashes, I dared to reach around him and grab his tight ass in both of my hands. His arms found their way around my waist, and his lips twitched into an insanely hot smile.

With too much to drink, my hand slipped between us and massaged him through his pants. He moaned in my ear, begging me to stop, but his body told me to keep going. Being a good girl, for now, my arm trailed back around him and I flashed him a devious wink.

His lips brushed mine then he brought them to my ear. "Why don't we go take a seat? I think I need a break... and a cold shower," he said. He adjusted himself, then followed close behind me to the table where I saw Hunter sitting by himself.

Edwin took a seat across from Hunter, and even though there was a vacant chair next to Edwin, his lap was too inviting. With an arm over his shoulder, he lifted me right where I wanted to be.

"Where's TJ?" I hollered.

"Last I saw, he was making out with some blonde chick," Hunter said, wearing a smirk, as he waved over a waitress.

Though Hunter looked like he already had enough to drink, he ordered something and swung his hand in the air to ask for a round of it. Shots lined our table within a matter of minutes.

When Edwin reached for a drink, we were both startled by Hunter's outrageous slur. "We have to wait for Maddie." He glanced around for her, then smiled. "Ah, there she is."

I flashed Edwin a quick look, only to find that he was equally as stunned by Hunter's high spirits when Maddie returned to the table. I had seen that look before. It was the same look he gave Aliah the first day we met. Trouble was brewing.

"What's up?" Edwin whispered in my ear, knowing something was wrong.

"Ally's in love with Hunter. She had planned to tell him tonight. That's why she reacted the way she did earlier. She was already devastated, and now this?"

"Aliah had her chance. Maybe Hunter doesn't feel the same. He seems to be having a good time with Maddie," Edwin said, then kissed my temple. "What's it going to take for me to get back that attention of yours?"

I smiled softly and kissed his luscious, wet lips.

"That's more like it," he growled, before kissing me again.

"Are we gonna drink these or what?" Maddie hollered. She was standing next to me, smiling, not at all bothered by our affection. Suddenly she was all confidence and comfort, which was probably exactly why Hunter was so attracted to her; being the same thing that attracted him to Aliah.

Edwin slid a shot glass my way and lifted his toward Hunter nodding his head. He gently tapped his glass against mine and then we all slammed it down in one gulp. The music was still bumping, but the drinks were starting to catch up to me. Once I was sure the drink was going to stay down, I locked my eyes on Edwin's.

"I take it you're ready to call it a night," Edwin said, laughing.

I nodded, only because I wanted some alone time with him.

"We're going to get going. Are you guys ready to go?" Edwin hollered.

Damn!

"Yeah," Hunter said, standing from his seat.

Double damn!

The place was still packed, as Edwin led the way through the mellow crowd. I didn't know why it surprised me when I caught Hunter accepting Maddie's hand when she reached it to him. I looked up into Edwin's eyes and smiled, trying to act ignorant to what was going on behind us. But it was hard.

As we entered the long hallway and walked toward the exit, I saw Kane chatting with a bouncer.

"Hey, you guys came. What did I say?"

Edwin and Hunter shared handshakes with him, giving me the opportunity to tug Maddie away.

"We're just gonna run to the bathroom real quick. We'll meet you outside," I told Edwin, then dragged Maddie off with me.

"But I don't have to go pee," she said.

"I don't care." I eyed the long line up stretching outside of the washroom. "I just want to know whether you know what you're doing here," I said.

"Going to the washroom?" she said, sarcastically.

"Starting a war with Aliah."

She rolled her eyes. "The war is over. I've won, fair and square. She blew it. Her problem, not mine."

I gave her a sideways glance. "Don't give me that. I know you're not that cruel; so stop acting like you are."

"You have no idea Abby. What you and Edwin have... I want that. With Hunter."

"You're playing with fire."

"You know I like it hot, and Aliah's the only one here who is going to get burned," she said, returning to her old selfish ways.

"Maddie, you know Ally's my best friend and I don't want to see her get hurt." I paused, taking a deep breath. "But Hunter is a big boy and I respect whatever he decides."

"Thank you for your blessing, Abby. That means a lot."

"Oh, is that what you thought that was? Hardly. You are not getting my blessing, little slutty," I said.

She giggled and turned her eyes to the floor.

"You do what you will, that's not my business. I'm staying out of it. It'll be Aliah's wrath that you'll have to deal with later, not mine," I said.

"I can handle Aliah."

I sighed. "Okay, I'll leave it alone then."

At last, we reached the front of the line. I quickly removed my panties and stuffed them into my small purse, before exiting my stall. Edwin deserved a reward.

After drying her hands, Maddie yanked me from the

washroom with her arm hooked in mine. As she pulled me toward the door, she looked self-assured and happy. Men hooted and hollered at us, as we walked down the hall.

Suddenly, feeling incredibly vulnerable, I wished I hadn't removed my panties. A pair of guys pulled away from their group and stalked up closely behind us, coaxing us to go home with them.

"Screw off," Maddie hollered.

We hurried for the exit, knowing that if they had balls enough to follow us outside, they would be scared off fast when they saw the two beefy men we had waiting for us there.

Maddie let me go, and crossed the threshold, as one of the guys caught up to me. He clutched onto my shoulder and yanked me back into the darkened hall. I stumbled backward falling back against him.

His grubby hand molested my breast, before I could react.

"Ugh!" I screamed.

"Oh yeah, you'll do just nice," he said, his voice as slimy as his hair.

As I tried to catch my balance, I felt his cold, cracked and calloused hand creep up my inner thigh. I instantly jabbed my elbow into his gut and stomped his foot with my long, skinny heel. He slumped to his knees on the dingy floor, hollering angrily and crying in pain, as I darted for the door.

CHAPTER SEVENTEEN

After escaping the steamy club, Maddie led me, quickly and silently, down the sidewalk to where Hunter and Edwin were waiting for us.

"You okay?" she whispered.

I nodded, panicked, and yet relieved that she was going to keep her mouth shut. Had she reacted differently, I would've been a teary-eyed mess for sure.

The only thing that held me together was the knowledge that if Edwin found out what happened, he'd go back in there, find the slime ball that touched me, and make him apologize for what he'd done, and then he'd beat him to a bloody pulp, or worse.

Despite all the night's drama, it was our last one, and it was almost over. I could still make it a memorable one. I wished there were some way to make the night last, wipe out the depravity and reinvest in the flame that was burning good and strong between Edwin and I this morning in the meadow.

"It's such a beautiful night out, eh?" Hunter asked Maddie.

"Way too nice to call it a night! What can we do?" she asked him, going for coy.

"We can go hang out at the beach, if you want," Edwin suggested.

"Right on," Hunter answered.

I shrugged my shoulders indecisively. I didn't want to share Edwin and I doubted that Maddie wanted us to tag along with them either.

"We'll catch up to you guys. You go on ahead," Edwin said, his eyes reaching mine.

Edwin slung his arms loosely over my shoulders. "What's up, Abs? You're not worrying about Aliah again are you?"

Without a need for words, after shoving my panties in Edwin's pants pocket, I kissed him on the nose and walked off for the beach. I glanced back, as he checked his pocket, to catch his reaction. His smile was priceless, when he realized I was sauntering away without panties.

"Wait up, guys," I called to Hunter and Maddie, as I hurriedly caught up to them, with my smirk firmly in place.

When we reached the sand, Maddie and I removed our shoes and we walked down the long, sandy beach toward the water. The only light was that from the headlights of a vehicle leaving the barren parking lot nearby. When the car was gone, darkness enveloped us.

"I want to walk up the beach," Maddie hollered back to Hunter, as she ran toward the swelling waves, appearing peaceful and carefree.

Hunter followed after her, and I started to follow suit, but Edwin stopped me and pulled me into his possessive arms.

"My feet are kind of sore," Edwin said, smirking. "We're just going to hang out here," he hollered, his eyes locked on mine.

"Okay, we'll meet you back at the resort," Hunter called back, without another glance.

I slipped my eyes off of Edwin long enough to watch Maddie kick her foot into an oncoming wave, intentionally splashing water at Aliah's man. She ran off giggling, so Hunter would chase her. That he did, and it was officially out of my hands.

"If you took a seat in the sand, it would be more convincing you know," I teased. Not that we needed an excuse to stay back. They understood, being caught up in their own *whatever you want to call it* to notice us anyway.

Taking Edwin by surprise, only because I was too drunk to care, I plopped down in the sand, being extra careful to keep my legs together. So, one outfit might not have made it out of the weekend alive. It was worth it. I leaned back to look up at Edwin, the backdrop a gorgeous, night sky.

He dropped to his knees and hovered over me, smiling, before he braced my neck and kissed me long and soft. Joining me in the cool sand, he wrapped his arm around my core, propping me against him, back to chest.

I took a deep breath of the fresh open air, leaned my head back against his shoulder, and listened to the noisy peace of the powerful waves crashing onto the sandy beach.

There seemed to be a few others lingering in the darkness, known only from the random hoot or giggle in the distance. At such an hour, it could only be assumed that the others were either utterly in love, like us, or had other naughty intentions, also like us.

The beach was massive and after a few minutes of total darkness and silence, it felt like we were totally alone.

Edwin caressed up and down my arm, incredibly subtle and totally hot. It drove me wild, reminding me that I was minimally clothed and it was just the two of us.

Being bold, I hiked my skirt and straddled Edwin's lap facing him. "I know what you want," I said, provoking him.

"Do you now?" he replied, with a slanted smile that hit me right between the thighs.

"I'm not that kind of girl," I said, teasing, touching. The warm summer wind breezed through my dark hair and my fingers rested on Edwin's irresistible lips.

He kissed them, his lips trailing toward my neck, and down farther until he brushed across my taut nipple. His mouth was hot and wet, and soaked through the barely there fabric, being the only thing separating his tongue from my skin. I shivered as he blew a breath over me.

He nipped and sucked gently, then slowly made his way back up to my neck, my chin, until his lips finally devoured mine, steady and sure. I slipped my hand between us and found him primed and ready for me, harder than ever. I stroked his length and he moaned into my mouth. His hands found their way under my skirt and skimmed my bare skin, making me tremble in anticipation.

I took my time popping his fly, as he kissed me everywhere but my mouth. Strained for space, I slowly unzipped his pants and tugged on his Calvin's. He sprang from his clothes and I clasped on, stroking him, warm and rigid. He tugged my dress below my breasts and, as his tongue teased my nipple, my head fell back, giving him full reign.

It startled me when his hands gripped onto my behind and he lifted me on top him. I gasped on a moan. *When did he slip on that rubber?* He filled me, with one stroke. It felt tight and warm and very, very good.

Hands clenched on my naked hips, he pressed me down onto him, thrusting himself deeper inside me. His strong, capable hands rounded to my rear, setting the pace, rocking me at a steady tempo. I knew we were in public and I still couldn't stop the incessant moaning.

It felt too good to stop.

Edwin chuckled, proud and amused, as I came undone in his lap.

"Oh, Eddie," I shouted. As heat coiled around me, I threw my head back and screamed out, not feeling at all comprised with my dress bunched around my waist, as deliciously violent tremors rocked through me.

Consumed with the tightening sensation, Edwin jerked me faster and harder and deeper, and I could see his own climax on the horizon. Another heat swirled inside me and Edwin, cupping my neck, pressed my mouth with hot, hard kisses.

I shivered with the awareness of the clenching, dragging me deeper into the abyss, as Edwin deepened the kiss, his tongue slipping along my teeth, dancing with my tongue. He swallowed my moan as another climax dragged me toward the swirling darkness, Edwin ready to crash right behind me.

"Yes, baby," he groaned. His hand was tangled in my loose tousled hair as a tidal wave of sensations made me gasp and convulse and Edwin filled me with his powerful release.

Staying incredibly still for a moment, our hearts thumped in magical harmony, and then Edwin lied back in the sand, taking me with him. After a moment frozen in time, he kissed me.

"I love you, Abs."

I adjusted my dress and rolled off of him, lying at his side in the sand. "That's just your penis talking."

He laughed. "He loves you too, but I assure you this is coming from my heart." He sighed, and turned on his side, smoothing his hand down my arm. "Trust me. You're the only girl in my world," he said, gazing into my eyes.

As the waves crashed the shore, creating a delightful, dark serenity, I leaned into him and shared a soft, meaningful kiss.

"Sorry about your skirt. It's filthy now," he said, brushing the sand off me.

I clambered to my feet. It took a second for me to readjust to being vertical again, but what a treat it was to see Edwin lying there, pants unfastened, shirt hiked up exposing his brick layered abs.

"Do you think I could get my panties back now?" I asked, sticking out my bottom lip. I reached into his pocket, but my hand came out empty.

Smiling, Edwin refastened his pants and flexed every muscle as he leaned forward to stand up next to me.

He retrieved my panties from his other pocket, dangled them in front of me, and proceeded to spin them around on his finger. "Looking for these?"

I tried to yank them from his hand, but he was too fast. He tucked them back in his pocket and took two long strides away from me.

"Oh, so this is how it's going to be?"

Edwin swiftly removed his socks and shoes, then ran off into the darkness toward the surf. "You can have them, if you can catch me," he hollered, as he ran ankle deep into the waves.

I was already filthy so I figured what was a little water going to hurt? I chased in after him and tackled him into the shallow water. He caught me around the waist and so I landed on top of him. He dipped me into the water, to make sure I got as wet as him.

We splashed around, rolling in the waves, kissing and touching, until I finally snuck my panties from his pocket. I got the panties, but now we were both soaked and dirty with sand from our ears to our toes.

I shoved him away to slip on the scrap of silky lace, and started toward the beach. Edwin leapt from the waves and carried me back into them.

He dropped back down into the water and pulled my slippery body on top of his. I couldn't stop giggling and smiling. His smile was just as big, his teeth gleaming in the moonlight. I was spellbound. I ran my fingers through his sexy wet hair and clung to his body, as I pressed a kiss to the corner of his mouth.

He ran his hand down my thigh and I shivered, though my cheeks were burning. He pushed me to my knees and lifted his wet sculpted body to a sitting position beneath me, his shirt clinging deliciously to every twitching muscle.

"You belong with me," he said, and wrapped my chilled body in his warm arms.

"I know," I said softly, a hand flattened on his smooth chest next to my head.

The waves continued to crash around us, promptly delivering me into a dreamscape. The night was warm, but the water was cold and my nipples were now protruding out of my top. Taking Edwin's hand, I stood up and dragged him out of the water with me.

"Where are our shoes?" I asked, frantically searching in the deepening darkness for my expensive stilettos.

Edwin located them farther up the beach with little effort. I teetered over to them and he laughed at me.

"That water didn't straighten you up?" he asked.

"I'm definitely awake, but I may still be under the influence," I admitted, having had way too much to drink.

He laughed again. "That's my girl."

Barefoot and soaked to the bone, we walked hand in hand. When we reached the paved sidewalk, Edwin squeezed the water out of his shirt.

"Yeah, we're going to have no trouble finding a cab tonight," he said, sarcastically.

"What should we do?" I asked, without any brilliant ideas of my own.

"Maybe you could drop your top again. That might get a few takers."

I slapped him hard and he acted hurt, but his grin returned on his face in a matter of seconds. "Don't worry, Abs. We'll figure something out."

We continued up the street toward some commotion outside a small local bar. It looked like Jay had gotten himself into a little trouble. He was throwing wild punches at some guy, and Tanner was providing his backup, getting right in on the action.

Aliah was casually leaning against the wall next to the door of the bar. She was alone. Edwin and I strolled over to her.

"What's going on?" I asked.

"Oh, you know, the usual. Turns out that Jay was hanging out with a slut. Big surprise. That dude over there thinks she's his girl. Jay doesn't think so. It actually makes for good entertainment. Go Tanner!" she cheered.

"It's good to see you're enjoying yourself," I said.

"Yeah, I am. But look at you. You're a mess; but you're totally glowing. What have you done to her?" she asked Edwin, smiling.

She had no idea. Then again, maybe she did.

"Whatever it is, I like it," she said, with a vulgar snap.

"I guess I just have that effect on the ladies," Edwin said, a sexy smile slanting across his handsome face.

Aliah laughed. "Whatever."

After the other guy was lying flat on his back and his friends ran off to hide, Tanner hurried toward us, with Jay limping up behind him.

"Let's get out of here. We're parked just up the road," Tanner said, dragging limping Larry after us.

I looked to Aliah. "Are they in any shape to be driving?"

Aliah nodded with certainty, as we rushed toward

Tanner's car. "Tanner hasn't had a single drink this whole time I've been with him," she insisted.

Jay got in the backseat of the two- door Civic, fat lip and all. Aliah and Edwin piled in next to him. It only left one vacant seat, and that was in the front. With Tanner.

"It's okay, you can fit," Edwin told me, suggesting I squish in the back with them. He was already soaking Aliah, but she seemed amused by that fact.

"Just get in," Tanner yelled, as he turned over the engine.

"It's fine, I can sit in the front," I said to Edwin, as I slammed back the passenger seat and scampered into it.

"Don't worry, I'm not going to try anything. You can give me a little more credit than that," Tanner scolded, as he pulled into the street.

I glanced over my shoulder again only to find Aliah pressed up against Jay. He was smirking at me; or maybe it was only his fat lip. I looked away quickly, but when I glanced back it was obvious he was smirking, getting off from making me uncomfortable.

"Hit Jay for me, will you?" I shouted over the loud music.

Aliah did, without question.

"Hey, what did I do?" he hollered at her.

Edwin reached his hand over the right side of my seat to catch my attention. I reached my hand over my shoulder to hold his; and it gave me some relief.

"What did you guys end up doing tonight?" Jay asked.

I smirked, blushing profusely, as I squeezed Edwin's hand. Tanner looked at me and figured it out right away. We were still drenched from frolicking in the lake after all.

"Right," Jay said, exaggerating the word.

"Sorry about your seats," I said to Tanner, ignoring Jay.

"No problem. They'll wipe right down," he insisted.

I could tell from how clean the car was that he'd be wiping the leather down as soon as my ass left the seat.

Minutes later we pulled into the resort and Tanner slowly pulled up to our place.

"Thanks for the ride," I said to Tanner, as I got out of his car. I caught him staring as I bent over to flip the seat to let

Edwin and Aliah out of the back.

It was apparent that Edwin caught him too, but he managed to contain his anger. Could he really blame him for noticing? My clothes were clinging to me.

"Thanks for the ride Arnold, I mean Tanner," Edwin said, as he pulled me into his arms and rested his hand on my ass.

Aliah kissed her fingers and tapped them on Jay's lips, since he seemed to have passed out. "Night, night," she called to Tanner, as she shut the door.

He pulled away in his car, looking at us in the rear-view, and I was sure that it was the last I would see of him. I stared as he slowly rode off. Edwin held me around my waist and rested his chin on my head.

"I'm going straight to bed," Aliah said, as she trotted for the door.

We followed her to the cabin to see what the sleeping arrangements were for the night. We quietly crept into the place and it was so very quiet. Maddie's bedroom door was shut. No doubt, she had a guest. Our bedroom door was wide open and it was empty, until Aliah stepped inside and started to undress.

"Abby, you coming?" Aliah whispered, oblivious to the situation.

"No, I think I'll head next door with Edwin," I whispered back, certain that I did not want to be there when Aliah figured it all out it the morning.

"What? I don't bite, and Eddie boy's welcome to join us," she said, hoping Edwin would change my mind.

"Another time," Edwin insisted, making Aliah laugh softly.

"Suit yourselves," she said, as she closed the bedroom door.

Edwin led the way, with long strides to his cabin. He stopped me just outside his door. "TJ may have company. I just wanted to warn you," he whispered.

"Is that all you were doing?" I asked, as I put my arms over his shoulders.

He smiled wickedly and leaned down for a kiss, slowly tasting me. He swept me up with a storm of emotions, but I was already head-over-heels in love with him.

CHAPTER EIGHTEEN

After our trip at the Southwind Inn, things were a little sticky between Aliah and Hunter to say the least. A few weeks had gone by and Aliah was still giving him the cold shoulder, unwilling to talk to him about what happened.

She was also giving me a hard time about going to the Westmount, where Hunter worked. If she couldn't, then I couldn't. It was a tough sell, but I finally convinced her that it was okay to step foot in the club again. She needed to let off some steam and what better way than to work it out with some cardio?

I cautiously approached the front doors of the Westmount, praying that we wouldn't come across Hunter. We hustled straight to our Zumba class and made it, without incident.

After a good, hard work out, and a quick shower, I hurried into the front hall ahead of Aliah. I thought I would head off any trouble, but my plan backfired brilliantly. When Hunter saw me, he excused himself from his private session to talk. *Shit!*

Aliah wasn't far behind me and was standing at my side when Hunter finally realized I wasn't alone.

"Hey, guys. I haven't seen you in weeks. Aliah, you haven't been returning my calls. We really need to talk," Hunter said, putting her on the spot.

I tried to stay out of it, backing away to remove myself from the line of fire, knowing it was going to get messy.

"You really should've kept it in your pants if you wanted a chance with me," she said, with her eyes narrowed at him.

"I had a moment of weakness. It's not unheard of. I am a man. But Aliah, it's you that I want."

"You should've thought about that before you did Maddison. If that was your way of getting my attention, well congratulations. You got it!" she hollered, hysterically. "Too bad I'm not one for sloppy seconds."

"It's not like that Aliah and you know it," he said, gazing at her through dark, brooding eyes.

Aliah didn't back down. She had plenty of time to decide what she was going to say to him, and she wasn't leaving anything out.

"Sorry to break it to you H-u-n-t-e-r, but life doesn't come with any guarantees or time outs. I can't just snap my fingers and forget it ever happened. I won't! Sorry 'bout your luck."

"You don't have to give me a second chance, Aliah. But you do need to know how I feel. I've made my choice and I choose you."

"Yeah, I buy that," Aliah announced, sarcastically. "I bet you told Maddison that to get her in bed too."

"This has nothing to do with Maddie. Leave her out of it."

"It's a little late for that, wouldn't you say? You fucked her, Hunter. This has everything to do with her!"

"I made my decision; granted it was the wrong one. I'll deal with the consequences."

"Yeah, you do that. A-L-O-N-E. Because I refuse to be your trusty old backup plan."

"Maybe you guys should take this outside," I suggested, trying to step between their heated stares. "Seriously, Hunter, you don't want to lose your job over this."

"Why not, then he'll have more time to fuck around with Maddison." Aliah stomped outside, madder than a wet cat.

Hunter chased after her. I reluctantly followed them, for moral support, though I wished I didn't have to witness the whole charade first hand.

"Back off Hunter! I don't need you to make me feel better. I'm doing just fine without you," Aliah shouted, swatting him away.

"That may be, but we are so much better *together,* Aliah. Please give me another chance," he pleaded.

I couldn't tell whether any of Hunter's words were

getting through to her now, but I knew it would hit her later. She stormed off to my car without a response.

"Sorry. I'll talk to her," I told Hunter, though I knew better than to make empty promises. Regardless, I still owed him one for helping me with Edwin. I hurried to my car where Aliah was waiting to be let in.

"Can you please unlock the door?" she snorted impatiently.

I clicked the button on my keychain and she got in. I slipped into the driver seat and immediately detected that she was on the brink of an emotional melt down.

"Take a breather or you're going to give yourself a heart attack," I said.

"Can you believe him?" she squealed, ignoring my advice. "He actually expects me to believe he's sorry!"

"I don't think he wants Maddie, Ally. Why else would he be going to such trouble?"

"Maybe you're right. But what's going to stop him from having another *moment of weakness*, as he called it? It's bull shit."

"It really sucks, I know. Chances are so hard to come by, and I was lucky Edwin gave me another one. I don't know what I would've done if he didn't take me back."

"It's not the same," Aliah groaned.

"How's it so different?"

"There was no sex involved. That definitely ups the ante."

"Fine, I'll give you that," I said. "It's still fresh. But that bad feeling in the pit of your stomach will fade eventually. And I'd bet he would do anything to prove himself to you, if you'd just give him the chance."

"Yeah, I just can't do it. It's still all too much for me. I believe that there's only one person you're destined to be with. I just can't see how that man-whore could possibly be my destiny."

"Well, that's your decision and you make a good point, but you know Maddie was making it very difficult for him to say no. She was throwing herself at him and he is just a man."

"Whatever. Please don't repeat his lame excuse. A cheater is a cheater."

She was right. And I agreed. But I also truly believed that Hunter was one of the good ones. Aliah thought so too, or she wouldn't have fallen so hard for him.

"I realize that, but you pulling Maddie's hair and all didn't exactly help the situation. It just made him feel sorry for her."

Anger was floating in Aliah's eyes. "That bitch totally took advantage of the situation. Ugh, I hate her!"

"Yeah, shit happens. What's new?"

Aliah crawled out of my car. "I'm not giving that bastard another chance. I don't care what you say."

The words came out of her mouth, but I could already sense the strength of them diminishing.

"Okay," I answered. "Call me if you need me."

She grunted some unintelligible words and slammed the door shut. I waved goodbye and barrelled back to my place, leaving just enough time to grab a bite to eat. Edwin and I had a date with the couch.

When I walked in my front door, Edwin was sitting at the couch already and had an iced-mocha latte and a bag from Timmy's waiting for me.

"You're here," he said. "I was starting to think you weren't going to make it in time."

"Babe, you're so sweet." I dropped my bag, plopped down onto the couch and curled up next to him, scooping up my treat. "Thanks."

I pulled a big hunk of muffin out of the bag and popped it into my mouth. Between my iced-latte, the icy air conditioning and my recent wet hair, I had to pull on a throw blanket that was conveniently tossed over the back of the couch. Our house was absolutely frigid and I loved it.

"My toes are cold," I said, inching them under my rear.

"I'll warm them up," Edwin said, reaching out an open palm.

I gladly leaned against the arm of the couch, and let

Edwin work his magic. He sniffed my feet sensually as he pulled off the fresh socks. The pressure of his fingers felt so good, but then Edwin brought my foot to his lips.

"Eww, stop!" I squealed. "You know I hate that. It's so gross!"

"If you say so," Edwin teased, dropping a wet kiss on the top of my foot. "I guess your feet will freeze then." Ignoring my wincing, he sucked on my baby toe.

I yanked my foot away and jammed it under his butt to warm them up, with an unconvincing pout on my lips. Edwin smiled and I knew it was because he would lick my every toe if I let him. I never would.

After watching a show together, we left the TV on in the background and talked about our day.

Before long Edwin was kissing me, but it was soft and innocent, being that I had already satisfied him earlier in the day. Twice.

By ten thirty, we were both ready for bed, the joys of working a nine to five, so we hit the sack. Our sleeping arrangements had been sporadic ever since our trip. Though we had slept in the same bed together every night since, we both loved our own beds so much that we had to agree to switch beds every couple of nights to be fair.

"My bed tonight, baby!" I cheered, skipping to my room.

Edwin followed me, though much less enthusiastic about it. I hadn't found the right time to have that serious conversation about our future together yet, but I knew it was only a matter of time.

If we were going to make our house a family home, then we would have to start living that way.

As I lay next to Edwin quietly in bed, I thought about how I would bring it up without totally freaking him out. He wasn't exactly commitment-phobic, but I knew stunning him with it was a bad idea. I would have to ease in on it.

"Want to have sex?" Edwin asked.

"We had sex this morning," I reminded him. "And at lunch."

"So. We used to have sex at least twice a day, usually

three times."

"Yeah, but it's not possible for a couple to keep that up forever. Besides, I had a long day and I'm exhausted."

"Fine," he replied, but from the tone I knew the pleading wasn't over.

A few seconds later, "Seriously Abby, I need sex. Your skin's so soft, it's turning me on. If you don't have sex with me I'll never fall asleep."

"Edwin!"

"I'll do the dishes for you tomorrow."

"Hah! You say that now. Are you willing to put that in writing?"

"Yeah, tomorrow."

"Mmm, hmm. I'm not in the business of giving the service before I get paid. I know the odds."

"You can bet on me," he said, deviously. "You know I always deliver."

He leaned in close and kissed me tenderly, his hands delivering a gentle caress. Though I tried to fight off his advances, so I could worry about our future, he won me over with his touch. We made love, quick and efficient, and before I knew it, I was back in happy land.

"That was quick," I said, still tingling from head to toe.

"Yeah, but it was good," he replied confidently.

"Very good. Can I go to sleep now?"

"I meant to ask you earlier tonight... but I forgot. Don't get mad," Edwin said, freaking me out.

"Forgot what?" I asked anxiously, instantly taking a roundtrip back to worryland.

"I want to take you to the Corsette Caves this weekend. I was going to surprise you, but I don't want to piss you off. Are you mad?"

"No. But isn't it the Festival of Lights this weekend? We can't miss it. We go every year."

"Oh shit, yeah. Well, if we go early in the morning, we should have enough time to explore the caves during the day and be back in time for the light show."

"Okay," I said, too exhausted to argue. "Night, Eddie," I

sputtered, through a hushed yawn.

He settled in and hooked his arm around me. "Night, Abs."

"Love you," I whispered, pulling his warm hand up under my chin and tucking him close behind me.

"Love you too, babe." He snuggled his face in my soft, messy hair.

Ahh, silence at last. Time to return to my worries in the safety of my own head. But as I tried to focus my burdened brain, a foggy haze swept over my eyes, closing my heavy lids and shutting out the night.

I am not a morning person. I have never been a morning person. I will never be a morning person. Nevertheless, someone had decided to wake me from my peaceful slumber at the bright and early hour of six.

To awaken to the sound of the insufferable ring of the phone could only be described as debilitating.

"Can you get that," I moaned, with aggravated frustration. I swept my hand over the bed behind me and found it vacant and cold.

The realization that Edwin was already out of bed just stoked my annoyance with a marshmallow roaster. The phone did not stop and, unable to bear another chime, I steam rolled out of the bed and jammed all the buttons with my eyes half closed.

"Hello?" I snarled.

"Abby, is that you?" a woman whispered.

"What," I growled incoherently, still having difficulty finding consciousness.

"Can you talk?" she continued quietly.

"Who the hell is this?" I asked, finally coming to.

"It's Maddison."

Stunned, I tried to conjure up why Maddie would be calling me at such an hour, but came up short. "Why are you whispering?" I asked, suddenly very curious.

"I don't want Edwin to hear what I have to say."

I could hear the hum of the jets and the water streaming around our deep tub. That would explain why Edwin didn't pick up the phone. "You don't have to worry; Edwin's in the shower. What is it that couldn't wait for work?"

"I'm so sorry for bugging you, but I didn't know who else to call. Can you promise to keep a secret? Even Edwin can't know."

"You know I won't do that, Maddie. But I can lend an ear if I must."

"Then promise me. Promise me that you'll help me first and judge later," she demanded. I could sense the tears trickling into her throat, stifling her voice.

"What is it?"

"Promise!" she cried.

Secrets can murder your relationship.

It was way too early to be thinking such heavy, unstable thoughts and attempting to rationalize them, but what was I so afraid of?

Secrets will murder your relationship.

"Fine. I promise. But you know as well as I do that secrets are a relationship killer. I doubt that Edwin would care anyway. Now tell me."

After a lengthy silence, I started to really worry. What could be that important? "Are you injured?" I asked.

"No!" she cried.

"Dying?" I asked softly, more concerned than ever.

"No, damn it! I'm pregnant."

CHAPTER NINETEEN

I'm pregnant? That was the last thing I expected to hear. The nightmare for Maddie had just begun and, at the risk of Edwin hearing my shock, I tried to reserve my tongue.

"What?" I gasped, and then covered my mouth with my hand after noticing my pitch.

"I know. I've taken like every test the pharmacy has and they all say pregnant. I thought I could sleep it off, you know? But nope... still pregnant."

Maddie started to cry hysterically and suddenly my selfishness stifled me. I recognized the sound of the shower curtain as Edwin flung it open.

Shit! Maddie needed a friend, a shoulder and a sounding board, and with Edwin on the prowl I wouldn't be able to console her.

"Maddie, Edwin is coming. I have to let you go. Where are you now?"

"I'm at home," she sobbed, wiping away the snot with her shirt sleeve.

"Okay, I'm going to get ready for work and then I'll be over as soon as I can."

"Hurry, please," she cried.

I cradled the handheld in the receiver, but it was too late. Before I spun around, I could sense that Edwin had entered the room.

He wore a fluffy towel, wrapped loosely around his hips, with his hair still wet and spiky. His eyes were warm and relaxed, but they still revealed his curiosity. He knew something was up. *Shit!*

Secrets can murder your relationship.

"Who was that?" he asked.

"Maddie," I answered, promptly.

"What did she want?"

Don't lie. Don't lie. Don't lie.

"She has a really upset stomach and is pretty anxious about it. She asked if I would come over to check her out."

"I wonder why she called you?" he said, honestly stunned. "Can't she drive herself to a walk-in clinic?"

Secrets will murder your relationship.

"I don't know. She's pretty upset. Sam must have been busy."

"Busy sleeping maybe. Since when did you and Maddie become best friends?" he asked sarcastically.

"Now there's a stretch. We're not *best friends*. Ever since the Southwind, we've kind of just reached a sort of understanding I guess."

"I hope that understanding doesn't start calling you every morning at this hour."

"No, I think it's safe to say this is a special incident. I promise to tell you more later." *There...not a total lie.*

"Okay, I'll drop you off at her place then and you can drive in with her later," Edwin suggested. "I wanted to get in to the office extra early this morning anyway."

Maddie would be incredibly disappointed if she knew Edwin drove me over. Hysterical and tear-ridden, she was also in no shape to drive.

"It's okay. I can drive myself," I said. I walked over to my dresser and could feel Edwin's curious eyes on me. I opened my top drawer and dug around in it, as deceit stabbed at my lower back with a large, heavy, ice pick.

"Are you sure?" he asked.

"Yeah, I'll see you at work." I pulled out a camisole and dropped it onto my dresser.

"Okay," Edwin agreed, stepping toward me cautiously.

He kissed me quickly on the lips and I watched his amazing ass disappear out the door. He knew something was up and I couldn't bear to face him again, until I could give him an explanation.

I sprang from my room and slipped into the bathroom before Edwin could catch me. I closed the door quietly behind me and, despite my urge to lock the door, I knew it would bite me in the ass later if Edwin had noticed. We never lock each other out.

I cranked the shower on hot and stripped from my night clothes. I stepped out of the pile beneath me and dragged open the curtain. Steam escaped from the shower and I hurried inside to retain some of the vapour.

Though I had promised Maddie I would be quick, a good thirty minutes passed before I finally retrieved myself from the bathtub. Another fifteen minutes spent on hair and makeup assured me that Edwin would be long gone.

I crept out of the room, just in case he was still there, and tip-toed to my bedroom. All was quiet in the house as I dressed for work.

It was supposed to be a scorcher out today, so I pulled on a thin grey pencil skirt and short-sleeved white blouse. I tugged a light sweater off its hanger, knowing the office was always extra cold on days like these, and hustled downstairs.

A chocolate-chip granola bar and bottle of orange juice would have to suffice for breakfast, since it was all my kitchen had to offer on the run. I yanked my keys off the hook and dangled my handbag from my forearm.

As I slipped on my last shoe, I heard noises coming from my driveway, and was struck with the realization that Edwin may not have left the building.

I carefully pulled the window covering oh so slightly aside to find Edwin getting in his truck. The engine rumbled as he turned it on, but he was taking his good old time with his a/c and music selection.

Edwin was definitely a morning person; relaxing, appreciating, enjoying and taking complete pleasure out of the simple things in life. After minutes of observing him, he unexpectedly looked up at the house. I removed my unprotected eye from the window and waited to learn my demise.

My heart raced a quarter mile before I finally I heard the roar of his truck engine, as he motored off to work. I gasped for a breath. I had been holding it ever since I thought

Edwin had caught me spying on him.

Edwin was gone but I was frozen in place for a good ten seconds before I took another deep breath and raced out to my car. Edwin had done a good job of making it look so pleasant outside. I was not expecting to be slammed with a wall of humidity.

Being miserably faced with the sticky heat of summer that was locked up in my car, I jabbed my keys into the ignition and cranked my air conditioner on full blast. As I sped out of the driveway at record speed, I eased my windows down, to let out the stifling heat.

With a light knock on Maddie's door, it opened; before I had even removed my knuckle from the hard surface. I walked into her living area and took a seat on the oversized blue suede chair, avoiding the mismatched couch with a mountain of used tissues piled up on it.

Apparently I had come in at a bad time. Maddie looked like she was on the brink of bawling again.

"It's going to be okay," I said. "You don't even know for sure that you're pregnant."

"I do know that my period's late and the damned tests all say that I am. And since when did I cry like a blubbering fool?" she squealed. "I am so pregnant."

"You should probably get a blood test done to be sure, you know, before you start announcing it to everyone."

She broke down in a flurry of cries and sniffles. "I feel so alone," she sobbed.

I reluctantly transferred myself to the couch and rested a hand on Maddie's shoulder. "You'll tell the man who did this to you and you won't be alone anymore," I explained, but the look on Maddie's face told me all I needed to know.

"You *are* going to tell the father, Maddie. You have to." After a pause, "Who is the father anyway? Please tell me you know."

"That's the problem!"

I gasped. "You don't know who it is? Maddie!"

"No, Abby! Give me some credit. The problem is I know exactly who it is. It can only be one."

I thought to myself for a minute and was stunned when I came to realize who it could be. *Jay? Hunter?*

I gasped again. "No."

"Yes," she cried.

"You didn't! No protection, Maddie, for God's sake. What did you think was going to happen?"

"It wasn't supposed to happen like that, but it just did. It was special, and not just for me, Hunter thought so to."

I was speechless. I knew I was there for Maddie at this very moment, but it was hard for me to stay on her side when Aliah was going to be so hurt by this new information.

"The thing is, I've only talked to Hunter a couple of times since then. I was hoping we could go on a date, but he never really showed any interest. I gave him my number, but he didn't call."

"Yeah, it's called a booty call for a reason. You know? A one night stand," I said, wishing I hadn't used such a harsh tone.

"It was more than that," she stammered.

"Really, then why hasn't he called?" I asked, softer now.

"Well, maybe he'll rethink that now that I'm pregnant."

"You can hope. But you knew that night that he and Aliah were sort of an item."

"Whatever. He couldn't have cared too much about her if he spent the night with me. The whole night. It was amazing, Abby. He was so sensitive to my needs."

"I'm sorry, but I really don't want to hear this. I'm in too deep already. How do you expect me to keep this from Aliah... and Edwin? You better figure this out and quick."

"What's there to figure out? I'm pregnant and Hunter's the father. I'm going to tell him today."

"It'd probably be a good idea to go check in with your doctor first. Those tests have been known to be wrong. As soon as the doctor confirms you're plus one, then you can tell him."

"Fine, let's go."

"What? I have to go to work."

"I think you can make this one exception," she insisted

sourly.

I was hesitant. Missing work was a bad idea. Both of us missing work was a disastrous rumor just waiting to happen.

"Please, Abby? I don't want to go alone."

"Well, you really shouldn't have to do this alone," I said, feeling sorry for her. "I guess I can tell Owen I'll be a little late."

Maddie immediately leapt from the couch for the kitchen phone, knocking tissues all over the floor. She dialed her Doctor's number, as I rummaged through my purse for my cell.

I dialed Owen's direct line and his voicemail picked up immediately. I couldn't fathom the thought of stretching the truth anymore, even if only on voicemail, so I dialed 0 and my call was transferred to reception.

"They can take me right at nine," Maddie chimed, as she returned from the kitchen.

Taylor's phone rang and rang until her voicemail finally picked up. I left her a message, begging a favour, that she tell Owen I have an appointment and I'll be a little late.

The doctor's office turned out to be only a few short blocks from our office. That made me incredibly anxious. I prayed that no one from our staff would see my car parked in the small, open parking lot. That would cause even more trouble for us both.

I followed Maddie into the small, white entrance, and down the long, white corridor. The waiting room was crowded but, to my surprise, when Maddie walked up to the secretary, she was welcomed right in to an examination room.

"I'll wait out here," I said, as Maddie looked back to me expectantly.

"Please come in, Abby. I'll owe you big," she begged.

Not wanting to fight with a pregnant lady, I agreed. "Fine." I sighed and followed her down the short, narrow hall to her room. The nurse smiled at both of us warmly and thoughtfully closed the door. We both took a seat in one of the grey padded chairs.

"I changed my mind. You should tell Hunter now, so I don't have to do all this crap," I groaned.

"It's a little late for that I would say. Seriously Abby, I'm lucky to have a friend as good as you."

"Sorry, but I have to admit, I was a little surprised that you called me."

"Well this situation is a little sticky. Not exactly something I want to call and tell my mother about... or even Sam for that matter. She wouldn't know how to deal. You really are the only one that knows the atmosphere from that night... you understand what happened," she said, dragging me deeper into the mess.

"What do you mean exactly? I knew you hung out with Hunter and went for a walk on the beach. The only reason anyone thinks otherwise is because he was in your room the next morning. I just figured it out for certain last night, when Ally called him out on it and he didn't deny having slept with you."

"I guess I just felt like you would be more understanding. I guess I was wrong."

"Hey! I'm here aren't I?"

"Yes. And I thank you for that."

There was a light knock on the door, and a short, large woman with fluffy, plain hair, and a long white overcoat entered the room. "Maddison! What brings you in today my dear?"

"I'm pregnant," she replied, cutting to the chase.

Her doctor chuckled heartily at her expression. "Congratulations."

"Thank you. My friend just thought it would be a good idea to get my blood tested. Can you do that now?" she asked, foot to the metal.

"Absolutely. But first I'll need a urine sample. You can take this cup to the washroom and I'll have a nurse prep you for the blood work. We can take a look at the calendar when you get back."

Maddie's mouth frowned and her eyes were filled with

an empty sadness.

I directed a quizzical look at her to amuse her. "You can do that yourself," I teased, and her doctor chuckled heartily again.

Maddie sheepishly left the room and suddenly I was very alone with her doctor. Without warning, as the doctor scribbled feverishly on Maddie's chart, a hit of jealousy knocked me over my skull.

Dizzy and confused, I tried to push those thoughts aside, but it was all too much for me. Sitting in the smallish exam room, I realized I was a selfish, jealous beoch.

Never had I imagined that tagging along with Maddie would drum up this response from my subconscious.

It's no secret among my close friends that I want a baby. Prior to our Southwind trip, it was all I could think about.

Find a man. Convince him to marry me. Demand a baby.

It seemed all too easy in my mind, but I didn't consider the latest development. Edwin. Though I've tried to find a good time to talk to Edwin about having children, I've learned that no time is ever a good time. Edwin being *that man* put a whole new spin on things.

Now that Maddie was going to have Hunter's child, I would have a situation to compare to.

No more waiting. The time had come.

Maddie's doctor had finished with her chicken scratch and was smiling at me across the desk.

"Abigail?"

I shook my head confused. "Huh? What?" I replied.

Maddie was not only sitting next to me, but announcing the news. "Did you hear that? I'm due April second! Can you believe it?" Maddie squealed, sounding overjoyed.

No, I can't believe I managed to block out a whole conversation while I drowned in my own thoughts. "Wow, congrats," I said, faking a smile.

Her sudden joy was depressing and I was sure my jealousy was written all over my face.

"We'll call you when your blood work comes back, but the urine test seems to indicate that you are indeed pregnant."

"Thank you, doctor," Maddie chimed, as she was escorted to the exit.

The walk to my car was quiet.

I broke the silence first. "Are you heading in to work?"

"No. I think I'd better go pick up some prenatal vitamins, and have a talk with Hunter. This isn't the sort of thing you put off. I already called Miller and told him I was taking the day off because I wasn't feeling well. Suddenly I'm feeling a whole lot better." She smiled softly and rested her hand on her flat belly.

Wasting no time at all, Maddie called the fire station. Apparently Hunter was at work. I wasn't even going to ask why she had his work number on speed dial. Hunter was on the phone in a matter of minutes. Their discussion was short.

"Well, here goes nothing," Maddie said. "Hunter will meet me at the café up the road in fifteen minutes. Wish me luck."

"Good luck," I said.

"Thanks again for understanding, Abby. I knew I could count on you. You really are a good friend."

"Such a good friend that you'll let me tell Edwin tonight?" I begged. "It's only a matter of time before everyone knows anyway."

"I guess it'll be okay, as long as you wait until you get home to tell him. I want to be sure Hunter is the next to know."

"Deal," I said, exchanging a friendly hug. "Congrats, by the way."

"Okay, thanks. And thanks for the ride," Maddie said, as she whirled away toward the café.

"Don't you want me to wait with you?" I asked.

She kept on walking. "I've wasted enough of your time. You should probably get to work. I can ask Hunter for a ride home and, if that doesn't seem like a good idea, I can always call a cab."

"Okay, if you're sure. Let me know how you make out."

"You know I will." She smiled and disappeared behind the next building, totally optimistic and utterly annoying.

Why couldn't I be brimming with sunshine? I should be happy for the girl. More confused than ever I headed straight for work.

"Good morning," I said to Taylor, as she greeted me in the office lobby.

"Oh! Hey, Abigail. Owen was just looking for you a minute ago. I never told him that you were going to be late. I thought you might get away without him knowing," she said.

Worriedly, I rushed to my desk. Why did she have to do that? I frantically clambered around my space, starting my computer and pulling out the pile of new work that lined my mess of a desk. My anxiety sharpened when I briefly checked over all of the deadlines.

"Just the girl I've been looking for," Owen said, as he peered in my doorway. My computer beeped, and on flashed the monitor, perfectly publicizing my lateness.

"Yes?" I asked.

"Is everything okay?"

"Everything's fine. Why do you ask?"

"You're half an hour late. That's unlike you. You usually you tell me when you're going to be late."

"Actually, I did call. You weren't in your office, so I left a message on Taylor's voicemail. I'm sorry you didn't get it. I was at the doctor's."

"Okay. Do you know where I might find the Jaxon file? I can't seem to find it anywhere."

It was such a relief to hear that he wasn't going to dwell on it. "Did you check the vault?"

He nodded. I stood from my desk, brushed past him and crossed the hall to the vault. He followed at a distance and stood in the doorway as I slid the large shelves of files on rollers aside. Three shelves deep, I located 'J' and thumbed through the files.

Jacklin, Jacobs, Jasmine, Jasper. Ah ha! Jaxon. "Here it is," I said, pulling it from the cabinet.

"Huh! I looked there twice and couldn't find it."

"I guess you just needed a fresh set of eyes," I said, hoping he'd forgive my tardiness.

It seemed to work too, because he took the file from me and headed for the door. "Thanks Abigail," he said, before rushing back to his office.

A few hours later, I rested my head on the table in the staff lunch room. I had to get away from my heaping desk. After munching on my flavourless snack, I closed my heavy eyes. It was an oddly lonely lunch hour, everyone else having either gone out or worked straight through theirs.

I crumpled up my baggie and figured it'd be smart for me to get back to business too but, before I could lift myself from my chair, Edwin appeared in the door and approached me with dangerously naughty intent in his expression.

"Doctors appointment, eh?" Edwin's voice sounded cool and sexy.

"What are you talking about?" I asked, figuring he couldn't have known.

"I overheard you talking to Owen this morning. I was in the copier room."

"Of course you were. You listened in on my conversation, did you?"

"Quit changing the subject. You told me you were going to Maddie's house for a cramp emergency. So, which is it?" Suddenly his tone was as sharp as a razor blade, making my knees knock under the table.

"I won't lie. I was at the doctor's. But it wasn't for me. Please don't make me break my promise. I have to keep my mouth shut for now. I will tell you all about it later."

"You can trust me. This is me were talking," Edwin pressed, testing my secrecy.

I sighed, closed my eyes tightly, and considered the consequences of telling Edwin before we got home. "You know I was at the doctor's office. You figure it out," I said, without giving him any more hints.

"Maddie?"

My eyes widened. "Very clever of you; now zip your lips before someone else hears you. I told you, I'll tell you all about it tonight."

"Tell him all about what?" Aliah asked, as she entered the room.

Great. Maddie's only fear was playing out right before my eyes. I'm a freaking gossip whore. Aliah was the last person who should be finding out about this from me. It's not my place. It's not my job.

"I can't deal with this right now," I exploded, and then thrashed past Aliah in a moment of senseless frustration.

"Okay then. Happy day to you too," Aliah replied, as I stomped off down the hall.

Back in the lunch room, Edwin and Aliah stared at each other for a long time, until they both agreed that it must be that time of the month for me.

"So. You and Hunter. You good?" Edwin asked.

"Yeah, I think Hunter and I are on the mend. We had a long talk yesterday and kind of figured things out. It'll take some time, but I think it might be worth the work."

"Good to hear. Hunter's a good guy."

"Yeah. That's what they keep telling me. Well, I gotta get back to work. I was just coming to say hello, but that didn't exactly go over very well," Aliah smirked at Edwin.

"Yeah. I'll go talk to her."

"Good man," Aliah said. She patted Edwin on the shoulder and scurried back to her desk.

Edwin veered for mine and found me frozen in my chair. My hands were covering my face, as I contemplated my crazy life. I spun around, worried that it might be Owen hovering in door, and then sighed.

"Don't worry. I'm not going to ask you any more questions. Tonight. I get it."

I took a deep breath and sighed again, this time with relief. I leapt from my chair and wrapped my arms around Edwin's neck. "Thank you," I whispered.

Edwin pried my arms off of him and smiled playfully. "As much as I like this; it's not appropriate business etiquette," he teased. "Later."

When he winked, my heart warmed. And when he pecked my lips, even though they were the only part of his body touching mine, it still ignited all of my senses.

"I'll see you at home then?" I asked. The sooner I could get the news off my chest the better.

"Absolutely. Ahh. Uhh... actually," he stuttered. "Shit. I totally forgot. I have a dinner meeting right after work with Miller. It's an important client. Looks like you're on your own for dinner tonight."

"No," I pouted.

I can come home right after, if you want. They'll probably do drinks though."

I was done being a selfish beoch for the day. "No, it's okay. Stay as long as you like. We'll talk later. Love you."

"Love you too, baby," he replied. And after another quick smooch, he disappeared down the hall.

Just then, Aliah peeked around the corner. "I don't have any plans, if you want to do something," she suggested.

Startled, I jumped back for a second, and looked around to see who else I was missing. "What is wrong with this place? Everyone's so damn nosy."

"S-o-r-r-y," Aliah snapped. Another time then. You're obviously having one of those days."

"Yeah, maybe. I'm actually not feeling all that great. I'll probably just pull on some PJs as soon as I get home and lay around the house; maybe even hit the hay early." I couldn't bear to spend another minute with Aliah, knowing the secret hanging over our heads.

"Okay, if you say so," Aliah replied, before trotting away wounded.

I was having one of those days. The kind where no matter how hard you tried, you just couldn't clear your mind long enough to get anything accomplished. At least I had managed to finish off my day at work without any more major catastrophes.

When I got home and walked in my quiet, empty house, my nerves were set on fire, though the air conditioning blasted on cold. I shivered with awareness, senses on high alert. But aware of what? I couldn't say.

The dead silence pierced through my ear drums, so I pulled my I-Pod from my purse and plugged the white headphones into my ears. Music always had a way of soothing even the darkest of days.

I jogged up the stairs, taking two at a time. I quickly stripped from my suit and dropped it in a heap on the floor. I pulled on some grey sweat pants and zipped a hot pink sweater over my camisole, with the music thrumming steadily in my ears.

Despite the loud distraction, nothing could disguise the hunger twitching in my gut that was growling a song of its own. *Maybe that's the cause of this ridiculously massive headache.*

After hanging up my dry cleaning, I turned the music up even louder, hoping to pound away the deprivation long enough to prepare something to eat. *Not gonna happen tonight.* I was starving.

I dashed down the stairs and hit the kitchen up for a bottle of pop and a slice of bread. A spoon and the jar of peanut butter came next. I carried it all to my comfy couch and sat in front of the TV, licking peanut butter from the spoon. Disgusting, I know, but so comforting.

My eyes were feeling sore from my early morning rise and a hard day's work. Though the show playing on the screen was broadcast in HD, it looked like a blur of colour to me. Music still droning, I shut my eyes and tilted my head back against the corner of the couch.

So many worries tumbled through my mind, the very things I had been trying to avoid all day. Apart from my own issues, I hadn't heard from Maddie and that caused me some concern.

I shunned all thoughts from my mangled mind and focused on mental imagery. Plain white ceilings. Four white walls. Bareness. Blankness. Emptiness. Nothingness... until I passed out from exhaustion.

I shivered suddenly, as an icy feeling spread across my entire body and woke me from a heady nightmare. I forced open my heavy eyes, and tried to focus them, but they burned with ache and delivered only blurred vision.

I was being watched. I could feel it. It felt like a single, dead, icy finger being dragged up my spine. The hairs stood on my arms and prickled my skin, an alarming unease attacking me. My unreliable eyes darted toward the front window and then across the room, with the loud hum of music only amping up my anxiety.

It was dark outside, but the nightlight in the kitchen was on and the television illuminated the house enough for me to see what I had to. The shadows spoon fed me impending doom. I ripped the earphones from my ears and threw them to the floor. The silence was deafening.

I tossed the open container of peanut butter on the couch and leapt up to grab the phone in my defence. I hugged it against my breasts and very slowly glanced into the kitchen, bracing myself for what I might find, but not being ready for what I found.

A shadow flickered across my kitchen floor and a dark silhouette swiftly appeared in the small window above my sink. My eyes locked on the dark figure, framed in my window.

I couldn't move, frozen in fright, in voiceless agony. The only indication of movement was my violently trembling hands clutching at the phone. Then the shadow slowly, sluggishly, turned to look in the window.

Terrified that I had been detected, I fumbled with the phone and jammed the buttons erratically with my thumb until a green glow lit my face. I frantically looked back at the window, but there was no one there.

A tree branch swayed in the wind, casting leery shadows across my kitchen floor that I couldn't explain.

Am I going crazy?

My heart beat rushed ahead of me, as I contemplated my next move. Had Edwin remembered to lock the back door after he took out the garbage this morning?

My nerves were shot, but I was convinced that someone was stalking me. Whoever it was, was still prowling my backyard among the shadows.

An ear-splitting beeping noise started to blare from the phone, telling me to hang it up, but I couldn't tear my eyes from the window. As I crept toward the kitchen, the phone stung my every nerve, my limbs jerking with vicious tremors.

Quickly realizing that the phone wasn't a very useful weapon against an intruder, I pounded a handful of buttons until it turned off. My eyes shifted to the patio door and stared at the dead bolt, begging for it to be turned over. It wasn't.

Petrified, and with one last shallow breath, I scurried to the drawer of knives and pulled out the biggest one I could find. I shakily crushed the large, shiny handle in my right hand, the cordless clung to my left.

My eyes darted from shadow to shadow inside my vulnerable home. The music had rendered my memory useless, my nap stealing the knowledge of whether the stalker was alone.

It has not been in the house. It was not in the house. It is not in the house.

Going only on a whim, for sanity's sake, I decided there was only one intruder; and it was outside. Though I kept telling myself that, I knew my false hopes could not deceive my eyes and ears. It was so dark. If I could only hear over the ringing in my ears.

I leaned restlessly toward the kitchen window and peered out the clear black pane. My eyes darted across the dark back yard, but found nothing in the shadows. I breathed a deep sigh of relief, believing that the peeping Tom had moved on.

With the knife gripped stiffly in my trembling right hand,

I held the phone to my heaving chest, as a sense of hasty relief washed over me.

Suddenly, my heart bored into my esophagus, when I caught a flash of darkness wash over the floor. I twisted abruptly to see what it was and found a pair of red, glowing eyes staring at me from the shadows, mere inches from the window pane.

I screamed in horror, the phone dropping from my hand and shattering to pieces around me, as I fell backward onto the hard ceramic floor. The shiny blade of the large knife sliced my delicate skin and spilled my blood everywhere.

Before I could comprehend what was happening, there was a knock at my front door and a harassing ring of the doorbell.

Could it be the intruder?

Blood continued to shower from my wound as I fumbled to pick up the knife, smearing dark patches across the cold floor. I stared at the growing pool of blood, but continued to cling to the knife for dear life. My eyes failed me, the room turning into a foggy shadow.

I tried to focus on the floor, but it only stunned me even more, the blood turning from a dark red to black. I tore my eyes away and reached for the dish cloth hanging on the stove. I wrapped my wrist and squeezed the cloth tightly in my hand, with my back pressing tight against the cabinets.

Tears began to sting my eyes as the doorbell rang again and again. All sense told me not to answer it. All sense told me to lock the door. I rushed to the back patio door and fumbled with the lock. As it turned over, more blood smeared across the white surface.

Feeling too exposed in front of the window, I hurried to the next room and wondered... *How many criminals actually use the front door?*

With the bloody weapon in hand, I took my chance, ready to strike. I sprinted to the front door, bumping my leg on the couch, but not taking it as a sign to back down. I flashed on the outdoor light with a bloody finger, and fearfully glanced out the glazed window.

CHAPTER TWENTY

I whipped the door open. The bloody knife dropped to the floor with a clang. I flung my arms around Maddie's neck and started to gasp for air, crying hysterically.

Stunned, she held me, comforting me like an adult would a battered child. "Is everything okay?" she asked, her hand smoothing over my back.

"Hurry," I cried, tugging her over the threshold.

She anxiously glanced over her shoulder as I tugged her inside and slammed the door behind her. I instantly rolled over the dead bolt with my uninjured hand, still visibly shaking.

"What's going on? Do you need an ambulance?" she shouted, noticing the bloody knife and the dark smears on the floor and wall.

"It's nothing." I gasped, trying to pull myself together. "I'm fine." But the tears still streaked my pale face and the blood continued to soak the towel in my hand.

"Then I hope you didn't get any blood on me." She checked herself over.

My wits urged me to regain some common sense. "It was an accident. It just happened. I'm okay. I just need to clean up this mess."

"Are you sure? It looks pretty bad."

"It looks a lot worse than it is... really," I persisted.

"Is Edwin home? I didn't see his truck outside."

"No. He had a dinner tonight. It's just me. Please don't call him."

"You're sure you're okay?"

"Yes. But do you think you could give me a hand? I really don't want him to come home and find this mess. He'd have a bird for sure."

Maddie sighed, then walked toward the kitchen. "Let's

get you cleaned up first and then we'll worry about the walls. And the floor," she added, as she stepped into the crime scene.

I couldn't argue with that, and Maddie did a fine job of wrapping me up. Her motherly instincts must have kicked in already. The walls were sparkling, as if they were never drenched in my blood. How she did it, I'd never know.

"Thank you so much for washing up for me. I owe you big."

"I'd say we're even. But that was a lot of blood, Abby. Are you sure you won't let me take you to the hospital?"

"I'm sure."

The house was back to normal, my wrist was covered in a clean bandage and, apart from my throbbing wound, it felt like the incident had never happened. Lucky for me the cut was superficial enough that I wouldn't need stiches.

Maddie was extremely understanding, and didn't judge me for freaking out over the *minor* incident. I may have left out a few tid-bits here and there, but why dwell on things such as glow in the dark eyes?

"You should really report it to the police. That's so creepy," Maddie said, when I finished giving her the sane version of events.

"I know, right? But seriously, it's fine. A one-time thing. Nothing to worry about. I promise I'll tell Edwin about it when he gets home."

"Okay. But in the meantime, are you still up for some company? I could really use someone to talk to."

I actually desperately wanted her to stay, so I wouldn't be left to my own crazy devise. "That'd be great. Stay. Please." I could use the distraction.

"You're sure you want to hear my troubles?" Maddie asked, giving me one last escape from the imminent storm of chatter.

"Yes, I do. Tell me... how did it go?"

Maddie walked to the couch and plopped down with a sigh. "It could have gone better. But I guess it could have been a lot worse."

Maddie stopped to take notice of my jar of peanut butter, with spoon still intact. She squinted at it and then glanced at me probingly, attacking my gluttonous snack.

"Hey, don't judge."

"Are you sure you're not pregnant too?" she teased, smirking at me. "Cuz that would be too convenient."

"Hah! Absolutely not! It's just been a long day. Now tell me what he said."

"Okay, well, first he said he couldn't believe he's going to be a dad and asked how I could be so sure that it's his. Then I explained that he's the only one. I told him that I wasn't exactly planning on having sex with him. Seriously, it all happened so fast. By the end of our discussion he agreed that he got me into this mess and he'd deal with it. Quite frankly, he's my baby daddy whether he likes it or not."

"Wow. Are you okay?" I asked, unsure how she'd feel about that.

"I feel much better now that I laid it all out on the table. Even though Hunter doesn't want to be with me, he's still here for me. That's got to count for something."

"What about Aliah?"

"He told me he's working on things with her and he wants to see where that goes. But he also admitted that this isn't entirely my fault. He even agreed that something special happened between us that night. So in other words, he's going to take care of me and the baby."

"Well that's good," I replied, shocked and impressed with Hunter's righteousness. I considered probing, to learn more about that *something special* she was talking about, but decided to stay out of it.

"It's a start anyway. I'm still banking on the fact that Aliah'll blow it with him and then he'll be all mine." She smirked, totally confident in Aliah's faults.

"Keep those comments to yourself, please. You know Aliah's my best friend."

"Best friend or not, you know she's always blowing it. She's no good for Hunter."

"Oh, and you're so much better?" I teased.

"Whatever. Now that I've tainted Aliah's image of Hunter, it's only a matter of time before she moves on to the next."

"You may have pegged Aliah, but Hunter doesn't look like he's going to give up that easily."

"He's not as persistent as I am," Maddie reminded me.

So true. And I laughed it off, only because if I didn't, I would have to strangle her for her blunt honesty.

"I bet we made a real beautiful baby though. Perfect tanned skin, dark luscious hair, just to name a few of Hunter's staggering qualities. Oh! I hope my baby gets his hazel eyes. They're so gorgeous." Maddie was beaming, lost in her own fantasyland.

Seeing Maddie so happy made it easier for me to forget about my mental instability and focus again on my superficial dilemmas. "Well, since you have your situation under control, maybe I can confide in you *my* troubles."

"Of course. I'm good at giving advice. Shoot."

"Okay, so it's about me and Edwin."

"There's a shocker. Trouble on the homestead?" she asked, eager to hear.

"No. Not yet anyway. But I have an ultimatum for him. And it scares me half to death when I imagine what he might say."

"What exactly are we talking about here?" Maddie seemed curious and intrigued.

"I'm not getting any younger. You're having a baby and you're twenty-seven. No offence, but I can't see waiting that long before having my first."

"Abigail, you're twenty-four years old. You have plenty of time."

"Before you know it I'll be thirty."

"Thirty is the new twenty these days," Maddie suggested.

While I agreed it was true, I still didn't think it was right. "Whatever. I've always planned to have all of my kids before I turned thirty, and here I am twenty-four and the discussion isn't even on the table."

"You'll have kids, in your own time. It will happen.

Edwin wants kids, so you're set. How many do you want anyway?"

My head was spinning from her rapid fire statements. I didn't want to feed off of her blissful optimism, but she made it difficult not to. "I've always wanted three; two boys and a girl. What about you?"

"I only want two. Never had I imagined that my first would come about this way," Maddie admitted.

"So... back to me. I was thinking of telling Edwin that I want to try to get pregnant in the next year or two. They say that you should go off of birth control for a year before you want to get pregnant. I'd like to plan for these things, and I really want to know what his plans are."

"And if they don't jive with yours?"

"If we aren't on the same page, then we'll have to call it quits. It's the only way."

"Your way or the highway?"

"Exactly."

"You guys are so perfect together though. It's like you're meant to be together."

"Yeah, yeah. I know we're great together, but kids are a real important part of my life plan. If Edwin wants to be in my life then he has to want the same things that I do. I can't waste any time with a man who doesn't want to have kids; and soon."

"What do you think he's going to say?" Maddie asked.

"That's what I'm afraid of most. From what he's said lately, I think he's pretty happy as is. I don't think he'd change a thing."

"Aren't you happy?"

I shrugged my shoulders. "I'm happy as a couple," I admitted. "But there's more to life than that."

"I hear you. I didn't exactly plan to get prego, but I'm not too disappointed that I am; and with a totally hot fire fighter at that. It couldn't have worked out better for me really. You should try and get pregnant now and our kids can have play dates together." Maddie was getting super excited, wiggling around like a newborn.

"Don't get too ahead of yourself, Maddie. I have to get past Edwin first. The last thing I need right now is to become disillusioned about having a baby. I'm not so sure Edwin will be quite as understanding as Hunter's being."

"I'm sure he'll go along with anything you say," Maddie said, sweeping her hand carelessly through the air.

I shrugged my shoulders again, this time heavy with doubt. "I used to think so, but now I'm not so sure. We've only been together for a month you know. This kind of thing isn't exactly the sort of thing you bring up in a budding relationship."

"Yeah, but you guys go way back."

"I know. I'm just totally freaking out about asking him. I guess there's no point in wasting each other's time if it's never going to work though. So when do you think I should do it?"

"You should take your own advice. The sooner the better," Maddie suggested. "It worked for me."

"I still have to tell him about you and Hunter. I guess I can use that to lead into it."

"You can do it. I'm sure it will work out exactly as you want it to." Maddie was brimming with hope.

"I hope so. Tomorrow he's supposed to be taking me to the Corset Caves. Maybe I'll tell him there."

"Uh, maybe you should wait until after your feet are planted firmly above ground," she teased. "Just in case."

We giggled together, but in the back of my mind I knew that it was an honest concern of hers. I was suffering from serious doubts myself.

The doorbell began to ring, again and again, tearing me from my insecurities.

"Who could that be?" I hurried to the door and peeked out the window. Aliah was standing impatiently outside it. "Shit!" I swung the door open wide.

"Hey. I was just coming by to check on you. I see you have company though." She was not impressed.

It was just a matter of hours ago that I was scampering around my house, like a lunatic, dripping blood everywhere.

Now I had a house full, wishing I could be alone. "Come on in," I said reluctantly, being careful to lock it immediately behind her.

"What's she doing here?" Aliah asked, while glowering at Maddie.

I was happy that she didn't ask about the huge bandage wrapped around my wrist, since it was already going to be enough of an event to explain to Edwin when he got home.

"Just visiting," Maddie replied.

"Aren't you supposed to be sick?" Aliah said, scowling at Maddie. "Stay back. I don't want what you got."

"I wouldn't be so sure about that," Maddie replied arrogantly.

"What is she talking about?" Aliah snapped, looking to me.

"Why don't you tell her yourself, Maddie? Maybe you should take a seat first," I suggested to Aliah.

"I don't need a seat. Tell me what?"

"You asked for it. Hunter and I are pregnant."

Aliah laughed instantly and looked to me for a hint that it was a joke. She found a blank stare on my face, without so much as a smile. "You're full of shit. I just talked to Hunter like ten minutes ago. He didn't say anything about a baby."

"Call him back and ask him, if you don't believe me," Maddie taunted.

"Believe it, Aliah. I was with her at the doctor's. She is definitely pregnant," I said.

"She may be pregnant, but it doesn't mean it's Hunter's. She's a whore. It could be anyone's baby."

"No, actually. It can only be his. It is his," Maddie stated, with one hundred percent certainty.

"*Well. Isn't-This-Just-Great.* I see you two are all buddy-buddy now too. And this whore's going to be my man's baby momma? Fuck this! I am so out of here."

"Aliah wait!" I called after her, as she yanked open the door and slammed it in my face.

I couldn't bear to follow her out into the darkness. "Seriously Maddie? Do you know all the trouble you cause me?"

"That's why you love me."

"No, that's why it's always been a love-hate relationship between us."

She giggled. "Aliah will have to get over it. I am having Hunter's baby. If she doesn't like it, then she can back off and let me have him."

"Go easy on her. This has got to be a total shocker for her. Even more, that Hunter didn't tell her."

"Well it's not exactly the kind of thing you tell your girlfriend over the phone. Uh, hi. I'm having a baby with another girl. Love ya. Bye," Maddie mocked.

"Good point."

"Well I should probably get going too. I told my parents I would stop by when I was done here. I'm just trying to muster up the courage to tell them. That should be fun."

"Good luck with that."

"You're welcome to join me if you like." She pleaded with her eyes.

"Not a chance in hell."

"Well, if you don't hear from me on Monday, it's because my mother killed me."

"Okay," I responded, laughing.

We exchanged a hug, her warmth wrapping my subconscious with a motherly security blanket, before she left. I closed the door behind her and turned over the dead bolt.

The house was quiet again, but it felt secure. I felt safe. In fact, I was actually feeling relieved to be alone again.

All fear of the attack of the glowing monster had disappeared after all that flowing chatter. Now my mind was only bombarded with thoughts about my station in life.

All the worrying in the world couldn't prepare me for what may or may not happen between me and Edwin. There was about a one percent chance that he would say he didn't want children. This would mean that I have no reason to worry. *Then why am I so damn anxious?*

I watched some mind-numbing TV and that did the trick.

My house was still chilly, but I knew it was only because of the effective air conditioning unit we had installed last year. I curled up on the couch, huddled under a blanket and stared at the clock that read ten o'clock.

I half expected Edwin to be late, but I didn't anticipate my solemn disappointment when he wasn't home by now. He couldn't be much longer, since he had planned a day trip for us tomorrow, but I couldn't seem to keep my eyes open to wait up. Closed they go, and off to dreamland I went.

When my eyes fluttered open, I winced from the brightness and covered my eyes with an arm. Squinting at the early morning sun, I saw my bandage was soaked with dried blood. And where was I? Lying in my bed? Unsure how I got there, I rolled over and there, right next to me, was Edwin.

"Babe, you up?" I asked, sleepily unaware that Edwin's eyes were closed.

He shifted next to me. "Well I am now," he groaned.

"What time did you get home?"

"Uh, it was maybe ten. But you were already fast asleep. Thanks for waiting up for me," he teased. "You must have been tired. I carried you to bed and you didn't even wake up."

Yes, he would make such a great father.

"I wondered how I got here."

"I may have taken advantage of you last night," he teased again, attractively raising his eyebrows.

"Did you now? Well I guess I'll have to get you back for that." I rolled all the way over, and drew my knee up his leg provocatively.

"Seriously? Cuz that would be awesome. You can use me any time. Really. Please do. I insist."

From the feeling of his early morning stiffy, I decided I would take him up on that offer. Right away. I wiggled out of my lacy panties and dangled them out of the blankets before dropping them to the floor. Edwin's hand skimmed firmly over my body, his grin stretching from ear to ear. It felt so good to have his hands on me again.

Driven by impulse, I ripped off my shirt and yanked down his underwear, freeing him from his only clothes. Edwin slipped his hand between us, where he found me wet, willing and ready. He groaned with desire, as he lifted me up and dropped me on top of him, his hands driving the heavy urge to unify us again and again.

I screamed out in pleasure as he continued to fill my request, forcing himself deeper until his body jerked deliciously beneath me. After the most satisfying ride of my life, I crashed next to Edwin on the bed to catch my breath.

"You must be feeling better," he chuckled.

"Huh?"

"You said you weren't feeling very well yesterday. You must have just needed to rest."

"I guess," I said, unable to think up something closer to the truth. It was true. I must have needed the rest, because I sure slept soundly last night. No doubt, the stress had finally taken me out.

"What happened to your wrist?" Edwin finally asked, still breathless.

"Long story." And I really didn't want to talk about it.

"I've got all day, baby," he teased, skimming his fingers over the curve of my hip.

I moaned, flattening myself into the bed. "It was just an accident. I fell and cut myself. No biggie."

"Well I hate to say this, but it looks like you tried to slit your wrist."

"How would you even know what that looks like?"

"I know you've been really stressed lately, and even though Jenny's been coming to you in your sleep you haven't started back up on your meds."

True, those pills would knock me out at night, but I doubt they'd stop Jenny from coming to me while I'm awake. "How do you even know that?"

"Come on, Abs. I know you like the back of my own hand. At least I thought I did. But now you're keeping things from me, and I'm not sure why. Is it Jenny? Did you try to kill yourself to be with her?"

I screeched with disbelief. "Hardly. If I wanted to kill myself, I'd be dead. I just dropped the damn knife and fell on it."

"That sounds absolutely ridiculous. You do realize that. It looks like you nearly chopped your hand off. You actually expect me to believe that you had this oversized knife out and your wrist accidentally fell on it?"

"Yes. Because it's the truth."

He pulled the bandage open and gawked at the fresh scabby gash across my wrist. His fingers trailed next to the wound and he shook his head trying hard to make sense of it.

"You're sure you didn't do this to yourself? I'm afraid this may be one of those warning signs of suicide. Like a cry for help or something. I would never forgive myself if something ever happened to you."

I smiled, foolishly happy to hear how much he cared. "Well, for one, I don't think that you ask the suicidal person that."

"So you are suicidal."

"Edwin! Please drop it. I know what it looks like, but I assure you it was totally an accident. I. Do Not. Want. To. Kill Myself!"

"Why don't you fill in the blanks for me then? I want to believe you. Make me believe you."

"What do you want to know?"

"Like why you had that knife out in the first place."

Shit! "I want to tell you, but you'll freak," I said, covering my eyes with my good hand.

"Now I'm going to freak either way, so you'd better tell me."

"Can I at least get dressed first?" At least then some of my dignity could remain intact.

"Make it quick. There's no more changing the subject. You're telling me now."

"Fine! I may have thought I saw someone staring at me through the window." I monitored Edwin's eyes, gaging his reaction.

"So you grabbed a knife? Why wouldn't you call me... or the police?" he hollered, suddenly swelling with rage.

I clambered out of the bed, walked to my closet and began to redress, trying to ignore the flames shooting from his ears. "I did grab the phone, but I thought maybe I was just seeing things. Then I saw that we forgot to lock the back door. I got scared, so I pulled out the knife." I spun around to face him. "I was just trying to protect myself."

His rage had already subsided, his blue eyes warmed to teal. "Nice, and instead you end up stabbing yourself. Worst of all, it's my fault."

"How could it possibly be your fault?"

"I'm the one that used the back door last, and I should've locked it. The kicker is, it would have been all fine had I been home to protect you. I knew it was a bad idea to go out last night," he said, frustrated with himself.

"Eddie. I'm fine. Nothing happened. I just overreacted."

"Someone was there though, right?"

"Yes," I replied calmly. Fully dressed, I walked back toward him and stood next to the bed. I reached my hand out and pulled him toward me.

Edwin continued to shake his head in disbelief, then pressed a kiss to my palm. "Maybe we should get a security system. I know I'd rest easier."

"We don't need a security system. I've got my own personal body guard right here," I said, cupping his stubbly chin.

"What good was I last night?"

He was really taking this bad. What can I do to make him see that it wasn't his fault? I want my sexy, sarcastic, boy toy back.

"I guess you'll have to keep a better eye on me from now on then," I teased, fluttering my eyelashes with a smirk.

Edwin pulled on his t-shirt. "You laugh, but I'm not taking my eyes off of you now. I would've killed someone if they hurt you. We're getting an alarm."

"I don't want to get into it, but I don't think an alarm will cure this problem."

"Damn it, Abigail. You *are* seeing Jenny again. I should have known; what with all your sleep-talking lately. Ever since our trip to the Southwind..." His voice trailed off. "I was banking on the possibility that you didn't remember it when you woke up, but I knew better."

"I've been talking in my sleep? And you didn't think to fill me in?"

"Abs, we've had full out conversations. It wasn't until recently that I figured out you were still asleep. I thought you'd remember when you woke up."

"I don't. But good then, now I don't have to fill *you* in."

"No, but maybe you should fill your shrink in."

"Maybe later."

"Definitely later," Edwin insisted.

I'm not going to the shrink. She thinks I'm crazy. I'm not crazy. I don't believe in ghosts. And yet my dead sister is haunting me. I can't explain it. She's just here. No shrink can ever fix that. I'm not going to the shrink.

"So... what did you do last night?" I asked, moving the conversation away from my craziness.

He rolled his eyes, acknowledged my stubbornness, and reluctantly moved on. "Just like I expected, the meeting ran late. Then we did dinner. Of course, after dinner the client invited us out for drinks. Miller couldn't stay, but he suggested I go to socialize. It was good as far as networking goes, but it was pretty damn boring."

"Did you make any good contacts?"

"Who knows? I guess time will tell."

"Well I certainly hope it was worth your while, because I missed you." I made a teasing pouty face.

"Well I'm here now," he said smiling, and pulled me between his legs. Sitting on the edge of the bed he tilted his chin up to me, silently pleading for me to come closer.

I dipped my head down for a sensual kiss and my lips matched his. "Are we still on for today?" I whispered, as he pulled me onto his lap.

"Oh, babe, I'm sorry. I was hoping to get an earlier start to the day. My head's still pounding."

"We don't have to go if you're not up to it." I didn't admit it, but my hand was pounding too.

"I told you I would take you and I will. You shouldn't have to suffer from my drinking." He looked deep into my eyes, assessing my keenness on going.

My eyes slipped away from his, and locked on my bare toe that I slid back and forth across the smooth, cold floor. "I don't know. I think I'd rather just hang out today and go to the Festival of Lights tonight, if that's good with you."

Edwin's eyes met mine and he didn't seem to be disappointed at all. "I'm good with that."

"You think you might be up for a walk this morning though?" I asked, eager to get out of the house. I was desperate for some fresh air.

"I guess I can handle a walk. Maybe it'll help clear my head."

I leapt from his lap and pranced toward the door. Edwin stood from the bed and stretched for the ceiling, letting out a loud growl.

"Where are you going?" he said on a yawn.

"To wash up."

"You look fine."

I spun around and stalked back toward him. "That's the worst thing you could tell a girl. Now I have to get in the shower."

"What I meant is, you look good to me," Edwin carefully corrected, but it was too little too late.

"Better, but we'll have to work on that. I promise to take a quick one."

"Oh, Abs. Wake me up in an hour," he teased, hopping back in bed.

"I told you I'll be quick," I said scowling, hands on hips.

"Yeah, that means you'll be at least an hour," he said, waving me off.

I grabbed a stray pillow from the footboard and hit Edwin over the head with it, leaving it on his face. He didn't seem to mind it too much, leaving it covering his eyes, ending our pointless conversation.

I was done looking *fine*. I wanted to look FINE! I planned on having a very important conversation with Edwin today. I would have to look super cute to make it as difficult as possible for him to say no to me.

After coating my hair with leave in conditioner, I looped it into playful braids that dangled over each shoulder. I couldn't get away with that look at work, so I thought I would play it up today; especially since I know how much Eddie loves it when I do. Being five minutes off of ready, I texted Edwin from the bathroom.

9:42 a.m.
Hey, baby. I'm ready to go. GET UP!!! :) ~ Abby

9:44 a.m.
I'm up. Btw, nice ass. ;) Edwin Santora

I whirled around, with phone in hand. There he was, standing in the doorway, watching me read his message, wearing a huge, devilish grin and an inviting cocked eyebrow. He looked all ready to go, in more ways than one.

"Don't even think about it," I said, though I was tempted.

"About what?" he asked, playfully.

"You know what."

"You're no fun. What's taking you anyway?" he asked, leaving his lusty libido alone.

"I just have to brush my teeth and I'm good to go."

"Then I'm one step ahead of you, because I'm all ready."

He insisted that he had brushed his teeth while I was in the shower, but I hadn't heard him. My mind was failing me more and more each day, between spazzing out and getting lost in my own head. Maybe I *should* consider making a visit to my psychiatrist.

After dabbing my mouth on the hand towel, I skipped after Edwin in my short jean shorts and white top. I hurried down the stairs, squatted next to my sparkly pink sketchers and quickly slipped them on.

Edwin and I walked silently, content for a time, but I knew it was only temporary. I had yet to tell Edwin first about Maddie's new development and then, more importantly, about mine. I didn't want to ruin the relaxed charge in the air, hoping to gain the courage as the day progressed. *Not likely.*

"There's something I've wanted to tell you," I blurted.

"Uh, oh. That sounds like trouble. Does it have to do with me?"

"It's about Maddison."

"Okay."

"And Hunter."

"Oh, this should be good. What did he do now?"

"Let's just say fixing things with Aliah is the least of his worries now."

"I don't get it. What did he do?"

"Maddie. And now she's knocked up."

"Oh shit! Hunter must be beside himself."

"Actually, from what Maddie tells me, he's taking it pretty good. He's stepping up."

"What else could the poor guy do? Trust me, he's freaking out."

"Well, it was his own dumb fault," I said, annoyed with Edwin's response.

"Oh, and Maddie's just a saint? I think not. I wouldn't be surprised if there was some premeditation going on there." Edwin's tone was cold and callous.

I disagreed. And I suddenly wished I had started with my own issues first. Hearing Edwin dish out his opinion about Maddie was not helping my situation. "I think we can agree that Hunter and Maddie can share the blame for this one. It doesn't matter which way you look at it now. They're linked together for life."

Edwin winced at the word *life* and it unexpectedly hurt my feelings. It should have made me more hesitant to slip in my own strategies, but instead it had the opposite effect. As we rounded the corner and headed back toward our house I got brave.

"About that... *life.* I want to talk about where *we're* going."

"I thought we were going home."

I chuckled at his ignorance, though anxious and disappointed that he wasn't meeting me on the emotional level I needed him at to discuss our life together. "No Edwin. I mean where our relationship is going. I know we've talked about our future plans a million times before, but we really haven't talked about it since we got back together. Now that we are, I need to know where things stand... where I stand."

We walked up our front porch and I could tell Edwin's muscles were tense. His thumbs were clamped inside his fists and his teeth were clenched as if he was in pain. "I thought we were just going to take it easy this morning?" he said.

"We are."

"That's pretty intense for this time of day if you ask me. Besides, we just got back together. I don't see why we need to rush into anything."

The answer of death. "I'm not asking you to marry me Eddie. I just want to know what way you see things going in the future. I *do* want to get married *someday* and have children of my own..." I didn't insert the word *soon*, though it was on the tip of my tongue.

"Oh, I see where this is going."

"Eddie, you know how I feel about it. You know I planned to have kids by now. My biological clock is ticking and I can't just go on forever like this. I need to know that we're on the same page."

He took a deep breath and growled under his breath as he stared blankly at the porch. "I need some time to think about all of this. I have to admit, I wasn't expecting it at all. I thought things were going great," he said, sounding hurt and confused.

"They are, Eddie. But there's more to life than just being a couple. I want a family."

"I need time."

I wondered whether he meant before talking about it or before he's ready to have a family. It choked the life out of me momentarily and I swallowed it down to maintain my cool. "Think fast, because I want to know how you feel now, not next year. You shouldn't have to think too hard about it."

Edwin looked stunned. His lips parted in shock. I decided to leave him alone so he could think.

I kept talking, with confidence, as I unlocked the front door. "I just want to know what it is that you expect out of this relationship. We'll talk tonight," I said, not letting up.

I let myself inside, leaving Edwin traumatized on the porch. Weird, I felt relief, when I should have been bursting into tears.

I pulled off my walking shoes, carried them to the back door, and slipped them back on before ducking out onto the back patio. Overwhelmed with unanswered expectations, saddened by Edwin's hesitance, it felt like I was contemplating how our relationship was going to end. Unfortunately, I had no other choice but to give him an ultimatum.

I sat on a cushioned rocking chair and sorted through my thoughts, as I rocked myself into a false sense of comfort and sanctuary.

I took advantage of my alone time to emotionally prepare myself for Edwin's answer. Though I believed in my heart, until today, that I had good odds of keeping Edwin, it was quickly becoming obvious that it could go either way.

Betting on Edwin's immediate reaction – like he had taken a sudden blow to his manhood – it would be smart to proceed with caution. As I feared, he's just not ready.

CHAPTER TWENTY ONE

It startled me when I heard someone walking up the side yard. Even though it was a bright, sunny day, I still felt a terrible sense of danger wash over me. The neighbour's dog barked at the intruder, as I stared at the treeline, defenseless, waiting to see who or what it was. I was relieved to find that it was only Edwin.

"Hey. I thought I heard you back here," he said, as he took a seat in the rocking chair next to me.

A shallow smile formed on my lips. "Sorry to lay it on so thick for you. I'm sure it was a lot to hear all at once."

"It's probably for the best. I see where you're coming from and I want you to be happy. We'll talk about it tonight, but for now we should eat. It's almost lunch and we haven't even eaten breakfast."

"I don't really feel like cooking. What about Tim Horton's?"

"That works for me, since I want to take you out for dinner later. You ready to go now?"

"Yeah, let's go."

Edwin took my hand and led me to the back door, where he carefully secured the lock and proceeded around the house to do the same in the front. He opened the passenger door to his truck and I let some steamy air escape before pulling myself up to get in. He pushed my butt, to give me a helpful lift, and swiftly rounded the truck toward his own door.

Over lunch we talked about superficial things: the weather, my hair, the food; anything but the elephant in the room.

"Are we still on for dinner?" I asked, after swallowing a bite of apple fritter.

"Yeah, I thought we would do dinner at a downtown

restaurant and maybe take a walk through the park after. It's supposed to be real nice out tonight."

"That sounds nice."

Edwin's gaze flicked to the exit and so I glanced over my shoulder to see who had stolen his attention. "Looks like we have company," he said softly.

Samantha noticed us immediately. Her latest victim, Caleb, did soon after and gave us a full arm wave. Sam shot me a cool gaze, as they waited their turn in the short line-up. Before long, they ordered their cold drinks and came over to our table to join us.

"Hey, brother. How's it going?" Edwin asked, sharing a handshake with Caleb.

"It's going," he said, then ran a hand through his dark hair with icicle highlights.

"Hey, Abby," Sam said. "Edwin."

I was amazed that she could manage to be pleasant with me when Maddie wasn't around. She was outright ignorant, more often than not, with her perfect little nose turned to the ceiling. "Hey. What are you guys up to?" I asked.

"Caleb thought we should go for a walk," Sam said, rolling her pretty eyes.

"How was I supposed to know it was going to be this hot?"

Edwin nodded his head. "It's definitely a scorcher, but there's a nice warm breeze." He stretched his bulging arms out in the air and then tucked his hands behind his head, his biceps displayed in a delightful package framing his equally as intriguing face.

"It's suddenly even hotter in here," Sam replied, fanning her face and flushing profusely.

If I didn't know any better, I would say she was flirting with Edwin. *Yes. She definitely was.* She tried to catch his eye with a seductive smile, lashes fluttering over her heated cheeks. She was hitting on him!

"Are you guys going to the fireworks tonight?" I asked, hoping to distract Sam.

Caleb lifted his chin toward Edwin with a smirk. "I've

been trying to convince Sam to come with me tonight, but she's giving me a hard time. Maybe you'll have better luck."

See? Even Caleb noticed Sam's slutty charade.

"Well, I'm definitely going," I said. "You should go, Sam." Yeah, I said it. But I really couldn't have cared less what she did.

Sam made a sour face and rolled her hazel eyes, suggesting she had no intentions of going. That seemed to hook Edwin's attention and, in turn, irritated me even more.

"I feel you," he said. "I could pass tonight too. I'm not really feeling it. Honestly, I could use a nap right about now."

I swallowed my disappointment, upset to hear that Edwin was dreading our night out together. It was having a debilitating effect on my self-confidence.

"Me too. I have an idea," Sam said to me and Caleb, acting all chipper. "Why don't you two go to the fireworks together and Edwin and I can go to bed."

My mouth dropped open in disbelief. Once I snapped my mouth shut, I squinted at her with a cold, vexed stare. She giggled at her own play on words, which was all too convenient to be unintentional. Edwin chuckled at her secret suggestion, though I knew he would never bed her. Caleb laughed out loud and then immediately called her out on it.

"You just want to get Edwin in bed."

"I didn't mean that. Oh, guys! That's not what I meant!"

Caleb thought it was funny, but I certainly didn't think it was. Angry, but with my best effort to stay calm, I stood from my chair. It screeched across the solid floor, but I didn't even care. I couldn't sit and listen to that whore for another minute.

"Anyways. We should get going. Maybe we'll see you there," I said, as I hinted for Edwin to get up. I smiled at Caleb and he looked like he wanted me to take him with us.

"Later," Edwin said, as we walked away.

"Gator," Sam replied, as if it was directed to her.

Silence followed us all the way home, until we walked

into the comfort of our open foyer.

"Can you believe Sam said that?" Edwin asked, taking the words right from my mouth.

"I know, eh? I don't think it was by accident either."

"I thought it was pretty funny. You really think she has the balls?"

"She said it didn't she? And in front of Caleb at that. What a whore."

Edwin laughed. "You're just jealous."

"Of Sam? Never! But I do notice I've been seeing her around more often lately." I stepped toward the living room, angry that Edwin was so amused by Sam's flirtations.

"You have nothing to worry about. She's got nothing on you." Edwin chased after me.

I spun on one foot and stood my ground, fists at my sides, catching him off guard. "Quit kissing my ass. I don't need your reassurance." I paused. Then with a huff, "You know what? I need some air. I'm going to go for a drive to Aliah's house."

Edwin reached his massive arms toward the ceiling and stretched them out. "You go ahead, I need a nap. Check yaaa..." he said with a yawn. "Later," he finished, dragging himself up the stairs.

He really had no clue. This was not a laughing matter.

Still pissy, I retrieved my cell from my purse and punched Aliah's number in. I stepped out onto my front porch, as my call went straight to voicemail. "Hey, Ally. It's me. I'm coming over," I said, and then ended the call. *Would she ever forgive me?*

Hours had passed since I had visited Aliah's empty house and Edwin still wasn't giving any indication that he planned to wake up any time soon. That was about to change. I went straight to his room, walked swiftly to the bed and stopped, hands on my hips.

"Are you planning on sleeping the whole day away?" I

grumbled.

He didn't budge, eyes sealed shut, and he looked so damn comfortable that I felt guilty for interrupting him. On a huff, I slipped onto the bed and curled up behind him.

"I wouldn't mind," he answered belatedly. He fell silent for another minute and I wondered if he had fallen back asleep.

"Well... I need you," I interrupted, acting like a greedy girlfriend.

Edwin tossed me aside, flung open the blankets and wrapped both of his substantial arms around me dragging me into his warm lair. It was amazing how he could make me feel so secure at such a dangerous point in our relationship. Our bodies were pressed close together, our legs intertwined, and Edwin nuzzled his nose in my hair, inhaling me like I was a dying flower.

Mindlessly, a tear fell down my cheek, but I quickly wiped it away before Edwin could notice. "I love you," I said, and I meant it so much.

"I love you too, Abs."

I tucked my chin in, hiding in his armour, the looming conversation hanging over my head like a storm cloud. The prospect of not making love to Edwin ever again smothered me. Emotions pooled thick in the air. Edwin stroked his hand along the curve of my lower back, cutting through the grey skies with a sharp, white-hot light. Immersed in his tenderness, he gently tilted my face up until our eyes met. His eyelids slid shut. Slow, soft and thoughtful, he kissed me.

Mouth still on mine, Edwin gently pulled out my braids and tousled my hair into loose waves. "That's better," he growled, and weaved his fingers close to my head.

His kiss grew hungry and I wanted to feed him. Emotions spilled from me and he consumed them, sharing my passion. I was breathless, desperate, as I gave him every ounce of myself. I felt every trace of his hands, every caress of his tongue, taking precise note of every tender touch, measuring every movement of his hard body, as he took his time undressing me.

He was attentive to my needs, tickling, touching and exploring every inch of me. As he exposed more flesh, his mouth covered over it, tantalizing me to the core, until my body begged for forgiveness.

"I need you," I cried. Desperate. Urgent.

Eager to satisfy, after skimming over me, once, twice, he entered me, filling me to capacity.

"Yes!" I screamed. Emotion blasted from every nerve ending, surrounding me in a rainbow of psychedelic colours and leaving me in limbo between illusion and reality.

"Yes, baby," he growled, his excitement mounting with every violent thrust.

My eyes rolled shut and Edwin expelled himself into me, clinging to my warm, convulsing body.

Still pressed deep inside me, Edwin's lips covered mine, slamming me back into reality. Unwilling to let him loose, I kissed him, fraught with worry, each kiss unravelling and interpreting my pain. He stopped me, sensing my excessive determination, and gazed at me with those amazing aqua eyes, revealing his own concern.

Without a word he scattered kisses tenderly across my lips, my chin, my neck. I ran one hand through his damp spiky hair, the other clutching desperately to his muscular back. I couldn't get enough of him. It was like our skin was fused together, but it wasn't close enough for me.

Time stood still, decisions on hold, while we touched with our hearts and felt with our thoughts. Staring into each other's curious eyes, wondering, worrying, we searched for the answers, probing, inquiring, but not finding anything.

My eyelashes fluttered shut, breaking the intimate gaze.

Edwin sighed. "We should probably clean up and get ready for dinner."

"Do we have to?"

"I've got it all planned out, so you'd better," he insisted, playfully steamrolling me to get out of his bed.

"That's funny, you didn't sound too keen on it this

morning."

"It was all part of my plan. I see it worked like a charm," he said, killing me with his sexy grin.

"Where are we going? You had better tell me so I know how to dress."

"I'm sure you'll look great no matter what you're wearing. I have a request of my own, if it's not too much," Edwin said, taking my hand and tugging me from the bed. "Leave your hair alone. I like it all wild like this." He tossed a wavy strand of hair in the air and tucked another behind my ear, before leaning down for another soft kiss.

After lingering for far too long, I ducked away to check myself in the mirror and gasped, shocked by my untamed hair. "My hair's a mess!"

"Leave it. It looks hot."

"Yeah, I suppose if you like the whole dishevelled, just-fucked look."

"I do. I really do." His smirk was honest and sexy as hell.

I glanced back in the mirror, a poised grin on my rosy, satiated face. I could definitely pull it off if I wanted to. "I think I can work with it," I said, knowing it would display Edwin's ownership of me to everyone we passed.

And that made him happy. I'd do anything to keep that bright, optimistic smile on his face for as long as I could. I kissed my fingers and touched them to his lips. "I'm gonna go get ready."

After I showered, with smooth shaven legs, I shuffled through my clothes with renewed hope. There was still a chance, I told myself, as I plucked an airy, strapless, blue leopard print shirt from my closet. It would match the wild look I was working perfectly.

I pulled on a pair of short black shorts that accentuated my long legs and then slipped on a pair of strappy high heeled gladiator sandals that I only wore in the presence of my monstrously tall and sexy man.

I strutted out of my room and down the stairs, feeling like a million bucks and hoping for a good response from Edwin. He was waiting patiently in the front room and glanced up when I walked in.

"Wow," he said. And the way that his eyes sparkled, I knew it was a good wow.

"So, how do I look?" I asked, doing a supermodel spin.

He approached with his hands out and, within seconds, he had me in his arms. "You look amazing," he growled, drawing my neck into his mouth. "If we didn't have reservations, I'd be taking you back upstairs right now." He kissed my mouth, his hands roaming over my soft bare thighs.

"You made reservations? Then we don't want to keep them waiting," I teased, flaunting my magical hips as I headed for the front door.

Edwin reached for my slim waist and lifted me out of his truck. He didn't let me go again until he opened the front door of the prominent downtown restaurant.

After mellow conversation and a fabulous meal, we went for a short walk through a quiet nearby park. The warm sun was settling low on the horizon and fluffy white clouds floated peacefully in the pastel sky.

"Are you up for a ride on the water taxi? I remember how much you loved it last time," he said.

"Absolutely." I was thrilled with the idea. Returning his beaming smile, I let him lead me to the boathouse to catch our ride.

The night was young, the sky a soft bluish-grey, just waiting to embrace a purple darkness. Riding the serene blue-green water was so surreal, the wind breezing through my hair, me tucked in Edwin's arms.

The sound of the water swooshed gently behind us. The crickets chirped from the nearby land, the warmth still radiating from the tired earth. Softened by the atmosphere, I relaxed against Edwin's hard chest, and soaked up all of his attention while I still could. It felt a bit like a dream.

After taking in the beautiful vista, I turned my loving

gaze on Edwin's gorgeous, thoughtful eyes. His lips touched mine, causing some onlookers to awkwardly glance away and others to gawk selfishly.

There was an amazing sense of calm in the air and I planned to ride that wave as long as possible. When we got off the taxi, we strolled among the light crowd to Del Ray Park to take in some music at the Festival of Lights.

Before long we were sipping on cold drinks and enjoying some decent entertainment under the darkening, night sky. A young couple got up from one of the many overcrowded benches and Edwin made a run for it.

We took our seat and absorbed the warm atmosphere. The first star of the night twinkled proudly in the distance over the water. When I drew my eyes away from it, I noticed that Edwin couldn't take his eyes off of me. His intense blue eyes made the night sky pale in comparison, mesmerizing me with their immeasurable depths.

"You look beautiful tonight, Abs," Edwin said.

"Thanks." I blushed seven shades of pink.

Edwin was proud and amused from his ability to affect me like that. He slid my butt closer to him, leaving just enough room behind me for a tall thin blonde woman to slide up on the bench next to me. The music was winding down, meaning the fireworks were about to begin, but Edwin was only aware of me.

We hadn't even brought up the issue we so badly needed to resolve, but it seemed so far from his mind at the moment. I gulped, ready to say what I had to say, but when I looked up, I found Hunter and Aliah sitting no more than thirty feet away from us.

Hunter's hands started to flag me down like I was an aircraft ready for takeoff. He pulled on Aliah's arm, dragging her toward us through the tight-packed crowd. When she finally realized where she was going, she didn't look too impressed about it.

"Hey, guys," Hunter hollered to us, well before we were in casual speaking distance.

"Hey," I said quietly to Aliah, as she stopped across from

me, while Hunter and Edwin greeted each other.

Aliah scorned me. "Oh, are we talking again?"

I stood up, but kept my leg tacked to the bench to make sure no one could steal my spot. I spoke extra softly, so our bubbly blonde neighbour would mind her own business. "Yes we are. It was a misunderstanding, Ally. I didn't mean for you to get hurt."

"Hurt? Who said I was hurt? You're the one that was all bandaged up," she scoffed.

I scowled at her, so angry that she brought up my ridiculous, self-inflicted injury, but glad that she was talking to me at all. I tucked my bandaged hand behind my back. "You know what I mean. Can we call a truce... please?"

She rolled her eyes at me, but in a friendly settling kind of way, and I knew we were good. "You look hot by the way," she said softly, smiling.

"She does look incredible tonight, doesn't she?" Edwin said, interrupting my private apology.

"Thank you. I'm just glad that you're talking to me," I said to Aliah.

"Okay, so I may have overreacted."

I gave her a hug and whispered in her ear. "We so need to talk later." When I pulled away from her, she smiled and nodded at me.

The guys looked at each other curiously, knowing that something was up, but didn't bother to intrude. The music ended and, just as I suspected, a jolly light-hearted fellow on the microphone notified everyone that the light show was about to begin.

"It's good to see you guys, but we don't want to lose our spot over there. We've got chairs and everything," Hunter said.

"Yeah, maybe we'll catch up with you later?" Aliah added, before Hunter pulled her back to their hideaway in the grass, eyes rolling.

"See ya," Edwin said with a chuckle.

I turned my attention back to him. He was looking extremely hot himself, his juicy pink lips calling my name.

"You look absolutely stunning tonight," Edwin said, reflecting my own thoughts.

"Thanks," I replied, another embarrassing blush causing me to submissively stare at my hands. I couldn't help but notice that the girl still sitting next to us seemed a little too enveloped in Edwin's compliments. She was staring all starry-eyed at him. *Back off bitch, they aren't meant for you.*

"Look, the fireworks are starting," Edwin said, pointing at the red glow over the water. He put his arm around me, pulling me into his little world and distracting me from the nosy lady next to me.

We cuddled under the twinkling stars as we watched the rainbow of colours burst into the dark night sky. The crowd oohed and awed over the array of lights. Some of the kids playfully tossed around their glow necklaces into the air as others enjoyed the show in their parents' laps.

A few parents had to leave the crowd as their young children screamed in fear, which might have scared off the thought of having children by most, but it only made me think of how badly I wanted a child of my own.

The grand finale was followed by a howling crowd and cheering children, who were ecstatic for being allowed to stay up well past their bed times. I admired the smiling families as they cuddled together on their blankets enjoying their quality time together. *I wanted that.*

I smiled at Edwin, who had been watching my eyes almost too carefully. He looked a little frightened and that worried me. We quietly waited as a rush of people hurried toward their parked cars.

After a few minutes, we casually made our way back to the water taxi. We had avoided the conversation long enough. *It was time.*

CHAPTER TWENTY TWO

The water taxi drove on, guided only by moonlight, as I looked into Edwin's soul. His arm was draped over the seat behind me and he stared out over the water at the colourless sky. I could sense a looming sadness weighing heavy on his eyes that hadn't been there the rest of the night.

My heart ached as I imagined why that might be and I knew I had to clarify a few things with him right away.

"We need to talk," I said, softly. I sounded so calm, even though I was a total mess inside.

He nodded in agreement, though hesitant. Then, without giving me a free second to collect my words, he pressed his lips hard against mine. When his mouth pulled away, it left me feeling cold, naked and defenceless.

I gulped the lump from the back of my throat and tears started to form in the corners my eyes. The suspense was killing me. I had to know. I had to ask. Now.

"I know how freaked out you got when you heard about Maddie being pregnant, and I have to admit that it worried me a little. Okay, maybe a lot. I've told you I want kids and honestly, I'm ready to move forward in life. Now. I'm looking to be in a committed relationship, so I can get married and start a family."

There. I said it.

I stopped, hoping Edwin hadn't heard my voice breaking up from emotion, but my breathlessness was choking me and I couldn't disguise it. The fact that he noticed, and squeezed my shoulder to acknowledge how difficult this was for me, just choked me up even more.

So, why wasn't he saying anything?

"I want to start a family with you, Eddie. But I can't wait forever. I need to know where you stand, and sooner rather than later. We can't go on like this if it's not going to lead where I need it to go." I stopped again, hoping Edwin would take his turn already. I had said my part, as hard as it was, and now it looked like it was my turn to take a lashing.

He took my hand, squeezed it tightly in his, and drew a sharp breath. "Abs, you know I love you."

I took a deep fearful breath, after taking my first beating. It was bad. The end was nigh.

"I love you so much," he continued, "but I know that it's not enough for you. I do want kids... just not now. I feel like we haven't had a chance to fully enjoy each other yet. I can just imagine the restrictions having children would put on us and I can't understand why you want that now. We wouldn't have the freedom to be able to up and do things as we please."

I put up my hand up in the air, like a stop sign, because his words were really starting to piss me off. I didn't want to fight, but he really had it coming. "You're acting like a child. It's called growing up," I said, growing angry and distant.

He must have expected a storm of emotion, because he didn't even try to fight me off.

"I know. But when I heard Hunter's going to have a little rug rat of his own running around, I just couldn't imagine that for me. I've just finished school, Abs, and I've hardly settled into my first job. I've always planned to settle into my career before starting a family. You know that. If you could just give me some more time..."

"How much more time do you need, Eddie?" I cut in. "Because I need to know. If you can't see it in your near future, then I'm afraid that our lives are turning in different directions again. If I get off the roller coaster ride this time, I won't be getting back on."

I swung my knees away from him and stared away at nothing in particular. Red had etched across every sparkle of light on the water, as I was reminded how many spectators we had. That same red fused across my cheeks, embarrassment joining all of my other spoiled emotions.

Edwin tapped me lightly on the shoulder. I didn't spin around until I had extracted every sign of weakness from my face.

"Okay, so say our life goals aren't entirely lined up at the moment," Edwin said, softly. "Does that mean that we can't be together? Am I expected to go back to being *just friends* with you? You know I can't do that."

My eyes met his and I wondered if my pain showed as excruciatingly clear as his did. *It hurts, I know, but it's now or never.*

"I'm not getting any younger, Eddie, and I'm ready for kids. So, unless you are too, I have to try something different. This just won't cut it for me anymore."

The truth hurt, but not as bad as the thought of breaking Edwin's heart. I was losing a lover who refused to give me children on demand, but he was losing his girlfriend, the love of his life and his future.

"We can try to work through this and figure it out together. It's worked for us before," he insisted.

Softly, "This is different. I think we've already done the figuring. It just so happens that this time it puts us apart. I'm looking for a lifelong commitment, Eddie. You've made it pretty clear that you're nowhere near ready to set your life in stone."

My next breath was sharp and, on an exhale, it felt like a piece of my heart was clawing up my wind pipe.

Edwin took my ice cold hands into his. "Abs, I'm ready to settle down with you romantically, if that's all you're asking. Marry me," he pleaded, dropping to both of his knees before me.

He pulled both of my hands to his mouth and pressed his lips against them. His imploring eyes took in my faint smile, but there was no humour in it.

I wished that it was enough for me: To spend the rest of my life with Edwin, baby or no baby. Tears threatened when I pulled him back up to his seat. Gasps sounded from the intrigued crowd nosing in our business.

I turned my shoulder to block out the others and faced

Edwin. "Eddie, you don't mean that. You don't even have a ring. That's not what this is. I don't want to pressure you into anything. Maybe the timing isn't right, or maybe we just aren't meant to be," I said, nearly choking on a soft cry.

"We are, Abs." He lifted my dipped chin and stared hard at me, with dark, fathomless eyes. "I want you to be my wife," he pleaded, desperate now.

His nose nudged my moist face and, despite the terrifying conversation, it gave me comfort to have him this close. Maybe it could work. But for how long?

Thunder boomed from my heart and tears stormed from my eyes. A trembling breath escaped my mouth, when his soft skin touched mine, but I shook my head. *No.* "This isn't how it's supposed to work. I want to marry out of love, not out of fear."

Edwin took my face in his hands and tilted my head up high, until my blood shot eyes met his, dark blue and intense. "I do want to marry you for love. I won't believe you don't trust that. It's just that I'm not quite ready to exchange my freedom for babies right now. Please understand."

What was left of my heart crushed at the sound of the Edwin's words. Heavy machinery came and leveled my dreams. "I'm ready for babies now. I'm sorry, I can't settle for anything less." I sobbed, a hysterical gasp echoing through the night.

"I just can't do it," he said, fraught with sadness. "If you would just trust me, it will happen. I love you so much and I have every intention of giving you babies. Later."

I suddenly wished I could jump from the taxi and swim to the shore. The ride was painstakingly slow and I'm sure we had entertained the other patrons to no end. I thought long and hard about what Edwin was proposing, but I couldn't imaging spending another year with him, for fear that he could swear off having children altogether.

Weary, angry even, I refused to leave anything off the table. "When then?"

He stuttered for a few seconds and stopped trying

altogether. With a sigh, "I don't know, Abs. When we're both ready."

"Honestly, Eddie, I love you now more than I've ever loved you. I want to be with you. But I can't play the waiting game. And this is not something I'm willing to leave to chance."

"I'll come around. You know I want a family too."

"It's cut and dry for me, Eddie. I want a family now. It's as plain as that."

As the ferry finally approached the dock, I hurried to the front hoping to make a quick exit. When we came to a full stop, I was the first one waiting at the door, impatiently begging the door to unlock so I could run away.

Edwin dragged up behind me and the other passengers formed a V behind him, allowing him to follow me uninterrupted. He rested his hand on the small of my back and I squeezed my teary eyes shut as he brought his lips to my ear. "You know where I stand," he whispered.

I spun around, seriously distraught. My eyes narrowed and my voice rose. "So, this is it?"

"That's up to you," he replied, calmly.

Leave it up to a lawyer to turn the burden on me. I choked back the gloom hanging in the back of my throat, but I couldn't stop the drops from sliding down my face. "What am I supposed to say to that?"

"I won't leave you, Abs. This is your decision. You either love me or leave me," he said, frankly.

The door latched open.

I leapt from the ferry and rushed down the dock. "I'm sorry," I wept.

CHAPTER TWENTY THREE

You know where I stand.

Those were the last words that Edwin said to me before I swallowed my courage, ended our relationship and terminated the only thing that was real to me. It's official: Abigail Jenkins and Edwin Santora are no more.

Standing next to his truck, I wept and wept some more.

If I get off this roller coaster ride this time, I won't be getting back on.

Why did I say that? Why? Oh yes, because it's true. That's right... I did the right thing.

No babies: no Abby.

Edwin took his time getting back to the truck as I waited alone in the shadows, unaffected by the darkness. My eyes were flooded with tears, my vision blurred, my mind cluttered with sadness. I could see a large man approaching me, but I couldn't tell who it was and I didn't care.

"Get in the truck," he barked, unlocking the door remotely.

It was apparent that Edwin had finally decided to grace me with his presence and he was extremely mad. For that I didn't give two shits because I was even madder.

The pain in my chest pulsed, and the chirping crickets were relentless. The sounds were almost deafening, ringing in my ears and pounding in my head. I scurried into the front seat to get away, but the sounds still hung in my ears.

I tried to concentrate on the steady rumble of the truck's engine, but that didn't help either, with the silent voices in my head taunting, blaming me.

Stop it! It's not my fault.

Edwin shifted the truck into reverse and punched the gas, showboating his anger, shooting stones into the grass. He slammed the stick into drive and punched it again, this time shooting stones at the feet of our trailing audience.

No doubt he wanted to get us home as fast as possible. I shared that desire. I pressed a cold hand to my forehead in an attempt to ease the tension, but I knew better. *Nothing will make this better.*

There wasn't a drug in the world that could make this feeling go away. We both knew it was over between us. There was no other way. Our stubbornness had caused us to butt heads in the past and surprise, surprise, here we were again. So much for learning from my mistakes.

I smeared the tears from my cheeks as they continued to drip from my eyes. Edwin stared at me through disappointed eyes, carefully inspecting my reaction.

What did he expect?

After the longest, most agonizing ride home, I hurried inside for some soul searching. From the sound of the engine and the squealing tires, as Edwin pulled away from the house like a psycho, I knew that he was pissed.

He raced off to blow of some steam and seek some lonely refuge, as he always did whenever we argued. And, on cue, I wept to myself trying to figure out where I went wrong. Hard to believe we were so blissfully happy a few short hours ago; that bliss now long lost.

I ran upstairs to my bedroom with plans of improving my outlook on life, but instead I sobbed and moaned about losing Edwin, the exact same way I had done too many times before.

How could I call it losing him when I intentionally pushed him away this time?

I tortured myself with desperate whimpers of regret and despair, until I finally cried myself to sleep.

The next morning came, whether I wanted it to or not. Though I barely slept a wink, I wasn't even sure whether Edwin had returned home last night. I laid there quietly, absorbed in my self-inflicted misery.

I listened carefully for any rummaging around the house. I couldn't face Edwin so soon. Unfortunately, it was Sunday and we typically laid low on Sundays. But it didn't matter how long I'd have to wait him out. I could not face him.

A couple of hours passed before I finally heard him settle in downstairs with the TV blaring. I had a desperate need to use the washroom, so I jumped out of bed, not wasting the opportunity, and tiptoed to the bathroom unnoticed.

When I returned to my room I closed the door quietly and hopped back in bed, still not quite ready to face the day. I pulled out my I-pod and turned on the music super loud. In a matter of minutes the music had me sobbing in my pillow.

The more I thought about Edwin's tender kiss and his hard exterior, the more I started to second guess my decision. Why do I put us through such punishment when we are so in love? At least I'm still in love with him. Who knows how he feels about me now, after what I did to him.

I can't believe I broke up with him.

There was a part of me that wanted so badly to run down the stairs, jump into his arms and apologize for my ridiculous antics. But this isn't the movies and things don't always work that way. I still had to fight the urge.

I'd better get out of the house before I really do something I regret.

I dragged my lazy ass out of bed and pulled my purse to the floor. I sat there cross-legged, rummaging frantically for my phone, so I could text my sister. It had been too long.

11:14 a.m.
Hey Aub, What's the bestest sista in the whole world up to? Could use a little R+R, preferably as far away from my house as possible!!! :(

11:16 a.m.
Uh oh!! That doesn't sound good. Just got home. Why don't you come over?? ~ Aubrey

As usual, in a matter of minutes she had messaged me back. Aubrey was always there for me when I needed her, and she had experience when it came to helping me get through a break-up with Edwin. Being that Aubrey was only a ten minute walk up the road, I decided to take her up on her offer. Immediately.

I slipped on some comfy lounging clothes and pulled on a light hoody. I plugged my headphones in my ears, pulled my hoodie over my messy hair and ignorantly walked out of my room, down the stairs and straight outside, without a glance in Edwin's direction or acknowledgment of his existence. I knew it would hurt him, but it would hurt me more to see him, and I was being selfish.

It was exceptionally cool for the first week of July, now that a cold front had moved in, bringing with it random thunderstorms and treacherous winds. I didn't care. Despite the unseasonably cool weather, the air-conditioners continued to hum and haw from every house thanks to the high humidity.

I turned up my music louder hoping to drown out the dreariness. It blasted my eardrums but it didn't work. I complained to myself, how my already muddled hair was kinking and curling into a horrible mess and became even more frazzled. Even the humidity was pissing me off.

As if it could get any worse, the light mist turned to droplets spitting from the sky. I could just see it, there was someone sitting high in the dark clouds, dangling their feet, pointing and laughing at me. A few steps farther and the spit turned into large drops showering from the clouds.

I let out an exasperated cry, staring up at the sky, flagging my hands at it like a madwoman. Was everything pitted against me?

I started a light jog toward my sister's condo, my aggravation still escalating. To my surprise, it was actually quite refreshing – real – even a relief to let off a little steam. I went a little faster, my legs stretching their full length as I started to gain speed.

That's when my phone vibrated. I slowed down to a speed walk and pulled my phone from my kangaroo pocket, rain splashing all over the screen as I checked the message from Aubrey.

11:21 a.m.
I called your house, but you're not there. Edwin says you took off. Tell me U R NOT walking in this weather!! You are, aren't you??!! :(Be there in a min. ~ Aubrey

Not more than three minutes later, Aubrey's car was speeding toward me, sloshing down the wet street. The rain had slowed back down to a dribble, but the top layer of my clothes were already drenched. I pulled my heavy shirt over my head, rung it out quickly, then dropped it on the floor mat, revealing my ribbed white tank top and tear stained cheeks. Of course, Aubrey noticed right away.

"I came as soon as I could. Are you okay?"

"No, I'm not okay." I broke into tears. Again. And I wished I could hide beneath my baggy sleeves and hood, now sopping wet on the floor.

After smearing away the initial downfall with my hands, I tried to pull myself together. I could see it was upsetting Aubrey. I was the big sister after all, and I'm expected to keep it together. Not this time. She stepped on the gas pedal and drove us to her stylish, upscale condo, as quickly as her four-banger could carry us.

Underground parking had its benefits, I thought to myself, sighing aloud as we headed toward the door. I held my soggy hoody away from me, like it had cooties, to keep from getting even more wet. I still couldn't bear the thought of the dreaded elevator ride. "Are the stairs okay?" I asked, hoping to avoid her nosy neighbours.

"You got it," she replied, as she flipped her long, wavy blonde hair over her shoulder. Aubrey stretched her arm up and over my shoulder to comfort me, as we trudged up the stairs from the basement to the second floor.

"Let's get you inside. There's no need for people to see you like this," Aubrey whispered, confirming my own concern. I looked like hell.

She unlocked her door and let me in first. After dropping

my shirt onto her marble floor, I shimmied out of my sweatpants, leaving them at her entryway while I scurried to her couch. I crashed onto it with a moan.

"Let me get you something to wear. Then you can tell me all about it," Aubrey said, leaving with my soggy clothes in hand. After tossing my clothes in her dryer, she returned with a dry pair of dark grey yoga pants. I slipped them on and plopped back on the couch, burying my face in my arms.

She took a seat on her red lounge chair and kicked up her feet. Even she knew she was going to be a while. "So, tell me. What is it now?"

"You say it like I always have problems."

She giggled, her green eyes glowing. "That's because you do. No offense, but it's like you're my own personal soap opera."

I was not amused, but I knew she was only being honest and that's what I loved about her most. "You know how I told you how great things were going with Edwin and me?"

"Yeah," she replied, seeming curious but hesitant.

"Well I had to go and throw a wrench into it and now my life's a mess."

"What did you do?"

Sobbing, "I broke up with him and it's for real this time."

Not giving me the benefit of the doubt, Aubrey smirked and pulled her knees to her chest. "Mmm, hmm. I've heard that one before."

I took a deep breath and pulled myself back together. I always felt like I had to put up a good front for my little sister. Sure she was only a couple of years younger than me, but she was still my little sis. I was supposed to be the strong one. Even my therapist told me so.

"But I don't get it. You're so happy when you're with him. Why'd you do it?"

"Babies."

"Babies?"

"Yes. I want babies and he doesn't. It's as simple as that."

"Well, I'd say that's a pretty good reason to break up with someone. You have to do what you have to do. It's his loss."

"Then why do I feel so wicked?" I was still very upset, but the tears had finally taken their leave.

"It's better now than later. Trust me. You saved yourself a shout-off. It really is better this way, Abby."

"It just hurts so bad, and for him to be in the house... ugh! It's all I can think about."

"It just happened, right? It'll get better. I promise. Once you get back to your daily routine, without him, you'll find your way. You always do."

"You're always so optimistic. That's why I had to see you. You're right, of course. I needed this."

"Anything for my big sis." She smiled her cheery grin and it warmed my heart one degree.

"I must be such a disappointment to you right now. I'm supposed to be the one helping you with your relationship problems, not the other way around."

"You've helped me through my fair share of stuff. You've always been there for me, and I'll always be here for you. Twenty-four, seven. And I mean that. If you ever need to get away, you can come stay with me."

"Deal."

"Good. So, are you up for some exercise? It might make you feel a little better. It sure beats eating like a pig and packing on the pounds."

"Let's do it." Jogging had made me feel a little more alive, so maybe this could help too. It was definitely worth a try.

"Okay, I got this new hip hop game for the Wii. It's a lot of fun." She plugged in the game and cranked the sound up real high. Side by side, we wielded our hips and imitated the dancers hand motions like professional dancers. Jamming to the music, I forced myself to work it out hard, in an effort to sweat away some of my worries.

"Want a bottle of water?" Aubrey asked, as we finished a low intensity dance.

"Please. I'm dying here. That was excellent. We

definitely have to do this again soon."

"You know where to find me," she hinted, smiling.

"Likewise. You know you can come over any time." I missed her little visits. They had become almost non-existent over the past few months.

"I know, but your relationship with Edwin was so intimidating. You two were attached at the hip and so in tune with each other. Nobody wants to mess with that."

"Ain't that the truth? It's going to be different now. I just keep telling myself that it's a change for the better."

"You'll be fine. You hungry?"

After dousing my sadness with hard work, waffles drenched in maple syrup and sisterly love, Aubrey drove me home and I was ready to face the facts. Edwin was in my life, no matter how hard it hurt, and so I'd have to deal with it. I jumped out of Aubrey's car, waved goodbye and headed right for the door.

Once inside, I locked the door and flicked the light switch on. A twinge of adrenaline spiked my nerves when I recalled my most recent incident. I guess my personal security system was out of the question now.

Edwin was still lounging on the couch. It looked like he hadn't moved a muscle since I had left hours earlier. I didn't speak to him as I headed for the kitchen to get some water, but when I walked by again, he didn't let me pass unnoticed.

Sitting in his spot, Edwin's eyes followed me. I ran up the stairs as quickly as I could. My heart skittered in my chest, my breaths sharp and laced with anxiety.

He hollered his threat, loud and smooth. "You can't avoid me forever, you know."

CHAPTER TWENTY FOUR

There I laid, back in my bed, wondering how to take what Edwin had said.

You can't avoid me forever, you know.

I did know that, and I was certainly avoiding him, but I couldn't imagine just casually hanging out as if nothing ever happened. Was he over it already? It didn't matter. *I* needed time.

I managed to stay out of Edwin's path for the rest of the day. That night, I cried before I fell asleep, but much less than the night before.

When I awoke in the morning, loneliness loomed over me like a dark cloud. Despite that, unexpectedly, I felt ready to see Edwin face to face. Regardless, I had to go to work. Whether I liked it or not, I would have to get used to the idea and fast.

I rubbed my eyes, pulled open my bedroom door and trotted down the stairs for breakfast. *No Edwin.* I ran back upstairs, showered in our shared bathroom, and returned to my bedroom. *No Edwin.*

I carefully unclipped a long black pencil skirt from a hanger, and slipped the fitted skirt over my hips. Before I topped it with a flirty blouse, I decided I should've probably brushed my teeth first. There's nothing worse on a Monday morning, than tooth paste splatter on your white shirt.

Acting quick and careless, I headed for my door, and when I stepped out into the hallway, I bumped right into Edwin.

"Whoa!" He seemed equally as stunned by the imposition, but he didn't budge an inch.

Being inside his personal space was incredibly awkward. It wasn't exactly the place I had expected to be this morning. But there I was, wearing nothing but a barely-there bra.

My eyes flashed away from his glimmering aqua glance and landed on his luscious smiling lips. Lower yet, my eyes focused in on his smooth chest peeking out of his crisp white, mostly unbuttoned shirt. *Damn it.* He looked like a tasty morning treat, his shirt fully tucked into those black slacks hung handsomely from his masculine hips.

I swallowed the lusty lump from the back of my throat. "Sorry," I said, softly. I didn't even know whether I was apologizing for getting in his face or eyeing his body like a piece of man candy.

It didn't seem to matter to him. He took my chin in his hand and looked right through me with a piercing gaze. "You can feel sorry for a lot of things, but this shouldn't ever be one of them."

His lips covered mine, his drugging kiss long and slow, as I struggled with myself to make him stop. I should have. I could have. But I didn't.

Edwin stopped first and smiled at my carelessness. I stood there a little stunned and a lot disappointed with my lack of judgment. With fists bunched at my sides, I forced a stern look to make its appearance. It was hard to keep it together.

"What do you think you're doing, Eddie?"

"I couldn't help myself, and you didn't stop me. What do you expect? I'm only a man."

How can I argue with that? I loosened my fists and took a deep breath, in an attempt to relax my tense muscles. "Well, maybe you can give me a little notice next time."

"I didn't plan for this. It just happened," he insisted.

"I'm sure. You're lips just bumped into mine."

"Like you just happened to rush out of your door at the exact time I was passing," he challenged. His arrogance was starting to make me angry, but I was relieved to feel any emotion other than sadness and despair.

"Wait a minute! That really happened! Don't try and turn this on me."

"Mmm, hmm," he replied, pressing my every button.

"Well, I hope you enjoyed yourself, because I'm not going to let you take advantage of me like that again." I backed away, more for me than for him. He smelled so good.

He laughed and just stood there, shaking his head, staring at me. His fresh aftershave and fragrant cologne mixed with his arousal in an enticing aroma. It had a terrifying effect on me, heightening my senses and messing with my mind. After being so dangerously close to him, I was desperate for some privacy to regain my composure. But his eyes never left mine and I worried that he was magically deciphering my thoughts.

With my nerves getting the best of me, I did what any reasonable woman would have done in the circumstances: I bolted for the washroom.

"I was just going to brush my teeth," I announced, trying to prove my innocence. I ducked into the washroom, feeling safe once I was out of the fathomless aqua force field he was wielding.

"Oh, really?" he replied, following after me. "Funny. Because that's exactly what I was coming to do."

My eyes grew wide with anxiety and as soon as I noticed, I glared at myself in the mirror. *Time. Space. I need...*

Edwin appeared nonchalantly in the reflection behind me. I tore my eyes from his firm chest and confident stare, and fixed them on my toothbrush, as I shakily applied the paste. I put the tube down and pressed both of my hands against the cold marble countertop to support my weight, stop the shaking and avoid his mystical eyes.

Continuing with his casual lack of concern, Edwin reached around me and under my outstretched arms to retrieve the toothpaste and his brush. I closed my eyes and inhaled his scent, totally disarming my anger and arousing my budding curiosity.

I took a deep breath, as I ran my toothbrush under the water. "What are you doing?"

"Brushing my teeth. Obviously."

"Hah!" I replied, with a mouthful of paste.

Edwin began to fight me for the sink bowl, playfully hip

checking and trying to shove me out of the way. I defended better than a seasoned veteran, boxing him out with my hips and rear-end.

"I'd better warn you," Edwin mumbled, with paste foaming around his lips. He nudged me aside and emptied his mouth into the sink. "I may try and kiss you again when you're done brushing."

I sputtered into the sink, reacting to his terrifying words. "Don't even think about it!" I was feeling extremely uncomfortable with the notion.

"You asked for notice and service is effective," he taunted, dipping his mouth to the tap. He slurped up some water and swished it around in his mouth as I took a mouthful of water myself.

I rinsed out my mouth and dried it on the towel as Edwin spewed out the last of his mouthwash. I wanted to be mad. I tried to be mad. But how could you be mad at that handsome face?

"Don't say I didn't warn you," he said, winking.

There was no denying that spending time like this with Edwin made me feel a lot better about everything. Playful was doable, and I was pleasantly surprised that he was being so good about it so soon. Taking my good old time, I flossed every tooth and gargled with mouthwash. Edwin watched me intently.

I acknowledged his presence, but tried to act emotionless. It was extremely difficult. An overpowering inquisitiveness hung thick in the air between us as I dried the wetness from my mouth. I found myself in desperate need of oxygen, the room entirely starved of it as Edwin stepped up beside me.

"We're going to be okay," he said, his low, sexy growl cutting through the hazy air.

I reached past him to put the bottle of mouthwash back where it belonged, and he didn't move out of my way. My sensitive sniffer caught a whiff of him again, as I nudged him aside to open the vanity door. *Mmm. That scent.*

Edwin stood, unmoved, blocking my path to the door,

making me brush past him to make my exit. As I walked away, he slowly followed, but stopped when he reached the hall. I pretended not to notice.

"You are pretty messed up," he said, stopping me in my tracks.

"Excuse me?" I spun around to face him, my expression cold and conceited.

"Did you forget already?" He hoped for a stunned response and so I acted clueless, as my eyes locked onto his heated gaze.

"I have no idea what you're talking about." If he only knew, I wanted him to try me on for size, something fierce. But I knew what was good for me.

I should stick to my original plan: evade, retreat and regroup. If I stayed away from Edwin I could move on a lot faster.

So, why won't my feet move?

"Oh, you know exactly what I'm talking about," he growled. His arousal swarmed the air around me, like a group of angry bees, and burned, fiery hot, through my lungs.

He took two long deliberate steps toward me, as I took one hesitant step backward. "I told you I would try again," he said, his voice sounding smooth and sexy, as he progressively got closer.

I should have turned and ran screaming for the stairs, but I could hardly make a peep. "I thought I had some time," I breathed, as his face drew near mine.

He brushed past my cheek, his breath on my neck and his lips against my ear. "You thought wrong."

My lashes fluttered shut, as Edwin slowly pulled away from my neck, his hand gently skimming across my cheek. I waited for his sensual attack, but it never came. I slowly opened my anxious, emerald eyes and looked up into his. His smile was soft and tantalizing, and his lips parted as he closed his eyes and titled his head for a kiss.

I gasped for air and pulled back, stunning myself with my own willpower. "I can't, Eddie. We can't do this anymore." *Though I so wish we could.*

"I realize we can't do this as a couple. But we're both single, consenting adults. We're free to do whatever we want."

I cocked an eyebrow at him, preparing to playfully test his crisis negotiation skills. "Do I look like that kind of girl to you? I don't just sleep around with random men like that."

He returned inside my zone, his lips delivering an enticingly cunning smile, shaking my confidence. "I'm hardly some random guy."

Yes! Yes! I thought, as Edwin's cologne doused my senses. At that moment, with my own hormones raging, I was unable to formulate a sentence, let alone verbalize one.

"It'd be just this once," he insisted. "No one even knows that we've split. I want to... no I need to feel you, Abs. One last time. Admit it. You need it too."

Just the fact that I was thinking about it was stressful enough, and Edwin thought that was his answer.

"What's the big deal?" he asked, smirking.

"It's not healthy!" I stammered.

"Get over it."

"But I have to go to work." I partly hoped he would give up, so I could stick to my guns.

"We don't usually leave for another half hour, at least. You know there's plenty of time for what I have in mind. Now quit with the excuses."

On a harsh exhale, I let my guard down only for a second, and Edwin didn't waste the opportunity. He kissed me, his hot lips on mine. He kissed me again, his icy cool breath in my mouth.

Stunned, I accepted the string of tantalising nibbles and devouring mouthfuls. Just last night I was worrying to myself that I may never find myself in this place ever again, and here I am the very next day wrapped in his amazing arms; his thorough hands exploring me with unguarded enthusiasm.

My mind was done fighting, my body begged me to stop

fighting and I couldn't fight Edwin off anymore, even if I wanted to. Did I want to? *Hell no.*

I pushed Edwin off of me and he froze in confusion, until I started to slowly, seductively, unzip the back of my long, fitted skirt. After it slipped to the floor, I kicked it aside. I was standing there in the hallway, with my breasts bursting from my lacy push up bra and my g-string barely covering anything, and yet Edwin's gaze was still locked on my face. He was speechless.

I knew this would be my last opportunity to touch him and so did my body. Together we intended to take full advantage of him.

A devious giggle tickled my throat, as I stepped toward him. His eyes grew wide with excitement as I yanked his pressed shirt from his pants and tore open the rest of his carefully buttoned shirt. The buttons sprinkled onto the floor like candy, as I stared up at him through dark lashes.

My hands smoothed over the rise and fall of his chest. They were cold compared to the heat radiating from his firm skin.

Edwin's lips turned up into a smile, finally revealing his arousal and forgetting about his surprise. I grinned back, provocatively, all anxiety piled back with my skirt on the floor. My hands scoured his bulky physique and my tongue found his hard nipple.

His eyes closed and his pants tented, as my aggression made him thicker and harder. Edwin licked his lips and gripped onto my behind with his large hands, letting out an excited moan as I nibbled at him.

My fingers skimmed over his rock hard abs, then deftly unclipped his leather belt. Dropping to my knees, my lips trailed down his body to where my fingers left off. Being slow and sensual, I trimmed the band of his fitted briefs with kisses and then pulled his belt off with a snap.

"Hey, I didn't say you could rip all of my clothes off," he said, his wicked grin being his demise.

Channeling all control, "Oh, are you making the rules now?" I stopped, acting like I could actually control my sexual rage. "Suit yourself." Yanking on his pants, I lifted myself to my feet and spun away from him. With one dainty step, my body trembled with an all-consuming ache for Edwin.

"No more playing, Abs. I need you."

I froze in place trying to shake the delicious chill chasing up my body. His serious response made my anxiety return full force though none of the excitement dwindled.

Stealing a few more steps away from him, I was met with the top of the stairs. I glanced down to our front foyer, reason returning to me, as I frantically reconsidered my options: fight or flight.

"Oh no you don't," Edwin said, reading my mind. Then, out of nowhere, he was just there; pulling me back and lifting me in the air like a doll. "You're mine," he ordered, looking up at me through deep, dark eyes.

Breathless, I wrapped my dangling legs around his waist, as he pressed me against the wall. He slowly drew my lips into his mouth, but when he grinded against me, we both became instantly frantic and obsessive.

We moaned in unison, desperate to fulfill our own fanatical desires. Edwin pulled me off the wall and turned for my room, his fly open and ready, his business attire flagging loosely from his hips.

"No! Take me now."

Edwin obeyed. He dropped his pants to the floor, laid me where he stood and boldly took me right in the hall. Arousal, pleasure, love and passion were among the many feelings blasting around me like a violent whirlpool as I quickly found my climax.

"Oh, Edwin. Oh God!" I wailed, as he thrust deep and exploded inside me, rocking me in a glorious second wave of pleasure.

He crashed on top of me, breathless and amused, his heavy chest driving the air from my lungs. Noticing my silent discomfort he lifted himself with a push up and kissed me gratefully on my lips. My head still swirled with ignorance and harmony.

"Now that's what I'm talking about," he growled, sensually. "We couldn't have done that if we had kids."

Edwin had to blow it with a smart-assed comment. *Who says that?*

Two minutes earlier, and that comment would have fueled and unleashed the already seething storm within me, but I was too satiated to be angry at the moment.

"Get off of me," I replied with a giggle, though I knew I shouldn't encourage him. My mind drifted, far, far away, in happy land. I giggled again, still caught up in the moment.

Edwin pulled his pants to his hips, zipped his fly and picked up his crumpled shirt from the floor. Motioning toward the buttons scattered across the floor, "Try explaining this to the cleaners."

CHAPTER TWENTY FIVE

Yes, the sex was good. Okay, it was better than good. And while doing it spur of the moment in the hallway was exciting, it was something I was willing to pass up to have children.

Over half an hour had passed before Edwin and I walked into work. One after the other, we entered the lobby, elation still spilling from our glowing faces.

Aliah was at the front desk, talking to Taylor, her green eyes glaring with speculation. "You two make me sick."

Edwin ignored her and headed for his desk, a smile still painted on his face.

"What?" I asked, smirking, still pretty damn content myself.

"You're both so damn happy all the time. It makes me sick to my stomach."

"They do make such a great couple," Taylor added, smiling. She was just happy to be involved in the conversation.

"Actually, Edwin and I aren't together anymore."

"Ha, ha. Very funny," Aliah said.

"I'm serious. Just ask him." My smile faded, honesty showing the severity of the situation. It stood true: Edwin and I are done. And now that Taylor knew about it, I was sure the entire office would be privy to it by noon.

"Am I missing something here?" Aliah asked Taylor, confused.

Taylor shrugged her round shoulders, just as startled by the news.

Aliah turned her pale green eyes on me. "You looked like you were on cloud nine when I saw you at the fireworks, and then you two couldn't wipe the smiles off your faces when you just walked in. What's up with that?"

"You wouldn't get it. Anyways, we've come to terms with our decision and we both agree that it's over between us."

"It sure doesn't look over to me," Aliah replied, looking to Taylor again for some support.

"I would have to agree with Ally there," Taylor said, nodding hesitantly.

I rolled my eyes, unwilling to spill all my beans in front of Taylor. There was some information best kept for other ears only; meaning not Taylor's. "I'll tell you more later, but I have to get to work now."

Aliah shook her head at me, solidifying the fact that they would be talking about me after I left, but that didn't concern me now. I had a new outlook on life. Life is what you make it. I wasn't about to boo hoo about it, all over again, and let another opportunity pass me by. Who knows what I had missed out on already.

This morning I was feeling a little saucy and had a little fun sharing my body with Edwin. But it was the last time. The love was still there, oh yes, but it was surrounded by a hollow shell. And right now that shell felt empty.

I had my first consensual adult experience as a single this morning, and I would make it my full time job to make sure it was my last. Getting it on with Edwin as I pleased, while dangerously enticing, was so not healthy.

The only way for me to move on is to put some emotional distance between us and let the passion fade. No more stoking the fire. And once the flames fizzle, I can just be me.

After yet another uneventful day at the office, Aliah attacked me in the parking lot. "What's the big hurry?" she hollered, chasing after me.

I stopped a few steps away from my car and waited for her to catch up. "No hurry. Actually I have no idea what the hell I'm going to do tonight."

"Hmm... wait! I know. Come out with me."

"Out? Seriously, Ally? It's Monday." My skeptical stare judged her, but it didn't seem to penetrate her flow.

"Don't look at me like that. Think of it as the first day of the rest of your life. We're going out! Whoop!" she cheered.

"Did you just say whoop?" I said, smirking.

"Oh yeah, I so did," she answered, ridiculously excited about it.

"I could do dinner. I definitely have to get some of this shit off my chest. We haven't had a good talk lately. You know, you still haven't told me how you and Hunter got back on good terms... or what you think about the baby."

"Whoa, whoa, whoa. We can talk later, but no baby talk. Please! We're going out. Woo hoo!"

"Okay, but I've saved up some pretty juicy stuff to tell you," I warned.

"Oh really? Try and top mine, because it's super juicy."

"We'll see," I wagered, playfully. "So, when are we leaving?"

"Just as soon as I change out of this stifling suit. I think I need to get into something a little more appropriate. You too."

"Are you going to pick me up?"

"You know it. And when I say 'appropriate', I'm using that term loosely. Dress hot," she demanded.

"Whatever you say. But may I ask where you're taking me?"

"Wherever the night brings us," she chimed, like an inspired damsel, as she shuffled toward her car. Textbook Aliah. She had no intention of telling me what was going on and I was sure that it meant trouble.

As I reached my house, I had already hashed over how surprisingly easy it had been seeing Edwin at the office over the past two weeks. I didn't get upset today, not once. I was okay with the fact that he wasn't my man to touch, boss around and love anymore. That was step one.

Now if I could only get the image of his bare, buff chest out of my mind; that and the look on his face when I ripped his shirt off last. That damned image was burned into my brain like a vivid photograph. *I suppose there's no harm in cataloguing it for future reference.*

The truth was: all I needed was time. Time was the only thing that would make it better. If I wanted to wipe clean my heart to open it up to a new man, I would have to put Edwin away.

After passing Edwin's shiny truck, I walked up my front steps and reached my key toward the dull door knob. I hustled straight to the bathroom to fix my hair and make-up, because I knew Aliah wasn't one to mess around.

At the speed that she drove, I knew I didn't have a whole lot of time to dilly-dally. Though I may have partly been trying to avoid Edwin again, I hoped that he wouldn't notice. I didn't want to have to go through the whole exercise again.

Before long, I had myself done up pretty damn good. I hurried to my bedroom, counting down the seconds before Aliah would show up. Just as I was about to pull a flirty shirt over my head, there was a knock at my bedroom door.

Damn, Aliah's fast!

"Come in," I called, as I wriggled into my perfectly fitted shirt.

Expecting Aliah's insistent, crude chatter, I was startled when the room fell silent. I quickly adjusted my shirt and spun around to face my door. "Oh, shit! I thought you were Aliah."

Edwin stood inside the door with a mischievous smile on his lips and his eyebrows curved for trouble. "Nothing I haven't seen before."

"Can I help you?"

"You just did." His eyes swept over me again and his smile stretched from ear to ear.

"Real cute, Eddie. What do you want?"

"Just checking to make sure you aren't avoiding me. You aren't all freaked out about everything again are you?"

I rummaged through my jewellery box for some dangly accessories. "Do I look all freaked out to you?"

"No, you look good."

I hooked some gold earrings from my ears, fluffy beige feathers dangling from them, and pulled on the matching long necklace. "Thanks. But if that's it, then I'll really have to talk to you later. I've got somewhere to be."

"Do you now?"

"Yes, I do."

"Don't tell me you have a date already," Edwin prodded, suddenly angry.

Why do I have to be such a meanie, pushing him like that? Because I'm feisty like that, that's why. "So what if I do?"

"You wouldn't do that to me. You wouldn't be so cruel. Did our relationship mean nothing to you?"

Ding dong: saved by the bell! And based on the incessant rings, it was definitely Ally at the door. I flashed a sassy smile at Edwin, breezed past him and sped down the stairs.

Edwin slowly walked the hall and waited at the top of the stairs to check out my visitor. "He sounds real classy," Edwin called to me, folding his arms over his buff chest.

Aliah let herself inside as I reached the bottom stair. She looked up at Edwin who was shaking his head, obviously disturbed by my insinuations.

"What's *your* problem?" she asked, scowling up at him.

"See, I told you I have a date," I said, smiling.

He slowly walked down the stairs, with his hands tightly packed in his armpits. "That's just mean."

"Oh, please. You asked for it. Give me some credit. Do you really think I'd be dating already? You know I took our relationship seriously. Probably even more serious than you."

"We'll talk about this later," Edwin said, with pause, "when we're alone." He glared at Aliah, as if it were somehow her fault that we were arguing.

"No, we'll talk about it now." I was not about to let him corner me again. Keeping out of those sorts of situations was the best move for me.

"I really don't want to hear it right now. And I'm sure Aliah doesn't want to either," he said.

"Don't let me stop you," Aliah insisted, loving the drama.

"Actually, you don't need to say anything," I said to Edwin, being firm. "There really is nothing left to talk about. Our relationship is over. Period."

"Fine, we don't have to talk about it, but you can't stop me from caring about you. I'll let you believe you're off the hook for now, but you aren't. Not by a long shot."

I gazed into his charming, heartbreaking eyes and quickly planted a kiss on his cheek. "Whatever you say, Eddie."

Aliah's smirk matched mine as she followed me out the door.

Edwin reached for Ally's arm and tugged her back gently. "Look out for her, will you?" he asked softly.

"Don't you worry, Eddie-boy. She's in good hands." Aliah swiftly pulled her arm from his loose grasp and twiddled her fingers in a wave. She left him standing in the doorway and that's where he stayed, staring at me through the windshield of her car.

Aliah slipped into the driver seat and pulled her door shut, flashing a quick glance at Edwin. "Wow, you really did a number on him," she said, as she turned over the ignition and slammed the car into gear.

"What are you talking about?"

"That boy is not going to let you out of his sight. You've still got him wrapped around your little finger."

"Nope. I don't."

"It sure looked that way to me. He's still got it bad for you."

"He'll get over it. When he sees that I'm moving on, he'll have to," I said, frankly.

"I suppose so, but he still seems pretty attached."

"Sex will do that for a man."

"But you said you broke up weeks ago. I doubt he's still dreaming about how great you are in bed."

"Well, about that..."

"Abigail Jenkins you tell me everything right now!" she demanded, eager for the dirty details.

"I might have bedded him after that, so to speak."

"You dirty, little, whore. And what do you mean so to speak?" Aliah was so intrigued she couldn't keep her eyes on the road. "Fess up. I want details."

"Well, we didn't exactly make it to the bed. I think saying I gave him a little action would better describe it."

Aliah's mouth dropped open and she slapped the steering wheel, swerving toward the oncoming traffic, her pale eyes still locked on me.

"Ally, watch the road!" I hollered, my eyes wide with panic.

She yanked the wheel and we escaped the near side swipe of the big red truck as it sped past us with its horn blaring. I was clinging to the door and had forgotten to breathe, but Aliah seemed undisturbed by it all.

"I knew you had it in you," Aliah said, as if nothing had just happened. "But I thought you said it was over."

"We agreed that there is no future for us as a couple, but as single, consenting adults, we couldn't resist."

"Hah! I cannot believe you! No wonder why you two were all googly eyed last Monday. So, now you've got him under your spell and here I am barely hanging on with Hunter." She shook her head, her thoughts rolling around in her head for only seconds before she blurted them out. "Eddie's still kickin' it with you. Unbelievable."

"Trust me, it was a one-time thing."

"Yeah, I'm sure you'll have no problem resisting him next time," she teased.

"I said I won't and I won't. If I ever plan to land myself another man, then Edwin can't be looming in my bedroom."

"Ain't that the truth. It's bad enough you have to tell your new guy that you live with another man. Oh, by the way, Eddie boy, he's my ex stud muffin."

Aliah hit the nail on the head. My dates had immediately red flagged me whenever I explained my living situation to them in the past, and rightfully so. Now if I can only stick to my one rule – no sleeping with Edwin – then I'm sure that the right guy will see past it. Spencer did.

"What are you thinking about?" Aliah asked, breaking me from my dangerous thoughts.

"Actually, I was thinking how funny it is that every time I imagine finding a new man, Spencer pops back into my head."

"Do you really want to go there again?" Aliah blasted me, curiously fast.

What is that all about? "When it was good, it was real good."

"Yeah, I've heard that before. Too bad it was mostly not so good."

"Take it easy. I didn't mean I was going to go crawling back to him. But he's a good guy."

"Oh, really? He was real good when he packed his bags and moved on without ever turning back."

"Trust me when I say this: I won't be wasting my valuable baby making years on my own leftovers. I left Edwin because he didn't fit my timeline. Why would I go back to another dead end?"

"Whoa, whoa, whoa! Back up a minute. What's this about babies and why did you leave Edwin?"

Had I been that unclear? Aliah and I had been drifting apart over the past few months, but it was hard to believe I hadn't slipped that into one of our conversations. "I told Edwin that I want to have babies soon and, if that didn't fit his plans then I couldn't waste any more time with him."

"Wow. I knew you were serious, but bam! I actually feel a little sorry for the guy."

Slightly angered, "That's not to mention that he hasn't put a ring on it," I added, making a point.

"Aren't you Ms. Demanding? You've been together for what, a few months, and you already expect a ring?"

"No, I don't expect a ring, but I do expect the prospect of a ring and some babies in my not so distant future. Ally, don't you realize how old I am? I ain't getting any younger, and I want to actually be able to chase after my kids. You know, keep up with them."

Aliah swerved off of the road and slammed on her

brakes. "You have got to be kidding me right now. You're twenty-four years old!"

"Exactly. I'm not eighteen anymore, and I'll be thirty before you know it. I don't care what you think, because I want kids and nothing's going to change that."

"It's no wonder Eddie was so stunned. I can't believe you wouldn't throw him a bone."

"Don't put it all on me. He knew how I felt about this. We've talked about it a million times before. I can't believe you're siding with him." My voice grew louder as I finished my sentence. "He shouldn't have gotten back with me if he couldn't handle it."

"Don't you yell at *me*. This is all *you*," Aliah retorted.

My face was turning into a ball of fire and I'm sure smoke was coming from my ears. "Suddenly I'm not feeling like going out with you. Take me home."

"Come on, Abby. I'm not siding with Edwin. You know I'm your girl. I'm just saying that I understand why he might have been a little distraught."

She still sounded like she was on his side. "I'm not going out with you."

She ignored my reaction and continued to rant in Edwin's favour. "He's a reasonable guy, but I bet he's thinking you're an evil succubus who's trying to steal his life away. And, I mean, can you blame him?"

I gasped with fury, as she pulled back out onto the street. And if she weren't driving, I would have rung her neck. "What's your point?"

"The poor guy just finished school and can finally relax and live a little and you wanna wife him up already."

"I cannot believe I am hearing this from your lips, what with the way you've latched on to Maddie's baby daddy."

"Leave Hunter out of this."

Ha ha, I think not. "No, he's fair game. While we're on the topic of *poor guys*, why don't you tell me how Hunter explained his way out of that one?"

"We weren't exactly in an exclusive relationship when he slept with Maddison."

"Oh, well when you put it that way, it's fine then."

"Stop."

"He can hold your hand by day and screw other girls by night, is that it?" I paused, letting the harsh truth of the matter sink in.

"You're a bitch," Aliah said, staring straight ahead.

I glared out the window at the lampposts speeding past us, but she wasn't taking me home. I scowled at my own reflection, a miserable bitch staring back at me. Why did I have to tear down Aliah too?

I was being unfair, when she had done nothing to me. Suddenly I felt terribly guilty for turning on her, but I couldn't bring myself to apologize. Silence hung light in the air as the car slowed down.

"You're lucky I know how to handle your bull shit, you know," Aliah said, glancing at me briefly. "I half expected this, but you're not getting away with it. You're stuck with me tonight." The light turned green and she stepped on the gas, swerving around the slow traffic.

A few more moments of silence passed, as I reflected on my rudeness and rummaged up some compassion. "I'm sorry for being such a bitch."

"Okay, so ignorance may be my new best friend. And yes, I may be dating a man whore, but it's still fun to play. Big deal, you and Edwin didn't work out. Close that chapter and move on to the next already."

She flashed a glance at me and barked another order. "We're going out, and you're gonna like it."

"If you say so."

"You'd better flip that frown around. I need my good old Abby back before we walk into that restaurant."

"Ally. What's going on?"

"You'll be fine. You're ready for this." She turned into the parking lot across the road from Riley's Pub, a local bar and grill that we frequented in the summer months.

"Ready for what, Ally?" I asked, hesitant and weary.

"You'll see. Maybe if you didn't lay into me, I would've told you. Now you'll just have to wait and see for yourself."

"Ally," I growled.

"I may have invited a few old friends out for dinner. Promise not to freak out."

I rubbed my forehead as the anxiety set it. The red returned to my cheeks. I absolutely hated the sound of that, but I had to suck it up. What was the worst that could happen: I might have a good time?

"I'm going to trust you on this one. I can't believe I'm saying this."

"It's about damn time. Come on. They're waiting for us."

CHAPTER TWENTY SIX

Aliah walked by my side, grinning from ear to ear. What had her so giddy, all of a sudden? She was up to something.

The street was packed with traffic. So when the cars came to a halt to wait for the nearby stop light, we made a run between the bumper to bumper vehicles.

A young gentleman saw us coming and waited, holding the wooden double doors open for us. His girlfriend rolled her eyes at him, none too pleased.

It was wing night, which was always a good excuse for people to come to the bar. For that reason, it was crawling with locals. Two couples and a group of six stood ahead of us waiting for a table. After scanning over the bar area, I flashed my eyes at Aliah.

"Don't worry. I have reservations."

"So do I," I said, sarcastically.

Aliah kept smiling at me, waiting for my reaction... for something. It made me more and more anxious by the minute.

"Why don't we get a drink at the bar first," she suggested, avoiding my narrowed eyes.

Without waiting for an answer, she dragged me through the bustling crowd to the bar. I was tempted to turn away the drink, but I decided to give Aliah a break tonight. Any time away from Edwin had to be better than being cooped up in the house with him.

"So, where are they?" I asked. My eyes anxiously skimmed across the room hoping to find a familiar face.

"Drink first," she insisted.

My growing unease stirred my stomach, as the cute bartender mixed my drink. The entire time, Aliah fought to wipe the smirk off her face. I took a sip of my drink. It tasted strong, but fruity. I took another gulp, as Aliah paid the bartender and left him a good tip.

"Are you going to tell me who's doing dinner with us or what?"

She took a sip from her sour drink and flashed me a devious smile. The death threat I issued with my eyes must have been enough because she answered me by nodding toward a private table at the opposite end of the room.

My eyes flashed over the booths and stopped at the one with two guys sitting across from each other. Squinting didn't help much. The booth was so dimly lit, I couldn't make out who it was.

Carefully studying the man facing my direction, I stared long and hard, until he glanced up and his sparkling eyes met mine. My head jolted back and I slouched a bit to hide behind the nearest person.

"Aliah, I am going to kill you. That better not be who I think it is."

"It is!" she cheered. Aliah stared back at the booth, giving me the impression that he wasn't looking anymore.

I hesitantly peeked over my shoulder to take another look. The instant my eyes adjusted to the lighting, he looked up again and caught my sneaky glance. "Oh, shit! He saw me."

I turned away quickly, then slowly looked back to see if he was still looking. He was, and so was his friend. I smiled, my cheeks raging red. Spencer stood up from the bench seat and waved for us to come over.

Aliah's mouth was forced into a perma-grin. "Go on," Aliah said, shoving me in his direction.

I mumbled profanities, but Aliah couldn't hear me over the upbeat music and the sociable crowd. "Tell me this isn't a double date," I pleaded. "You have a boyfriend and I've been single for all of two weeks. Eddie would have your head if he knew about this."

"Take it easy. It's not a date. We're just out as *friends*. I owed him one."

As we reached the table, Spencer made direct eye contact with me again. The lights glimmered in his icy eyes and he smiled, his lips mysterious and sexy. He stood up again to greet us, and flagged a hand at his friend.

"Abigail, you might remember Dex. You've met before," Spencer said, his English accent as sexy as ever.

"Of course I do. How are you?"

Dark and handsome, Dexter reached out his hand for a shake and then pulled me in for a hug, knocking me to my knees on the bench seat. "I'm great. How've you been?" he asked, planting a kiss on my cheek with his pale pink lips.

"Honestly, I've had better days," I admitted, "but I'll try not to be too much of a downer." I dropped my rear onto the seat next to him, trying to act calm and casual. It was difficult under Spencer's penetrating stare.

"I wasn't expecting Spencer to bring company. What a pleasant surprise," Aliah said, devouring Dex's shiny dark hair and soft blue eyes. "Abbyl, aren't you going to introduce me?" She remained at my side, her facial expressions quickly changing from sweet to perturbed.

"What, you haven't met? Didn't you set this up?"

She bent over and whispered in my ear. "No. He really is a pleasant surprise."

I rolled my eyes and smiled at Dexter, who was watching me intently. "Dexter Allbright meet Aliah Brooklin."

"It's Dr. Allbright now," he gloated.

"Oh, that's right. You were just finishing your last exam at med school when we last saw each other. Where are you working now?"

"I've actually been at the Regional Health Centre for the last year. I specialize in urgent care in the emergency department."

"Do you mind?" Aliah interrupted, clearing her throat.

I looked back to her and she was still standing at my side. Her eyes were darting at me to move out of her way. I doubt it was the smartest move for me, especially with seductive Spencer undressing me with his eyes, but I gave in anyway. I flashed a glance at Spencer, who raised his eye brows and smugly shrugged his shoulders at me.

"Ugh," I groaned, as I slid out of the booth to let Aliah in.

"You don't have to worry, Abby. I won't try anything," Spencer said, the words just rolling off his sexy tongue.

I sat next to him, hesitantly. He reached his arm over the seat behind me and leaned in close, startling my nerves.

"Okay, I lied. But you're free to do as you like," he whispered in my ear, tickling my eardrums with his smooth, sexy voice.

It didn't matter what he was saying because his charming accent was already seducing me. "You can try to chase me, but it's pointless," I insisted, trying to be cool about it.

Aliah was intently listening to one of Dexter's hospital horror stories, absorbed in his blue eyes and soft spiked hair. As I peered over my shoulder, a cheery waitress appeared at the end of the table with a mysterious drink for me.

"What's this?" I asked Spencer.

"I may have ordered you a drink. It's your favourite."

"No, it used to be my favourite," I corrected.

"I can return it if you don't like it."

"I'll have it," Aliah hollered across the table, reaching for my drink.

I put my hand firmly on the glass and gave Aliah an evil eye. "Thank you for the drink. It may not be my favourite anymore, but I still like it a lot." Another raging blush heated my cheeks.

Spencer smirked, hearing exactly what he wanted to hear. "So you're saying I have a chance?"

I shoved him playfully and played the ignorant. "If Aliah's never met Dexter, then how did you set this whole thing up?"

"That was all Spencer," Aliah chimed.

I looked into his eyes to read what he was thinking, but came up empty.

"What? Don't look at me. It's your friend over there who doesn't know how to obey the law."

"Aliah?" I glared at her, waiting for an answer.

"He may have caught me driving a little faster than I

should have, on my way home from work tonight," she said. She batted her eyelashes at him and he chuckled. "He didn't have to pull me over, but he had ulterior motives. See? No ticket."

I looked over to Dexter who was listening attentively. "Don't they call that unlawful coercion or something like that?" I asked him.

"Certainly bad judgment," Dexter said, smirking.

"It's actually called police discretion," Spencer asserted. "In other words: what I say goes. Lucky for Aliah, I'm a flexible guy."

I broke out laughing. "Listen to you," I said, smiling.

"Oh, but I am," he insisted, his voice smooth and charming.

"Since when were you a *flexible guy*?" I asked, arching an eyebrow.

Dexter laughed at him. "She's got you there."

"Wait one minute," Spencer hollered at Dexter. "I changed our plans in a flash tonight, didn't I?" Then he turned his accent on me. "I'd say that's a perfect example of my new found flexibility."

"Oh, so you weren't talking like flexibility in the bedroom then," Aliah teased.

I scowled at Ally for moving the conversation to the bedroom. Though Spencer did have mad skill in that department, it was the last thing I wanted to think of now. Lucky for Aliah, the waitress interrupted my cruel plotting against her, when she placed the bread and salads on our table.

"The soup will be right up, sir," she said, her smiling eyes lustily locked on Spencer.

I sensed Spencer flagging his arm behind me, even though my drink was far from empty. Textbook Spencer: trying to get me drunk so I'd loosen up. Not this time. One more drink and I was done.

As I suspected, when Spencer's soup arrived so did another fruity drink. It went down smooth, just like the next mysterious drink that arrived when I finished off my meal. It tasted like heaven. I couldn't turn it away.

"What's in these anyway?" I asked, slurping out of my straw to drink up the last drop. I was starting to feel a little woozy; then a lot woozy.

"It's rum," Spencer said. "And he wasn't going easy on the shots."

"My brain's on fire," I said, rubbing my temples. "If it's possible, I feel even worse than I did before."

"Well, it's been fun, but I think this is where I call it a night," Dexter said. "I have an early morning ahead of me."

"Yeah, I'm gonna bounce too," Aliah said, standing with Dexter.

"Aliah, would you mind taking Dex home?" Spencer asked. "I'll take care of this one."

"For sure. Let's go," Aliah said to Dexter, totally ignoring me.

"Oh, no you don't. This is all a part of your elaborate plan," I babbled incoherently, pointing a wobbly finger, eyes narrowed at Spencer. "But it's not going to work!" Dizzily, I stood from my seat and staggered after Aliah.

Spencer grabbed my arm to catch me from falling. "She's drunk," he announced, as if everyone in the vicinity hadn't already noticed. He helped me toward the door.

I stuck out my bottom lip in a pout. Transforming my eyes into a scowl, I turned them on Aliah, who got stopped up at the doorway. "You did this," I said to her.

"You know what?" Aliah said pointing a finger at me. "Screw you. Let's go Doc." Aliah spun away from me and slammed through the double doors. Dexter saluted us as he followed behind her.

"I have no idea what just happened here, but I'm glad that it did," Spencer said.

"Great!" My arms flailed like a crazy lady, causing the other patrons to back up and stare. "Why is this always happening to me?"

Spencer, just as confused as the other patrons, grabbed firmly onto my elbow and yanked me through the entrance like a criminal. "What is wrong with you?"

I tore my arm away from him, fists bunched at my sides, a mean stare locked on him. I didn't say anything.

"Come on. I'm taking you home," Spencer ordered, his icy blue eyes penetrating the hard barrier I was trying to erect. "You've obviously had too much to drink."

I considered hailing a cab but, before I could even formulate a sentence, a warning drop of rain splashed on my head.

"Take it... my arm," Spencer insisted, as I stumbled onto the sidewalk toward the road.

"Why should I?"

"I am not going to fight with you, Abigail. If you prefer to fall into traffic, then by all means."

After a brief brooding silence, I clutched his arm. He glanced down at me and flashed a sexy, knowing smile. He smoothly tugged me across the road and through the city parking lot by the river. A warm rain started to sprinkle over us.

"Can you slow down?" I whined, stumbling over my own two feet.

He slowed his speed to a near stop and flashed me another smart, but incredibly sexy look, raindrops tipping his spiky hair. "How's that?" he asked.

"Better," I stammered, though nothing could stop the spinning in my head. It was difficult enough to place one foot in front of the other.

"I thought maybe you would like to stay dry."

"I really could care less what you think," I said crisply, still clung to his arm. My eyes skimmed over the large parking lot that mostly serviced the main street businesses by day, but at this hour was nearly empty. After passing the last vehicle bundled near the main street, and listening to Aliah's incessant horn honking as she passed us, I started to wonder if he had even parked in the lot at all. "Where's your car?"

Spencer only chuckled, his eyes flashing toward the only car left in sight. Beyond the small pockets of light under each of the randomly spaced lamps, a shiny car sat in the last space lining the river, surrounded by a foggy mist of shadows. Yes, it was the farthest possible spot in the lot. It had to be his. *How annoying.* A blister started to gnaw at my ankle, causing me to limp in my wet shoes.

"I've been thinking of you lately," Spencer said, his voice too low, seductive.

"Is that so?"

"Yes, and I think you should be inclined to listen to what I have to say."

"Save it, Spencer. I've got enough shit to deal with."

"Like Edwin?" he asked.

"Yeah. I guess you could say that."

"It's always about him isn't it?"

"Not this time," I slurred. "Edwin and I aren't together anymore. There, I said it."

"Glad to hear it."

"You would be," I said with a growl, as I pulled away from him. "Some things never change."

"Like my feelings for you?" he whispered softly, more to himself. Frustrated, he rubbed his hand back and forth through his wet hair, messing it up. It only made him look sexier.

Funny, I didn't care how I looked. My hair was a mess. My night was a mess. My life was a mess. "Tell me this one thing," I asked. "Why is it that you could have any girl in that place tonight – I mean they were practically throwing themselves at you, begging you to take them home – and here you are with good old, bitchy me?"

"Am I that transparent?" he asked, smirking. Spencer was as transparent as they come, always saying exactly what was on his mind.

Fine, don't answer my question. "Where are you taking me?" I pressed, wondering how much longer it would take to get to his car.

"To my love nest. Where do you think? To my car."

Startled, I stumbled over a small rock and began to fall in slow motion. Alert and agile, Spencer gathered me into his arms before I landed on the hard ground.

He looked down at me, his icy eyes sparkling. Dizzily trapped in his embrace, I let him hold all of my weight in his arms. So close to the damp, hot pavement, I thought I would fall into the steamy puddles, but Spencer's grip never wavered. The blue-grey mist that was his eyes wrapped around me, putting me in a foggy fantasy state. I felt the urge to kiss him, but knew it was a very, very bad idea.

"Tripping over reality?" he said, lifting me back to my feet and dragging me out of my daze.

Feeling defeated, "Yeah, and I smacked my head on the cold hard truth."

Spencer dug into his pocket. Lights flashed on the lonely charcoal Charger as he led me to his car. Suddenly feeling very lightheaded again, I linked my arm around his trim waist for support and rested against his shoulder. The cool black leather relieved the heat storming my forehead.

Stiff and stunned, mistaking my faintness for affection, Spencer stopped before we reached his car. He must have forgotten how friendly I got when I drank.

He turned to face me and slipped his arms around my waist, drawing me close. "Do you still want that answer?" he asked, smoothly.

"You've lost me."

"The reason I chase after you, even after all we've been through, Abby, is *this*."

"*This?*"

His breath tickled my ear, his heartbeat pounding strong against my chest. He tilted my chin up, to meet his gaze and motioned his index finger in the small space between us. "*This*," he said again.

I sunk into his misty grey-blue eyes and found myself falling into his trap. He was a beautiful, charming man, with a voice so smooth and cool that Mother Theresa would have dropped her panties at his request. I tried to swallow the sour lump from the back of my throat, but it didn't go away.

"I can be myself when I'm around you, Abby. I can say what I want and you'll tell me like it is. I like that."

"Ahh, I see. You're a sucker for punishment."

"I guess I am," he admitted, with a mischievous grin. His hypnotic eyes and charming words were leading us to a place I was sure I didn't want to go, and yet I couldn't escape his allure.

My eyes fluttered shut, as his hand swept across my cheek and along my jaw. My lips parted, an open invitation, and his lips massaged over mine, with a sensual kiss. Slowly, I drew my mouth away from his, and took a long breath. "I'm sorry. I can't do this," I said, my slurred voice soft and breathless.

"What, you don't like it?" he said, in his erotic English accent.

God damn, that's sexy. "No. I definitely like it. But it goes a lot deeper than that."

He chuckled to himself. "Sucker for punishment."

"Can you please take me home?"

Disappointed now, he took my hand, making me feel like a scorned child as he delivered me to the passenger door.

"You don't have to take care of me, Spencer. I can take care of myself," I said, as I struggled to open the car door.

"Yeah, I can see that," he replied, sarcastically. He pulled the door wide and eased me into the seat. Within seconds he was sitting next to me. He slowly reached over and pulled down my seatbelt, inhaling me as he clicked the belt. He sat back in his seat and sighed.

"Are you waiting for something?" I asked.

"Yeah. I'm waiting for you to tell me why you don't want to give *us* another try."

"Oh, Spencer. Do we have to do this now? I really don't want to get into it."

"Just tell me straight up."

"You're asking for it!" I warned, ready to let him have it.

"It can't be worse than my reality. Before you left me, I had dreams. Plans. We could've gotten married, maybe do a little travelling, then start a family..."

"Wait a second. You've been talking to Aliah, haven't you? And for the record: you left me."

"What does this have to do with Aliah?"

Great. He didn't know about my hang up on having a family, but he does now. Why did I have to go and open my big mouth? "It doesn't."

"Still the same old cold shoulder. What I would give to know what's going on in that mind of yours right now," he said.

"So, I'm selfish. Sue me! Besides, what's your damage? You realize you'd only be my rebound guy."

"The only damage I suffer is from a broken heart. I thought I was okay. I thought I was ready to move on. Then I saw you with Aliah that one day. Now, no matter how hard I try, you're all I think about." Spencer started the car and stared into the fogged up windshield.

"You've got issues," I said, shaking my head with disbelief.

"And you don't?"

"Yeah, maybe I do, but they don't involve you."

"It *has* to be about Edwin. It's always about Edwin with you. You two are perfect for each other, you know that?"

"You can't be mad at me. I didn't do anything wrong," I snapped, while my tummy did a flip-flop.

"Then why aren't you and Edwin together anymore?" he asked, selfishly curious.

In the heat of the moment, "Because I gave him an ultimatum and he made the wrong choice."

"*You* gave *him* an ultimatum?" he said in disbelief.

"Yes. I told him if he didn't plan to put a ring on it and make me some babies, then I'd to move on with someone who would."

"And he told you no?" Spencer looked stunned.

"He's not ready for kids. He loves me, but... blah, blah, blah. Edwin did what Edwin does when things get intense. He backs off. You know my theory? If you don't know how to swim, then get out of the damn pool!"

Spencer chuckled.

"Oh, you think this is funny? Am I funny to you?"

"Stop it, you're killing me," he said, still smirking. "You fed me this whole story, only for me to find out that you are completely single. Forgive me if that makes me sadistically happy."

"For your information Spencer, you're not in the pool. In fact, I'm swimming solo. Regardless of what you might think, I do have a heart and it's really hurting right now."

"I'm only asking you to keep an open mind."

Staring at my feet, I kicked off my shoes. "And then what? I let you back into my life and we live happily ever after?"

"Not necessarily. There are no guarantees. But does that sound so bad to you?"

While the idea of having Spencer's children wasn't revolting, the fact that I was even considering it so soon after being with Edwin was. I felt sick to my stomach and it wasn't from the conversation. The dry, moisture-less air in the car began to suffocate me. I needed fresh air and fast. He shifted the car in reverse, not noticing how ill I had become.

"Wait!" I hollered, as I frantically grasped at my seat belt.

He finally realized something was wrong and turned on the interior light to investigate. He assessed my face, as the light caused tears to fall from my eyes and I began to gag on my humility. Urgently forcing open the door, I burst out of the car, but I couldn't clear the sense of asphyxiation. I heard the car power down as I bent over the tall flower beds and decorated the manicured riverbank with my dinner.

Spencer hurried to my side and held my hair as I dry-heaved a few more times. When I finally caught my breath I began to cry. "See? I make myself sick."

"Either that, or I make you sick. I shouldn't have pushed you so hard. Now I blew it," he said, releasing my hair.

"You didn't blow it," I said softly, then tip-toed barefoot a few feet away from his car. I took a seat on the damp concrete parking slab and pulled my legs to my chest. After wiping my mouth with my wrist, I buried my face in my arms. Spencer came and sat next to me, but I was empty to the pit of my stomach. So very empty.

"Does that mean you'll give me a chance?" he asked, gently rubbing my back.

I pulled my head from my arms and stared off into the darkness in disbelief. "Spencer, I feel like my world has been crushed. I just puked my guts out in front of you and yet you're still trying to get fresh with me?"

"I don't stop feeling this way because you're a little ill. If I could have you in my life again Abby, things would just fall back into place for me."

Spencer was laying the charm on thick and he knew it was my weakness. He also knew I was a sucker for that sexy English accent and I wondered if he was toning it up a notch just to appease me.

"Are you sure I'm the one you're waiting for? I see you've painted this brilliant picture of me and I'm finding it hard to live up to. I just wonder where your imagination begins and reality ends."

I looked deep into his eyes so he would truly feel my words. Intensity was thick in the humid air and Spencer leaned in for a kiss. I turned away.

"Ugh," I groaned, as I shoved him off of me. "You're nasty!"

"You worry too much," he said, shaking his head in disapproval. With a sigh, "I'd better get you home before Edwin starts to worry."

I couldn't even tell whether or not he was being sarcastic. "Do you need your ears cleaned? I already told you, Edwin and I are done."

"I'd believe it more if you'd stop swooning every time you heard his name. It's just as well. Maybe this will serve as a lesson for both of us."

I stood up, steadied myself, and then walked back to the car. "Why don't you enlighten me?" I slipped into the car and Spencer poked his head in his door, so I could see him before he took a seat.

"When something seems good don't fuck it up, because it definitely isn't going to be any better on the other side." Lost in his own disillusionment, he got in the car and turned it on.

"Where were you two months ago? I could've used that lesson then."

Spencer stared at me for a second, sharpening my nerves. Then, without speaking, he threw the car in reverse and quickly drove off. From that look he gave me and the speed he was travelling, I figured he didn't appreciate me trying to apply his lesson to my relationship with Edwin.

"You're dangerous you know," I said. And I wasn't referring to his driving.

"Am I?"

"Yes. You're just like my friend, Maddie. When you want something, you go for it, even when the odds aren't in your favour. Unfortunately, like Aliah, you always expect to win in the end and that can be dangerous." I glanced out my window, at the passing houses.

"Why is it that I'm pulling into your driveway after dark and I know you're not going to invite me in? I thought you thrived on dangerous men."

"Are you really asking that?"

He slipped the car into park. "Not an answer."

"Fine. Bad timing," I said, briskly.

"There's more to it than that. You can't fool me, Abby."

I spun around to face him, my eyes narrowed in on his. "Fine! My turn to teach you a little life lesson: You can't always get what you want and the cold hard truth hurts. I'm sorry, but it's just not ever going to happen between us."

"I'm glad we had this talk," Spencer said, staring out the front windshield.

I cracked my door open but, suddenly feeling incredibly guilty, I couldn't leave him like this. "Are you ready to move on now?"

"I've definitely learned a lot tonight. I have to quit trying so damn hard. Who knows, maybe the right girl will find me. Until then, you're stuck in my dreams." A wicked smile curled onto his lips and it was almost as sexy as that damned accent.

"Enjoy me there then," I said, sarcastically. "At least I

won't be a plastered wreck. Thank you for dinner."

He reached for my hand and squeezed it, then drew it to his mouth, his kiss soft, his icy eyes gleaming at me. "You're everything a guy could ever want, Abigail. Don't ever let anyone tell you otherwise. Edwin's a fool to let you go."

I closed my eyes to hide my expression from the sudden squeeze on my heart. With a deep breath, I pushed open my door. "Goodnight, Spencer."

Not releasing my hand, he drew my eyes back to his. "Are you sure you don't need help getting to your bed?"

"Goodnight, Spencer," I repeated, more forcefully this time.

"Goodnight," he replied, his devious smile still lurking on his handsome face.

I closed the door and gracelessly stumbled up my stairs. Spencer flashed his lights and honked his horn to acknowledge my clumsiness, despite the hour. I fumbled with my keys at the door, until it creaked open. I pushed the door open and found Edwin standing on the other side, Spencer still backing out of the driveway.

"It wasn't locked." Edwin's voice was stern and angry.

What's his problem?

Aside from awakening all of my neighbours, Spencer's ignorant honking and light show had done exactly what he had set out to do. It solidified Edwin's distance from me, by making his presence known. Spencer honked two more times before he squealed off in his fast car. I scrunched my eyes shut, hoping if I held them long enough that the night would just be over already. But when I opened them, Edwin was staring at me, his eyes dark and angry.

"Who the hell was that?" he boomed.

"Spencer. Who do you think?"

"Who?"

I rolled my eyes. "Don't play dumb. Spencer. Spencer Caldwell."

"What were you doing with him? Tell me you were not on a date," he snapped.

"It wasn't a date. We're just friends. Aliah was there and

so was Spencer's friend Dexter, if you must know."

"Sounds like a date to me. You know there's no such thing as being *just friends* with a guy. He only wants in your pants."

"Oh, really? And what is it that *you* want?" I stammered, still feeling the emptiness in my gut and whirling in my head.

"That's not fair."

"Who said anyone was playing by the book? What's truly unfair, Eddie, is how you're acting. If we're not together – *and we're not* – then we're free to date whoever we like, as single consenting adults," I added, mocking his own ridiculous concept.

"You're sleeping with him again," he stated, as if he knew it for a fact. And when I didn't answer, Edwin flagged his hands in the air in disbelief.

"I didn't say that," I slurred. "All I'm saying is, it's time to move on. If I learned one thing tonight, it's that all this bull shit arguing is useless."

"In other words, you're dating him again and you want my permission to sleep with him," Edwin growled.

"Edwin! You seriously need to get over yourself. I don't need your permission. And for your information, it's not always about sex. Spencer understands me."

"Yeah. He understands what he has to say to get back in your pants. I see how drunk you are, Abby. Look at yourself!"

"I'm not sleeping with him!" I screamed, yanking off my shoes and throwing them to the floor. "Are you happy now? You've fucked me up so bad that I can't even enjoy a night out with a good friend! Well guess what? Tomorrow's a new day."

ABOUT THE AUTHOR

Christa Simpson is a Canadian Indie Author and mother of two. She loves reading, writing, music, movies and dancing. She likes her men muscled, her music loud and her kids happy.

She lives in a small town in Southwestern Ontario with her husband and two beautiful little girls. She is a dreamer and has always believed that you can do anything you set your mind to.

You can visit her website:
http://christasimpson.com

Follow her blog:
http://christasimpson.wordpress.com

Or find her on Facebook:
www.facebook.com/authorchristasimpson

THE TWISTED TRILOGY
By Christa Simpson

Book 1: Twisted
Book 2: Twist & Turn
Book 3: A Twist of Fate

SUPPORT THIS INDIE AUTHOR!
LEAVE A REVIEW!

CHRISTA SIMPSON
Rules were made to be broken...

FINDING DESTINY

When Skylar is forced to invite Destiny back to his cabin, he can't ignore what is subtly unravelling between them. Skylar has rules. He has never strayed from those rules. And yet Destiny has him breaking every last one of them. But when tragedy strikes, torn from her arms at lightning speed, Skylar is left to wonder whether he would ever find his *destiny*.

For the full synopsis, please visit:
http://christasimpson.com

The Twisted Trilogy: Book 2

Twist and Turn

Excerpt:

After I loaded the dishwasher, I clambered to the living room where Edwin was relaxing. Lying casually on the sofa, his muscles still looked incredibly defined, to the point where I could have just stood there and stared at him all night. Instead, I picked up his shirt off the otherwise empty chair and tossed it at him. He caught in one swift motion and then rested it on the arm of the couch.

Can't you take a hint? Put on the damn shirt!

"Thanks," he said, his aqua eyes glimmering at me.

Sigh. As if his flexing muscles weren't enough to get my attention, he had to turn those gorgeous eyes loose on me.

"Are we still on for tonight?" I plopped on the chair across from him and tried to remind myself why I had called it off between us in the first place. The chair was comfy, but it was only a temporary seat. Edwin was parked in my spot and he knew it.

"You know it," he replied, smiling. He looked rather comfy with his heavily muscled body stretched out on my couch, and he didn't make a move as the show started.

I dramatically cocked my head, to display how awkward it was for me to watch the TV from where I was sitting, but I realized then that Edwin wasn't going to shove over without a fight. Ignoring the delightful way he filled the sofa, I walked to the end of it and sat right on his feet. He groaned, but reluctantly moved his bare toes out of my way.

That had gone a lot easier than I thought it would. A winning smile spread across my face. We were finally getting the hang of being friendly roommates, *without benefits*, and it was incredibly therapeutic for me.

With my soft, brown hair draped straight down my back, I stretched my arms for the ceiling and moaned softly. "Oh, my aching neck. Can you believe it's still sore from my hip-hop class yesterday?" I groaned, not really expecting a reply.

Edwin pressed both of his bare feet onto the area rug and slid up next to me. "I can massage it for you," he said, his voice a deep seductive growl.

My achy-breaky muscles made it an easy decision. The TV was flashing commercials anyway, so I turned sideways and let him ease my tension with his magical fingers.

He swept my hair from the nape of my neck and brushed his fingers across my suddenly sensitized skin. I shivered with awareness as his fingers spread out over my shoulders and closed around them. His skillful hands massaged my tight muscles and whispered across my skin in such an erotic way.

I closed my eyes and enjoyed the instant relief, verbalizing my approval with a guttural moan. *It felt nice to be touched by him. So why did it feel so naughty?*

"Does that feel good?" Edwin smirked. He already knew the answer.

"Mmm, very."

When his fingers loosened, I wanted to cry out for him to keep going. Harder. Deeper.

"Why don't you lay on the floor so I can do a better job?" he suggested.

I knew it was a bad idea, but I couldn't resist the allure of Edwin's massage. I scurried to the floor, laid on my stomach, and then tucked my eyes into my folded arms, eager for more.

Edwin dropped to his knees and crawled over me, until his heavy muscles were resting on my thighs. "You getting shy on me all of a sudden?" he asked, as his hands slid under my shirt and whispered all the way up to my shoulders.

His hands explored all over my bare skin, overloading my sensory system with a guilty treat. I couldn't help but be turned on by his touch, whispers of pleasure escaping my lips as he caressed my lower back and wrapped his hands around my sides. His fingers tickled up the curve of my spine, gently teasing my sensitive skin, until he refocused a little higher.

"This is in the way," he explained, as he slipped his fingers beneath my bra strap. "Do you mind?" he asked, as he pulled my shirt over my head.

"No," I whimpered softly, hoping he didn't know the effect he was having on me.

Edwin unfastened my bra and slowly drew the straps over my shoulders, exposing my entire back and leaving but a small piece of fabric between my bare skin and the floor. He mounted my hips and touched me again, working his way from my shoulders downward. His fingers tickled down my sides, arousing the soft flesh only inches from my nearly naked breasts.

He gently tucked my hair behind my ear and brushed it all over my right shoulder, before deepening his massage. Suddenly the muscle pain was gone, but a new ache was spreading through me. Instead of stopping him, like I should have, I let out another moan, a little more provocative than the last.

Edwin's touch only grew more aggressive. He was intentionally tantalizing me. "How's that?"

"It's a little too hard," I groaned, craving his gentle touch.

"You used to like it hard," he said, his voice low and smooth. Then, without pressing his erotic suggestion, he lightened the pressure.

Unable to produce a constructive sentence, I ignored his point and enjoyed his gentle fingers. I had an incredible urge to flip over and pull him onto me, taking what I knew could be mine. *Whoa, what?* My own thoughts startled me, breaking through the thick fog hanging heavy over my brain.

It was now apparent to me that Edwin was trying to seduce me. And though my body ached with desire, I couldn't give in to him. We had made such progress over the past few months and it would be too painful to turn back that clock. I took a long deep breath to douse the flames licking across my body, hoping it'd be enough.

It wasn't.

I felt Edwin's warm body hovering close to mine, his steady breath warming the back of my neck. Every hair on my body stood on end, every nerve sensually aware of his closeness. I wanted to stop him, knowing how dangerous these intimate moments could be, but when his lips touched my bare shoulder, I couldn't breathe let alone speak.

Available now!

http://christasimpson.com